A GOD
IN THE
SHED

J-F. DUBEAU

Published by Inkshares, Inc., San Francisco, California
www.inkshares.com

Edited by Adam Gomolin, Matthew Harry, and Kaitlin Severini
Cover design by M.S. Corley and interior design by Kevin G. Summers

ISBN: 9781942645351
e-ISBN: 9781942645368
Library of Congress Control Number: 2016942387

First edition

Printed in the United States of America

"Those Old Ones were gone now, inside the earth and under the sea; but their dead bodies had told their secrets in dreams to the first men, who formed a cult which had never died."

—HP Lovecraft, *Call of the Cthulhu*

PROLOGUE

REGRETS ARE THE INSTRUMENTS by which we learn. We tend not to repeat the mistakes we truly regret. They may cause us pain, but regrets push us to better our lives. We regret how we treat our first love, but it teaches us to be a better partner. We regret being lazy in school, but it reminds us to apply ourselves in the workplace later. We may be troubled by our regrets, but we don't carry them with us for the rest of our lives. Instead they become milestones, honor badges that remind us how we've grown.

Remorse, however, is a much deeper feeling. What wouldn't we do to take back the circumstances that birthed those scars? For Nathan Joseph Cicero, the answer was "nothing." He was a man well acquainted with remorse, and most of his came at a young age.

Back then, the small village of Saint-Ferdinand was little more than a crossroads encircled by a handful of farms and orchards. All told, a little over a hundred individuals inhabited the region. But that was on the verge of changing.

It was the summer of 1873. The province of Quebec was then part of the nascent confederacy of Canada. The recent changes in the political landscape had taken time to trickle down to rural areas, but it was anticipated that villages like Saint-Ferdinand would see an influx of inexpensive labor and new residents.

Nathan was twelve at the time. His father had decided that his son would to be sent to boarding school in the fall to receive a formal education. It was a significant investment for the Cicero farm, but one that would pay for itself with the knowledge and contacts Nathan would bring back with him. The family was putting their hopes and dreams on Nathan, but the boy felt more than up to the task. It would be an exciting adventure.

But first, he planned to enjoy his last summer in Saint-Ferdinand. To climb the orchard trees with his friends, fish in the local pond, and explore the depths of the nearby virgin woods. The whole while, there was much ribbing from his playmates about how much the big city would change him. Nathan, they said, would come back with a snooty attitude and fancy clothes. He would forget his roots. But they were only teasing. They knew that the Ciceros were not the type to get carried away by their own success, least of all Nathan. So it was that he; his best friend, Jonathan; and the Richards twins decided that exploring the forest would be their big summer project. To modern sensibilities this may not seem like much of an adventure, but in the late nineteenth century there were still thousands of acres in North America where no living man had set foot. Places either forgotten or forbidden. Venturing deep into those woods was not a journey of imagined risks and make-believe dangers. This was to be an adventure as real as the boys had ever experienced, one with more peril than they could have anticipated.

The first few days were all fun and games. They knew which parts of the forest were used by hunters and trappers and kept clear of those areas, preferring to delve into unknown territory. At first, their day trips were shallow and timid. They'd walk perhaps an hour before marking their progress and turning back. However, as the first week came to an end, the boys felt emboldened. They packed their bags with provisions and water, calling them "rations," to give their preparations an air of importance. None of their parents would allow them to sleep in the woods, so Nathan and his friends had to leave at sunrise in order to return before the daylight vanished.

There is a hypnotic quality to walking in the wild for extended periods of time. After the first half hour, talk between the boys ceased. All that remained was the sound of their own footsteps and thoughts, set to the background music of birdsong. They'd chosen their day well. While the weather was warm, there was a slight breeze that managed to find its way between the trees. Although the sun was harsh, its light was filtered by the thick canopy of leaves and pine needles.

They walked for what felt like an eternity. Eenis Richards, the younger twin by a full four minutes, had initially complained about the boredom. He'd wanted to play games or sing songs to alleviate the tedium. But soon, even he was taken over by the serenity of the journey. Like four ants, they walked in a line, their trance unbroken as they crossed clearings, jumped over narrow streams, and wound their way between increasingly large and ancient trees.

It was the silence that eventually broke the spell. How long they'd been walking without the accompanying cacophony of forest noise, it was hard to say, but all four boys noticed the quiet at the same time. Nathan, who had been in front, stopped dead in his tracks, half-expecting the others to bump into him. Instead his friends all stepped up to stand beside him.

They were in a small clearing. The area was bursting with life. Tall, wild grass covered the ground, a chaotic mix of plant species that could be hiding all manner of rocks and hazards. The trees that towered overhead were old and ominous. Yet, of all the things that could have played on their nerves, it was the eerie silence that tugged at the imagination.

"Nathan?" Jonathan's voice felt alien to him as he spoke.

The Cicero boy didn't respond. He was transfixed by something at the opposite edge of the clearing.

"Look," he said, and pointed after a moment. "A cave."

It was difficult to see, buried behind a curtain of tall brush, but there it was, low to the ground, a dark hole in the limestone. The opening was framed by the roots of a particularly large oak tree that stretched toward the clouds. Of all the vegetation in the clearing, it was the only thing devoid of life.

The boys approached the cave entrance carefully, both to avoid taking a misstep in the thick weeds and also because of the clearing's unsettling atmosphere.

"Whoa!" Nathan cried out all of a sudden. His arms went akimbo, blocking his friends from stepping farther. He couldn't tell if they'd seen what he had, but he was certain that they were no longer alone. Something was in the cave. Its eyes glinted in the darkness.

"I see it," Jonathan confirmed in a whisper. "What is it?"

"Not a bear. The eyes are too close together," Eenis said.

"They look almost . . . human." Nathan dropped his arms but forced himself to not run away.

"We should go," Jonathan said, voicing what the others were ashamed to admit.

"*Pleeeease . . . stay.*" The words had been issued from the cavern, piercing the air with a sound that soothed the soul and eased the mind.

As the voice dissipated, a body crawled from the shadows of the cave. At first, it walked on all fours, awkwardly scuttling on the ground like a beetle or a spider. Its limbs were clearly human, though pale as porcelain, and its elbows and knees were bent at odd angles. Twitching and shuddering, it rose up on its feet. The creature seemed to study the boys as it stood, adopting their stance and posture. It was naked, but neither male nor female. Its body was roughly the same size as Nathan's and his friends', but smooth and featureless. Its skin had the texture of unscarred moonlight.

Nathan wondered how the thing knew English. It was like no Native American he'd ever seen, nor any other human. It didn't resemble any of the creatures he'd heard of in stories, either. Neither society nor folklore had a name for whatever had crawled out of the hole beneath the dead oak tree. Then it occurred to him that whatever the thing was, it hadn't spoken. Not words, anyway, but rather clear concepts, sent directly into their minds.

"Who are you?" Nathan finally asked.

The creature studied its hands like it had never seen them before. *I'm not . . . sure how to explain.*

There was a sort of vulnerability to the thing. It seemed fragile, almost swaying in the wind that blew through the weeds. Nathan gave up on figuring out what the creature was, and chose to feel sorry for it instead. As the seconds ticked on, however, the thing appeared to be increasingly disturbed by its situation. The feeling was so strong as to be contagious, infecting the boys with a growing sense of dread.

"Do . . . Would you like to play a game or something?" Nathan offered, desperate to break through the creature's apparent anxiety.

It cocked its head to consider the offer. The cloud of panic that hung over the clearing vanished immediately. *Yes. A game. I think I'd like that.*

Nathan, Jonathan, and the Richards twins spent the rest of their afternoon playing with a creature they couldn't begin to understand. Their games were simple. They had no ball, and little room to participate in anything too elaborate. What they did have was plenty of places to hide, so they spent their time improvising a half dozen variations on hide-and-seek.

Eventually, it came time to leave. The creature showed signs of alarm until Nathan and the boys swore that they'd be back the next day. Why wouldn't they? The cave-thing might be strange, but when else would they be able to spend time with such an inhuman curiosity? This was especially true for Nathan, to whom the stranger represented everything he would be losing when he moved to the big city.

The rest of the summer passed quickly. On most days, the boys would go into the woods to visit with their new playmate. They eventually settled on calling it "him," mostly because doing otherwise while it remained naked would have been uncomfortable. Though they had decided on a gender, they could never settle on a name for their new friend. They also didn't ask much about the creature. Not where it came from nor why the area around his cave was devoid of animals. They were at an age where such details held little importance. He was their playmate, and their secret, and that was all that mattered to them.

He, however, was learning a great deal from the boys. Most of what he learned regarded games and their rules. Rules were very important to him. On more than one occasion, Eenis might cheat a little, and that would send the stranger into a fit of rage. It was as if he couldn't understand the mechanics of rule breaking. Each time, Nathan would soothe him and try to explain. He could not change the creature's attitude nor get to the core of why even the slightest bending of the rules upset his bizarre friend to unreasonable levels, so instead he had to settle for simply appeasing his rage.

"Rules are like promises. Why make them if you intend to break them?" That was the closest thing to an explanation Nathan got from the stranger. Of course, the boy knew that life wasn't that simple, but how to explain that to something that had crawled out from a hole in the ground?

Perhaps he should have tried, though, as things inevitably came to a head one day in late August. There was less than a week before Nathan was to leave for Montreal. As usual, the boys were playing with their friend in the forest.

Guilt was already wearing heavily on Nathan's shoulders. It was clear that, among the four children who ventured into the woods to visit the creature, he was the one who related to it best. It trusted him. Either in spite of or because of that, Nathan had yet to tell his friend that he would be leaving, and each day it became that much harder to bring up the subject. As he debated the issue in his mind, another incident erupted.

"You cheated!" the creature admonished. A quick look immediately determined that it was Jonathan who was the culprit.

It wasn't the first such occurrence, and each time, the stranger had become more and more enraged. They were playing a variation on the game of tag that the creature seemed especially fond of. The rules were simple: as long as you were being watched, you could not move or run from the player who was currently "it." The trick was to try to distract "it," then stay out of sight, adding an element of hide-and-seek to the game. As with all of their games, the creature took the rules extremely seriously.

"I wasn't cheating!" Jonathan countered. This was a first. Before, he had always been too intimidated by the strange creature to defend himself and instead admitted fault, hoping to move on from the confrontation. His new bold attitude did not sit well with his accuser.

"You did . . . ," said the cave-thing, surprised at the boy's contradiction. *"You did, and now you're lying about it!"*

Throughout the summer, the creature's skin had become darker and more textured, losing some of its ethereal quality. The boys had assumed this was due to it being in the sun for the first time in God knows how long. Now, as they watched, rage seemed to consume the stranger, sending a ripple through its skin and leaving it a shade darker. Its posture also changed, going from an almost regal stance to the low, looming crouch of a predator.

"N-no!" Jonathan wasn't contradicting the creature, Nathan was sure of that, but rather expressing his sudden fear at the situation. The subtlety was lost in his panic as the stranger crept closer to Jonathan.

Trying to get away, the boy stumbled and fell to the ground. A cry broke from his lungs. Nathan could have sworn he saw a look of concern flash over the creature's face before it leaped toward Jonathan. And then things fell apart.

Jonathan, still in the grip of his increasing fear, threw a rock at the stranger, hitting it square in the jaw. At that moment, the creature went from friend to monster. Nathan ran toward the scuffle in the hopes of once more disarming the conflict, but this time he was too late.

The creature turned back to Nathan, its face an inhuman mask of apologetic concern. Whatever it had done, it regretted it dearly, but all of that was erased by just how much of Jonathan's blood covered its mouth.

"He broke the rules, Nathan. You can't break the rules." The thing spat Jonathan's finger into the grass, globs of blood and shards of bone staining the forest floor.

Nathan looked around, only to find that the Richards twins had already run off, scattered by the escalating situation. Only he, the creature, and a screaming Jonathan remained, the latter still pinned to the forest floor.

"Nathan . . . forgive me. I will make it up to you. I will fix this!" the creature pleaded.

Without breaking eye contact, Nathan backed away slowly, desperately trying not to stumble over the branches and rocks that littered the ground. The creature stood but couldn't follow, abiding as always by the rules of the game. An eternity passed before Nathan could once more hear the sound of birds in the trees. An eternity of listening to his two best friends, one screaming for his life and the other pleading for his forgiveness. Only when the two voices had faded entirely did he feel safe turning around and running back toward Saint-Ferdinand.

Later, on his way to his new life, Nathan Joseph Cicero carried something new in his baggage: the weight of his first remorse.

CROWLEY

THE SUN IS A TRAITOR, thought Inspector Stephen Crowley as he pushed the trailer door open. *It shines bright and cool in the morning but stabs you in the back by the afternoon.*

A putrid stench rolled out of the trailer, enveloping him and his second-in-command like a fog. The foul odor pressed against their bodies, refusing to dissipate in the hot and humid air. When they would tell the story later, the two officers would describe the smell as almost tangible. With every whiff, the stench betrayed its source: rotten, moldering flesh. The cops weren't here by coincidence. They had come to make an arrest, and whatever was giving off the retch-inducing stink would likely become important evidence.

The day had been so promising. Crowley had planned on taking his son, Daniel, fishing in Magog. The cool breeze on the water would have balanced out the harsh heat and humidity. The sun would have been a glorious luxury instead of a discomfort.

Summer vacation had just started, and Crowley knew Daniel would have welcomed the opportunity to knock back a few cold ones with his old man. His son wasn't of drinking age, being just shy of seventeen. However, out in the middle of a lake, supervised by his police inspector father, it wouldn't have mattered. Instead

Crowley was called in just as he was making breakfast so he and Lieutenant Bélanger could make this most unfortunate house call.

The trailer was as run-down as could be expected. It had been dragged deep into the woods almost two decades ago, and Crowley could see no sign of upkeep since. Every piece was falling apart; even the front doorknob had been replaced by a rusty padlock. All around the trailer, a generous variety of furniture and appliances created an odd forest that contrasted with the majesty of the surrounding trees. Within the piles of junk, the inspector's trained eye noticed a strange preference toward refrigerators.

Everyone in Saint-Ferdinand knew the trailer's owner wasn't completely sane. Old Sam Finnegan had come from a farm on the outskirts of Knowlton, where he'd lived a quiet life, breeding dogs and raising ducks. There were even some clues that he had been married once. But when he moved to Saint-Ferdinand, there was little trace of that man left. He was but a husk, his eyes distant yet oddly focused. He'd purchased a plot of land from a local farmer and driven his trailer there to rot. It was deep in the woods, with little more than a dirt path leading to it. Finnegan frequently came to town to buy food, stock up on booze, and perform odd jobs for local residents. He never caused any trouble and frequently helped out the locals for favors and a bit of cash. Occasionally, he could be seen muttering to himself. "Eccentric" was what polite townspeople called him.

His trailer, however, was that of a man driven stark raving mad. Sam was quite obviously obsessed with dark things. The cramped two-room residence, if it could be called such, was littered with letters he'd penned and drawings he'd made. There was a large and disturbing collection of knives on the counter near a filthy sink. More knives than any sane man should own. Stacks of books from a dozen religions, each dog-eared and annotated, were piled in every corner.

The first room, which seemed to function as a combination living room/kitchen, turned out not to be the source of the smell.

A thick cloud of flies pointed instead to the second room. Inspector Crowley already had a good idea of what he was going to find there.

The door was ajar. Neither of the two officers expected to be met with any resistance, but just in case, Crowley drew his sidearm. He nodded for Bélanger to nudge the door open. As it creaked ominously, light spilled into the pitch-black bedroom. Lying restfully, almost serenely on the bed, was the body of Ms. Annette Benjamin, a retired schoolteacher, volunteer at the local library, prize-winning gardener, and latest victim of the Saint-Ferdinand Killer.

Stephen put his 9-mm Smith & Wesson back in its holster, sighed loudly, and scratched the back of his thick neck. The inspector had never considered himself much of an intellectual. He'd skipped or slept through most of his training sessions on blood-spatter analysis, crime-scene assessment, and other modern investigation techniques. Not that he wasn't qualified to do his job, but creeping into his midfifties, Crowley was from an older school of crime fighting, one that relied on gut instincts, hard questioning of witnesses, and even harder interrogation of suspects. Still, he knew that when a body turned up, it was time to call in the eggheads.

"Jackie?" the inspector croaked into his radio. "Send for Randy and let the boys know to pick up Finnegan if they spot him in town."

He turned down his radio and took a better look at the bedroom. Officially, his job was to wait for Randall McKenzie, the medical examiner, to show up. It was going to be a long wait. Randy didn't work exclusively for the department, and doubled as one of two physicians in Saint-Ferdinand. Also, he was notoriously nonchalant about his duties. Crowley had plenty of time to make his own observations about the scene.

First and most obviously, Ms. Benjamin had been killed elsewhere. The dark patches of blood covering her light-blue flower-patterned dress suggested she'd been stabbed multiple times in her ample belly. Lack of blood in the room meant the body had probably been dragged there. No mean feat, considering Finnegan weighed at most 150 pounds, while his victim must have hovered near 250.

The more Stephen observed the body, the stranger it all seemed. The corpse had been positioned faceup, both arms lying to her sides. It seemed Old Man Finnegan had been worried about his victim's comfort. The body was also fully clothed, reducing the likelihood of a sexual motive. Ms. Benjamin wasn't known for her wealth, making theft another unlikely motivation.

The heat and humidity seemed amplified within the cramped trailer. Sweating profusely, Crowley took a step back out of the room. The smell was becoming a bit much to tolerate, and a little fresh air wouldn't go unappreciated. But before he could walk out, Stephen's attention was drawn to the many flies that crawled over the body. Death and decomposition, while unpleasant, had never bothered Crowley. Nor had the sight of blood or gore. Flies, however, touched a nerve. They reminded him that people were nothing more than walking, talking bags of meat, ready to become something else's meal.

The flies on Ms. Benjamin were especially numerous, which wasn't surprising considering the weather and circumstances. But for some reason, the repulsive insects had congregated around her eyes. Ignoring his disgust, Crowley shooed the flies away from the body. As the insects scattered into a small black cloud, the inspector got a good look at the dead former teacher's face. He had to crouch down in the dim light to make sure, but there was no mistake. Someone had removed Ms. Benjamin's eyes.

"Crowley!"

Bélanger's call cut through the stillness. The lieutenant was phlegmatic by nature, unruffled by even the most traumatic crime scenes. Inspector Crowley knew that when Mathieux Bélanger raised his voice, it was for a good reason and, accordingly, he double-timed it outside.

There he found his lieutenant crouched next to one of the many refrigerators, a small pile of bright pink clothes at his feet. The door to the refrigerator stood open, giving the impression the old appliance had disgorged the pink bundle.

"I heard a hum from one of the fridges and took a look," Bélanger explained.

Crowley looked down and saw that the bundle was in fact a second, tiny body. He immediately recognized her as Audrey, the eight-year-old daughter of William Bergeron, a local business owner and friend. Crowley had seen her alive the previous day, sitting at the counter of her father's drugstore, telling long stories about everything she was going to do during the summer. She'd been wearing the same pink dress, her blinding platinum hair tied in the same ponytail. Her body had neither obvious wounds nor signs that she had suffocated while in the appliance. Her eyes were open and, more important, still in their sockets.

"Christ . . . ," whispered the inspector.

The news of this discovery would destroy William and his wife, Beatrice. Audrey was their only child and precious not only to them but to all of Saint-Ferdinand. More than a few of William's acquaintances attributed his recent sobriety to Audrey's presence in his life. She had been a fragile thing from the day she was born, over a month premature, but sweet as sugar. It was no surprise that everyone was so protective. Even older kids would allow her to tag along with them, ever doting on the delicate child.

Once news of her death got out, the villagers would tear Finnegan apart if they found him before the cops did, and Crowley had half a mind to let them. Anger came easily to the inspector. Affection for his own son aside, Crowley wasn't an openly loving man. Frustration was his language and he could speak it louder than most, often by punching inanimate objects in order to vent. But it was his job to tell William and Beatrice what had become of their only child. He'd had many similar conversations since becoming a cop, but they never got any easier.

For almost twenty years, Saint-Ferdinand had been home to a very long stretch of unsolved murders and disappearances. When they'd chanced upon evidence that might put a definite end to the killings, there had been much reason to celebrate. But it was quite a different feeling for Crowley to realize that he'd known the killer for so long and had never once suspected him. It was embarrassing. For that reason alone, the inspector felt like administering a legendary beating to Finnegan himself.

Thankfully, decades of professional experience soon took over. The inspector stood and walked to the nearest refrigerator, putting his hand on its back. Frowning, he walked over to another and did the same. Crowley repeated the process with another six refrigerators before he stopped, looked around, and realized something.

"They're all working, Matt." There was an unmistakable gravity to his voice. "Every one of 'em, humming like a diesel."

Crowley was partially right. There were seventeen fridges on Finnegan's property. Some were in plain sight; others were overgrown with vegetation. Eleven were running off of a hijacked power line.

The inspector and his lieutenant had suspected that more of the fridges contained bodies, but they dutifully waited until the medical examiner, EMTs, and as many other cops as they could round up arrived before going through the grisly task of opening them. By late afternoon, Sam Finnegan's property was swarming with law-enforcement professionals gathering a gamut of forensic evidence from fingerprints to blood samples, to casts of shoe prints and tire tracks. Only then was every refrigerator opened and documented.

When the lion's share of the investigation was done, their biggest fear was confirmed. Each of the functioning appliances was revealed to contain the body of a victim. Of the six that were no longer in operation, two were stuffed with putrefied remains. This brought the confirmed body count to fourteen, which was shocking until a shallow trench was discovered near the edge of the woods. In it, bones of clearly human origin had been dumped. Once these were sorted and counted, the number of victims would increase dramatically.

Most of the corpses were easily identified. No effort had been made by Finnegan to hide who they were. Personal items were left untouched. Their wallets and jewelry had remained with them. They were unmolested, apart from the slashed throats and missing eyes.

Many of the victims were familiar to Crowley. They'd been neighbors from his childhood, high school classmates he'd lost track of, or faces he recognized from the case files of the Saint-Ferdinand Killer. Some were residents of the small village, while others were hikers and campers who had vanished in the surrounding woods throughout the years. The media had blamed bears or hiking accidents for the disappearances. The locals knew better. So did the inspector.

"You can't start blaming yourself, Stephen." Randy McKenzie was bent over the body of Melanie DesPins, a middle-aged mother of three who had disappeared four winters before. Her throat had been slashed mercilessly, her eyes ripped out. Randy was short, balding, and rotund. His was the physique of a man who spent his time sitting or eating, often both. His eyes, however, displayed uncanny intelligence and care that made him almost attractive, in a friendly neighbor kind of way. "Till today we've barely had a thing to work on with this case."

"Doesn't matter," Crowley grumbled. "People have been disappearing on my watch for years. What do we have? Eighteen? Twenty dead people? And Audrey Bergeron in the mix. I didn't get into this line of work to count corpses like notches on a belt."

"We had nothing to work with. No prints, no witnesses. Hell, most of these people I've never even heard of, and I grew up here! And no one would have thought Sam Finnegan capable of this."

On this, Randy was correct. There had been other, more likely suspects over the years. Outsiders, mostly, as the people of Saint-Ferdinand were reluctant to imagine one of their own capable of such horrors. Just nine months ago they'd brought in a trucker called Patrick Michaud, who frequently camped in the surrounding woods. He had been through town frequently enough to be responsible for the crimes, and a watch he wore had belonged to one of the victims. Michaud claimed he'd found it in the forest. He was grudgingly released for lack of evidence.

So, yes, Randy was right. Crowley had no reason to blame himself or anyone in his department for missing the obvious. They had all worn the same blinders. They'd all ignored what had been staring them in the face. Yet it was difficult not to feel responsible, especially for poor dead Audrey.

"Doesn't it seem strange that she's here, though?" asked Randy as if reading the inspector's mind.

"None of them should be here, Randy," Crowley said, and frowned.

"Yes, of course. What I meant is that she's the only victim below thirty-five, and she has no apparent wounds." The medical examiner snapped off his latex gloves dramatically. "I know there wasn't much of a victim profile when we only had one or two bodies, but now? Now we have an MO."

"And she doesn't fit into it." Crowley scratched the back of his neck again.

"Hell, I doubt she was even murdered. I don't think she was part of Sam's plan."

That was an odd statement. The girl was found less than twenty-four hours after her disappearance, trapped inside the refrigerator of a madman. Eight-year-olds rarely died of natural causes. On the other hand, there was no sign she had struggled. No bruises or lacerations. Audrey had always been a tremendously fragile child as a result of her birth. She had a weak heart and suffered from severe asthma. Either of these things could have killed her from within. The coincidence nagged at Crowley, though.

"Randy?" the inspector asked. "Do me a favor, will ya?"

"Sure."

"Figure out where she died for me. If it was within city limits . . . well, you'll have some work."

Randy hesitated, looking nervously around for a moment. "I would really rather not," he answered at last.

"Randy. She was just a kid."

"Fine." A shiver went up the medical examiner's spine in spite of the heat. "But God dammit, Stephen . . . ."

A few silent moments passed as both men surveyed the scene. A dozen officers from Crowley's department and other regional stations were busying themselves securing the perimeter and identifying evidence. The Saint-Ferdinand officers had become somewhat comfortable working a crime scene. It bore witness to the morbid history of Saint-Ferdinand that small-town cops knew so much about how to handle a murder scene.

"What about the eyes?" Randy asked, breaking their contemplation. "Any idea what that's about?"

"Not sure. I'm really hoping he wasn't eating them, though."

"Depersonalization," someone interrupted.

Both men turned around to see a woman in her late twenties wearing a gray pantsuit, her shoulder-length brown hair held up by large sunglasses. She looked up from the body of Ms. DesPins and smiled apologetically.

"Disfigurement is used to dehumanize a killer's victims. Makes killing easier. Especially if the murderer knows his prey." The woman walked over to kiss Randy on both cheeks.

"This is Erica Hazelwood," Randy explained to Crowley. "She's a doctor in criminal psychology and one of my favorite students. I figured she could drop by and give us a hand."

"Great. Another expert." Crowley clearly didn't like surprises. He was about to vent the day's frustrations on the medical examiner but was interrupted once more by the new arrival.

"I just want to help out with the case, not step on your feet, Inspector." Erica's smile quickly turned to concern, and she empathetically put a hand on Crowley's arm. "But I mostly work with victims' families. I'm here about the little girl's parents."

Crowley realized he'd been clenching his fist during the exchange and relaxed, a little embarrassed at his temper.

"If you'll allow her, she'll break the news to William and Beatrice," Randy added. "You've got enough on your mind, I imagine."

"You're right, Randy." He turned to Erica. "Sorry, Ms. Hazelwood."

"It's quite all right, though I must ask: How long have you been working today?"

Stephen had been woken up around three in the morning. One of his officers had been called in to break up a fight at a local tavern. Sam Finnegan had arrived at the establishment around two thirty in the morning. He'd tried to purchase a beer, revealing his hands were stained with blood. Arnold, the bartender, was immediately suspicious and refused him service. Things became agitated when Finnegan wouldn't take no for an answer. Old Sam fled the scene, but the complaint had been reason enough for Crowley and Bélanger to visit his trailer. They'd knocked on his broken door ten hours ago.

"Not that long," Crowley lied.

Erica was about to contradict him, but the inspector's radio scratched to life.

"Crowley?" came Lieutenant Bélanger's distorted voice. "I found the eyes."

Sam Finnegan, it turned out, had not eaten the eyes of his victims. Instead he'd put them to a more industrious use. Lieutenant Bélanger's location was deep in the woods, roughly ten minutes' walk from Finnegan's trailer and obscured by thick evergreens. He stood outside a small cave opening. Moss-covered rocks lined the entrance, which was barely visible through the foliage. The cave itself wasn't very imposing. Less than six feet in diameter but burrowing almost straight down into the ground. It would have been a claustrophobic fit for most adults.

Sam's handiwork was evident in the way he had arranged the area. He'd set up a dark brown couch facing the cave like a lunatic's living room. The piece of furniture was covered with branches in a crude but premeditated attempt to camouflage the setup. Empty liquor bottles and cigarette butts littered the forest floor, testifying that old Sam had spent a large amount of time there. But most disturbing was a semicircle of half a dozen thin metal rods, planted firmly into the ground and meticulously spaced at regular intervals. Speared at the tip of each of these metal rods were the eyes of Sam Finnegan's victims.

"So much for dehumanizing his kills, huh?" Crowley commented, his own eyes riveted by the bizarre scene before him.

"Sam...," Randy murmured, crouching to examine the nearest rod. "What the hell were you doing?"

"How did you not notice a pattern of missing eyes in the bodies that were found, Inspector?" It was Erica, carefully tiptoeing through the ferns and branches while trying to get a better vantage point on the gruesome tableau.

"The bodies we found were all at various stages of advanced decomposition," Crowley said while studying one of the eye rods. "We have a lot of hungry critters in these woods, Ms. Hazelwood. They tend to go for the soft tissue first. Eyes, tongues, and balls."

Erica's face twisted in concern. "Then why haven't these been devoured yet?"

Crowley ignored the question. He already knew the answer, and anyone with ears could figure it out. Aside from the rare gust of wind disturbing the branches of nearby trees, the area was completely silent. No birds chirping, no squirrels rustling through the undergrowth. The eyes had not been eaten because, for some reason, there were no animals to eat them.

The inspector opted to keep this observation to himself. He knelt down to investigate the skewered eyes further. The one closest to him was bright blue. Incredible care had been taken not to damage the globe of the eye or obstruct the pupil. The inspector reached out slowly toward the rod, but before he could touch it, Randy interrupted him.

"Stephen!" The name broke the silence, the sound echoing in the nearby cave. "Don't touch. Look at them."

Everyone started paying more attention to how the eyes were arranged. The tiny white-and-red dots surrounding the cave were horrifying and eerie. Despite the strength of the late-day sun, a chill seemed to permeate the area.

"They're all looking at the cave. . . ," Erica said, and let out an audible breath.

Once Crowley noticed it, everything became clear. Each eye pointed directly at the cave entrance, as if waiting for something.

"In death, they are ever vigilant." A raspy, tired voice broke the quiet behind them. Instantly, Inspector Crowley and Lieutenant Bélanger spun around and drew their sidearms. Both recognized the voice. Both had been expecting it.

"Sam Finnegan . . . ," whispered Erica Hazelwood. Her words were lost in the din of threats the two officers shouted as they moved in to arrest the old man. Sam didn't put up a fight. He lifted his arms and, in an almost practiced move, put his hands behind his head, all while slowly collapsing to his knees.

The old man was a pitiful wreck. Eyes sunken and cheeks hollow, his body was malnourished and filthy. In fact, the only patches of skin on his face not covered with grime were the two pale streaks left by flowing tears. Old Sam Finnegan's lips moved as he repeated words that were swallowed in the tumult. It was Randy who somehow deciphered what the madman was saying and repeated it:

"I'm sorry. I'm sorry. I'm so very sorry."

VENUS

VENUS MCKENZIE LOOKED UP at the sky, squinting as the sun mercilessly beat down upon her face. The few shops and restaurants that made up Saint-Ferdinand's main street were each stirring to life, slowly preparing for the inevitable noon rush. Owners unlocked their doors and put out their wares. The florist busied herself transforming the sidewalk into a veritable garden. The aromas of her inventory fought against the nearby burger joint's greasy smells of fries and onion rings to be the dominant fragrance. Saint-Ferdinand didn't have much of a downtown area beyond the wide street that bisected it. From where she stood, Venus could easily see where the village started and where it ended, along with every business in between. She could observe Gaston, the operator of the gas station, scratch his generous rear end as he removed the padlock on the sole pump that served the town's need for gasoline. She took note of two nurses in blinding white uniforms as they walked into the medical center, chatting loudly. She knew them both, a mother-daughter duo that also sang together in the town's annual talent show and were frequent customers at her mother's tea shop. The village was coming alive as it had every single day for the last hundred years. Today, however, things were different.

Behind her, she heard the click of a lock, followed by the creaking of a door and the gentle song of wind chimes. She smiled with contentment and turned to see that her friend Penelope had figured out how to use the keys her boss had left in her care. She'd swung open the door to let the stale air out of the converted trailer, a hollowed-out mobile home that had been transformed into an ice cream parlor. Venus didn't wait for an invitation and pranced right in ahead of her friend.

Both girls had been here hundreds of times, but always as paying customers, funneling the better part of their allowances into milk shakes and ice cream cones. As Venus walked toward the three bright red barstools at the counter and passed a seafoam green wall decorated with paintings of sundaes and parfaits, she was discovering the ice cream shop all over again.

"This place is going to be packed this afternoon!" Venus declared, sitting down on the middle stool and spinning back to Penny, who was busy securing the front door. The summer had so far been withering, hot, and unusually eventful. Teenagers from the surrounding farms would be eager to come here to waste time and money. Normally, the shop was open earlier in the season, but the owner, Mr. Bergeron, had been preoccupied this year.

"Ugh, I hope not," Penelope answered, giving one final kick to the wedge of wood under the door. "Mr. Bergeron never really showed me how the machines work, and I'd like to get a little practice before my first customer. I'm surprised he even let me open at all."

"Well, I know someone who'd be more than happy to serve as a guinea pig while you train."

"I bet you do."

Penny was a little over a year older than Venus. Both were smart girls, but where Penny focused her sixteen-year-old intellect toward long-term goals, Venus had a purely academic mind, allowing her to skip ahead a full grade. The older girl tied her shoulder-length blond hair into a ponytail before slipping it under a sheer net. The accoutrement did little to damage her looks. Penny was considered a striking young lady, and there was no doubt that she knew it. To her mother's infinite relief, her daughter seemed to have little interest in playing the dating game, focusing instead on her plans to become an athlete or, failing that, a prestigious lawyer in Montreal. Once her hair had been secured and she'd washed her hands, she started the various ice cream machines and carefully poured a generous cone of soft-serve chocolate ice cream for her friend.

"There you go, Aphrodite."

"That's not my name," replied the younger teen, accepting the frozen treat despite her obvious irritation.

Penny often teased her about her name. Venus had explained at length that she was named after the planet, not the Roman goddess of love. Her mom had told her she'd one day be among the stars, a whimsical prediction that delighted Venus to no end as a child. It had made her want to become an astronaut, which was probably the driving force behind her academic success. That career goal was eventually replaced with plans to become an archaeologist, then a marine biologist. These days, academics seemed to be enough on their own. Her focus would shift from one subject to the next, dancing between biology, physics, and math. She was often skipping one class to read about another in the library.

"Are you gonna let me work behind the register once in a while?" Venus asked before taking a bite out of her cone.

"Nope." Penny leaned on the counter, looking out the front window. "Mr. Bergeron had three strict rules. Number one: never close if there are still customers who want something; and number two: don't let Venus behind the counter."

"Damn . . . Wait! He has a rule just about me?"

"Well, not you, specifically. Anyone, but I'm pretty sure you're no exception."

"What's the third rule?" asked Venus as she finished off her cone, flicking the crumbs at her friend.

Penny fell silent and turned around to prepare another frozen dessert. She mumbled an answer that was drowned out by the sound of the ice cream machine. Venus spun back around and was presented with a perfect chocolate-and-vanilla swirl ice cream cone. She dutifully ignored it.

"C'mon, what's the third rule?"

"The third rule"—Penny swallowed—"was not to give any ice cream to Audrey."

"Oh."

Both girls became very quiet. Audrey Bergeron, the daughter of the local entrepreneur behind half the businesses in town. The jolly, rotund, middle-aged man was a powerful force in Saint-Ferdinand, driving the local economy and, with the help of his wife, leading the community's social activity. His daughter's bright, innocent smile and unbound enthusiasm had charmed everyone in the village. Her body had been found a week earlier at the home of Sam Finnegan.

Audrey's death was a terrible loss not just for her parents but for the whole community. Yet it was the shock of finding out that Finnegan had a second life that had most people talking. The old man may have been strange, but he had never been considered dangerous.

"You know he used to help me practice batting for Little League?" the older girl said, breaking the silence. "And Abraham's dad hired him to clear his driveway every winter."

"He got my cat out of a tree last summer," added Venus. In truth, everyone in Saint-Ferdinand had a story of Old Man Finnegan doing something for them. Even though he might not have been all there, he could fix a bike and build a tree house better than anyone. Between Audrey's death and the discovery of Finnegan's blood-soaked secret life, the village was deeply shaken.

But something positive had come out of the tragedy. With Sam behind bars, it signaled the end of a killing spree that had lasted nearly a generation. The murders and disappearances had become so much a part of the townspeople's routine that stress and fear had also become part of their everyday lives.

"My uncle Randy says she died of natural causes," said Venus. "So Sam didn't kill her."

"Doesn't make the other people he killed any less dead," Penny was quick to specify. "Ms. Benjamin used to teach my mom in grade school. From what I hear, her body was stuffed in a fridge, arms and legs sawed off, eyes and tongue plucked out, and something had eaten her liver."

Rumors about the bodies discovered on Finnegan's property had run wild in the last week, and they'd gotten more gruesome with every telling. Penny's grim description silenced the younger girl, but only for a moment.

"Poor Audrey." Venus sighed. "And poor Mr. and Mrs. Bergeron. That girl was their whole life."

"It's been a messed-up week. Are you going to the funeral?"

Venus leaned her chin on the counter and stared into the distance behind the register. The funeral was today, and it really felt like she should be there. After all, both she and Penny had spent enough time with Audrey. Penny frequently babysat the child to make a few extra dollars, and Venus often joined her. In time, the two had become like big sisters to the bubbly little girl. Venus had loved Audrey as much as anyone, but she was afraid she'd feel like a fraud going to the church. Her parents, having their own, more secular set of beliefs, had never taken her to church, which would make the proceedings all the more alien and awkward.

"Nah," said Venus. "If I go, I'll just start crying again. And . . . I wouldn't know what to do there."

"Duh, it's a funeral," Penny said, picking up a bottle and a rag. "It's just a way to say good-bye. Pay your respects. People expect you to be there."

"Not my parents. They're not going. Besides, it's easy for you to say that; you have a perfect excuse not to go." Venus waved her arm, indicating the ice cream shop.

"I'd go if I could. I'm gonna miss the little mouse."

Penny kept on cleaning while Venus absentmindedly ate her second cone. As the minutes wore on, the weight of their conversation dissipated. The girls had already gone through the worst of their grieving. When Lieutenant Bélanger had walked up to William Bergeron's farm with a lady from out of town, it hadn't escaped the attention of Ms. Dwight, who lived across the street. When William broke down, weeping on his front porch, the neighbor had no trouble figuring out why and immediately got on the phone. By sunset, not a soul in Saint-Ferdinand was unaware of the tragedy. At that time, the medical examiner had yet to turn in a verdict about the little girl's cause of death. The population separated into two camps: those who went to the police station, demanding the monster who had done such a thing be brought to justice, and those who rallied at the Bergeron farm, offering what comfort they could. Venus's parents stayed home, of course, but she went to the station, according to her curious nature.

She also knew she'd run into her uncle Randy there. As luck would have it, she arrived just as he was about to leave for the hospital. As she wiggled between the other bystanders, her attention was immediately drawn to the bright yellow ambulance. She'd known what she would see before she had cleared the last row of onlookers, yet she'd persisted. When she had gotten close enough, she managed to catch a few words of her uncle's conversation with Inspector Crowley and Lieutenant Bélanger. She didn't hear much, just that Audrey had no wounds beyond a few scrapes and bruises, and that it was likely her defective heart had given out. The conversation took a strange turn from there and Venus had been intent on eavesdropping, but then her eyes settled on the stretcher and her interest evaporated instantly.

The black plastic body bag had seemed almost empty, only a small lump suggesting its contents. The rest of the world sort of vanished at that moment. Venus didn't know how long she stood there, staring at the tiny remains of Audrey Bergeron. Venus only snapped out of her daze after the ambulance had driven away. By that time her uncle was long gone, and only a handful of people still congregated outside the police station. Venus cried the whole ride home, struggling to keep from falling off her bike.

It all seemed like so long ago now. So surreal. Perhaps that was why she didn't want to attend the funeral. As long as she stayed away from any reminders of the events, Venus could pretend they'd never happened. Penny seemed to be holding herself together much better. Venus found herself envying her friend's strength.

Just as these stray thoughts crossed her mind, a series of cars drove by the shop. Penny stared, putting a hand over her mouth. Other bystanders stopped to look at the procession too. Alice Merret's grandmother crossed herself. David Radford, who did accounting for most of the village shook his head while his partner Shawn blew his nose in a tissue. In the middle of the line of cars was a hearse, and inside it they saw a pile of colorful stuffed animals.

"Penny?" Venus stood slowly from her stool. "Mind if I come back in an hour or so?"

By the time Venus caught up with the funeral procession, the cars were already empty. Her father had once told her that Saint-Ferdinand boasted a graveyard twice the size of any similar village. It had taken her a few years to learn that this was due almost solely to the Saint-Ferdinand Killer. The cemetery had perhaps two dozen rows of headstones and a small mausoleum. Once she made her way past the wrought-iron gates, she could easily make out the small crowd of people that had gathered to pay their respects to Audrey.

Everyone was wearing their Sunday best, and Venus suddenly felt self-conscious about her jean shorts and white tank top. Thankfully, there were plenty of large maples and dense weeping willows behind which she could conceal herself. She got as close as she dared before kneeling behind an ancient headstone (she didn't think the owner would mind, his name having been all but eroded from the monument) and resting her arms and chin on top. It was a perfect spot: close enough to hear everything but far enough that she wouldn't be seen.

Venus took stock of the scene. A sharp stab pierced her heart when she laid eyes on the tiny white casket resting next to a diminutive hole in the ground. She couldn't help but wonder what kind of cruel world made coffins for children a necessity. Equally heartbreaking were Audrey's parents, William and Beatrice, who were huddled together, their eyes swollen from days of grieving.

This wasn't the first time Saint-Ferdinand had rallied around the Bergerons in their time of need. When Audrey was born over a month premature, she was underweight and too weak to survive on her own. The doctors at the hospital in Sherbrooke had kept constant vigil on her, despite the odds of her survival being very low. The community had stepped up as well. Many of William's employees volunteered to cover his shifts at his many businesses, while several villagers, including Penny's mom, had cooked meals for the new parents and delivered them to the hospital. It had been three weeks before Audrey was able to breathe unassisted. Twenty-three days after giving birth, Beatrice Bergeron had finally been allowed to hold her baby. She and William had been warned that their little girl's heart and lungs would always be fragile, and they'd doted on her accordingly.

A priest whom Venus didn't recognize, probably from another village, went through this same history, regularly interrupted by Beatrice's loud sobs. He did his best to comfort the mourners by reminding them that while Audrey was gone, her time spent among them had been happy. From the very day she had come into the world, she had brought out the best in everyone, and in her eight short years had done more good than many could aspire to in a lifetime.

Venus decided that the priest was right. The little girl had been a positive presence in her life since Venus's family had moved to the village. Every time she stopped at the ice cream shop or ran an errand for her mother at the drugstore, Audrey had been there, making customers smile. Every winter for the past four years, the little girl could be found skating on the lake or sledding down a hill. She wasn't the only child her age in Saint-Ferdinand, but she was easily the happiest, and her joy was infectious.

Eventually, the tiny white coffin was lowered into the tiny dark hole. It was troubling to think that the button-nosed, platinum-haired little girl would be covered in dirt and left to rot. Once the grave was filled, each person filed past the shiny new headstone, depositing one of the stuffed toys that had filled the hearse. Most left behind brand-new plush bears, Audrey's favorite, while closer friends and family members left behind older toys that had belonged to the child. The most battered of all was a small, dirty, matted, and obviously much-beloved bear with a red felt hat sewn to its head. Beatrice lovingly laid it at the foot of the mountain of plush toys. She knelt there, her husband crouched next to her, leaving the priest and the rest of the attendees to quietly depart.

By the time the Bergerons pulled themselves to their feet, the only other people in the graveyard apart from them were Inspector Crowley and Venus's uncle Randy. The four of them spoke for a long while in quiet whispers that Venus strained to hear, but without success. Once it became obvious that the bereaved parents were ready to go, the inspector exchanged a few words with Randy before escorting the Bergerons to his car and driving them away.

Curiously, Venus's uncle did not immediately leave after watching the inspector drive around a bend. Venus was almost tempted to step out from behind the headstone to talk to him, but something in her uncle's eyes made her decide against it.

At a brisk, almost nervous pace, Randy made his way back to where the attendees had just paid their respects. Once standing on the freshly turned earth, he looked nervously around before crouching to pick something up. He stowed his prize inside his jacket and walked back to his car.

As Randy drove off, leaving her alone in the cemetery, Venus slowly crept out of hiding. Curious, she went to see which of the stuffed toys her uncle had pilfered from the plush shrine to Audrey's memory. As she suspected, the battered old bear with the red hat was gone. Less obvious, however, was why her uncle, a respected doctor and gentle human being, would stoop so low as to steal a dead child's toy.

Venus was no stranger to the bizarre occurrences Saint-Ferdinand could serve up. She wasn't originally from the village, having only moved there with her family a little over four years prior. To its residents, the little town seemed so normal, but through the eyes of a girl who'd spent most of her life living in the suburbs of Montreal, every little quirk and eccentricity stood out. It had taken her a while to figure out how deep the idiosyncrasies went, and after a few years she'd simply given up. There seemed to be no end to how weird the little village truly was.

Passing through the winding old roads that connected the farms, orchards, and occasional residential developments, Venus was reminded of the unique layer of personality that the village and its residents exhibited when you looked past the surface.

Riding by her friend Abraham's place, she could see the large windows installed on the second floor of his family's barn. Abraham's father had gone from farmer to artist at about the same time she arrived in town, renovating the structure into an immense studio. Almost across from that farm was Old Man Richard's orchard. The owner was a cantankerous old man who seemed to hate everyone yet took meticulous care of his trees, going so far as to name each of them. A short detour would lead her to Ms. Livingston's house, a lady who raised rabbits for no reason in particular. Venus had never done it herself, but all the kids knew that if you went over for a visit and named one of the bunnies, she'd force you to take it home with you. But none of their eccentricities could explain her uncle's disturbing behavior at the cemetery.

While the village didn't have a school (all the kids had to travel over an hour away to Sherbrooke for their education), it did have a church. Easily one of the oldest structures on Main Street, the Jonathan Moore Church stood as the center of the community. Services were held there, but in the four years since she'd moved to the area, Venus had never heard of a priest or other church official ever residing in town. Rather, it seemed that a few of the more influential locals took turns playing the part. Of all the places in the village, the church was the only one that had never locked its doors, despite the threat of a serial killer terrorizing the area.

Venus could see the tall bell tower looming over the tree line, indicating that she was close to the village center and also nearing the ice cream parlor. For a moment she entertained the hope that Penny would give her another free ice cream cone. But her thoughts of cold desserts quickly vanished as she got closer to one of the crossroads that led to Main Street.

There, Venus spotted three other teenage cyclists. Her heart immediately sank. While the village was strange to her, Venus and her parents were, in turn, strange to some of the villagers. Some thought the McKenzies simply had weird city ways, but others weren't as accepting. Particularly the three teenagers who were now blocking her progress.

Venus could put a name to each of their faces: Nick, Brad, and André. "Good kids" as far as anyone else was concerned, but Venus knew better. While they never picked on the other kids at school or in the village, when the three were together, they would torment her endlessly. They called her names, pushed her around, and the previous summer she'd gotten a vicious skinned knee after they'd run her off the road while she was riding her bike. These assholes weren't intimidating individually. They weren't even that rebellious. Venus knew each and every one of their families, and they were, by Saint-Ferdinand's standards, normal people. While the McKenzies certainly could not be called that, her family's "weirdness" wasn't why the boys harassed her. It was out of jealousy.

The parents of Saint-Ferdinand kept all their children, no matter how old, rebellious, or independent, under a tight watch. Early curfews, constant supervision, and a demand for absolute transparency from their offspring were common—a well-understood consequence of having a killer loose in their town. For most, this had been going on since birth, and no one was exempt.

No one except Venus.

Even before moving from the city, Venus had always had more freedom than most kids. She could come and go as she pleased, whenever she pleased. For as long as she could remember, she never had to follow any family rules or give an account of her whereabouts. "Free-range parenting," her parents called it, and even with the shadow of a gruesome murderer looming, they never bothered to tighten their watch on their only child. Of course, this garnered her no small amount of resentment from the other kids.

Preferring to avoid another unpleasant confrontation, Venus opted to take a longer route back to Main Street. She had her own kind of envy to deal with. For starters, the reason she couldn't more easily ride through the woods or take a shortcut over rougher terrain was that her bicycle was designed for the city. With narrow, fragile wheels and a light frame that wouldn't survive any of the obstacles common to Saint-Ferdinand's back roads, her bike was yet another oddity that made her stand out. As she pedaled away from the bullies, Venus envied the more rugged mountain bikes that most kids rode around town.

Her alternate route took her through another part of the village, where the more successful members of the community, those who either owned businesses or chose not to live on their farms, resided. The styles of architecture ranged from large two-story

Colonials, to modern aesthetics, to sprawling ranches. All were built on beautifully landscaped properties that boasted stone driveways, gazebos, and extensive flower beds.

This was where the Bergerons lived. On a normal day, their house would have been one of the easiest to distinguish. It had everything: plenty of square footage, a large inground swimming pool, and a beautiful tree house in the back. Weeping willows decorated the front lawn, barely hiding the plethora of brightly colored toys that littered the grounds. The immense stone construction was flanked by two large chimneys, and the pool house mirrored the design and architecture of the main house. Today, the Bergerons' home was even easier to spot. It was the one with dozens of cars parked out front.

Venus couldn't help but become choked up. For the second time today, she felt compelled to give William and Beatrice Bergeron her condolences. To let them know how she felt about Audrey's death and try to offer some solace to the grieving parents.

She slowed her pace, hoping to catch a glimpse of what was going on inside. Looking through the house's large windows, she could see dozens of people inside. It was the same group she'd been spying on at the cemetery less than an hour ago, except more villagers had joined them. A quick look at the guests' cars told Venus that some of the visitors were from out of town. The Bergerons' influence wasn't limited to Saint-Ferdinand.

Her eyes settled on a large emerald-green Ford Taurus station wagon. It was cleaner than she had ever seen it. This was her uncle Randy's car, and seeing it sent an unexplained chill down her spine. For a moment, she wanted to go peek inside the vehicle. See if perhaps her uncle had left the toy he'd stolen in there. Just as she was about to get off her bike, however, a car drove up the street.

It was another unfamiliar car, a shiny gray Acura sedan. As it passed, Venus couldn't help but notice a rental sticker on its trunk. It parked in front of the Bergeron place, the driver being especially careful to stay away from other vehicles. The woman who stepped out was not an experienced driver, that much was clear.

With brown hair and wearing a gray suit, the woman looked to be in her late twenties. Too young to be one of the Bergerons' friends. She glanced around for a moment, making eye contact with Venus. After an uncomfortable beat, the woman double-checked her phone for the address, a poor excuse to look at something else and break the awkwardness. Without looking back up, she made her way to the front door, where she was greeted and allowed in without question.

For the second time that day, Venus decided not to express her condolences. Between her uncle's bizarre behavior, a house full of strangers, and simply not wearing the right clothes, she decided that this wasn't her place.

Then again, the same could be said of Saint-Ferdinand.

RANDY

A CHILL WENT down Randy's spine. Though it was a relatively cool night, sweat began to bead all over his body. He would much rather be rid of this unsavory task in the daylight. But at least the cemetery was out of the way, and most of the village had gone on to the reception to offer their condolences to William and Beatrice. Everyone, that is, but his niece, Venus, whose bicycle he'd noticed outside the graveyard as he'd driven away from Audrey's burial plot.

It was pointless to hope she hadn't seen him taking the stuffed bear from the grave, but that was a problem for another day. The business at hand would require his full attention, something that would be difficult enough given that it was past midnight and the old graveyard made him so uneasy.

It wasn't that Randy had a problem with dead bodies. Part of his job was to perform the occasional autopsy or, as he'd been called to do the previous week, identify and sort through the bodies of the recently and not-so-recently deceased. What made the medical examiner nervous wasn't the dark, either, though it certainly didn't help. Nor was he superstitious. Superstition was fear born of ignorance, and he knew better.

No, what made Randy's nerves fray was what would become of him if he were discovered, or worse, what would happen if he failed at his task. If the townsfolk learned what he was about to do to Audrey, their current rage toward Sam Finnegan, who had merely placed the girl's dead body in a fridge, would be redirected at Randy. *They wouldn't understand.*

Still, the doctor set himself to the task. First, he carefully removed the toys that covered Audrey's grave. As emotional as this initial step might be, it was by far the easiest. He kept his mind busy by trying to memorize the exact position of each stuffed animal so that he could move them back into place once his work was complete.

Then came the more physical part of his job. Randy wasn't an athletic man, and the two hours that followed underlined that fact. Measuring five feet nine inches, he had nurtured a modest but growing pot belly over the last two decades. As a result, his cardiovascular ability was far below what was necessary to shovel six feet of dirt off the child-sized casket. Thankfully, his arms had remained somewhat powerful; otherwise, he doubted he could have finished the job.

Having cleared off the coffin, Randy allowed himself a few moments to rest. Sitting at the edge of the hole he'd just dug, he stared at the box inside, where they'd put little Audrey's body less than a day ago. It seemed to glow as the light of the moon hit the glossy white surface.

Once he caught his breath, Randy jumped back into the hole and stood on top of the coffin. He whispered an apology that seemed directed at the sightless stone cherub on the headstone above him, then struck downward with his shovel. The wood on the lid cracked like thunder. The doctor waited a few moments in silence, his ears pricked, listening for any reaction to the noise. Apart from the occasional cricket, however, it was quiet.

"Well, here's hoping no one exhumes you again anytime soon, darling." He was surprised at how loud the words sounded in the night air, but if anyone were going to hear his activities this far from town, they already would have.

Randy pried loose the top of the coffin. Underneath lay Audrey Bergeron's body. His own autopsy had revealed that her little heart had given out while she'd been riding her bicycle. The scratches and bruising indicated that she'd fallen from her ride, but the pattern of her wounds suggested she'd been limp and probably unconscious when she fell. Finnegan claimed that he'd found her on his way home from the bar and, not wanting to abandon Audrey on the side of the road, had taken her with him. The child's bike was recovered where Sam claimed he'd stumbled upon the body, and the medical examination supported his story. Oddly, Audrey's death was the only one that seemed to weigh on Old Sam Finnegan's shoulders, even though he had nothing to do with it.

It was difficult to look down at her and not expect Audrey to sit up and giggle. Even in the pale moonlight it seemed as if there were life in her tiny frame. A sudden, irrational fear took hold of Randy. Carefully, he kneeled down and gently peeled back her left eyelid with his thumb. What he was looking for in the child's dead eyes no other medical examiner could have seen. In fact, only a handful of people alive would have believed, let alone understood, what the doctor was searching for.

"Still in there?" he mumbled to the cadaver. "Good girl."

Reassured, Randy reached up and grabbed the leather bag he had left by the grave. He carefully untied the straps that kept the worn, tanned flaps closed, and opened the bag with reverence. In it, he found a handful of crude iron nails. Roughly four inches long, each seemed to have been forged long ago. A thick layer of oil prevented them from corroding. The doctor pulled out four of these nails before closing the bag and exchanging it for a hammer he had also brought with him. It, too, was an antique, its iron head worn and chipped, the wooden handle gray with age.

Gently, Randy laid down the tools on Audrey's chest. He carefully took off the child's shoes and then socks. The doctor picked up a handful of dirt from the loose soil around him and smelled it. Satisfied, he then vigorously rubbed the bottoms of the corpse's feet with the earth, only stopping once both were thoroughly black with dirt. Anyone watching him would have wasted no time labeling the doctor a madman. Yet he still had one last insanity to perform. There was no point in stopping now. He kept reminding himself it was for the best.

With a deep sigh of resignation, Randy picked up the hammer and a single nail. Aligning the point of the nail between the middle metatarsals, he expertly drove it through the soft white skin of the child's right foot. In two hits, the nail had gone straight through the delicate little extremity.

Either tears or sweat blurred the medical examiner's eyes. Randy brushed the moisture away, picked up a second nail, and repeated the process on Audrey's left foot. He then took up a third nail and touched its tip to her right eye, but hesitated. He cocked his head as if listening to a silent voice, then said, "Don't worry, darling; you'll be able to see in a second."

Then he hammered the nail into her eye. Before he could take stock of what he had done, he picked up the final nail and drove that one through her left eye.

The deed was done. Randy McKenzie stood over his handiwork. He knew his actions were an abomination. All of it, a clear violation of the law, common decency, and his personal and professional ethics. Yet, despite the atrocities he had just committed, to have *done nothing* would have been far worse. How could doing the right thing feel so wrong?

Before climbing out of the hole, Randy bent down one last time. Tenderly, he brushed Audrey's bright blond bangs away from her face. Her lovely eyes were destroyed now, punctured by ugly iron spikes. The doctor touched her cheek one last time before grabbing a pendant from around her neck, a gold medallion with two doves and a candle, and yanking it off.

"Sorry, love. Your father's going to want proof I did as promised."

It took most of Randy's remaining will to pull himself out of the grave. He still had another hour of work ahead of him, refilling the grave and erasing as many traces of his unspeakable activities as possible. Before he started shoveling, however, he picked up one last item he had brought with him and threw it down into the hole. Once that was done, he picked up the shovel and began tossing soil back into the hole, burying little Audrey for the second time and, with her, a worn stuffed bear with a red felt hat.

CROWLEY

"MR. CROWLEY! WHAT an unexpected pleasure. Come in! Come in! Make yourself at home."

Sam Finnegan gestured toward the door of his cell with an affable smile. He'd been cleaned up and dressed in fresh clothes. The Saint-Ferdinand police station didn't exactly have prison uniforms, but someone had found a loose-fitting jumpsuit and T-shirt, along with a pair of white socks and Velcro sandals.

The confessed murderer had spent the past few days recuperating from whatever drunken state he'd kept himself in for the better part of his life. He'd either been less of a drunk or was more resilient than assumed, and had sobered up quickly. Sanity, however, remained an elusive trait. In fact, Crowley quickly noticed that without the drink, Finnegan seemed even more on edge and disconnected from reality than before. He'd transformed from a bumbling, semicoherent old man to a somewhat cunning, ever-regretful husk. Behind his eyes lurked a silent threat while his face was nothing but remorse.

"I am at home, Sam."

It was a matter of fact. Everyone in town knew how many hours the inspector spent working, whether on duty or not. It went far beyond that, however. While the station physically belonged to the municipality, its soul was Crowley's. The building, facilities, and even officers were but an extension of himself. A status he'd built out of hard work and good will.

"Right, right . . . Well, welcome anyways," Sam said. "I'm sure you're here on business, but I wanted to thank you personally for treating me so well. Especially after . . . well . . ."

"After you spent eighteen years terrorizing my city, murdered . . . How many, Sam? Twenty? Thirty of the people under my care? Including my friend's daughter?"

"Stephen." Finnegan stepped up to the door and grabbed on to the bars of his cell. "I didn't kill Audrey. You gotta believe me."

Finnegan, the Saint-Ferdinand Killer, had eyes as blue as evening snow. Pale and cold. In them, Crowley wanted to read the man's soul, but the curtains of madness covered all the important facts. It was tempting to let the old man dangle. Let him suffer in doubt as he'd tortured others with grief. It would serve him right, but Stephen knew that if he wanted to get something from Sam, he'd have to give something first.

"I got Randy's autopsy report on Audrey," he said, stretching the information, then paused for both effect and to twist the knife. "Heart failure."

Relief. It went through Finnegan's body like a reverse shock. Instead of tensing his body and muscles, the fact seemed to release him. For a moment his grip on the bars lessened. There might as well have been no jail, no cell. In that instant Sam was more free than he'd been in a long time. Perhaps decades. His was the easing of a man who'd found forgiveness or peace with his god.

"Thank God," he whispered.

"What difference does it make, Sam? I have a twelve-page confession stating you've killed twenty-two people. You ended it by *explicitly* stating these are only the ones you remember. So what's one little girl?"

It was infuriating to Stephen. This psychopath acting like he somehow cared about his friend's daughter. The worry appeared genuine, of course, but that didn't matter. He had no right to pretend, let alone feel honest remorse. Yet the inspector had to show restraint, which was not his specialty. He was here for information. To solve a problem. Not to vent his feelings about the old man.

"I ain't no monster, Stephen," Sam said, scratching at his face. "I know, I know . . . I've killed. A lot. But it was necessity! I ain't got an ounce of malice in me, Stephen. World's gonna remember me as the Saint-Ferdinand Killer, the beast who killed to steal people's eyes. Their precious eyes."

He looked up at Stephen, fingernails still digging into his short gray beard. Ever since his arrest, Sam had been little more than a whining, crying old sack of bones. He'd offered no resistance and spent the bulk of his time mumbling to himself. There was no threat left in him. He was ancient, weak, and incoherent. For the first time, however, Crowley saw the killer. There was something in Finnegan's eyes, a focus and determination. This is the person his victims must have seen moments before their demise.

"I ain't no child killer, Stephen," Sam continued. "I ain't no rapist, no sadist, and I ain't no necrophile. Necessity, Stephen! I killed outta necessity!"

"All right. Settle down."

Up to now, Finnegan had made himself at home in his cell. He'd gone in peacefully and had enjoyed his meals quietly and been cooperative in answering questions. While Crowley hadn't visited his prisoner more than a handful of times, he'd always seen a placid old man resigned to his fate.

Not today.

Being alone with the murderer brought out a new side. Finnegan, no longer the obedient captive, paced his cage and fidgeted with the bars and his clothes. A picture of barely restrained panic.

"How about you tell me who you've been working with? Share the blame a little so you don't have to shoulder it all yourself."

"There's no one else. Alone, Stephen! I was left alone with that thing. Alone to hold the keys and watch the door. To keep an eye, to keep as many eyes as possible, on that cave."

Eyes. Always eyes with this village. Crowley wasn't a native of Saint-Ferdinand. He'd moved here because of the job opportunity and because of his wife. He stayed for his family and the community. In time, he'd become such an integral part of the village, he might as well have been a native. Yet in all that time, he never got the fascination with eyes.

"Well, you don't have to worry about that anymore."

"Oh, I don't, do I?" Sam said. "I ain't bad people, Stephen. You and me? We ain't the same. But our jobs? They might as well be the same."

"Sam," Stephen said, and smiled, trying to keep his tone from being too condescending, "you don't have a job."

"Mincin' words, are we? Call it a responsibility, then. Whatever floats your boat. But these?" Sam hit the bars of his cell with an open palm. "These mean nothing! When it comes for me, and it will, a few metal bars ain't gonna keep it out."

Crowley frowned, walking to stand less than a foot from the cell door. He wanted to leverage his size and imposing frame to browbeat some answers out of Finnegan, but either the bars separating them or something in Sam himself made that impossible. The killer held his stare. Whatever agitated him was more threatening than the mild posturing from the inspector.

"What's coming for you, Sam? Is it the thing from the cave?"

"You know what it is, Stephen. You ain't no fool who don't know the fox in your henhouse."

"Humor me. The thing from the cave, where is it now?"

"Heh." Sam shrugged, then pinched his thin skin. "I ain't dead. So I suppose it must still be there. Or maybe trapped somewhere else? One of your friends, maybe?"

That cave. Someone would need to go in there eventually. Crowley could only stall that part of the investigation for so long. For now, it was easy to simply request that the cave be left alone. Stephen's superiors up the chain of command somehow had enough confidence in his judgment that they trusted his instincts. If he waited too long, however, he'd have to start throwing red tape over the process like so much tinsel on a Christmas tree. Better to have it be done with sooner rather than later, but first he had to make sure no one would find anything they shouldn't.

"So the lock is still on the door? The thing is in there." There was hope.

"You didn't take my eyes away, did you? Them eyes are what's keepin' it in the cave. It's the thin line keepin' me alive right now. Without those eyes—"

"I had the forensic team take those as evidence. The eyes of your victims? We removed those. They're gone, and you"—Stephen pointed a finger in Finnegan's face—"are still alive."

Sam was a bit shocked. If Crowley could trust his instincts about the man, the surprise was genuine.

"Then maybe somethin' else is keeping it there? Or it's stayin' there on purpose. Plannin'. Plottin'."

"Or maybe it's trapped in the cave. Maybe it just doesn't dare come out into the sun. How long has it been in there, Sam? Almost two decades? More? It's gotta be weak at this point."

Gleaming white but crooked teeth peered out from between Finnegan's cracked lips as he smiled without humor. It was a knowing man's grin. The kind of expression one had when realizing one spoke with someone who was at a disadvantage.

"You have no idea what yer dealin' with, do you?" Sam said, fingers dancing on the bars as he explained. "This is a god, Stephen! Not just a fancy name for something mystical and magical. It don't get weak. Do you know how lucky we are that there's a way to keep it trapped at all?"

"Then, since you're still alive, maybe it's not as evil as you make it out to be."

"Oh, you damn fool, Crowley." Finnegan shook his head. "This ain't no bear. It's a vessel. A container in which we've been pissin' our greed and hate for decades. This ain't just no random god no more. It's a god of death. *A god of hate and death.*"

DANIEL

UNLIKE MOST BOYS his age, Daniel Crowley usually woke along with the sunrise, even during summer vacation when nights were already short. Being raised by a single father who was also head of the town's law enforcement had bred in him a sense of discipline that few teenagers understood, let alone practiced. Not only did he wake up early and follow a strict exercise regimen, Dan also ate a surprisingly healthy diet and displayed impeccable grooming habits. While his buddies were discovering the joys and pains of alcohol abuse, Dan was content to nurse a single beer for the whole evening. Because of this, he was often asked to be the designated driver, or to cover for his friends whose parents wouldn't let them drink.

Dan also took it upon himself to earn his own spending money. For the past three years, he had spent summers and weekends at Luke Howard's grocery store, bagging purchases or hauling inventory. It wasn't the best salary in the world, but it covered his gas and the upkeep on his old Honda Civic, the cornerstone of a healthy social life in Saint-Ferdinand.

Thankfully, he wasn't scheduled to start work for another two weeks. This gave Dan plenty of time to catch up on a few things. There was a lot that needed to be done during those empty days. For starters, his Civic could use a little maintenance. It wasn't in bad shape for a used car, but it was beginning to show its age. Some amount of time would also have to be dutifully wasted by the lake. Summer demanded it. Then there was Sasha Lindholm, his longtime girlfriend, who would monopolize as many hours as she could before his job swallowed him whole. Finally, he wanted to hang out with his dad.

Dan genuinely enjoyed his father's company. The two had built a strong relationship after Dan's mother had abandoned them both when he was still in diapers. Stephen relied on his son to maintain the household while he kept up the odd and demanding hours of a high-ranking police inspector. In return, Dan counted on his dad to fill in the roles of both parents, a task he was usually very capable of.

Usually. The events of the previous week had already sabotaged several planned activities between father and son. Dan understood that the situation with Sam Finnegan and the shocking death of the city's most beloved child took precedence over a fishing trip. But now that Finnegan had confessed to everything and they were waiting for a lawyer to be appointed for his defense, Dan was hoping he and his father could get back to their normal routine.

The teenager rolled out of bed and made his way downstairs to the kitchen. They shared a two-story Colonial, large enough that both men could go all day without seeing each other if they so desired. So Dan wasn't surprised when he didn't cross paths with his father during his morning rituals. It was only when he sat at the kitchen table to eat a breakfast of eggs and bacon that he noticed his father's Ford Explorer was missing from the driveway.

"You can't be serious," he muttered. He dropped his fork and stood to have a better look through the window.

The situation was far from unprecedented. Often, Stephen Crowley was called upon to work through the night or leave before dawn on some emergency. Which was why Daniel had made sure his father was prepared for any and all eventualities.

He had even gone through the trouble of pulling out a cooler, buying some crushed ice, and preparing sandwiches for the trip. The Finnegan case would be stagnant for the next few days, and any other situation could easily be handled by Matt Bélanger for twenty-four hours. No radios, no cell phones, no interruptions: that had been the arrangement.

Furious, Dan called his father for an explanation. Of course, his cell phone was out of service range, but that didn't stop the boy from leaving an angry message he'd probably regret later. Still seething, Daniel abandoned his breakfast, grabbed his keys, and made for the door.

Saint-Ferdinand was a small town, but the territory surrounding it was significantly larger. Composed of wheat and cornfields, orchards, and a couple of dairy farms, the municipality radiated far around the village. For such a small populace, it was an inconveniently huge area to cover when looking for someone. These circumstances had likely kept Sam Finnegan's dark secret hidden for the last twenty years, and now Stephen Crowley was benefitting from them as well. Hence, Daniel had no choice but to make his way to the station and see if anyone knew his dad's whereabouts.

With just under two thousand permanent residents, Saint-Ferdinand didn't require more than nine or ten full-time police officers, and only the most rudimentary of facilities. Located at the edge of town on the main road, it boasted three floors of very limited square footage. The ground floor housed a reception area, where three dispatchers shared shifts throughout the week. There were a handful of desks and three offices, the largest of which was Stephen Crowley's. The basement had a couple of offices that were, to Dan's knowledge, used for storage, most of it for files related to the Saint-Ferdinand Killer. There were also a couple of prison cells that were primarily used to shelter farmers who weren't in a condition to drive. Finally, the top floor was reserved for archiving and booking.

When Dan walked in, he was politely greeted by the dispatch-er, Jacqueline Tremain. He'd known her since he was a boy, and she'd treated him like a favored nephew for a long time. Now that he was six-foot-one, square-jawed, and had respectable stubble, her demeanor toward him had become more professional. Were he the manipulative type, he could have exploited that to get away with just about anything, but Dan barely gave it a second thought.

"Morning, Jackie. Have you seen my dad anywhere?" he asked as he crossed through the doorway.

"Good morning, Dan. He dropped by 'bout an hour ago." The dispatcher looked up from a hunting magazine. "I assumed he'd be back home by now. Want me to page him to see where he's at?"

The notion had its appeal. It would be expedient and cut out the guesswork. But Dan's anger and resentment demanded that his father be given no warning.

"Nah. Do you know if he was stopping off anywhere before heading home?"

"He was supposed to check out something at the Finnegan place."

Dan barely had time to thank her before storming out the door.

"I thought we'd agreed: no work."

Daniel Crowley was busy reapplying a layer of sunscreen. Af-ter spending half of the morning driving around Saint-Ferdinand, he had found his old man's car right where Jackie had told him it'd be. However, when Dan had arrived at the Finnegan property, a patch of land located deep in the woods behind the Peterson farm, his father wasn't there.

Dan had slipped under the yellow tape that delineated the borders of the crime scene, a line he knew took him into a re-stricted area. Everything and anything of importance had been removed, sent to a lab out of town, leaving the area cleaner than it had probably been in ages. Yet, even with the property picked clean, Inspector Crowley was nowhere to be seen.

Eventually Dan did find his father. Following a trail that led deep into the woods, he'd spotted his old man crouched next to a cave entrance. Daniel had heard about the cave. It was there that Sam Finnegan, the Saint-Ferdinand Killer, had been arrested, and where some of his most gruesome pastimes had taken place.

They'd had a huge fight in front of the cave. Daniel accusing his father of forgetting their fishing trip, and the inspector admonishing his son for potentially contaminating a crime scene. The argument was one for the books. A rare occasion when Dan was so sure of the righteousness of his position that, as his dad had taught him, he refused to back down. It took a while, but eventually he was able to do what no one else in Saint-Ferdinand could: wear down his old man.

So they struck a deal. Crowley would make good on his promise, and the two of them would go fishing. In return, the inspector would forget that his son had essentially broken the law by walking through a crime scene. Now, a little more than two hours later, they were on the waters of the lake in Magog, fishing rods in hand.

"What work?" said Crowley, taking mock offense.

"That rock you picked up back at Finnegan's place." Dan pointed with a bottle of sunscreen at the stone in his father's hand. "Isn't that evidence?"

Crowley turned it over a couple of times. "Nah. If it were, one of the eggheads would have bagged it."

It was a peculiar stone. Smooth and round, it belonged in a riverbed, not near a cave entrance. More interesting was the symbol sculpted into its surface. An eye with a spiral iris.

"I've never seen one that old," Dan said. "The symbol, I mean."

The teenager cast his line into the lake. After their fight, they'd taken the boat out and driven to Lac Memphrémagog. The day was old, and any fishing would have been better done at the crack of dawn, but catching fish wasn't the point of these trips. These little escapes were for the Crowley boys to spend time alone. Stephen needed the break before diving back into his investigation, and the coming days would likely offer few opportunities for this kind of relaxation.

"All right," said Daniel. "Put that thing away before I skip it across the lake."

With a smile and a nod, Stephen Crowley tossed the stone in his hands a couple of times before stowing it in his coat shirt pocket. He leaned backward, letting his face bathe in the hot summer sun. He even allowed himself a brief smile of contentment. This would come to bite him in the ass during the next few days, but he was too proud to put on sunscreen. The burns on his features would turn his already-red skin a vicious shade of crimson, and his temper would be made even more volatile by the accompanying irritation. Even as the light turned his vision a bloody orange red through his closed eyelids, Stephen knew all that, but at this moment, he was fine with it. It was worth the sacrifice.

The inspector exhaled in satisfaction. "Thanks."

"What for?"

"Twisting my arm and forcing me to do this."

Daniel loved his father's boat. Twenty feet long with a powerful outboard motor, it was quite luxurious and roomy for two people to go fishing on. They could have comfortably been six on board with room to spare, but on most occasions it was just the two of them and a cooler filled with drinks and sandwiches. For as long as Daniel could remember, this had been the teenager's favorite thing to do with his old man.

Stephen, however, looked tired in a way that his son hadn't seen in a long time. Year after year, he'd seen his old man work himself half to death after each Saint-Ferdinand murder was confirmed. Sleepless nights, absent clues, and evidence that would constantly lead to nothing but disappointment pushed the inspector to his limits, but always he'd been able to get back on his feet. Usually a day off and a long, uninterrupted night of sleep were enough to undo any of the damage.

This time, even though the case was, for all intents, solved, it seemed like the toll had been deeper and had left a more permanent mark on the man. Between smiles and short bouts of serenity, Stephen would get a strange look on his face. A rare combination of worry and frustration. Daniel might have been tempted to call it fear had he not known that his father was incapable of that particular emotion. Besides, the inspector would dance in and out of it so fast that there had to be something more to this new state of mind.

"Beer?" Stephen offered while riffling through the cooler and pulling out a couple of foil-wrapped sandwiches.

"I dunno. What if the pigs come rolling in?" Dan joked.

Of course there would be police patrolling the lake, but Stephen knew these guys by name, and none of them would bat an eye at seeing Daniel with a drink in hand.

"You and I can take a few cops." Smiling, Stephen tossed the beer to his son and picked one out for himself.

"By the way, I never got to ask you: How was the service?"

The Crowley boys weren't known for small talk. They'd briefly discussed the death of Audrey Bergeron but hadn't brought up that subject, or Sam Finnegan, since the funeral.

"Funerals are funerals," he answered, casting his line into the water. "People say dumb things they think are touching."

Dan nodded. He knew his father's views on the local community. By virtue of his title, the inspector was privileged to know a lot of private information. In an area the size of Saint-Ferdinand, where secrets were hard to hide, that meant he knew everything.

"So . . . when?" Stephen asked with a level of hesitation.

"When what?"

"When do you join?"

Daniel sighed loudly and turned his eyes to the horizon. Without looking at his father, he tried to come up with a dignified answer. "I don't know, Dad. I'm not much for religion, you know that."

They were talking about the church, or rather the social club focused around it. Part chamber of commerce, part gentlemen's club, its members included Stephen and others of the village elite, and it met at least once a week. It was both an offshoot of the Saint-Ferdinand Craftsmen's Association and an evolution of the community that had existed around the congregation a long time ago. Now it was mostly an excuse for the local bigwigs to drink together.

"It's not about religion," Crowley explained between bites of his sandwich. "I mean, there's a bit of ceremony—"

"And an initiation," Dan interrupted.

"Yes, there's that, and a few rules, but it'd be good for you to get to know how the town really works, Dan."

"Nah."

"Nah?"

"Nah," the teenager repeated with a certain degree of flippancy. "I love Saint-Ferdinand, but I don't see myself spending my life there. Probably going to try to get some kind of business degree from Sherbrooke or McGill. Find work in that field."

Stephen quit eating for a second, that weird look crawling back to his face. This time he didn't break eye contact with his son. He studied him instead, peeling back unseen layers in search of something immaterial in Daniel's features.

"Dad?"

"Sorry." Crowley shook his head and forced a smile. "I just forget sometimes how much you look like your mom."

Ah, thought Daniel. So this was what was bothering the old man. It wasn't the first time this comment had come up, and it probably wouldn't be the last. As he grew older, his father would keep seeing similarities between him and the woman he'd loved. If Daniel were ever to have kids, he expected Stephen would see hints of his ex-wife in them, too. The wound of abandonment was cut open again and again, always by the most pleasant and familiar of knives.

"I'm not vanishing, Dad." He leaned in and gave his father a gentle shove on the shoulder with his fist. "But if I get a good degree, I don't want to waste it in Saint-Ferdinand."

His argument was met with silence and a stern, doubtful stare from the inspector. Daniel had been too young to feel the full blow of his mother's inexplicable departure. The way Stephen had described it, Marguerite Crowley had one day just picked up and left. It was first assumed that she might have run afoul of the Saint-Ferdinand Killer, but after a year, divorce papers showed up in the mail with instructions to return them, signed, to a PO box in Sherbrooke.

"Besides," the teenager continued, "I still have a few years before university, and even if I move out of town, you know I'd be back here every weekend anyway."

"Right . . . ," Stephen said sarcastically.

"Sure! Where else can I get access to a sweet fishing boat?"

The inspector shook his head but finally smiled. "Y'know, you turned out all right. Your mom fucked up."

"She's no mother of mine." Daniel felt awkward but tried to hide it by taking a swig of beer. "Did you ever hear from her again?"

"Not a word."

Melancholy was taking over. The past few days of investigation had been exhausting, and although Inspector Stephen Crowley wasn't one to let emotions bring him down, he was too tired to do anything about them anymore.

"Dad?"

"What?"

"We're the Crowley boys," Daniel stated, raising his beer can toward his old man. "We don't need nobody."

"Yeah." Stephen toasted with his son, a tentative smile beating back the dark cloud. "The Crowley boys."

VENUS

"HEY! HIPPIE!"

Venus had been calmly walking home from the post office when the familiar voice cut in with an equally familiar insult. The week was circling further down the drain with every passing moment, as if some dark god had cast its hateful gaze upon the young girl.

First there was the rain. It came down in thick, wet sheets, showering the village from dull gray skies. In the beginning, it was a refreshing break from the harsh sun that had been beating down on Saint-Ferdinand for the past two weeks. But it soon became a different kind of ordeal. Once the sky cleared, the sun would turn the rain puddles into clouds of sticky humidity that would hover over the town for days. Saint-Ferdinand would become an unbearable sauna. For now, however, the unexpected deluge was its own annoyance.

Then there was the clerk at the post office, Anaïs Bérubé, who wouldn't release Venus's package until the teenager brought her some form of identification. Anaïs had known Venus for years and had released hundreds of packages to her, but she was so hung up on protocol that she couldn't make one tiny exception. As a result, Venus either had to walk home, get her medical insurance card, and walk back, under the marginal protection of her umbrella while diluvial torrents fell all around her, or she'd have to wait one more day for her new video card. Ironically, a day like this would have been perfect to install her computer hardware—if it wasn't being held hostage at the post office.

Now, in the middle of this monsoon, she had to run into André Wilson. A smarter boy would have picked a better time and more pleasant weather to practice his half-witted bullying, but not André. He was as dedicated to his craft as an artist, but his medium was childish insults, and his canvas was Venus's ego.

"Really, André?" Venus turned around to face the boy. Her exasperation was cut short when she realized he wasn't alone. He had his two cronies, Nick and Brad, with him. Judging by their sodden uniforms and muddied shin guards, they had just come from soccer practice.

"Heading back to the commune?" André laughed.

When she'd initially moved to town, André had been Venus's first friend. They built snow forts, went swimming in the lake, and camped in André's backyard. Then, nearly two years ago, Venus had skipped to tenth grade. She had lost a lot of friends that year, but she had been closest to André. She tried to comfort herself with the knowledge that it was going to be worth it in the long run, but losing his friendship still stung. If it hadn't been for Penny and Abraham, she might have just given up on making friends at all. Especially since André had become her worst enemy.

"I'm not a hippie," she said. "You don't even know what that means!"

"Your parents are hippies, so what does that make you? Huh? *Venus?*"

André and his dumb friends laughed again. Her parents were indeed "free-spirited." They owned a tea shop, where they sold artisanal kettles, imported teas, and herbal drinks. Her mother also cooked homemade, organic baby food that she sold to the mothers around town, while her father padded the family income by doing some carpentry. Both were staunch vegetarians and vocal pacifists. But as far as Venus was concerned, their philosophy of "free-range parenting" was synonymous with "child neglect." Her parents deserved to be called names for their weird New Agey behavior. What Venus resented was that she was associated with their dumb lifestyle choices. Especially since she worked so hard to not be like her parents.

"Look, André, it's raining cats and dogs. Can't you reschedule being an idiot till tomorrow?" The words escaped her mouth before she realized no good could come of them.

"I don't know if it's the rain, but you're awfully clean for a hippie," said the bully, nodding to his friends. "Grab her."

Venus turned to run, but her short sandaled feet couldn't outpace three young men in running shoes. Within three strides, they had caught up to her and kicked her umbrella aside. Lifting her by the arms, they unceremoniously tossed her into the muddy ditch by the side of the road.

"There you go!" said André. "Ain't that more comfortable for a dirty hippie?"

When Venus finally got home, she was livid. Dirty, wet, cold, and humiliated, her only saving grace was that no one could see her tears as she barged into the house. Her mother Virginie immediately dropped her book and ran to get a towel. As she helped dry her daughter off, it was easy to see the link between Venus and her mom. Both shared a similar delicate bone structure. However, the teenager had inherited much of her father's Scottish heritage, with freckles and fiery red hair, while Virginie had thick dark brown locks. She still looked young, despite the long years she'd spent under the harsh sun of equatorial countries, working as a volunteer for the Red Cross and Doctors Without Borders. It had made her skin tan and given her eyes crow's-feet that conveyed a mischievous squint.

"Oh, sweetheart! What happened? Did you fall?"

Venus snatched the towel away and answered in gasping breaths, "No! I was thrown! Into a ditch."

"Who did this? Why?" her mother asked.

"Because! Because you and Paul can't just be like the other parents in town! Because you can't just vacation in Florida instead of Burning Man! Because you can't just give a curfew and chores and an allowance, and you can't call me Mary or Suzy or something *normal*!"

Slowly and gently, Virginie took a corner of the towel and wiped the mud away from her daughter's face.

"Venus," she began as soothingly as she could, "we raised you like this because we believe it will make you a better person. We don't treat you like a normal girl because we believe you are more than ordinary. We think you're special."

"No, I'm not! Parents always say that to their kids, but I'm not falling for it. What's wrong with normal? Just because *you* want to stand out like circus freaks, that doesn't mean I should pay the price!"

Before she allowed herself to regret her words, Venus shoved past her mother and stormed upstairs to her room.

VENUS

"I'LL BEAT THE snot out of him."

Abraham Peterson spoke as if it were a matter of fact. Then again, as far as sixteen-year-old boys went, Abe wasn't prone to empty threats or hyperboles. Not that he was pathologically phlegmatic, but he rarely bothered with hesitation or burdened himself with such things as plans.

"No, you won't," Penelope said, setting a large chocolate sundae in front of the boy.

"Why not? I'm twice André's size. I'd obliterate him." Abe was a large boy who had no physical reason to be afraid of anyone. A voracious appetite conspired with constant farmwork to grant him a powerful, if rather graceless, physique. His piercing eyes were too small for his face, which made him look dumber than he actually was. This combined with his economy of words made him as much a target of ridicule as Venus was for her eccentric parents. Though other kids tended to keep a safe distance from Abraham.

"Because I told you so, but if that's not enough, because André'll take it out on Venus if you do."

Abraham growled an acknowledgment before stuffing an enormous spoonful of ice cream and syrup into his mouth. Penny grimaced at the display of gluttony before continuing.

"I don't need anyone beating André for me," Venus said, looking up from her own bowl of ice cream.

"Say the word and I'll—"

"No!" Penny interrupted.

"I'm thinking of moving out," Venus announced between bites.

"You can't move out. You're not old enough to get a job." Penny picked up a rag and some stray dishes to dry. "Besides, where would you move? No one rents apartments here."

"You could move to the farm," Abraham offered, carefully swallowing before he spoke again. "There's plenty of room, and Pa would probably find a use for you."

"The shed," Venus said. "I'll move into the shed in my backyard. I've got it all figured out."

This only made sense in a Venus kind of way. The young teen had always been fiercely independent, having essentially raised herself since she could walk. She knew she was smart, too, but impulsive, often lacking common sense. The shed would be a comfortable place to sleep and work on her computer, assuming the Wi-Fi could reach it. She'd have to go back to the house to shower and use the bathroom, making the place little more than a grounded tree house. It was another harebrained idea that Penelope would have to talk her out of. It wasn't the first, and it certainly wouldn't be the last.

"You're just upset and need some time to cool off," Penny said. "Maybe you can spend a few days at my place?"

"But if you do move into the shed," piped in Abraham, his mouth once more filled with fudge and ice cream, "I can help you move your stuff."

Out of patience, Penny slapped her hand over his mouth, but before she could get to lecturing him about the basics of table manners, the door chimes rang, announcing a new customer.

Wearing the kind of suit-and-tie attire seen only at weddings and funerals in Saint-Ferdinand, the man looked around the shop expectantly. With his gaze settling on Penelope, he smiled and walked in, letting the door slam behind him. Young and relatively short with unkempt brown hair and a face that seemed like it wouldn't grow a beard for several more years, he strode to the counter and took a seat right next to Abe, nodding to the boy as he did so.

"Can I help you?" Penny asked with a sincere smile, wiping her hand on her apron.

"Do you serve any of those float things with soda and ice cream?" the man answered with a perfect smile.

"Sure. Any particular flavors?"

"Root beer."

As Penelope turned away to make the float, Abraham swiveled to his side and leaned dramatically on his elbow. Taking on airs of self-confidence that fit him as well as a cocktail dress, he smiled and made sure his mouth was free of food.

"So, are you a cop or a reporter?" Abraham asked with his best attempt at conviviality.

"Abe!" Penny scolded him. "Don't bother the customers!"

"It's quite all right," said the newcomer. "I stick out like a sore thumb, don't I?"

"Yeah," continued Abraham after shooting Penny a victorious look. "Actually, I'm surprised the place ain't crawling with city folk, considering the news and all."

"You have your chief of police to thank for that. Kept the lid on things pretty tight."

"We don't have a chief here," interjected Venus while Penny handed the man his float. "Inspector Crowley's good enough for our little corner of the world."

"Whatever the man's title, he's a genius at understating important news. If it weren't for a friend at the hospital in Magog who told me an odd story about a dead little girl—"

"So a reporter, then?" Abraham asked a second time.

"Guilty." The man smiled and took a deep sip of his float. His eyes rolled up in his skull, expressing blissful joy. "What is it about small-town floats that are so delicious?"

"So, if you're a reporter, what are you doing drinking sodas with high school kids instead of getting the big story?" Venus asked, apprehensive.

"One scoop at a time, I figure." The man grinned and looked to Abraham, who seemed to appreciate the pun. "Besides, I'm probably not that much older than you."

"What newspaper do you work for, mister . . . ?" Venus squinted as if trying to recognize the man.

"Chris Hagen. Freelancer."

"I'm Abraham. They're Penny and Venus."

There was a moment of silence as the older girl glared at him, annoyed at being introduced by her nickname.

"It's Penelope, actually. So, Mr. Hagen—" Penny began.

"Chris," the reporter said, and smiled.

"Whatever," Penny said. "You still haven't explained why you're here and not interviewing important people."

"Beside the delicious float? It's mostly because all the 'important people,' as you put it, have already told me, with little room for misunderstanding, that they are too busy for the media."

"So you're taking a break before giving it another shot," Abraham said with confidence.

"Nope," replied Hagen. "I'm befriending locals in a not-too-subtle attempt at finding someone who'll put in a good word for me."

Penny sneered at the reporter's attempt at charm. Her natural cynicism kept her from accepting anyone at face value, especially if they were too open about their intentions. Venus had once called it "interpersonal paranoia." Her friend was hard-pressed to disagree with the expression, though she'd never admit that.

"Well, you're barking up the wrong tree," Penny said while picking up and rinsing out Hagen's glass, which had been swiftly emptied during the conversation. "You should look for Daniel Crowley, the inspector's son. He's probably going to be harder to charm, though."

"So the inspector has a son?" Hagen said, delighted. "See? It was worth my dropping in here after all. A refreshing drink, good conversation, and a bit of work done."

Hagen got up and fished in his pockets, pulling out five dollars in bills and coins before putting them on the counter. "Maybe I'll see you guys around. Thanks for the float, Penelope," he said, putting special emphasis on her full name before leaving with a wink and a smile.

The teenagers watched as the door closed. After a beat, Abraham turned to Penny.

"I'll have another sundae if you don't mind."

Penny rolled her eyes, exasperated at her friend's voraciousness.

"What?" asked Abe, sincerely confused.

VENUS

VENUS CARRIED A large bucket of water from the back door of her home and across the yard. As her arms strained not to spill the contents, she gave her father the stink eye. It wasn't that Paul McKenzie didn't offer to help, which was all part of his "hands-off" parenting style, but that he almost seemed to be openly mocking her intentions. As was often the case on these devastatingly hot days, he'd decided to close the tea shop for the afternoon. After all, scorching weather didn't do much for hot beverage sales. Both of Venus's parents had considered selling gourmet ice tea in the summer, but winter sales more than made up for slower months. There was no need to be greedy, they said.

Despite what everyone thought of Paul's laid-back attitude, Venus's father was a surprisingly hard worker. While his wife took care of the tea shop, he kept himself busy by creating handmade furniture for local businesses, tourists, and connoisseurs of artisanal carpentry. He also restored antique pieces and sold them back to antiquity shops in Montreal. His work was prized and admired by the nouveaux riches that inhabited the trendier parts of the metropolis. But this afternoon, he was taking the day off.

"You sure you want to move in there? Doesn't seem that comfortable to me!" he shouted to Venus.

"Is that a parental decree?" she shouted back, huffing and puffing as she dragged the pail to her new home.

"Not at all," Paul said, and laughed. "That wouldn't be cool. You do what you gotta do, man. It's just a real shitty shed."

Venus dropped the bucket next to an arsenal of cleaning products she had already assembled at the door of the shed. Half the water spilled into the grass, but she didn't seem to care. She dumped some all-purpose soap into the water and stirred it with a rag.

"Don't care. I just want my own space for a while, Dad."

Paul leaned back and kicked off his sandals before taking a swig of his lemonade. He'd always tried to raise Venus as an independent thinker. He and his wife figured there was nothing they could teach their daughter that life experience wouldn't teach better. So far, the experiment had been rewarding. Venus was a smart and resourceful young woman. She had grown into more of a friend than a child. The three of them could talk and relate in a way most families didn't, and he really felt like she was comfortable telling him anything. Sometimes, though, especially over the last year, Venus would announce that she would rather have "normal" parents. During those episodes, Paul thought it best to just let her have her way. Until it passed.

"Groovy," he said. "Let me know if you need a hand."

The job of cleaning out the shed was colossal, and Venus quickly decided that it would take more than one day. Simply emptying out all the broken-down junk that had accumulated over the years took the better part of two hours. To her delight, she found that the storage area was wired for electricity. An old electric lawn mower was still plugged into the single outlet. A simple test quickly confirmed that it had current, opening up a whole new realm of possibilities for her future domicile.

Soon after, Venus stumbled upon an unexpected surprise. Hidden deep behind the disused gardening equipment and forgotten lawn care products, where no one should have been able to find it, sat a bird's nest, complete with five perfect eggs. Venus couldn't figure out how a bird might have found its way into the shed, but it was a clever hiding place. She left it where it was.

It was only after another hour of vigorously sweeping and scrubbing the floor and walls that she saw the nest's owner. Venus had been focused on her task of ridding a corner of cobwebs and dirt when a loud chirp echoed through the shed, nearly making her jump out of her skin. She turned to look but couldn't recognize the species. Venus could pick out a blue jay or a red cardinal, but on average, if the bird's name wasn't color-coded, they all looked the same to her. This particular specimen was especially boring. A football-shaped bundle of gray feathers topped with a tiny head and eyes that reflected very little intelligence. However, the animal's behavior enthralled Venus. It danced around its nest, chirping and flapping its wings to defend the unborn chicks.

Quickly but carefully, Venus abandoned the shed, coming back a few minutes later with her arms full of electronic equipment. Her hygienic endeavors had been forgotten in favor of an entirely different project. Her father, bearing witness to her rapid change in focus, bit his lip to stifle a laugh. Smart but scattered, that was his daughter.

Penny arrived just as Venus was plugging in the last cables to her setup. She looked appraisingly at the complete disaster the McKenzies' yard had become. Cleaning products littered the lawn among piles of discarded junk.

Penny walked into the shed to see her friend perched on a stool, tying up some wires into neat bundles. The older girl held out a plastic cup of half-melted ice cream and put on her most disapproving glare.

"Y'know, Veen, for a straight-A student, you sure come up with stupid ideas."

Venus was startled and nearly fell off her perch. "What are you talking about? This is a great idea." The younger girl hopped off her stool and accepted the dripping treat.

"Oh, sure! If you're planning on getting twelve more cats or writing a manifesto."

"Speaking of cats," said Venus, glancing around the area. "Have you seen Sherbet?" Sherbet was the name Venus had given to her smoke-gray half-Persian cat." I don't want him getting into the eggs."

Penny gave her friend the same kind of look most people reserved for those with diminished capacities. "What are you even talking about? I thought you were moving into this . . . place, and now you're going on about eggs?" She switched to a mocking tone. "Are you medicated? Should you be?"

"I don't take drugs," Venus said. "And I found this nest at the back of the shed and there're eggs in it. Never seen this kind of bird around here. I want to see the babies when they hatch and how the mother takes care of them. So I'm installing a camera. Maybe I'll cut the footage and put it on the Internet."

"So you're going to be spying on a bird in your own empty shed through your computer?" Penny asked, leaning on a wall while picking at her own cup of ice cream. "Oh yeah, that'll really get back at your parents."

"I guess. I don't know. I just . . . I feel like it's their fault I get picked on so much."

"You get teased because you're in high school. Everyone does. Besides, your parents aren't *that* weird. I mean, they're . . . *unique*, but in a cool way."

"Unique?" said Venus, sitting back down on her stool. "You and Abraham only see the surface. Paul and Virginie aren't just unique; they're downright bizarre!"

"Oh?" Penny raised an eyebrow.

"They keep bursting into scenes from back in their theater days. And I don't mean once in a while when they're bored. I mean all the time. Do you know how annoying it is to hear Andrew Lloyd Webber at breakfast three days in a row?"

Penny giggled. "I can't imagine, no."

"They keep acting like horny teenagers, too. How awkward is that? I'm their daughter, not some . . . roommate! It's gross.

"Do you remember last summer? When they up and left for three weeks without warning? Just a note on the fridge. 'Dear Venus, gone on vacation. Back soon. Money on the dresser for food.' Aren't there *laws* against that sort of thing?"

Penny was suddenly lost in her own family reminiscence. Her smile changed from amusement to melancholy as her eyes stared into the past.

"Oh . . . Penny. I'm so sorry." Venus covered her mouth in embarrassment. "I'm such an ass . . . ," She grabbed her friend in a tight hug. "I'm so selfish."

"It's fine. Just, y'know, remembering." Penny shook her head. "Living vicariously through you."

Venus finally let her go. "Fine, you can borrow Paul for the weekend. We barely use him anyways."

"Funny. Still, you do have it pretty good, Veen." She wiped a tear from the corner of her eye. "My dad being gone aside, I don't see my mom very often. She got home so late last night and left so early this morning, I didn't even cross paths with her. Choosing work over her daughter yet again."

"Okay, you're right. I do have it good," Venus said. "So . . . how high on the self-absorption meter did I score this time?"

"Nine? Nine point five?" the older girl confirmed with a smile. "That your bird?"

The mother bird had waddled through a small hole at the back of the shed that, with much effort, allowed her to come in and out. She looked around with apprehension, carefully moving toward her nest while glaring at the girls.

"That's just a partridge. They're absolutely everywhere around the Richards farm."

"How come I haven't seen one before?" Venus asked, trying to justify her ignorance.

"I don't know. Maybe because you hate nature and stay indoors playing on your computer all the time?" Penny nudged her with her elbow. "Why don't you join me at work tomorrow and we can go watch movies at my place with my mom when I'm done? Maybe that'll remind you how boring normal parents actually are."

GABRIELLE

GABRIELLE LAFOREST USUALLY didn't walk home from work. In the wintertime she took her car, but during the summer, rain or shine, she made a point of taking her bicycle. Not that she was a dedicated athlete, but she liked to stay fit and her schedule didn't allow her much time for exercise. So she made do with what she had, and the most efficient thing she could come up with was cycling.

It was a hobby she wished she could share with her daughter. While they were close, especially since Gabrielle's husband had passed away nearly five years ago, they didn't have much time to share common interests. Gabrielle was extremely busy putting food on the table, and as Saint-Ferdinand's sole notary, her days and evenings were often full.

So it was particularly frustrating that Gabrielle's bike chain had broken just as she'd left the office. She had planned on dropping by to see her daughter, Penny, for a cone sprinkled with a bit of quality time, but the broken chain had sabotaged those plans. At this rate, it would be well after dark by the time she got finished walking home. Twilight had already descended, and she could barely see the road in front of her as the sun bid its final farewell to the horizon.

Not much more than a week ago, Gabrielle would have been hesitant to walk alone after dark on such an isolated road. She would have jogged to the nearest farm, eyes peeled for shadowy figures, and begged for a ride. She would have gotten it too, no questions asked, even if her Good Samaritan didn't know her very well. No one wanted to be responsible for the next Saint-Ferdinand murder victim.

Tonight that threat was gone. Sam Finnegan was behind bars, and while there were still many issues to resolve, such as finalizing the list of victims (of which her late husband might be one), the danger was behind them. There was an intoxicating giddiness at being able to walk alone in the night. Part of it, she had to admit, was the thought of seeing the monster who had nearly ruined her life hang for his crimes.

Gabrielle still had roughly half an hour of walking ahead of her. The lights from the Richards farm were far behind her, and she could see the glow of familiar porch lights from the Demers' stables ahead. Her little house was just beyond that, at the edge of a small residential area on the north end of town. Though it looked close, she knew from experience that the distance was deceiving.

She was surprised when her meditative solitude was interrupted by a voice. The sound was so faint, so ethereal, that at first she thought she'd imagined it.

A familiar panic set in. All the fears that had plagued her for eighteen years rose from their grave, more powerful and more real than ever. Then she heard the voice again, and her soul was gripped with a different kind of terror.

The voice was that of a little girl. The words it repeated were unintelligible, but the recent death of Audrey Bergeron had left a deep scar on the community. Especially on those parents who had daughters of their own.

So Gabrielle's motherly instinct overcame her fears, and she walked toward the voice. She had to step off the road and jump across a ditch, walking several yards into the forbidding shadows of the forest. As she looked behind every tree, she expected to find a wounded or lost little girl, terrified and alone, much like she thought Audrey must have been the night she died.

Before long, Gabrielle was deep enough among the trees that she could barely see the road anymore. She stopped, listening carefully for the voice. Again, silence was her only answer. Not even the rustling of animals or the chirps of insects could be heard. She was about to dismiss the whole incident when she saw the little girl.

She was a tiny little thing, with alabaster skin and pale ivory hair. She was wearing her Sunday best, but her feet were bare. Crude iron nails had been driven through the milky flesh and into the ground beneath her. Similar nails had been rammed into her eye sockets. In her arms she held a stuffed bear with a bright red felt hat.

As Gabrielle stared in stunned silence, the apparition spoke one more time. They were the same words as before, but she could now make them out clearly: *"Run away . . ."*

CROWLEY

CROWLEY STOOD AT HIS DESK. His office was air-conditioned, but still, beads of sweat were racing down his broad back before being absorbed by the cotton of his light brown shirt. He'd been standing like this for a few moments. Dedication commanded him to make the call, but fear of losing control of the touchy situation begged him to stay his hand. His thick fingers brushed the receiver of the office phone in almost soothing strokes.

The eyes. He could feel them on his back, freezing him in place, watching him through the window to his office. The entire station was tracking his every move. Officers from neighboring municipalities, the medical staff from Sherbrooke Hospital . . . Even his own staff was frozen. Waiting for him to make his next move, to give his next order.

First, however, he had to make the decision.

Crowley's own eyes, tired as they were, could not look away from the corkboard behind his voluminous but tattered leather chair. It was filled with photos—photos of the eyes from the Finnegan crime scene were the freshest additions to the mosaic, but there were other things. Other eyes not from the crime scene.

The inspector pulled his fingers off the receiver, slapping a hand on the back of his neck to secure his choice, then turned to face his audience. The decision was made, the events set in motion.

"All right." He addressed the exhausted professionals assembled in his precinct as he stepped out of his office. "It's been a rough day. It's going to be just as rough tomorrow. Anyone from out of town who doesn't want to go home, ask Jackie, the lovely brunette at the front desk, and she'll tell you where you can go for the night. There's some room at the bed-and-breakfast down the street for a few people; for the rest, we got some locals to volunteer a spare bedroom.

"Because of the scale and duration of Finnegan's murder spree, there's good reason to think he might have been working with someone else. So before you go, I need to lay some ground rules."

A rumble went through the assembly. Everyone in town wanted to believe the nightmare was finally over. Sam Finnegan had agreed to confess. The bodies had been found. The crime scene was under investigation. It was over. All that needed to be done was the cleanup. After nearly two decades of endless investigation, why could the inspector not let this one rest?

"I hope I'm wrong, but just to stay on the safe side, we need to keep the investigation out of the media until we know more. We do our jobs right, and we'll either catch the accomplice or prove there wasn't one in the first place. We fuck up, and there could be another murderer on the loose."

Nods of approval replaced shrugs of confusion. The troops were reenergized, focused once more on the task. Years of coaching Little League for his son had done wonders for Stephen Crowley's ability to inspire a small crowd. They would wake up early and be back at it tomorrow, and the next day, and the next. As long as it took to get all the clues and evidence. More important, everything would go through the inspector. Body parts, autopsy reports, crime scene photography: he would see it all and hopefully find answers to his own questions.

One by one, the officers and volunteers emptied from the station, some waving good-bye, a few taking a moment to shake his hand on the way out. They left behind a battlefield strewn with the eviscerated bodies of doughnut boxes and the bled-out remains of coffeepots. From the cacophony of work was born an almost-absolute silence, broken only by the soft click of the copy machine, signaling that it was out of paper.

Dutiful as always, Jackie started picking up the trash so the office would be ready for the second round of serial murder investigation in the morning.

Crowley considered going home. He'd need energy for the days ahead, and a comfortable, if lonely, bed would be the wisest decision. Unfortunately, when it came to his own health and well-being, Crowley was the kind of man who made bad decisions on the best of days.

Sitting at his desk, he swiveled his chair to stare once more at the corkboard. Almost two decades of investigation stared back at him. Each precious clue had been as useless as the last. Eighteen years of chasing leads, following hunches, and interrogating suspects, only to have the killer trip up like an imbecile.

Then again, if Finnegan was an imbecile or a cretin or whatever the medical term was for his mental condition, how did he manage to evade capture for all those years? A clumsy idiot with a lopsided grin couldn't have outsmarted him and his officers for this long, could he?

"You really think he had an accomplice?"

Crowley didn't need to turn around to recognize Randy McKenzie's voice or the sound of his rotund body settling into one of the other office chairs. Randy knew almost everything about this case that Stephen did. They'd both worked their own sides of the investigation. Two men at the top of their professions, outsmarted by a moron.

"How else could he have done this? Forget that Finnegan is about a hundred and fifty pounds wet and my son could beat him up on a bad day—"

"Your son could beat *me* up on a bad day."

"Anyone could beat you up on any day, Randy. What I mean is, how the hell did that old man overpower all these people?"

Crowley turned back around, wanting to read the answer on the doctor's face as much as hear it from his lips. A quirk of being an investigator for so long.

"Same way he kept us in the dark for eighteen years: no one suspects the village idiot. Sam is like our very own Ed Gein, only multiplied by ten."

Careful not to disrupt the carefully stacked papers and empty coffee cups, Crowley swung his legs up onto his desk, crossing them while leaning back in his chair. His boots were still crusted with the dirt from the investigation. The cleaning crew would have a depressing amount of work come Wednesday. Between the tracked mud and spilled coffee, the floors of the station were a disaster.

"I never trusted him."

"Ha! C'mon, Stephen. We all trusted him. You said it yourself: the man was harmless. At least we all thought he was."

Silence fell between the two men. The witching hour had long passed, and the effects of caffeine were quickly dissipating. Crowley gave a sidelong glance at the empty cups on his desk, victims of his need to stay awake, and considered having another. Or perhaps his friend across the desk could give him something a little more powerful. It wouldn't be the first time he'd made such a request.

The inspector could feel the eyes on the corkboard boring into the back of his head. There was Finnegan's collection, of course, but those didn't nag at him. It was the others that kept preying on his mind. Drawings they'd found in library books, spray-painted on the sides of buildings, even carvings dug into the bark of trees, all depicting the same image: a stylized eye with a spiral iris.

For as long as he'd lived in Saint-Ferdinand, these acts of vandalism had been appearing all over town at irregular intervals. Some had been cleaned up, others painted over, but still they cropped up, carved into a park bench or imprinted into the cement of a sidewalk.

"If not just him, who else?" Randy said, cleaning his glasses.

"I don't have a name! But between that cave, those eyes, and this town's history? You can't tell me this"—he waved at the board behind him—"is a coincidence."

"What? The Craftsmen?"

The Saint-Ferdinand Craftsmen's Association. An organization as old as it was defunct, whose symbol had been an eye with a spiral iris. Like a Freemason guild or a chamber of commerce, the Craftsmen had once been the driving force behind most of the village's business. Their icon used to be on every building, in every farm.

"Why the hell not?"

"Because they're gone, Stephen!" The rotund medical examiner smiled at the inspector, trying to communicate the mirth in the situation. "Just because their logo was an eye, doesn't mean there's a connection."

"You don't know these old geezers like I do, Randy."

"You're insane. Kids are painting those symbols. What are you thinking? That old men are skulking through the night, spray cans hidden in their nightgown pockets?"

"Keep laughing, asshole. Someone else was working with Sam. I know it."

"Fine, but who? Who looks at Sam and thinks, *This is the guy who should be the muscle behind a murder spree*? Who does Finnegan even associate with?"

"God dammit, Randy, I don't know." Crowley pinched the bridge of his nose, exhausted and frustrated. "Maybe someone was manipulating him into it. Sam's a suggestible sort of guy, right?"

Randy leaned on the desk, trying to get a better read on the inspector. His own clothes, pressed brown slacks and a white shirt, were soiled from a day's work in the field. Only his hands had remained perfectly clean, having been covered by latex gloves most of the time.

"Stephen? Why do you need there to be an accomplice so bad?"

"Because." Crowley wheeled his chair to the side, giving McKenzie a clear view of his corkboard. Old, yellowed photographs and sketches of the symbol joined by new and shiny printouts of the eyes found at the crime scene. Some were still speared to metal rods, while others were putrefied and found in the ground near the cave entrance. "Finnegan wasn't just randomly doing that thing with the eyes. There's something in that cave, and it all ties back together."

The inspector pointed to the closest image of the spiral iris. That particular photograph had been taken before his son was born. It depicted a barn wall with the same symbol in white paint, covering the majority of the surface.

"They knew, Randy . . ."

"So what if they did? They're gone. You made damn sure of that."

Crowley grunted, a mix of dismissal and pride. His eyes returned to the corkboard, his attention shifting slowly from photograph to photograph. The inspector scratched his chin.

"Could Finnegan have been one of them?"

The doctor shrugged and leaned back again in his chair. "Maybe. There's a whole lot we don't know about the guy, but I doubt anyone stayed behind to pull his strings."

"We should have searched the cave," Crowley mused.

Behind him, Randy frowned, his jovial and cavalier attitude melting away for a moment. The thought of the cave and its contents tainted his laissez-faire demeanor, curdling it into a forbidding worry. His brow furrowed under the burden of knowledge. "No, Stephen. We should leave that cave alone for as long as possible."

CROWLEY

"WHAT THE HELL is this?"

Crowley gestured to the boxes that now crowded his desk. Three overflowing containers had replaced the painstakingly accumulated paper cups and piles of paperwork that had lived there for so many weeks.

Each box was filled with twice as many documents as it could normally fit. Stacks of folders were held together with elastic bands, and brightly colored notes stuck out, indicating their purpose and content.

Fortunately, the boxes were labeled. The one closest to regurgitating its contents was marked VICTIMS. These would be the autopsy and forensic reports, testimonies, and all related files for each person Finnegan had killed. The box next to it was labeled RECORDS. These documents formed the archives of the investigation. Crowley had committed most of what was within to memory. Hell, he'd written over half of it himself.

The final box was one he'd requested, and was by far the most manageable of the three. Files only extended about an inch or two beyond its rim. No one had to assemble this box for him. It was a well-known entity in the filing room upstairs. The garbage can where the department threw everything that had to do with the random acts of vandalism attributed to the Craftsmen. It was labeled JUNK in the handwriting of Crowley's old boss.

When Stephen had requested these documents, he hadn't considered the volume they would occupy. He'd also assumed that they would take a little longer to gather and wouldn't be dropped in the center of his desk. Someone would need to get chewed out for that, but now wasn't the time.

The inspector had planned on stopping in for just a moment before going home. He wanted to grab a few papers, but those papers were gone now. Probably buried under the boxes, or relocated to wherever the genius who had delivered these boxes thought they belonged.

With a grunt of both effort and annoyance, the inspector began to pick up the boxes and move them next to the wall. If he could find his papers, he'd be able to get on his way and salvage whatever was left of the evening. Maybe even spend some time with Dan.

The first and second boxes posed no problem, though it was becoming clear that the papers he had come for were no longer on his desk.

The final box was so light compared to the other two, Crowley picked it up with one hand. While his arm was strong enough to carry it with ease, the cardboard handle on the box was not. It tore, tilting the box and vomiting piles of carefully ordered folders and files onto the floor.

"God dammit!" the inspector shouted. The two officers still in the room didn't even bother to look up.

Stephen bent down to pick up the mess, hoping the order of the files had been somewhat maintained. He had no time to spare reorganizing old documents.

Page after page he picked up had the same symbol printed on them. The eye with the spiral iris. It was painted on a sidewalk, drawn on a traffic sign, and etched into an electric pole. All the locations were familiar too. Some were innocuous and had been easy to remove, like a crudely painted version on the door to Bergeron's Drugstore from a decade ago. Others were more bizarre and permanent and could still be seen today. Like the one expertly carved into Neil McKenzie's headstone in the cemetery.

The assumption had long been that the vandalism was started by the Craftsmen as a way to claim the village as their own. They were a group of self-described entrepreneurs and scholars, an old-school gentlemen's club. When Stephen moved into town, they were already on the decline. Their members were old, and with people like William Bergeron muscling into the area with success-ful businesses, it left little room for the aging social club. Now-adays, the symbol was little more than local color. It was mostly kids who used it, ignorant of the eye's original meaning. Or so most people thought.

Inspector Crowley knew better. The Craftsmen had been more than a social club; they'd been a cult, born from a nefarious purpose. They were students of ancient, forbidden arts, unafraid of the consequences of their acts.

Not all of them had been bad, though. Without the Craftsmen, Randy McKenzie would have never learned the necromantic rituals he'd mastered. Even Harry Peterson wasn't a bad egg, but he'd definitely fallen in with the wrong people.

Fortunately, Stephen Crowley had chased that sort out of town a long time ago.

His own group was different. They had, he hoped, a much more focused plan for the town's future. More important, they now had the means of accomplishing their lofty goals.

The inspector lifted a pile of documents off the floor, but in-stead of stuffing them back in the "junk" box, he brought the files to his desk. There, he sat and looked down at the assembled reports and photographs.

Reaching back around the armchair, Stephen dipped his hand into the pocket of his uniform jacket. He pulled out a moss-covered stone, the same one Daniel had threatened to throw in Magog days ago. The inspector stole a glance into the station bullpen. His two employees were still at their desks, filling out paperwork or responding to e-mails.

Confident he wouldn't be bothered, Crowley put the stone on his desk next to the papers. He traced the lines of the carving carefully with his thumb, hoping for some sort of epiphany. When none came, he opened the files.

The Craftsmen and their dumb little symbol. After all these years, Crowley had hoped that the collection of old men was now little more than a footnote in the history of Saint-Ferdinand. That he'd seen the last of them eighteen years ago.

But what if he hadn't? What if the old cult was somehow behind Sam Finnegan's murder spree? The cause of the village's overpopulated cemetery? That was difficult to swallow.

So he found a rock with their symbol. So what? These things were all over town, and the stone was clearly of some age. Finnegan had probably found it and kept it near the cave as a souvenir. Or maybe he was the one responsible for the vandalism in the first place, imitating the eye with the spiral iris for whatever sick reason his mind had constructed.

Or Crowley could follow his gut.

The inspector looked at the first file photo. The barn with the crudely reproduced icon on its wall.

Trusting the small voice at the back of his head, Crowley rolled his chair to where the boxes lay on the floor. There, he dug through them, caring little for how badly he was messing up the classification of the documents. Pulling autopsy report after autopsy report, he kept going deeper into the box until, at long last, he got to the bottom.

Jackson Conroy. The first presumed victim of the Saint-Ferdinand Killer. The man, a local business owner who operated the only pizza restaurant the village had ever known, had gone missing almost nineteen years ago. A week before the first sighting of the eye with the spiral iris.

Crowley retrieved one of the more recent autopsy reports from the discard pile. Graham Henderson. A large man, his body had barely fit into one of Sam's refrigerators. In fact, his arms had been broken at the shoulders, his legs bent until the knees cracked in order to get the door closed.

The autopsy didn't seem to reveal much. Cause of death: stabbing. Time of death: more difficult to establish, but could be narrowed down to within a few weeks. It didn't matter; everyone knew when Henderson had vanished. His truck had been found in the woods off the highway last November, the front seat covered in blood. It was presumed that the man had been murdered, and his name was added to the list. The only peculiarity on the report was the presence of long scratches on Graham's back, along with a few thistles stuck to his clothes.

Last November. Going through the files on vandalism, Crowley found the closest event, two weeks after Henderson was declared missing and only a couple of days after his car was found. The photograph attached to the report with a paper clip depicted a patch of sidewalk that had recently been redone. Someone had traced an eye with a spiral for an iris while the cement was still wet. Next to the sidewalk, blurry but recognizable, was a clutch of thistle plants.

His gut lurched.

It wasn't a strong connection. Not even something that would normally be worth pursuing. After all, thistles grew almost everywhere in town.

However, there were two boxes full of autopsy and incident reports, and a full night to connect as many of them as possible. By morning, Crowley would know if the Craftsmen were a relic of the past, or a threat to the present.

DANIEL

THE CROWLEY HOUSE wasn't the most ostentatious in Saint-Ferdinand, but it reflected the status of its owner well. The only undeniable luxury was the two-car garage, which contained a large black Ford Explorer and an expensive array of sports equipment, ranging from skis to golf bags and even a fiberglass kayak.

In front of the garage stretched a long asphalt driveway that led to the road. The sun beat down on the black surface, creating heat ripples in the air just over the ground. In the middle of this forbidding desert of burning pitch stood a white Honda Civic. Impeccably clean with dazzling chrome hubcaps, its hood yawned open as Dan Crowley, shirtless, leaned over the engine.

"Nice car!" a voice called out from within a few feet of the Civic.

Dan pulled himself up from under the hood of his car and, squinting in the sun, took an appraising look at the stranger. How the man could stand wearing a full business suit in this heat was baffling to him.

"I used to have one of those when I was your age," the man continued. "Red hatchback. Nowhere near as well maintained as this one, though."

"Thanks," Dan replied. "If you're looking for my dad, you're out of luck. He's working today."

"Why doesn't that surprise me?" the stranger said. Disappointed, he stuffed his hands into his pockets and leaned against the car.

"If you tell me who you are, I can let him know you dropped by," the teenager countered, wiping grease from his hands.

"Oh! Where are my manners? Chris Hagen, freelance reporter."

Chris extended a hand, which Dan accepted with some hesitation. People in Saint-Ferdinand, especially the Crowley boys, were wary of reporters. There was something unsettling about people whose job it was to dig into the lives of others.

"So my dad's been dodging you, I gather?"

"You could say that. Or you could say that the entire village has been avoiding me." Hagen put on a smile. "Not that I blame them. I wouldn't want to talk to me either if I'd gone through what you folks have."

"We're a private people around here, Mr. Hagen."

"Chris, please." Hagen wiped nonexistent sweat from his brow. "Look, I'll level with you, Dan. I would rather not bother a man like your father, but it's kind of traditional to get the authority's point of view when it comes to criminal investigations. I'm really trying to be respectful of his position and his community by making sure I get the story straight from the horse's mouth."

"Well, you're in for an uphill battle then, Chris. My old man is a master at avoiding people, and pretty damned pigheaded to boot."

"All right. Who should I be asking then?"

"Well . . . there is this criminal psychologist who's been in town. She's helping out some of the victims' families. She can probably answer most of your questions." The teenager suspected that having two people from out of town digging into Saint-Ferdinand's dirty laundry wouldn't sit well with his dad. Normally, he'd be first in line to defend his father's values, but he'd also been brought up to help others whenever he could, and it was a hard habit to break.

"Interesting. Any idea where I can find this fellow visitor to this lovely village?"

"Her name is something Hazelwood. She's set up at the station."

"The station, you say? Well, you've been a great help, Dan." Hagen produced a business card and passed it over. "If you could give that to your dad, I'd be grateful. Maybe he'll change his mind."

Chris Hagen strolled back down the driveway, hands in his pockets and still apparently unbothered by the scorching summer heat. Finally looking at the card, Dan noticed an odd but familiar symbol at the corner: an hourglass with wings. While trying to put his finger on where he'd seen it before, another mystery dawned on him. Turning back to the now-distant reporter, he yelled: "Hey! Chris! How did you know my name was Dan?"

Hagen either didn't hear, or he intentionally ignored him. Either way, a second later he was gone.

RANDY

RANDY MCKENZIE WALKED under the yellow plastic ribbon that cordoned off the crime scene. Already he could smell the distinct stench of rotting flesh in the air and reached into his pocket for a pair of latex gloves. He had no doubt that they would come in handy soon.

The scene before him was a nightmare. Quite easily the most gruesome spectacle the medical examiner had ever laid eyes on, and that was saying a lot. If this turned out to be a murder, and there was very little chance it wasn't, it would be the bloodiest in Saint-Ferdinand's history.

The doctor found Crowley in a trance, standing over a pulpy chunk of the body, his eyes locked in quiet revulsion on the hundreds of flies that had settled in the victim's exposed chest cavity. There was obviously a lot going on behind his eyes at that moment. Randy didn't cherish the idea of increasing the inspector's burden, but he would be remiss not to tell him what he knew. Sooner rather than later.

"I hope your little friend has a strong stomach, Randy."

"Erica? I think she can handle this." The medical examiner waved his arm in a slow arc, signifying the insane carnage all around them. "Though I don't necessarily think she should have to."

"Too bad. I need someone to talk to the LaForest girl."

"She doesn't need to see the—Wait, this is Gabrielle LaForest?" Randy turned green and lost his balance. For a moment he was convinced he would lose his lunch as well, but somehow he kept his gag reflex under control. Gabrielle LaForest was the mother of his niece's friend, but she was also a relatively close acquaintance of his. She had helped him with the paperwork when he sold his house in Saint-Ferdinand and moved to Sherbrooke to work at the university. It was one thing to see a human body in this condition, and another to find the corpse of a friend. But the two combined was a difficult pill to swallow even for someone as experienced with death as Randy.

"How did you identify . . ."

"Her wallet," explained Crowley.

"What was it? A bear?" The question felt hollow, grasping at straws.

"God dammit, Randy, you know damn well it wasn't a bear. We both know what did this."

The doctor did know. Just from the sheer volume of violence on display, no animal could have done this. Blood was absolutely everywhere. The ground was sodden with it. Tree trunks were painted red in large splatters. There seemed to be enough to fill the veins of three people the size of Gabrielle. Large sheets of skin were stretched across the ground. Organs lay in ruin, strewn across the forest floor with odd-looking lumps of bloody flesh. Only her intestines had remained intact. Those had been hung from the branches above like a grotesque garland. At the foot of a particularly massive maple tree, most of Gabrielle's bones, including her flayed skull, were gathered in a bloody pile. A butcher had committed this atrocity, and had done so with impudence and barbaric yet deliberate care.

"We're having a meeting tonight, Randy. I want you there." Crowley's eyes were still fixed on the mass of flies covering the bloody sternum like a writhing blanket.

The doctor knew what kind of meeting Crowley was talking about. He wanted no part of that sort of gathering. Randy had always considered himself an outsider. A neutral party.

"No. I've done what I could."

"You can't ignore this kind of thing, McKenzie. You're part of it."

"Exactly," Randy said, adamant. Crowley was surprised by the sudden display of spinal fortitude. "You think I have power over this? I'm more at risk than any of you."

"You don't say?"

"What do you expect me to do, Stephen? Show up at church, say a little prayer, and then tell you there's a magic spell that will stop all of this?"

Crowley turned to look the medical examiner square in the eyes. For a second, Randy wasn't sure if Stephen would hit him for daring to refuse. Thankfully, the larger man seemed more preoccupied by other matters.

"You've always known more than you let on. Now more than ever, every little piece of information counts." Crowley started to nervously scratch the back of his thick neck. "We're well past the time for holding back."

"The best I can do is try to find someone actually qualified to help." Randy crouched down to take a closer look at the remains. "That would have been a lot easier to do if you hadn't chased all the Craftsmen from town. Hell, maybe Finnegan knew what he was doing after all."

"Are you going to start defending that monster now?" Crowley growled.

"Monster? Look around you; this is just the beginning. There's no bargaining with it anymore. You need to get your shit together and find another solution. Sam probably saved more lives by keeping that thing—"

"Oh God . . ."

The voice came from a few yards behind them. Had it not been for the stillness of the forest and the reverential silence the rest of Crowley's staff were exhibiting, neither would have heard the swallowed outcry. As one, they turned to see Erica Hazelwood walking carefully among the debris that had once been a woman.

"Erica . . . ," began Randy, almost panicked. "You shouldn't be here."

But the psychologist kept walking silently toward the two men, a hand firmly covering her mouth, as if stifling a scream. She stepped carefully, making sure her feet did not touch any of the bits of flesh and viscera that littered the ground.

"Well, Ms. Hazelwood, you wanted to be involved in the investigation process," Crowley said with questionable tact.

Erica did a double take but kept calm. "You're right, inspector. I'm sorry for my . . . outburst." She kept all traces of being shaken from her voice. "You must admit: this isn't your average set of remains, is it?"

Crowley nodded his agreement, taking another long look around. "No. It sure isn't. How's that for depersonalizing a victim?" asked the inspector, not expecting an answer.

"Stephen . . . ," Randy warned, a weak attempt at being the knight in shining armor.

"It's okay, Randy. He's got a point. I think this goes far beyond depersonalization," she said to the inspector. "If I'd have to venture a guess, I'd say it was a cult killing."

Crowley and McKenzie looked at each other for a moment, neither admitting to the irony of her statement.

"I mean, look at this scene," explained Erica. "This killing obviously had a ritualistic element to it. The pile of bones, the stretching of the skin, the hanging of organs. It's like the Manson murders on speed. Are the eyes still in the skull?"

"No," answered the inspector. "Both were pulled out of their sockets and crushed." He pointed to a bloody pile of leaves at the foot of a slender birch tree marked with a small yellow flag, where what remained of the eyes had been found.

"Whoever the killer is, he had plans for almost every part of his victim. The eyes are destroyed, where Sam had preserved his victims'. The body is obliterated, where Finnegan had kept those he killed neatly in freezers."

"You think there's a connection?" asked Randy, though he and the inspector already knew the answer.

"I'd be surprised if there weren't," said Erica. "Maybe the inspector is right. Maybe Sam had an accomplice. Maybe he had many."

"I don't think Sam was working alone, Ms. Hazelwood," Crowley said. "But I think it's a stretch to say he was part of an organized cult."

"What makes you so sure?" Erica asked with overt suspicion. "Considering the nature of the murders and the condition of these remains, I can name several experts who would agree with my recommendation. Randy, you know I'm right about—"

"I hear your concerns, Ms. Hazelwood," Crowley cut in, "but I know the residents of this village personally. A pair of murderers is hard enough to imagine. Look, I'll have Matt see what he can find about cult activity. In the meantime, I have another job for you. Talk to the victim's daughter, if you don't mind."

Without another word, Crowley turned and started on his way back to the road. Randy was quick to hobble behind him, leaving Erica to stand in the middle of the field of horrors.

"Weren't you a little hard on her?" he asked the inspector.

"Your 'girlfriend' is asking a lot of uncomfortable questions, Randy. You don't want to come to our meeting? Fine. Here's your new homework: you keep her out of my hair. Unless you want to explain to her the finer points of who the Craftsmen are and what you do in your spare time at the morgue."

"Threats, Stephen?"

"How'd you put it? This is just the beginning."

With those words, Crowley stormed off in the direction of some of his officers.

Randy McKenzie looked back at his friend. Dr. Hazelwood was leaning down next to a tree and studying an object on the ground. It had been a mistake, bringing her in on this case. Randy had wanted an opportunity to work with Erica again and hopefully give her the opportunity of a lifetime working on a unique case. This was the stuff careers were made of, but it was beginning to sink in that it was also how lives were lost.

This wasn't just a chance at professional advancement. There was real danger here, and Erica was that much more at risk for not knowing it.

As Randy observed her, both worrying and admiring, he noticed something peculiar about the item his friend was looking at: a soft-looking brown object with a shock of red on top. It looked perhaps like some piece of flesh that had found its way onto a chunk of wood. However, there was something familiar about it.

Thinking no one was looking, Dr. Hazelwood reached down and picked up the item. At that moment, Randy recognized it for what it was. His skin grew cold, and he was so overwhelmed with shock that he failed to acknowledge the potentially illegal breach of protocol his protégé was committing.

Not only did she touch the piece of evidence, Erica snuck it into her purse. Normally, Randy would have intervened, reminding her of the consequences of what she was doing, but he couldn't.

What Erica Hazelwood had stolen from this crime scene didn't exist anymore. Or rather, it should be unattainable. Out of reach of any mortal. Yet there it was: a brown stuffed toy with a red felt hat stitched to its head.

VENUS

THEY SHOWED UP midafternoon. Inspector Crowley, Lieutenant Bélanger, and that woman from out of town who, as far as Venus knew, was helping out with Old Man Finnegan's case. Calmly, they asked everyone to leave the ice cream parlor except for the new woman and Penny, who turned as white as a sheet. At first, Venus thought they were there to reveal that Sam had confessed to killing her best friend's dad. A lot of people had been getting these kinds of visits over the last two weeks. Usually Lieutenant Bélanger handled it, but he wasn't the best candidate for giving a teenage girl that sort of grim news.

But this was about more than Penny's father. That much became clear as Venus and Abraham heard their friend bellow a gut-wrenching cry of distilled anguish as they were led from the shop.

Abraham dropped his milk shake as the truth of the situation dawned on him. Something must be wrong with Mrs. LaForest.

"Inspector Crowley? What's happening?" asked Abraham in the hope of getting a better picture of the situation.

"We found the body of Penny's mom in the forest this morning," answered Lieutenant Bélanger, straight-faced.

"Matt!" admonished Crowley upon seeing the shock and distress on the two teens' faces.

The lieutenant shrugged apologetically.

"Look, guys. Lack of tact aside, what Lieutenant Bélanger said is right." He paused to let the news sink in. Crowley made it a point to know most of the people in town. He was aware that Venus and Abe weren't idiots, and hoped he could count on them to be levelheaded. Venus kept staring, wide-eyed, but Abraham nodded steadily.

"All right, son," the inspector continued, putting a hand on the bear-framed teen's shoulder. "It's clear we have a situation to take care of. I need you two to keep your mouths shut and wait here. Ms. Hazelwood's gonna have a talk with Penny, but when she's done . . ."

"We have to be there for her," Venus finished in a quiet voice.

"Right. You guys can handle that? Don't leave your friend alone, and do what Ms. Hazelwood tells you."

"We're on it, sir," said Abraham.

Crowley nodded at Bélanger to follow him, and they left the teens behind. Without a word, Venus and Abraham backed up to the ice cream shop, while curious villagers stared in their direction. Christine Bowler, a girl from Penny's class who had been about to walk into the shop when the inspector showed up, approached the two friends who were silently leaning on the trailer. She was a tall, athletic girl with a stern face and a permanently humorless expression.

"What's that all about, then?" she asked once within earshot.

"Store's closed, Christine. Something happened to Penny's mom," Abraham said.

"Shut up, Abe," Venus cut in. "We're not supposed to tell."

"S'all right. I won't babble around. So what happened?" Christine continued, hungering for good gossip.

"We . . . don't know," Abraham tried to explain, his eyes darting back and forth between the two girls, measuring Venus's level of irritation.

As Abe continued to make excuses, Venus's attention shifted to a spot across the street. After a moment, she pushed herself off the wall and, without a word, walked toward her target: Chris Hagen, still wearing his crisp business suit, was sitting at a coffee shop table with a large glass of lemonade. His sunglasses sat on top of his stylishly unkempt hair, and his soft blue eyes locked on to Venus. She stood before him, her hands on her hips. He smiled at her, bringing the glass to his lips.

"You spend a lot of time staring at teenagers, or are we special?" Venus asked defiantly.

"Huh. I *have* been spending an unusual amount of time talking to kids over the past two days," he answered, as if coming to the realization himself. "That must come off as a little creepy."

"It comes off as very creepy." She sat down opposite the man without knowing why. "Have you considered a different hobby?"

"I'm sorry. It's part of my job to observe. You and your boyfriend looked distraught." He closed a small weathered notebook and slipped it into his jacket pocket, but not before she noticed the strange spiral patterns sketched onto the cover.

"Don't bait me," she responded. "I've met creeps like you before. You don't impress me."

"Oh, a city girl, then?" The man leaned over the table, his eyes drilling into hers. "I'm sorry I made you uncomfortable. I was just . . . curious. After all, I'm pretty sure the whole street heard your friend Penny cry out earlier. Can't blame me for taking an interest, but you . . . What are you doing here talking to me?" Hagen jerked his chin in the direction of the shop. The front door was ajar. The psychologist was talking to Abraham, who pointed in Venus's direction, a confused look on his face.

Hagen took another sip of lemonade. "You'll want to be there for your friend in her darkest hour, Ms. McKenzie."

Venus stood up and ran back to the shop. She didn't bother saying good-bye.

"What was that all about?" asked Abraham when she got close.

"I . . . I don't know." Venus glanced toward the coffee shop, seeing Hagen jot a quick note in his book before standing and leaving. "I just saw him sitting there and . . . There's something gross about the guy. Like, this was all his fault somehow?"

"Venus McKenzie?" a woman interrupted. Venus recognized her from the day of Audrey's funeral. "I'm Dr. Erica Hazelwood. May I have a word with you?"

"I'd rather talk to Penny," Venus said.

"In a moment. I understand you and Penny are very close?"

Venus nodded. They'd only known each other for a year and a half, but the girls had latched on to each other like two halves of a whole. Their differences, and the fact that Penny seemed incapable of tolerating most other people her age, had made the teens inseparable.

"Good," continued Erica. "I've already talked to her, and I'll be meeting with her once a day for the next little while. But right now she needs friends, and every ounce of support you can give her."

"Can I see her now?" asked Venus after a moment.

Erica stepped out of the doorway and let the girl rush in.

Penny was sitting at the counter. Her eyes were puffy, and her cheeks were wet with tears. She stared into the distance, only half-aware of her friend's presence.

"Turns out, she didn't stand me up the other day." Penny sniffled. They both knew what this meant. At the very same time she'd been complaining about her parental issues, Penny's mother had been lying in the forest, dead.

Both girls stood in silence for a few moments. Venus was no stranger to awkward and uncomfortable situations, yet she didn't know how to handle herself. The whole situation was too surreal. It felt like at any moment she would wake up, and things would be back to normal. She knew this wasn't a dream and that she should go to her friend and hold her, hear her cries, listen to her rage against a universe that would so callously take away both of her parents. Yet she couldn't move. It was as if acknowledging the situation would make it real.

Slowly, Penny turned to look at her. Her face was a visage of impossible distress. Seeing such despair, Venus broke from her trance. She took a step, then rushed forward to take her friend in her arms.

The girls remained entwined for a long time. Venus stroked her friend's hair while Penny cried herself into near senselessness. Before long, the younger girl broke down too. Gabrielle LaForest had cooked for her, had welcomed her for sleepovers, had driven her and Penny to school. In the last year and a half, the dead woman had been more present in her life than Venus's own parents.

Eventually both girls pulled away from each other. Penny, who had always been more practical, was the first to break the silence.

"Can . . . Can you get Abraham?" asked Penny between sobs. Venus quickly nodded and walked to the door. "I just want to hang out here for a little while with you guys."

The big teenager walked in, his head held low. He was surprised when Penny leaned against him. The three friends sat in silence. Periodically, Penny would break down in fits of tears. This lasted perhaps two hours before Penelope would weep herself to sleep, exhausted by the emotional toll.

"Where's Ms. Hazelwood?" whispered Venus. "I don't know what I'm supposed to do now."

"She said she had to go. She asked if either of us could take Penny for the night since she has no one in the village to take care of her. There's room at the farm and Pa won't mind, but . . ."

"No," she said. "Penny's slept over dozens of times. I'll take care of her."

"All right. I'll call your mom to pick you guys up," Abraham announced, standing to get to the phone.

"Is that necessary?" she asked, remembering her fight with her mother.

"Yeah," he said, picking up the receiver. "There's still a killer out there."

DANIEL

DAN HAD FIGURED it out. It had taken the better part of an afternoon, tearing through the house like a madman, but he'd finally remembered where he'd seen the strange symbol on Chris Hagen's business card before. He hadn't seen the winged hourglass since he was a child, but once he remembered where it had come from, it took him but a minute to find the artifact.

He pulled a large trunk out from underneath his father's bed. It was an unusual piece of furniture for a practical person like Stephen Crowley to own. An ornate and weathered antique carved out of several different essences of wood to create what was more a work of art than a storage container.

A chill went up Daniel's spine as his fingers traced over the inlaid design on the cover of the chest: an hourglass with stylized wings. The symbol and the chest were holdovers from a long time ago. From a time when father and son weren't the house's only occupants. The box didn't fit with Stephen Crowley's tastes, but it would have easily caught the eye of Dan's mother, Margaret Crowley.

What could be hidden inside the trunk? Maybe it was the souvenirs that his father had elected to keep from his ex-wife. Maybe the box itself was the only souvenir. Maybe it had nothing to do with Dan's mother at all. The teenager knew he would never find out by just looking at the lid. Somehow this trunk and Chris Hagen were connected. So after another moment's trepidation, he opened the box.

Inside were stacks of documents. Files, photos, letters, all sorts of information that had been tossed pell-mell into the chest. The papers were yellowed and delicate, the pictures faded. The whole thing smelled of salt and mothballs.

"Sandmen?" Dan whispered to himself.

One of the first papers to grab his attention was a list of names. It was scrawled hastily in what was unmistakably his father's handwriting. There were two rows of names, though one was almost completely blacked out with a marker.

The names in the first column were all familiar to him— members of his father's social club. Bergeron, LaFrenière, Parcs, all people who held influence in Saint-Ferdinand.

In the second column, only one name remained unmarred: Harry Peterson. At the top of the list, in big block letters was the word *CRAFTSMEN*.

Dan set the list aside and picked up the next piece of paper, a yellowed letter signed by William Bergeron. The letterhead bore the winged hourglass symbol, the word *SANDMEN* below it in a fancy serif typeface. All very official looking. The letter itself was barely legible, but before he could make sense of it, Dan's attention was drawn to something else. A photograph. From the looks of it, the picture was taken twenty years ago. It showed a carnival or circus that must have been on a field somewhere, as evidenced by the farmhouse in the background on the edge of the photo. In front of a popcorn cart stood a familiar young woman, holding the hand of a little boy. He was about five, with oddly familiar features. Next to the boy was a young and dynamic Stephen Crowley.

As his mind struggled to process what he was seeing, Dan was startled by the sound of the front door opening. Immediately he closed the trunk and slid it back under the bed. With quiet haste,

he made his way to the bathroom and started the tap, splashing
water to make it seem like he had been washing his hands.

"Dan?" his father's voice called out as he came up the stairs.

"Just a minute!" the teenager replied as he ripped a hand towel from a hook on the wall. He stepped out of the bathroom,
making a show of drying his hands. "What's up?"

Stephen Crowley looked like he'd walked to hell and back
barefoot. His eyes were sunken, and his short graying hair was
tousled badly, having been tilled by nervous fingers. With his un-
done tie and soil-stained shirt, the man appeared as if he might
have forgotten how to care for himself at all.

"Look, buddy," he said apologetically. "You're gonna have to
have dinner without me. I've got work tonight."

"What happened?" Dan was smart enough to recognize that
there was a particular tension in his father's voice, an urgency that
signaled something important was going on.

"There's been another murder. A bad one." Crowley's haunted
look confirmed the truth of the statement. "There's a . . . monster
out there. I want you to stay in, all right?"

Being raised in Saint-Ferdinand meant living in the shadow
of the Saint-Ferdinand Killer, a beast that had taken at least one
life per year for almost two decades. Before Finnegan was caught,
people had accepted that a handful of them would most likely
disappear at the hands of the murderer. Property values had plum-
meted and remained low. A slow exodus had drained the town of
a third of its residents. Yet Dan couldn't remember a day when his
father, the man most aware of the area's danger, had so emphatically demanded that he avoid the outdoors. If Dan hadn't known
his father better, he would have sworn the man was terrified.

"All right. Where are you going?"

"Following a lead." Crowley quickly changed into civilian
clothes: denim pants and a plaid shirt. He did, however, keep his
police belt and sidearm.

"Dad . . . who died?"

"Gabrielle LaForest."

"Oh."

Dan hadn't known Gabrielle. But his own friend Bernard's father had disappeared two summers ago and was only found the previous week in one of Finnegan's freezers. Yet the tone in which his father said the name couldn't help but make Dan feel as if this particular murder was something of a different nature. Something alien. It hit Dan that he, and probably all of Saint-Ferdinand, had gotten used to the killings because, despite their obvious horror, they were familiar. It was the devil they'd known, but now it seemed there was another on the loose.

As Stephen finished buckling his belt, the phone on his nightstand rang. Dan started walking across the room to answer it, but his father cut him off, answering it himself.

"Crowley," he said. "Hey, Will . . . I don't care. This is important."

Stephen Crowley's temper rose quickly as he listened. Dan could see the skin on his father's neck turn crimson. As quick as Crowley succumbed to anger, there were only three things that could frustrate him quite this fast, and Dan had spent the greater part of his teenage years learning what they were: being disobeyed, being contradicted, and personal failure.

"Listen to me very carefully, Will. You will drag your drunk carcass to this meeting, and you will drink coffee and sober up every step of your way there. If you don't, I will personally tie you to a tree for the night and use you as bait." Crowley wasn't exaggerating. Dan knew it, and Will probably knew it too. "You knew what you were getting into; we don't get sick days!"

He hung up and turned to his son once more. No one in Saint-Ferdinand wanted to mess with Stephen Crowley when he was in this kind of mood, especially not the boy who knew him best.

"You!" He pointed at Dan while walking to the stairs. "Not a foot out of this house!"

"Yes, sir!" Dan saluted, but the attempt at mirth fell flat. His father walked out the front door and loudly locked it behind him, leaving Daniel alone to contemplate what was going on.

Briefly, he considered looking online for more information on Gabrielle LaForest's murder. Knowing his father's pathological hatred of the media, though, he figured no information would hit the television or papers for a long while. Then he contemplated going back upstairs to take another look at the trunk under the bed. Maybe discover who the boy in the picture was, or what the man who had called his father had to do with it.

"Will," Dan mused out loud. "William Bergeron."

Why would his father, hot on the trail of a dangerous murderer, need to meet with Bergeron? Why would he threaten a grieving father and family friend?

Before common sense could overcome his decision, Dan ran downstairs, grabbed his car keys, and rushed outside.

It wasn't difficult for Daniel to figure out his father's destination. The original plan was to follow his old man discreetly. It wouldn't have been that hard in such a rural area. He knew the roads well enough to drive without headlights, and there were no streetlamps except on Main Street. At this time of night, even his white Civic would be almost invisible.

Even that was too much of a risk, though. Dan knew the fury he'd unleash for this level of disobedience, and after a bit of thinking, he realized there were only three places his father might go: the station, which was improbable, as he'd just changed out of his uniform. The cave on Finnegan's property, since he seemed so obsessed with it. But in the end, the most likely place was the church.

If Dan's father was meeting with Bergeron at this time, it surely related to the village's welfare; the two of them never met officially without the rest of the congregation. Whether it was Mrs. Bergeron going into early labor, someone disappearing because of the Saint-Ferdinand Killer, or even simply when there was an unusually large snowfall, Stephen Crowley always went to church to meet with his peers. It's simply what they did in emergencies.

Gabrielle LaForest's death certainly qualified.

During the quiet, nervous drive to the village proper, Daniel contemplated his choice in turning down membership to his father's social club. How much more would he know about what was going on if he'd simply said yes?

Main Street was empty. The only business still open at this hour was Kelsey's Tavern, and that dive was far down the road, in the opposite direction of the church. Daniel made a point of parking on a side street and walking the rest of the distance to the steps of the Jonathan Moore Church. Stephen's familiar black SUV, along with the cars of several other important villagers, was parked in front, confirming his suspicions. Every step he took, Dan felt like eyes were watching him. Between the bright white sneakers he wore and the echo each of his steps made on the stone stairs, he expected someone to shout at him at any moment.

Thankfully, there was no one to call him out. Only the moon and the impeccable silence kept him company as he snuck to the large oak doors that dominated the front of the building.

Daniel had been inside a few times. He also knew a fair bit about the structure's history. Originally called the Saint-Ferdinand Church, after the same saint for whom the village had been named, it had been rechristened the Jonathan Moore Church in the mid-1870s, after a prominent member of the congregation. It was the largest building on Main Street, but not the oldest in the village. That honor belonged to Pascal Begin's farmhouse, which, while having been renovated extensively, had kept most of its stone facade for over two centuries.

An interesting feature of the church was a little-known secret about its front doors. Most villagers assumed that the large oak panels were kept unlocked to offer a more welcoming atmosphere and be an example of what kind of village Saint-Ferdinand wished to be. The truth was, the lock was broken. It had been for decades, and the pieces required to repair it were too expensive and difficult to obtain. So Dan was able to enter quickly and quietly.

Inside, the teenager made a point to ignore the conversation echoing through the vast ceiling of the main chamber. He knew all the voices and could have made sense of the words had he paid attention, but his focus was on the second-floor mezzanine. It was designed for the choir and offered both a good view of the altar and wonderful acoustics. In that sense, it might have been the worst place to quietly hide and observe, but Daniel had been in the choir as a child. He knew that there was a spot in the corner where sound didn't carry at all. It was meant for the choir director to stand and give instructions without his words interrupting the church services.

It was in this spot that Dan settled to watch as his notion of the Sandmen was shattered.

Eyes unblinking, the police inspector's son observed as an assembly of the village's most distinguished, most-respected individuals stood in a circle around the altar. There, where every child baptized in Saint-Ferdinand had lain, the elite were bent down over a large flailing ball of fur. It was one of Ms. Livingston's rabbits. Almost every kid in town had owned one at some point or other, but this one was not intended to be a pet.

Instead Mrs. Bergeron held it down while the ancient Gédéon LaFrenière plunged a thin blade into the animal's neck. Blood erupted from the wound, but it wasn't enough to silence the dying animal. Shrieks resonated on the church's walls, similar sounds to what a child being burned alive might make.

This mockery of a holy choir lasted only a minute longer before LaFrenière, his wrinkled face painted with disgust and annoyance, plunged the knife into the animal's heart. Once the unsavory task had been completed, he put the knife down with reverence, onto a plate covered by a clean white linen sheet decorated with an embroidered winged hourglass. Flowers of crimson red erupted where drops of blood had fallen.

"What now?" The gruff and unpleasant voice of Hector Alvarez had pierced the fresh silence. As the owner of a slaughterhouse just outside of town and the meat shop and deli on Main Street, he was accustomed to blood and the cries of animals.

"Now we hope that a fresh kill will bring Finnegan's prisoner forth," LaFrenière said.

He sliced open the belly of the rabbit, playing the tip of his fancy ceremonial knife in the animal's entrails. As disgusting as the sight was to Dan, there was nothing in the old man's behavior that came as a surprise. Gédéon had long ago lost his family, bitterly outliving everyone he'd ever known and loved. If a soul had an expiration date, his was long past.

"Hmph," Stephen Crowley scoffed. "For once, I'm glad you're all such idiots."

If the inspector was trying to get a rise out of his peers, it was a success. Considering what he'd just witnessed, Dan silently cheered his old man on.

"Pardon?" Beatrice Bergeron asked, the insult having bitten deep.

"You think killing a rabbit is going to bring a god of hate and death to our doorstep? You're all morons. Animals like that die by the hundreds in the woods no more than twenty yards behind this church."

"A sacrifice to attract a god," LaFrenière explained, vitriol dripping from his voice like the blood on his knife. "What's so hard to understand about that, Crowley?"

"That ain't no sacrifice." Stephen thrust his chin toward the baptistry. "The Craftsmen knew what sacrifice meant. Finnegan knows what sacrifice means! It means loss! It means giving up something important. That? That's just a dumb animal. This is why we've always been a step behind them and always will be!

Besides, what if this had worked? Have you thought of that? Have you?"

The old man frowned, and the butcher stepped beside him in support. Beatrice's face was also getting darker, her mannerisms more agitated.

"Listen, you incompetent moron!" Beatrice exploded with anger. "This god is the key to getting my daughter back. If you think I'm worried about a little collateral damage getting in the way, you are sorely mistaken!"

"Come now. No reason to lose our tempers," William interceded. His voice still maintained a hint of a slur.

"Weren't you listening?" Crowley spat out, volatile and angry. "If that stupid ritual had worked, we'd all be like Gabrielle right now. All of us! Guts, blood, and bones, everywhere in this church! This is why we have McKenzie!"

Stephen waved his arms, pointing around him for emphasis. Daniel ducked down, making sure no one noticed him.

"Well, maybe if you'd been able to bring Randy here tonight, things would be different, Crowley," LaFrenière said, his own anger rising to match the inspector's.

"You think I didn't ask?" Crowley stepped forward, his mass and height casting a shadow over the frail old man.

"Ask? And you call *us* idiots, Stephen? If you were half the man you pretend to be, McKenzie would be here whether he wished to or not. No! If you did your fucking job, we'd have the god by now!"

The old man didn't have time to blink before Stephen Crowley's massive fist rammed the words back into his mouth. Blood sprayed as LaFreniere's lip split. The speed and might of the assault made Daniel gasp. The teenager stifled his breath, convinced the entire group had heard him. However, the assembled villagers were more focused on Stephen Crowley's handling of LaFrenière. A second punch, to the old man's gut this time, had already been delivered.

"Stephen!" William called out, the alcohol finally gone from his voice.

Inspector Stephen Crowley interrupted his assault on LaFrenière, shooting a look of red-hot fury toward Bergeron. The sheer force of his anger made William take a step back and raise his hands, palms out, in front of him.

"Calm down, Stephen," he mumbled, the fear of being next in line to get his teeth knocked out sweating from each syllable.

At this point, Daniel had seen enough. He'd been witness to his father's anger in the past. He'd watched Stephen put his fist through a wall after being unable to repair a lawn mower. Anger wasn't the inspector's favorite emotion, but he was often its victim and had sampled every flavor and shade of the feeling. Yet, in over a decade and a half, Dan had never seen his father succumb to his rage with such abandon. Never had he seen his old man lose control so thoroughly, nor beat a man so mercilessly.

Nothing was worth seeing his father like this. No revelation could erase seeing his hero fall this low.

CROWLEY

THAT STUPID CAVE.

Stephen Crowley's mood was one of his blackest ever. Everyone had more or less legitimate reasons to be part of the Sandmen; he understood that. Bergeron, of course, had lost his daughter, but even predatory assholes like LaFrenière had motivations that made sense. The old man had seen his whole family, including both sons, taken by cancer, and he knew in his fetid old gut that his destiny would be no different. Archambeault was more vain, wanting the riches and security that came with power. He'd already had his wish granted simply by associating with the group, but once the eyes to greed were open, it was difficult to ever get them shut again.

Their motivations were understandable. What Crowley couldn't comprehend was the lack of commitment. Everyone wanted their share of the pie, but it seemed that the hungrier each individual became, the more reluctant they were to put in the effort. They couldn't possibly expect him to do all the heavy lifting and then simply collect at the end.

Were these the kind of people Stephen wanted in his camp? They were getting close to opening Pandora's box, but what would happen then? Who would stand by him to corral the forces that would be unleashed? It was times like these he wished Dan would have joined the group. Maybe he should have been more forceful with the boy. Twisted his arm a little. That way he'd have at least one ally he could depend on. The Crowley boys.

Randy was another disappointment. The inspector loathed using the word, but there was genuine *magic* to what the medical examiner could do. Yet, when offered a place among the Sandmen, he barely hesitated before refusing. While Randy enjoyed a great position at the university and didn't want for most earthly things, there were benefits to having friends like the Sandmen. Especially for someone who dabbled in practices best left out of the public eye.

No, instead Stephen had only himself to rely on for everything.

Before the meeting had concluded, Crowley stormed out of the church. He wanted to make sure they were the ones left to clean up. If they were all too afraid to get their hands dirty, the least they could do was put away all the paraphernalia from their ridiculous ritual. Crowley didn't feel the slightest hint of guilt over having the rich and powerful of Saint-Ferdinand pick up after him, even if the group included grieving parents and sick old men. While they'd be in the comfort and security of the church, he had to deal with that goddamned cave.

Hopefully, his hunch was correct and the place was now deserted.

About a mile before he arrived at the Peterson farm, Crowley cut his headlights and slowed down. The lights to Harry Peterson's barn were still on. The sick artist was awake and painting. Another one of the village's disappointments. Someone who had the knowledge and experience that Crowley needed to complete his job but who selfishly chose not to share either. It was a well-known fact that Peterson had been part of the Saint-Ferdinand Craftsmen's Association before the group disbanded years ago. He knew more about the history of the town than anyone else. The inspector had long suspected Harry of being the one behind the Craftsmen graffiti, but he couldn't prove it.

It wasn't the only thing that Crowley suspected him of either. It was probably no coincidence that Sam's home and the stupid cave were at the edge of Peterson's property.

Crowley drove his Explorer down the road that separated two of the farm's unkempt fields. The path had been well trod over the past week, and a few more tire marks wouldn't raise an eyebrow. The inspector parked near the line of yellow tape that delineated the crime scene. Reserving his anger in case he might need it, he climbed out of the SUV.

Even before the bodies were discovered, Finnegan's property had been a depressing place to visit. Everything spoke to the man's broken mind. The weird collection of appliances was eerie long before their purpose was found, and the lone trailer was a reminder of the miserable life Sam had lived every day.

Night did no favors to the trailer and the area around it. Even Crowley, whom Lieutenant Bélanger had once said was unacquainted with fear, found himself getting anxious as he walked through the property. He pushed his anxieties aside. The trick, he found, was to remain too angry to be afraid. Tonight, despite the creeping shadows, the inescapable stench of decay, and the ghosts of the events that had transpired here, there was more than enough rage to keep the terror at bay.

Without a clear path to the cave, Stephen had to take out the floodlights from the back of his vehicle and haul them all the way to the entrance. Each step of the journey allowed Crowley to stew in his anger anew, pushing away thoughts of the blood that had soaked the ground, and the powerful forces he was investigating. He'd need every ounce of courage available for what was to come.

Harsh light sprayed across the entrance to the cave, illuminating every detail, every crack in the rocks, and every branch of the dead oak tree that framed the entrance. It did nothing to remove the location's ominous nature. Shadows were starker, and the cave itself became a black vortex that refused to give away anything about its contents.

Crowley felt his hairs stand on end. It wasn't the nature of the cave but a coldness to the air around him that he simply couldn't shake. As he was about to take his first step through the entrance, the second battery-operated floodlight in his hand, the inspector took a moment to stop. Holding his breath and closing his eyes, he tried to hear if there was any noise coming from within the cave. Rustling of leaves, movement, anything to give him a clue whether the thing he was seeking was still hidden inside. There was rustling in the trees and the hoot of a barn owl, but nothing from the black hole in the ground.

Crowley remembered how things had sounded when Bélanger had first found the cave. How, under the hot rays of the sun, the place had been completely silent, devoid of life, with an emptiness that did not belong to the forest. The sounds that were usually a source of fright for those who ventured into the woods at night were now like a comfortable blanket to the inspector. A reassurance that things were back to normal here.

Still, it took one last push of his willpower for Inspector Crowley to crouch down and walk through the low archway of dirt, roots, and rocks. The light from outside cut through the shadows, but the twists and turns of the shallow tunnel prevented it from digging too deep. After a few moments, he had to pull out his service flashlight to better navigate the cave.

The walls seemed oddly textured. There wasn't much room to either side and none to stand. After a minute of squeezing through a bottleneck, the inspector was disgorged into what felt like a larger chamber. The beam of his flashlight seemed insufficient to the task, and he set the floodlight on the ground. The location was finally getting to his nerves, picking at his worries and teasing his imagination with shadows that looked like creatures but in the end were nothing. Fumbling in a way he'd never admit to another living soul, Crowley flipped the switch on the floodlight, illuminating the chamber by casting its beam toward the ceiling.

Considering what had, at one point, inhabited this place, the inspector thought it would be desolate, dry, and sterile. Instead he was presented with a tableau of madness that could almost be considered beautiful.

The texture he'd seen on the walls was finally revealed to him in all its terrible glory. Every surface was covered in desiccated organic remains. An untrained eye, unfamiliar with the appearance of organs and broken bones, might have missed the subtlety, but to the inspector, the textures were obvious. Every inch of the cave had been decorated by a gruesome mural. The bas-relief of interwoven spirals and elegant curving patterns was sculpted from skulls, bone fragments, nearly fossilized viscera, and the leathery remnants of animal skin.

A voice from the back of Crowley's mind cried for him to leave, but he stood rooted in place. Anger, fear—none of it compared to the awe he felt at the hypnotic patterns surrounding him.

This was not done by the hands of men. Despite the terrible nature of the art confronting him, the inspector couldn't help but get closer to it. With a hand trembling not out of fear but reverence, he touched the wall. For the first time since his eighteen-year search had begun, Stephen Crowley had a tangible link to his quarry.

VENUS

IT WAS A minor triumph, but well worth it.

The past two days had been difficult. Penny had been the easiest thing to manage, being reduced to little more than a zombie by her grief. It was devastating how little she would talk and how the strong, willful girl had given up her autonomy. Paul and Virginie had been as helpful as they knew how. Going back and forth between wanting to be of assistance and staying out of Venus's way. Staying true to their parenting style, they didn't interfere, but instead stocked the kitchen with the girls' favorite snacks. Not that Penny would eat anything. To their credit, they had talked with Penny's grandmother, who lived in Florida, and had worked out that the grieving girl could stay at the McKenzie house until things settled down.

It had also been up to Venus to go to the LaForest house to gather essentials for her friend. As expected, it was a painful visit. Every room in the house had a memory linked to it, like that time Mrs. LaForest had brought them brownies in Penny's room while they were watching horror movies, or all the dinners they'd shared in the living room, sitting on the couch. Should Penny be allowed to keep the house and live there, it would be a difficult homecoming.

None of these things were the success Venus was so proud of, though. What she had accomplished reassured her that, although it would take some time and the road ahead was going to be difficult and painful for her friend, Penelope was going to be mostly okay. After hours of sitting with her in silence, listening to her cry, and attempting to come to terms with the unimaginable, after much begging and prodding on Venus's part, she had finally succeeded in getting Penny to eat something.

Both girls had chatted calmly well into the night. Venus had tried her best to keep conversation topics away from the tragedy of the previous day, but they could only ignore the elephant in the room for so long. Inevitably, conversation returned to the subject of Penny's mom: why she had to die and what would the orphaned girl do now. Eventually Venus's friend went to sleep, drained by the tragedy.

Venus, however, was still very much awake. The recent events only served to fire up her brain with questions. Who was this "Chris Hagen"? Why had she been compelled to talk to him? Who had killed Mrs. LaForest? Having no way to find answers at two in the morning, Venus looked for a way to distract herself until she, too, was able to sleep.

She turned to her computer, browsing through web pages while petting Sherbet. Yet, after an hour of reading, and in spite of her friend's snoring and Sherbet's purring in her lap, Venus was still no closer to sleep.

She decided to take a look at the feed from the camera she'd installed in the shed. At this time of night, there shouldn't be much going on. The mother bird would probably be covering her eggs and sleeping with one eye open for predators, Venus thought to herself as she switched the feed on.

Something was in the shed.

It was difficult to determine what she was seeing. Between the camera's low resolution and the terrible lighting, the image quality wasn't up to the task of properly rendering the interior of the shed. It was enough, however, to let Venus know that something was wrong.

In the middle of the empty room was a stain. A shadow that obscured the bird's nest she had meant to observe. At first glance, it could have been a smudge on the lens or perhaps a compression error in the signal, but after double-checking the equipment, she knew that wasn't it.

Even more disturbing was the mess around the shadow. Seeping from the darkness appeared to be a pool of dark liquid. It looked dreadfully familiar.

Venus leaned in, her nose almost touching the monitor, trying to get a better look. Suddenly the shadow turned, and she jumped back. Eyes. Glowing eyes had appeared inside the shed. Her heart raced. The eyes seemed to be staring directly into the lens, as if they knew she was watching.

Venus stared back, both petrified and fascinated. She observed for several minutes until it hit her. This was a prank. It had to be. André and his cronies were playing a sick joke on her. They had broken into her shed and messed with the lighting to create the play of shadows she was seeing. The eyes were probably LEDs or pocket flashlights. As for the liquid, that was the telltale sign. Whoever was trying to scare her had knocked over a can of paint or a bucket or something. It seemed a curiously elaborate plan, one too sophisticated for André to have come up with. In fact, none of her usual tormentors had the wit or skill to invent anything like this.

Whoever was behind it, they had Venus's attention. She stood, dumping poor Sherbet onto the floor and walking downstairs to the back door. The cat followed in her footsteps, still offended at being dropped.

The night was dark, lacking a moon or the streetlights of larger communities. The only source of illumination came from the shed itself. The soft white glow of the camera's light emanated from the various cracks in the wall and the small window in the door.

Venus walked as calmly as she could, her bare feet leaving footprints in the wet grass. She was too preoccupied to enjoy the feeling of it between her toes.

When she stepped into the shed, Venus realized that part of the reason for the terrible image quality on her monitor was that the lighting was even worse than she'd assumed. The brilliance of the bright bulb she had installed seemed to be obscured, as if a black veil had been thrown over the whole shed.

Something shuffled in the corner. A soft rustling, like cloth being dragged on the floor in an empty room. She jumped and spun around, her left foot stepping in something wet. Eyes wide and pupils dilated, she looked into the darkness . . . and the darkness looked back at her. The glowing eyes. She had their full attention. They were not LEDs. This was no prank.

Venus stumbled back, trying to make her way through the doorway of the shed and into the night, but something caught her attention. On the wall opposite the shadow was something new. A spiral pattern, artistically laid out. It looked like a cross between an arabesque and the spiral of a nautilus shell. Beautiful in its complexity, the mural was painstakingly drawn with intricate details and curves that pleased the eye and soothed the mind. However, the realization of what glistening and wet materials were used in the creation of this art slowly sank in. Venus was disgusted. There were eggshells, delicate skulls, and the occasional tiny feathers in the mural. Ingredients taken from the eggs and their fetal contents. Bone, viscera, and blood. Such was the media used to create the enthralling mural.

As she was deciding between screaming and running away, the door to the shed slammed shut. Venus slipped and fell against the wall. The whole shed shook under the impact. She sat for a moment, staring at her left foot. The toes were darkened by a thick liquid. She wiggled them, feeling a stickiness that she remembered from many a skinned knee and scraped elbow.

The shadow crept closer to her, and Venus tried backing up farther against the wall. If she could have somehow squeezed between the boards, she would have done it. Anything to be out of the presence of whatever these eyes belonged to.

Suddenly the shadow stopped, as if it had run up against some invisible wall. It writhed and swirled like smoke caught in the wind, yet refused to disperse. At the edge of her hearing, Venus could barely perceive screams of fury, strong in their anger but dim, as if coming from inside a grave. The shadow focused its eyes on her once more, and the screams vanished. For a tense moment, she considered that perhaps she had indeed fallen asleep upstairs and was now having a nightmare.

Then it spoke.

The voice that came out of the shade was like nothing Venus had heard before. Both beautiful and terrible at once, it could be compared to a heavenly chorus chanting from within a cave inhabited by a hundred thousand bats. It echoed majestically, while tearing at the soul with voracious hunger.

"Release me." The demand writhed in the young girl's mind, more like burrowing worms of thought than sound in her ears.

The shadow lashed out once again, and Venus pulled her legs in to get out of its reach. Through the fear, she tried to identify her attacker. If she couldn't figure out its name or recognize its face, at least she wanted to know what it was. So far, all she could come up with was blood and shadows.

The creature, whatever it was, seemed to have given up on reaching her physically. It swirled slowly in the darkness, shapes existing only on the very edge of perception. Dancing over the line between something seen and something imagined.

The two of them stayed that way for several minutes, each minute stretching on forever. It gave Venus time to think. Occasionally a wet crack would echo from the darkness, breaking the silence and making her jump. The eyes would look around, the stare from them raising the hairs on the back of her neck like nails on a chalkboard. The more she looked at the thing, the smaller she felt. This wasn't the feeling of being in the presence of a predator; it was something greater, more humbling.

"Who . . . Who are you?" she said, squeezing out the words with much less confidence than intended.

The shadow receded for a moment before pushing forth once more. Less aggressive, more akin to a wave pulling back before crashing onto a beach.

"I just want to know who you are! Your name!" she found herself screaming.

"No name. I am unique." More swirling, but not as predatory as it had been. Venus thought it almost looked majestic.

"What are you then?"

"To you? A god."

She believed it.

The voice dug deep into her soul, not just transmitting the sound of its words but implanting ideas into her mind. They were seeds she had to consciously pluck out, lest they take root against her will. She quickly found that when she weeded through the words, she could compose her thoughts more calmly, giving her back some control of the situation.

"Then what are you doing in my shed?"

"You set this trap. Release me."

I should do this. That was the thought that immediately appeared in her mind, at least until she weeded through that idea and realized she couldn't. The shade would kill her. In fact, it had tried to kill her before ever giving the order to be freed. Venus swallowed hard, praying she would soon wake up at her computer. Instead her eyes fell once again on the mural, the handiwork of the so-called god, painted with the remains of the unborn birds.

"Why?"

A quiet moment passed before the creature spoke again.

"Because I know you. It's what you do."

The voice was now velvet-smooth, couched in unspoken promises so real that Venus almost felt she could touch them. The shadow crept close again, its menace stripped away, replaced instead by a seductive slithering, graceful, like a snake.

"You don't—"

"But I do. You were called Neil last we met."

"You . . . You're wrong. Neil was my grandfather."

The shadow crashed against the invisible wall, attempting to get to her, to move past the immaterial barrier that kept it contained.

Thoughts blossomed unbidden in Venus McKenzie's mind once more. She knew what the voice meant, and for less than a second, the lifetime of a spark, she *was* Neil McKenzie. The so-called god didn't see the difference and, through its eyes, the line became blurred between the man and his granddaughter.

"I forget," the shadow said in words of sound and thought. *"Your kind loses itself between iterations, but you smell like Neil. You fear me, like Neil. And you will help me, like Neil."*

Venus pulled herself to her feet, leaning on the wall for support. Her bare feet slipped a few inches as she stood, but her eyes never left the torrent of darkness that now occupied most of the shed.

"I'm not my grandfather," she stated, once her footing and her voice had found firm ground.

The eyes in the shadows receded and flickered in a clumsy imitation of blinking. The swirl of black clouds themselves backed away from her, coagulating in the corner, revealing the horrid mural once again. Was the creature proud of its handiwork and showing it off? The seductive curves and spirals begged for closer observation, but the knitting of wet tissue and organs made her gag.

"Strong. Like Neil," it added. The compliment was like a peace offering. *"But your strength is weighed down by fear and doubt. Are you sure you are not him?"*

"My name is Venus," the girl said, pushing herself away from the wall as a demonstration of her will and courage. "And I'm not afraid; I'm careful."

The bulb flickered and Venus nearly bit through her tongue, trying to keep her composure. With each flash of light, the creature of shadow and blood moved, twisting in the air like a barely contained hurricane. It was beautiful.

"Free me, Venus."

For the first time, its voice did not hurt her ears and mind. There was no obvious attempt to implant alien thoughts among her own, only the three pleading words, spoken with the soft whisper only a shadow could manage.

"How?"

"The eye of glass and metal. Remove it, Venus. Free me."

The girl rapidly put the pieces together. The invisible line that the shadow seemed incapable of traversing, it coincided with the limits to her camera's line of sight. Somehow this so-called god, for all the power it emanated, was kept in check by a fifty-dollar webcam from the computer store.

"Free me."

Curious, she took another step. Her bare foot, moist with drying blood, intruded an inch into the creature's invisible cage. Her heart pounded so hard that she could hear her own blood rushing through her veins. Venus waited for something to happen. An attack, an assault. A way for the shadow to physically impose its will upon her.

Nothing.

Another step. The darkness moved once more. Where it had snapped like a predator when she had last walked within its reach, its motions were slow and deliberate. There was no mistaking the raw power of the thing whose space she now shared. Swimming with a great white shark would have been a fraction as intimidating.

A third step. If the god had any plans for her, she would be unable to avoid them now. In a moment of cold terror, Venus wondered if somehow it had indeed charmed her into its arms. She'd never felt the seeds of foreign thoughts take root in herself, but somehow there they were. Or perhaps these were her own feelings? The line had become impossible to see.

A vortex of black velvet, hungry for light, danced between her feet. Dervish-like, the shadow spun around her. The lack of light somehow moved her hair like a soft wind, blowing strands of it over her eyes. There was, at this point, only darkness and the smell of blood.

Venus closed her eyes, delighting in this communion of flesh and spirit. Her own weight was taken from her along with her will as she ascended to the tips of her toes, drinking in the abandon of otherworldly forces. The freedom of letting go was intoxicating. An embrace that touched parts of her soul she didn't even know existed.

She could see now. The line that could be drawn directly from her grandfather to her. Hints of the relationship the god had shared with Neil McKenzie and how, to a creature so immortal, the difference in generations might be meaningless.

"Stop," she murmured.

Venus thought she would have to struggle, to argue, to fight. That she had stepped too far into the trap, and that everything from this point on would be outside her control. Through the dance of shadows, she could see the mural again. Beautiful yet terrible, and it sobered her.

In the span of a breath, the dance was over and the god of shadows and blood had pulled back into the dark corner of the shed.

With careful steps, Venus made her way back to the safety of the wall. Her eyes never left the place where the god was huddled, looming over a puddle of blood. The shed seemed to expand forever beyond the corner, reaching into all the dark places at once.

"Why did you let me go?" she asked, having reached the safety of the door.

"You'll be back," the god said, scratching at her mind once again.

Venus nodded. Her heart still raced from the experience, though it was difficult to decide if it was fear or exhilaration that drove each beat. She looked outside the shed and into the night for a moment, then back inside at the shadow with whom she had just danced.

"I will . . . ," she said. Or thought. It didn't matter. The god understood.

CICERO

IT WAS GOOD to be back in Saint-Ferdinand. The town hadn't changed too much in the years he'd been gone. It wasn't quite the same feeling as coming home, though. There was no warmth or security. No, it was more like visiting one's old high school. Every building whispered memories to him, every street begged him to reminisce, but not every scrap of nostalgia was pleasant. There was some loss here, a bit of fear there, and tremendous amounts of suffering everywhere.

He parked his rickety 1968 Volkswagen Beetle at the Peterson farm and walked to the village from there, intent on experiencing the past as it presented itself to him.

After stepping out of his seasoned vehicle, Nathaniel took a look around, his eyes lingering for a moment in the direction of Finnegan's trailer. Somewhere in these woods was the home of his old friend. Oh, how it pained him to think on how they'd failed each other.

Just before the tree line was the field Peterson had lent him, and a few feet away, the farmhouse he and his family had lived in back in those terrible days. There was a boy in the field, working to clear it.

Nathaniel started the long walk toward Saint-Ferdinand proper. It had been a hot day, and the old man was thankful he'd arrived in the late afternoon. If he'd gotten here much earlier, he would have had to take the car to town or be broiled alive on the walk there.

The farms he passed all held strong memories of the friends who had lived there so long ago. Now most of the farms had been renovated and modernized almost beyond recognition. Yet they all kept at least a small fragment of their original charm: an old fence, a dilapidated barn, or some other vestigial element from back in the day. To his left was a corn farm where his friend and accomplice, Jonathan, had lived until the day he died. To his right was an orchard that used to be a small potato farm. He remembered a pretty girl had spent the summer there when he was eleven. So long ago.

Nathaniel used to visit Saint-Ferdinand annually. He did so against the better wisdom of Katrina, one of his employees and his oldest friend. Indeed, his last visit had rewarded him with a short stay in jail. He'd stayed away for almost twenty years after that, waiting for the appointed time. But as it turned out, he was a few days late. So was the nature of prophecy: vague and conveniently veiled in innuendos.

Not far down the road, a little past the Richards farm, which he remembered fondly as the home of a pair of twins with whom he'd gone hunting and fishing, Nathaniel's sharp nose detected the nauseating odor of putrefying blood. There was a time when he wouldn't have noticed or recognized the smell. Today he wasn't just familiar with it, but attentive to it.

Taking a few steps into the woods, he quickly found a portion of the forest that had been roped off by bright yellow plastic ribbons. The area was large. A chill went up Nathaniel's spine as he considered whether this was the site of a massacre with many victims or a single, extremely unfortunate one.

While he had strong suspicions about what had happened, some of the details didn't fit. He'd expected a great darkness to have befallen this place, but somehow he also felt a small light shining through the shadows. Something dark and cold had taken place here, but it hadn't gone unnoticed. There was power in that. Nathaniel could feel it.

Still, there were things to do and people to see. So many people to see. Nathaniel didn't linger. There would be time for that later.

By the time he walked into town, it was almost five in the evening. Some shops were already winding down. Tables and chairs were being moved indoors, signs and placards being taken down. Exhausted employees from a variety of jobs were eagerly packing up, praying there would be no last-minute customers. Some of the older villagers gave him odd looks, like old schoolmates who couldn't quite remember his name. He, however, remembered them all.

Nathaniel felt a spark of shame at avoiding the police station. The building he was heading for was the only other municipal office in town and was located right next to the station. He had nothing to worry about, at least officially, but there were certain people he'd rather not run into quite yet. There would be time for that unpleasantness later.

Saint-Ferdinand's town hall served the limited number of functions necessary for the village to run smoothly. It housed the mayor's office, administrative offices, and even a small courtroom that hadn't seen much use, as the small town hadn't had a residing judge in a few years. Fortunately, Nathaniel was only there for a trivial but necessary task. A formality.

The old man squeezed in through the door at the very last moment. The woman at the front desk let out an audible sigh at having her workday so rudely prolonged. She was rather young, Nathaniel noticed. Young enough that she would have been an infant the last time he visited.

"I'm very sorry to come in so late, mademoiselle," he said, approaching the counter. "Allow me to make it up to you by keeping my request a simple one."

"How may I help you, sir?" the clerk inquired mechanically, his apology flying miles above her head.

"I am merely here to pick up a permit, dear. Two, actually: one for temporary residence and the other for commercial zoning." He smiled broadly and announced, "The circus is coming to town."

The woman remained unimpressed. She pushed a strand of brown hair from her face before walking over to a nearby cabinet behind the counter. Nathaniel remembered a time when the mere mention of a circus would have men and women, young and old, beaming with pleasure and anticipation. Nowadays, people were too blasé. The traditional circus, the traveling carnival, had lost most if not all of its luster. Attractions were either considered too ordinary compared to the wonders one could see at the theater, or too politically incorrect because they made use of animals and freaks. Such a disappointing turn of events.

"Your name, sir?" the young lady asked with as little interest as she could muster.

The old man smiled again, not with pride or joy but rather like a child unveiling a secret.

"Nathaniel, dear. Nathaniel Joseph Cicero."

The clerk remained unimpressed.

DANIEL

IT HAD BEEN a long, introspective weekend for Daniel Crowley. After witnessing his father's bizarre gathering at church, he had come home with more questions than answers.

For the past two days, Dan had been avoiding the outside world. Sasha, his girlfriend, had left a dozen messages that he'd ignored. Two sunny days had come and gone without him going outside. He ignored his routine and neglected his usual workout regimen. Most of all, he avoided his father. Not out of fear, though there was certainly a portion of that. It was mostly confusion. Daniel wasn't used to lying and didn't know if he could keep a straight face in front of his old man. More likely he'd break down, succumbing to a rare bout of Crowley anger and demanding an explanation. And his father didn't react well to demands.

Thankfully, Stephen Crowley was easy to avoid. The inspector had barely set foot in his own home all weekend. This allowed Daniel to spend more time investigating the contents of the chest under his father's bed. So far what he'd discovered made him question either his father's sanity, or his own.

From what he could gather, the social club his father belonged to and the Sandmen cult were one and the same. If the papers and photos Dan was sifting through weren't evidence enough, his memories of the bizarre meeting he'd witnessed confirmed it.

More baffling, however, were the notes referring to the old Saint-Ferdinand Craftsmen's Association. Daniel had found several papers, some of them official court documents, mentioning the Craftsmen. One that stood out was a subpoena for his father, requesting his testimony regarding a violent altercation between one Stephen Crowley and "Cicero's Circus and Performers." The charges had been dropped due to lack of evidence.

Yet no matter how deep Dan dug into the documents, the name Chris Hagen went unmentioned. This particular fact felt wrong. Hagen's business card bore the icon of the Sandmen. Obviously, he had ties to the organization. Was he a new recruit? Shouldn't he have been at the meeting at the church, then? Why would his father avoid a member of his own group? None of it made sense.

The final piece of the incomplete puzzle was the photo of his father with the strange boy and familiar woman. Even the location felt vaguely familiar. The antiquated popcorn machine with ornate, old-fashioned lettering. The white-and-turquoise circus tent dominating the background. Even the farmhouse on the edge of the photo teased the fringes of Dan's memory, like a souvenir dangling at the tip of his mind.

Dan sat on the floor of his father's bedroom, the contents of the chest sprawled around him. He was very careful to keep the documents organized so he could place them back in the chest in the exact same order he'd found them. The tension that had been slowly rising between him and his father would spill over if the inspector found out his son had been rummaging through his affairs.

The phone rang, shattering the silence like a sledgehammer through a plate-glass window. Dan gasped, a little embarrassed by his own skittishness. Then the phone rang again, and he scrambled to his feet to answer it.

"Hey."

"Hi, Daniel?" came the familiar voice of Jackie, the dispatcher on staff at the station. "Is Stephen there?"

Of course not, thought Dan. *He's probably too busy gutting rabbits and having secret meetings. When would he find the time to be home?* But he didn't voice his thoughts. What if Jackie was one of "them"?

"Nah. He's off somewhere," the teen answered as nonchalantly as possible. "Can't you reach him on the radio?"

"No, that's why I thought he was home." She sounded unconcerned. "It's okay. Not an emergency."

"Hey!" Dan figured he might as well try to gather as much information as possible. "Do you want me to give him a message?"

There was a pause. He could tell that the dispatcher was weighing her options. Deciding whether revealing too much might put her on Stephen Crowley's bad side.

"All right. Just tell him when he gets a chance, to check out the Peterson farm."

Dan attempted to push his luck. "This is my dad; he's gonna want to know why."

"Tell him Cicero's Circus was just granted a permit to set up shop in the field next week."

"You make it sound like that's bad news."

"Yeah, well, you know your father."

"I guess. All right, I'll let him know," he said, his eyes darting to the various stacks of paper strewn around the wooden chest at the foot of his father's bed.

As soon as he hung up, Dan went back to the chest and grabbed the subpoena, along with copies of the Saint-Ferdinand Killer case files. Quickly, he leafed through them, looking for something he'd seen not moments ago. He pulled one file out of the stack, staring down at the photo of a suspect. He placed it next to the picture he'd been obsessing over for the past few days, putting two more pieces of the puzzle together.

"Nathaniel Joseph Cicero," he murmured, reading the name of a suspect from the case file. "Cicero's Circus. Ex-member of the Saint-Ferdinand Craftsmen's Association."

VENUS

"DO YOU TRUST ME?" the god asked.

Venus had spent the last two days taking care of Penny and staring at her computer monitor. Whenever her friend left the house to meet with Dr. Hazelwood, Venus would look at the images the camera sent her from the shed. When they were both supposed to be asleep, Venus would stay up and spy on her prisoner instead.

There wasn't that much to see. For the most part, the creature kept to the shadows. Not once had she been able to see it in its true form. Somehow it knew when it was being watched and did something to pull and tease at the light, making itself disappear into the folds of darkness.

She could see that its mural was getting bigger. It was more complex and, though she was loathe to admit it, more beautiful. The grainy picture from the cheap camera hid the true nature of the materials used, leaving only the exotic intricacies of the curves and spirals that seemed to bend in on themselves forever. The pattern was like music tossed onto a wall. Each part led into the next, combining in a symphony of shapes. So long as she didn't think about where the paint for the canvas was coming from, she could enjoy the art.

For two days she'd observed the thing in this way. Studying and watching, hoping that it would slip and reveal itself. *You'll be back,* it had whispered, and she'd agreed without hesitation. Despite the certainty that she would indeed return, Venus was hesitant to do so. Distance and time had allowed her cooler instincts to prevail.

When the girl had first seen the self-proclaimed god, she had known, with absolute certainty, that she was facing a predator. A monster that could annihilate and devour her. Whether a primal memory was warning her or she was simply terrified, she could tell where the balance of power lay between them. And it did not favor her.

Still, she was alive. She had danced with a god, allowed it to touch her soul, and she had lived. The feeling had been intoxicating and otherworldly. Whatever the monster was, and she had no doubt of its malevolence, the embrace she'd experienced had given her unparalleled comfort. The god had known her deepest wish, her need for security, and it had delivered. Even now, knowing she had been in the arms of death, she longed to return.

So of course, she did.

It was long past midnight, after Penny was sound asleep, that Venus crept from her room. Her parents always slept like the dead, so she wasn't worried about waking them. Not that they'd care much if she did. Sherbet was the only annoyance. The furry little pest weaved between her legs like a shadow as she walked through the house. Once they reached the back door, Venus shooed him away. This was her time now.

Her time, and her god.

Venus padded barefoot through the dewy yard. A low-hanging fog hid most of the ground, and she was careful not to step on the myriad garden tools she had pulled from the shed. She opened the door to the building, finding herself before a towering mass of shadows, wearing nothing but a T-shirt and pajama pants covered with cartoon characters.

"Do you trust me?"

These were the words it chose to greet her with.

"No," she said, her voice cracking despite her best effort. It wasn't out of fear, though, but rather an unfamiliar shyness.

The dancing darkness crashed at her feet, bouncing off the invisible barrier that kept it prisoner. A mist of moisture, like the spray from the ocean, hit her face with a gentle caress.

"Free me." The voice encroached into her mind once more. Needles in her thoughts.

"But you'll leave," she said.

Speaking the words crystallized her fear. The creature had demonstrated that, while it wasn't harmless, it had no ill intentions toward her. Venus was too tough to be impressed by the spectacle of blood and shadows, but she was afraid. Afraid that the monster would escape. She had wanted to study a bird's nest but had stumbled upon so much more. She couldn't allow it to slip away. This was *her* god.

"My gratitude would be the stuff of legends."

It would, wouldn't it?

Venus lifted her foot, again in the thrall of her prisoner. She may have caged a god, but it held her mind in its grasp. The smell of blood was what snapped her out of the sudden trance. Before she'd completed the first step, the metallic tang in the air reminded her of exactly what kind of deity she was dealing with.

This was a god of hate and death.

"I can't let you go," Venus said.

"Can you keep me here?"

She couldn't. Not for long. How long before someone else entered the shed? The god might be trapped, but anyone with a hammer could break the padlock and walk in. Then what? Would the creature be so kind to them? There was so much blood on the ground . . .

Venus closed her eyes and took a step forward. Shoving the smells and sights out of her mind, she tentatively crossed the barrier that separated her from the god. The simple act of pushing through that boundary was worth it for the adrenaline rush alone. Abandoning morality and safety in favor of a thrill no one else could possibly experience. All for the promise of something beyond the reach of human sense. Again, the voice in her mind turned to a smooth caress. Realms of possibility opened to her as she allowed her mind to be touched by the god. For a brief moment, she felt the embrace of security that her parents had never offered. Here she was safe from the world. All she had to do to make the feeling last was agree to one simple covenant.

"You trust me."

"I don't . . . ," she said, clinging to her own strength.

Again, inscrutable darkness danced around her. Even with her eyes closed, she could see how the light was devoured by the shadows. Her flesh shivered at the touch of whatever it was that possessed such immense power but cowered from the light and could not escape a camera's gaze. Every sense was on high alert, the prey ready to bolt at the first sign of a threat. Every sense was in turn rewarded. Her skin enjoyed sensations she had only dreamed of as guilty pleasures. Comfort and intimacy holding hands with her. The voice whispered wordless promises and kindness while her smell picked up on the wet grass from outside the shed. Even her sense of taste, though it could perceive nothing but the tangy bite of blood, learned to enjoy the flavor in a new and unsettling way.

These weren't her senses. These weren't her feelings but the god's imposed perceptions upon her own. It longed for its freedom, to be back in the wild and revel in the still, dark night. More unsettling was how it hungered for blood and the lives that gave it. She felt the echoes of countless victims who had died, either at the monster's hands or not, but whose souls it had consumed.

When Venus opened her eyes again, the god had receded to the corner.

"You . . . eat them?" she said, emotionless.

"Not the body. The soul, or essence, or whatever you wish to call such things, is drawn to me, bright and sweet. It offers sustenance beyond enjoyment. Without it, I cannot starve, but with it, I can remake the world."

Dazed, Venus walked back to the shed's door. She couldn't look at the shadow-creature. She knew what she'd see, and the impossible lack of light had lost its sense of wonder and mystery.

"My honesty disturbs you," the god said, then echoed its words from their first meeting. *"You'll be back."*

"I . . . I don't know that I will."

Venus walked out of the shed. She took a few steps in the wet grass then remembered to double back and secure the door properly. There was a faint glow of sunrise on the horizon, turning the sky from pitch black into a bruised purple.

She made a point to wipe her feet thoroughly before walking into the house, and tiptoed with unusual care back to the second floor. It was later than she'd thought, and she did not relish the prospect of explaining to Penny what she had been doing.

In the bathroom, she looked at herself in the mirror. Pinpricks of blood covered her face. Venus reached for the faucet and noticed that her fingers were stained red too, though she couldn't remember touching anything.

She washed her face and scrubbed her hands. The warm water felt good and helped Venus distance herself from the night's events. What was she doing?

Looking into the mirror, she was disappointed to see that despite her skin being spotless, the god had left a scar on her soul.

"You look exhausted."

Venus glanced up from her cereal, a sweet but fruit-filled granola her parents bought in the health food aisle of the grocery store. On a normal day, she could devour a couple of bowls of the stuff, but today she had no appetite for food.

Meeting Penny's eyes, she could only imagine what the other girl saw. Disheveled and haggard, with all the symptoms of someone who had not had enough sleep and who had too much on her mind. How was it that Venus was getting sympathy from someone who'd just lost her mother?

"You don't look so hot yourself," was the best she could reply.

It was a lie. Her best friend looked better than anyone could expect. Her hair was brushed, her back was straight, and while her eyes were still puffy and red, they were focused. If Venus had been paying better attention, she'd have noticed the signs of anger lurking underneath, but at the moment she was simply trying to keep herself from falling asleep in her cereal.

"Thanks?" Penny's answer was peppered with sarcasm. "I don't want to make this all about me, but I do think I have a pretty good excuse."

Venus dropped her eyes back to her cereal. She was right, of course. Venus wanted to tell her best friend about her discovery, but she didn't know how to begin. *There's a god in the backyard shed* sounded ridiculous, even if Venus had all the proof she needed locked up right outside. In fact, all she had to do was crane her neck a little to see the god's prison through the kitchen windows.

Plus, she couldn't put her friend through another life-altering event. Penny might be putting on a brave face, but she had a tough day ahead. There was another meeting with Dr. Hazelwood and some questions from the inspector. She was also supposed to have a preliminary phone call with a lawyer from Sherbrooke so they could get the paperwork started to decide if she would be allowed to live on her own before becoming an adult in the eyes of the law. She didn't need the existence of a supernatural entity piled on top of all that.

"Venus?" Penny poked her friend in the forehead. "What's up with you?"

"Hmm," Venus growled. "I haven't been sleeping well."

The noncommittal answer didn't impress her friend, but Venus shoved a spoonful of cereal into her mouth to avoid more talking.

"Maybe if you got off your computer and went to bed at a reasonable time."

"I always browse the Web before I go to sleep. I mean, do you know how much you snore?"

The words weren't done spilling out before Venus wanted to swallow them back in.

Penny bit her lip before coming back with an answer. They both knew how important it was that she stayed with the McKenzies, but Penny was a proud young woman. If it weren't for the pain and isolation, she'd be more than happy to stop being a burden and go back to her empty home.

"Maybe I should just sleep on the couch?" she said stiffly.

"No, Penny. That's not what I meant." The last thing Venus wanted was for her friend to feel guilty about her grief. "This isn't about you. Or your snoring."

It's that thing in the shed. She wanted to say it, but the words simply wouldn't come out. It wasn't only about putting more weight on Penny's shoulders, though. Even through the haze of exhaustion, Venus could recognize that. As far as she knew, no one had done what she was doing. She'd stumbled upon something that made her unique. This was her god, and she wasn't sure she wanted to share it. What need did she even have to be like everyone else anymore?

"Listen, I might not be in the best position to assess other people's mental well-being, but I can tell it's not just lack of sleep." Penny pointed her spoon at her host. "I've seen you go without sleep, Aphrodite—"

"Don't call me that!" Venus snapped.

Penny frowned. She carefully put her spoon down next to her bowl. She picked up her napkin, a folded piece of paper towel, and wiped her mouth. Finally she took a deep breath.

Venus could tell that she'd made a mistake. Again, she'd let her own problems take precedence over her friend.

"Penny—" she began, but stopped at a look from the older girl.

"One last time." The tremble in her voice betrayed that Penny was on the cusp of either anger or a breakdown. "What is wrong with you?"

"Nothing. I'm sorry."

Venus quickly got up from her chair and snatched the half-empty bowls from the table. Emptying, rinsing, and setting them to dry—every move was meant as a way to avoid further conversation.

She'd invited her friend to move in so that she could cheer her up, not weigh her down with drama. Her mind raced to find another topic of conversation, perhaps an activity they could do together that might distract Penny. However, every turn her thoughts took brought her face-to-face with the swirling vortex of blood and shadows. The only thing on her mind was the seductive creature that she had tucked away all for herself. She had a god in her power. More than anything, she wanted to go back and see it again.

She was about to suggest they visit Abraham at the farm. Fresh air would do Penelope good. Also, it would get Venus away from the shed. Before she could voice her suggestion, however, Penny sniffled.

"I found a message on my cell phone."

"You don't have a cell phone," Venus said.

"I do. I just never use it."

Venus looked at her friend. The rising sun had finally crested over the tree line in the backyard, pouring in through the kitchen window and onto Penny's back. The only shadow cast was that of the shed.

"The message said: 'I know you won't get this, but if you do, can you come pick me up?'"

The meaning of the message hit Venus in the gut with the force of a moving train. She moved her lips, mouthing the words that would soothe her friend, but no sound came out.

"Why didn't you tell me?" Venus finally managed to say, unable to bear the silence any longer.

"'Cause I'm tired, Veen. I'm so tired of being the victim. I'm not good at it. Every time your mom shoots me that look of pity, I just want to punch her in the face. Oh my God . . . I'm sorry. I don't mean that."

Venus smiled. Every time a little crack in the shell of her friend's sadness would appear, she could see Penny as she used to be.

"It's sad, Venus. To find a message like that? I just don't want to deal with it." Finally she looked up at her friend, her blue eyes dry but angry. "But I also don't want to deal with your bullshit. Just tell me. Distract me. Give me something else to think about. I don't care what it is."

The young McKenzie girl's eyes darted around the kitchen before settling onto the shadow of the shed on the table. She struggled to articulate what she wanted to say. Iterations of her confession came and went in her head as the seconds ticked away. Again, before she could formulate her thoughts and voice her situation, Penny took the initiative.

Pushing her chair away from the table with a loud sigh, the older girl got to her feet. She walked passed a petrified Venus, stopping for a second before going upstairs.

"Forget it. I'm going to the shrink. I need to go shower."

VENUS

YOU'LL BE BACK. It was a promise and a threat. The god had spoken to her this simple prophecy, and Venus hadn't doubted it the first time.

There was a god trapped in the backyard shed. It filled her head with promises, but Venus was no fool. She could sense the toll behind the offer. If only for that, she'd have avoided the shed from then on. But she couldn't just leave the thing in there indefinitely. If such a creature was real, what else was out there?

After Penny walked out of the kitchen, Venus didn't see her again that morning. Her best friend had left for the village and was now at the station, talking to Dr. Hazelwood. Venus wondered if would they talk about her. About her selfishness and callous behavior. What would the doctor think of her?

Venus shook the thoughts away. She had no time to waste on them. Her parents had also left the house, taking their cream-colored VW bus to run errands. They wouldn't return for a few hours. Plenty of time to visit her god. To get answers and to maybe see what the creature was truly capable of.

The shed padlock yielded without effort after she entered the numbers. As soon as she pulled it out from the door handle, she heard a soft rustling from within.

The door creaked open, releasing a foul odor into the backyard. The smell was enough to make her eyes burn.

Through watery eyes, she examined the shed. Immediately Venus could see signs of her presence there from the night before. Dried blood in the shape of her foot, tracked from the door and back into the shed. Streaks of dull brown testified to her struggle to get up, slipping in the red liquid that had oozed from the shadows.

Against her better judgment, Venus pulled the door closed behind her, the desire for privacy outweighing the need for a quick escape route. It was foolish. It was dangerous. It was her god.

"Again, you return." The voice was soothing this time, a caress on every sense. *"More like Neil every time we meet."*

The shadows moved to hide the creature as Venus looked at it. Sunlight seeping in from the open door fought against the swirling darkness, revealing, for the span of a thought, the shape of the god.

It wasn't what she expected. Nor was she sure that the form that had flashed before her eyes wasn't just what the creature wanted her to see. The god, for all the power it radiated, was the size of a child. One perhaps a few years younger than Venus. The thing's eyes glowed with inhuman intensity and it wore the flesh of an alien anatomy, but there was also a vulnerability that took her by surprise.

"I'm not Neil," she repeated. Venus had never really known her grandfather, but from what her parents had told her, he wasn't a person she'd have liked very much.

"No, but I own you just the same."

Her god.

Or was it?

"You don't own me. I'm the one who holds the keys to your jail."

Shadows spiraled over the floor like dervishes before the voice came back into her mind. The words were gentle, but the edge to its thoughts was a little sharper.

"Yet you came back to me."

"I did." The attempt to inject authority into her voice had failed.

"You want something."

Venus sat on the ground, in the very spot where she had fallen, terrified, on the night she'd first found the creature. Circumstances were slightly more comfortable this time. Her abject horror, at least, had been replaced by a dull, manageable fear.

"What happens if I free you?"

It wasn't an idea she had seriously considered until the words fell from her lips. Darkness, blood, glowing red eyes: the thing had all the traditional hallmarks of evil. She could feel the malicious intent in its voice every time it spoke. Freeing it would spell disaster. And yet here she was, considering the ramifications.

"Rewards beyond your wildest dreams." Warm thoughts accompanied its answer.

"You keep saying that, but what does it mean? Be more specific."

"How can you define infinite possibilities?"

It was not a question but rather a confirmation that the sky was the limit. She'd read enough books to know that these sorts of Faustian bargains always came with a price. Nothing came for free. Not without consequence. Before her was a genie, and the shed was its lamp. She'd rubbed the thing three times; maybe it was time to make a wish.

"Bullies," she said.

She'd mulled it over. It wasn't the most important thing in her life, but it was probably the safest thing to ask for. So many other things could backfire. She'd considered asking for Gabrielle LaForest's life back, but in such a potential "Monkey's Paw" scenario, what shape would the results take? What if the god brought her back . . . wrong? It was better to keep the stakes low and the investment minor.

"I get bullied. A lot. For dumb reasons."

The shadows hung low to the ground as she spoke. She could see the eyes through the dark fog, but somehow they had lost some of the malice that animated them. Instead there was a sort of alien understanding. It was the same look she gave Sherbet when she thought she might relate to what the animal was thinking.

"Bullies?" The god sampled the word with curiosity. It was the first emotion not laced with hatred to filter through its speech so far.

"Kids my age who pick on me. They treat me like crap because I'm not like them. I don't come from here, so I don't act or think or dress like them. I don't like the same things and I don't play the same games. I don't know why that offends them so much, though.

"It's not the end of the world, I guess. They push me around and call me names, but . . . it's just so exhausting. I want it to stop. Can you make them stop?

"I don't know how you grant your so-called rewards. I'm not sure I want to know, or that I'd even understand. I don't want you to kill them, but I want the bullies to stop. Is that something you can do?"

During the explanation of her wish, Venus had focused on the tip of her running shoe. She had wanted to put her thoughts in order and make sure her request was clear.

Now she looked up to find the creature sitting cross-legged before the hideous mural it had created. The shadows were gone. The god was naked, exposed for the first time for Venus to see. Even as a physical creature, it was hard to describe. Dark skin and smoldering red eyes on the frame of a child. The anatomy was wrong. An elegant caricature of humanity. And although its flesh was intact, the god looked wounded.

If there were a crossroads of vulnerability and magnificence, that would be where this god could be found at that very moment. *"Yes,"* came its chilling answer.

BRAD

FREEDOM!

It was a feeling that Brad Ludwig hadn't fully experienced since moving to Saint-Ferdinand. But today? Today was all about freedom.

Of course he still had a curfew and of course he couldn't leave the city limits, but for the very first time since as long as he could remember, Brad could go where he wanted, do what he wanted. A pocketful of allowance money and a new bike gave him access to a world of possibilities. The sun was shining and his friends were waiting for him.

This was going to be the best day ever.

Brad didn't realize it, but it wasn't only his parents' ever-watchful presence from which he was finally released. He had also been freed from the resentment it engendered. Back when they'd lived in Saint-Jérôme, his older sister, Heather, had been in a car accident. She had been out riding her bicycle alone, much like he was right now, when the Ford pickup had sideswiped her.

It wasn't a terrible accident, but when she fell from her bike, Heather's head struck the pavement. She was admitted to the hospital with a concussion that eventually turned into a coma, all because they simply couldn't stop the bleeding in her skull. Three weeks later, after two surgeries failed to stop the hemorrhage, she passed away.

The event took its toll on the whole family. Mourning led to depression, which in turn led to professional difficulties. Soon Brad's father lost his job, and when he was offered a new position at the local drugstore, the Ludwigs became one of the first families to move to Saint-Ferdinand in years.

Needless to say, when his parents heard of the Saint-Ferdinand Killer, not wanting to go through the sorrow of losing another child, they clamped down on Brad's activities. From that day forward, the fifteen-year-old boy was never allowed out without his father or mother shadowing him. If he wanted to go to a friend's house, he was driven there. Under no circumstances was he ever permitted to be alone.

Until today. Today the killer was behind bars, and as the village embraced its freedom, so did Brad. Tentatively, he'd asked his father if he could bike to André's place, alone. His dad gave it a long minute of thought before he agreed. There was still reason to be careful. The local paper had an article about how Gabrielle LaForest's body had been found in the woods, but the police had issued a statement that it was most likely a bear attack, judging by the remains. This had made negotiations more difficult between Brad and his father, but after copious promises to be careful and to call once he reached his destination, Brad was on his way.

He rode through the back roads, cut through the Hawthorn apple orchard, and drew close to the edge of the village where his friend lived. This, he thought, must be how it feels to be that McKenzie girl. To do whatever you wanted without supervision.

"Hey, kid!"

Brad turned to look at whoever had called out his name, stopping his bike with what he thought was a particularly smooth skid brake.

"Can you help me look for something?"

The voice was coming from the woods. He couldn't make out the source of the words, but they sounded friendly enough. Savoring his newfound independence, the boy propped his bike on its kickstand and walked into the woods to see what was up.

When Brad woke up, the road and the forest were gone. He was in a dark place, lying on the ground. No. Not on the ground—he was elevated. On a table of some sort, but he couldn't move.

He could hear a clinking noise. What sounded like a belt being removed, then a rustling of clothes, and some humming. He didn't recognize the tune, but it sounded like one of those old songs his grandparents used to listen to. The boy had seen enough horror movies to know what was going on, but he suppressed his desire to scream. Whatever had happened, whoever was in the dark room with him, there was no need to attract his attention.

"How's your head?"

The same voice from the woods. Calm and pleasant, if a bit cold and detached. His head felt fine, though he was hesitant to move it.

Bare feet padded toward him. The shadow of a hand reached over him to pick up something else on the table. A knife. It came and went from his line of sight.

"Do you feel that?" the voice asked with some concern.

Brad couldn't answer, shaking his head instead. The motion did reveal some level of discomfort in his skull. The same feeling he had when diving to the bottom of the deep end at the pool.

"Good! Then this won't be too bad." The voice seemed genuinely relieved, and for a moment so was Brad.

Then he saw the knife again as it passed in front of his face. It was covered in blood.

"You should be glad. You know you were chosen for this? Not by me, but by something greater than us both. I heard the call, and it told me to pick you. I don't know who you are, kid, but you should be proud. Now, don't move. This will only take a little while."

The next hour was a nightmare of surrealism for Brad. It was hard to tell what exactly was happening in the dim light, but as the minutes drained off the clock, so did the blood in his body. He couldn't feel anything, however. Either drugs or some kind of damage to his spine prevented him from moving and experiencing any pain. Judging from what was being pulled out of him, though, he was glad for the reprieve.

He couldn't be sure at what point he died. Some level of distress started to seep into his mind. Images became blurry. Thoughts, elusive. Eventually he knew he was no longer alive. Enough blood and organs had been removed that his body had given out. Whatever had kept the hurt at bay also prevented him from giving his death too much thought. The loss to his parents, the erasure of his hopes and dreams, all of that meant nothing in the numbing haze that protected him from the depredations done to his flesh.

There was no need to fight it anymore. His spirit was no longer tethered to the meat-and-bone vessel he'd occupied for fifteen years. He was no longer in the dark room, though where he found himself was no brighter. He could somehow perceive the silhouette of the man with the voice. He was still speaking to him.

"Don't fight it, boy. Let the shadow call to you. Help me find it."

As the words filtered to this place in between life and death, Brad understood what the man meant. There *was* a call from a shadow. Terrifying, repulsive, yet pervasive and inescapable. It was pulling him to a specific location in the complete and implacable darkness.

No. Not complete. There was a light in the shadows. A young girl, about eight years old, surrounded by a blinding glow, like a lighthouse in a storm at sea. *Heather?* he thought, rejoicing at the thought of seeing his sister again.

Ignoring the shadow and the voice, Brad went toward the light. Maybe he was dreaming after all. Only, when he got close, he recognized that this wasn't Heather. It was another girl, about the same age as his sister had been when she'd fallen. Her hair was straight, while Heather's had been short and curly, and this girl wore a fancy white dress, whereas his sister had refused to wear anything but overalls and T-shirts.

"Don't listen to it . . . Don't go . . . ," the girl in white said.

Brad almost obeyed. He tried to walk toward her and take the hand she was offering, but as he got close, he saw her eyes. Dark nails, driven into the sockets. The stuff of nightmares. The shadows were calling to him. Brad turned from the girl to follow the voice in the darkness. She cried out to him again, but he ignored her, focusing instead on the lure of the shadows. Maybe that was where he'd find Heather?

VENUS

THE OFFICE WAS COLD. Much colder than Venus had expected it would be. Clad in summer clothes, denim shorts, and a loose T-shirt, she couldn't help but shiver.

Dr. Hazelwood, who sat across the desk from her, noticed and smiled. The psychologist was better equipped to deal with the temperature, wearing a beige pantsuit that would have been unbearable outdoors.

"The AC's been in overdrive the past few days," she apologized. "It's like a meat locker in here."

"Yeah, I'm sorry. I've asked Inspector Crowley to get it fixed. Drinking hot coffee helps. Would you like a cup?"

Venus shook her head. She'd already been drinking more than a healthy dose of caffeinated products. With her nights taken over by worrying about the contents of her shed and the days trying to act as if all was normal, her consumption had gone through the roof.

"All right then. Shall we get started?" Dr. Hazelwood ripped off a page from the legal pad on her desk. "First let me say that I was getting curious about when you'd be paying me a visit."

"Why is that? I haven't lost anyone in my family."

Dr. Hazelwood took a note, but Venus couldn't see what it was.

"No one immediate to you, perhaps, but you can't say Ms. LaForest's death didn't affect you. Or Audrey's."

"Penny's been talking to you about me, hasn't she?" Venus asked.

The doctor took another note. She had a friendly smile and was young enough that Venus could almost feel like she related to her. Also, Dr. Hazelwood was a city girl, much like her. The village was alien to both of them—a far cry from the noisier, more hectic streets of Montreal, or even Sherbrooke, for that matter.

"Obviously she has," Dr. Hazelwood answered. "We talk a lot about her mother and father, of course, but also about her friends and relationships. The whole point of grief therapy is to process the feelings. Confront any issues of guilt and, if I can, offer some guidance about how to emotionally handle the difficult task of moving forward."

"Right. And I'm a relationship."

"To Penny? You are much more than that, Venus. I don't think I'm exaggerating when I say that you're the sister she never had."

The girl shivered again, passing it off as a symptom of the cold. Truth was, the words cut deep. Even before moving to Saint-Ferdinand, Venus couldn't remember getting along as well with anyone as she did with Penny. It made lying to her grieving friend much more shameful.

"I get it," she said. "You told me, back at the ice cream parlor, to take care of Penny, and . . . I haven't been doing that very well."

Dr. Hazelwood frowned, tapping the tip of her pencil on the paper. She looked at Venus as if the girl had given her the wrong answer to a simple question.

"No one ever said that. If anything, Penny has expressed a lot of worry about you. You seem like a smart, capable young lady, so I hope that if you weren't processing the last few weeks' events well, you'd come to me."

Venus couldn't ask the doctor to understand the breadth of what she'd been dealing with. Dr. Hazelwood knew about the murders and, through her grief counseling, probably a lot about Saint-Ferdinand. But she didn't know about the thing in Venus's backyard shed. Just thinking about it, she felt her blood turn to ice.

"So let's talk about you," Dr. Hazelwood continued. "How are you, Venus? Be completely honest with me."

"I'm fine."

Dr. Hazelwood took down another note. The act irritated Venus. She'd come here for help. To learn more about how Penny was doing and maybe figure out how to get her friend back in control of herself. Venus knew she wouldn't be a fan of therapy. Talking about her feelings was something she was only comfortable doing with her best friend. Spilling her guts to a stranger felt wrong.

"Then why did you ask to see me then?"

"I want to be better at helping Penny."

"Have you ever flown on a plane?"

"Uh, a few times, I guess. I went to Germany with my uncle once, and my parents used to take me out west to Vancouver when I was a kid. Why?"

"Oh! I love Vancouver. Such a beautiful city. I've never been to Germany, though," Dr. Hazelwood said. "Anyway, you know during the safety demonstration? How they tell you in the unlikely event of a loss of cabin pressure, et cetera, et cetera, you should always put your mask on first?"

Venus sighed, figuring out where the doctor was going. "Best way to help Penny is to first help myself?"

"Bingo," Dr. Hazelwood answered with a smile. "So where do we start, Venus? Do you want to tell me you're fine again?"

"No."

"Good. How are you?"

"I don't know."

Dr. Hazelwood leaned over to jot down yet another note. Anytime Venus pushed back at the questions, the doctor would write something about it.

"Okay, you know what? I'm not fine! I'm doing terrible, and I don't know what to do." Venus became agitated, almost yelling at the doctor. "I'm not sleeping and I'm not taking care of my best friend and I can't tell you why. I don't know who can help me with this. Probably no one and certainly not you!"

Slowly, Dr. Hazelwood put the cap back on her pen. Her smile gone. For a moment, Venus thought she'd gone too far by losing her temper. But then Erica put the pen down, calmly turned her notepad around, and pushed it over the desk so Venus could see what she'd written so far.

Salad, carrots, dressing, feta cheese. A grocery list.

"You . . . baited me . . . ," Venus said.

"You're right. I probably can't help you with whatever's eating at you. I'm not here to offer ready-made solutions. I'm here to listen to whatever you have to say. I get it, though: it's difficult to open up to a stranger. Especially about intimate stuff. That's fine, but you have to talk to *someone.*"

Venus fell silent, her eyes still stuck on the notepad. She'd gone from being livid about Dr. Hazelwood's manipulation to being ashamed of her own childishness. The solution to her problem was simple: she wanted to take better care of her friend, but to do so, she needed to get things off her chest. She needed to tell someone about the thing she was keeping prisoner, this god of hate and death. And the best person to talk to was Penelope. The thought gave her another shiver, or was it the room?

"Stay here," Dr. Hazelwood said while getting up. "I'll get you something warm to drink while you think of what you want to talk about next."

As the doctor left, Venus silently agreed that the temperature was getting a little out of hand. At this point, Venus was convinced she was going to walk out of the station with a cold. The teenage girl's skin was covered in gooseflesh, and her nose was beginning to run. In fact, she was about to follow Dr. Hazelwood out, thank her for her help, and run out into the warm sun, when a voice stopped her, cutting their appointment short.

"Here . . ."

The words were like icicles breaking in the wind just at the edge of her hearing. Alone in the room, Venus was startled by the voice and turned toward the source of it, but there was nothing. Just the desk, covered in file folders, and that notepad with the stupid grocery list.

And Dr. Hazelwood's purse.

For no reason that she could understand, Venus became convinced that the voice had come from the purse. In fact, the belief was so clear that before she gave it a second thought, her hands were pulling something out of the bag. A familiar plush bear. The same one she'd seen her uncle take from Audrey's grave.

"What are you doing?"

Dr. Hazelwood stood in the doorway, holding a pair of steaming coffee cups. She was shaking with outrage.

"Where did you find this?" Venus asked.

"That's none of your business! What were you doing in my purse?"

"I'm sorry, Dr. Hazelwood," Venus said. "I don't know what came over me, but where did you get this bear? Did my uncle give it to you?"

Still boiling with anger, Dr. Hazelwood closed the door with her foot and set the cups down on her desk. She went to retrieve the toy from Venus's hands, but the girl pulled it away.

"Did he?" she insisted.

"No. I found it."

"Where?"

"I can't tell you. Why would you think Randy gave this to me?"

Venus considered her next words very carefully. She'd come to see the doctor for help, for an outside perspective. She wasn't prepared for the decision she was about to make. One that might have a dire impact on her uncle.

"Because I . . . saw him take it from Audrey's grave. After her funeral. Where did you find it?"

The doctor seemed to lose her footing for a moment. She sat down, holding a finger up, silently asking for a moment to compose herself.

"We have to talk to Inspector Crowley," she finally said.

"Why?"

"I found it at a murder scene. Gabrielle LaForest's murder scene."

CROWLEY

"SIT."

Crowley wasn't in the best mood. His ex-wife had once described that as "marginally tolerant." It was meant as a joke at the time, but the years since the divorce had made it more real.

The last two weeks should have been a victory lap for the inspector. With Sam Finnegan behind bars, he should have been in a position to finally relax. Instead he'd been caught in a wild-goose chase trying to find a supernatural entity that was supposedly hiding here in Saint-Ferdinand. The inspector had spent many nights trying to connect the Craftsmen, the god, and Finnegan, but with no tangible results. He'd tried interviewing Sam again, but this resulted in nothing but further frustration.

When they found a second body, that of Brad Ludwig, Stephen thought they'd have another trail to follow. Instead he wound up with another dead end and wasted days keeping the Ludwigs placated and away from the media.

He was working too hard and was keeping those he used to trust at arm's length.

One of those people was Randy McKenzie. The inspector and medical examiner had been a good team for a long while. A small-town Holmes and Watson. Neither tackled a crime scene without the other.

But today Randy had come to Crowley's office not as a friend or coworker, but as a potential suspect. It was an awkward situation. Years of chasing a monstrous killer together, and now one of them suspected the other was a homicidal maniac.

Randy did as instructed and took a seat. Crowley stared at him with his pale blue eyes, frowning, measuring the potential ways to handle his colleague.

"Randy. Help me out here . . . ," began the inspector. "Tell me why I shouldn't put you in the cell right next to Finnegan."

"What?" Randy's eyes bulged in disbelief. "How about because you know exactly who—what—killed Gabrielle!"

"Maybe," said Crowley, rubbing the back of his neck. "But maybe I don't. Not one hundred percent. I'm pretty sure it's not you, but I can't ignore what the rest of the town, the rest of the office, and the flood of reporters waiting at the gates are going to make of this. And there's always a chance that you're taking advantage of the situation for your own ends. I can't ignore that."

"What the hell are you talking about, Stephen?" Randy's surprise was slowly turning into anger. "I don't have any 'ends' that would require me to kill someone and decorate the forest with her entrails."

"You don't?" Crowley sat on his desk and picked up a file. "I know for a fact that you dug up a little girl's grave to mutilate the corpse. So explain to me how different that is from killing someone in"—he flipped through a few pages and read—"'an obviously ritualistic fashion,' as your friend Erica calls it."

"You bastard. I saved Audrey from a fate worse than death, and you're going to feed me to the dogs as a scapegoat?"

"Listen, Randy, we knew it might come to this. You and I weren't going to end up on the same side. I just happen to have prepared better for it."

"Careful what you're about to say, Stephen. You think I don't have a few tricks up my sleeve too?"

Crowley plucked a fresh photo off his corkboard. Like so many others, it featured a specific symbol. The eye with a spiral iris.

"Your friends are back in town. Cicero, Katrina, and all those other idiots." He handed the photo to McKenzie. It showed a crudely designed poster for Cicero's Circus, which had been stapled to a telephone pole. "If you've got any leftover tricks, I'd use them to help me find the god. Otherwise, you might as well get used to the idea of spending the next little while in jail."

Randy shot up from his chair, his finger pointed dangerously close to Crowley's face. The inspector looked at him with disdain, his brow furrowed as if he smelled something foul.

"Don't you dare do this, Stephen. You have no idea what you're dealing with."

"What are you going to do?" The threat had fallen flat before the might of Stephen Crowley's self-confidence. "Summon up some ghosts? Raise an army of zombies?"

"It doesn't work that way. But if you hang me for this, you'll be in more trouble than you can handle."

There was a spark of worry in the inspector's eyes as he stood and slowly paced the office. He knew Randy couldn't just call on the undead to do his bidding. That kind of magic took sacrifice. What he didn't know was the actual extent of the medical examiner's occult knowledge and power. Still, Stephen wasn't the kind of man to back down when threatened.

"Listen, Randy, it's not like I want to do this, but you've said it yourself: Finnegan was right under our noses the whole time. I'm not willing to take that kind of chance again. Until we've found the . . . our 'friend,' I want you where I can keep an eye on you." The inspector gave his colleague a hard, penetrating look. "Unless you already know where it is?"

"I don't. You can't hold me, Stephen. You have no grounds. Any accusation you level against me would put you in the spotlight too. I'll be out of here in one phone call."

"Wrong. I've got a couple of people pointing the finger at you. Tell me where the god is, and we can work together to finish all this."

"Wait," Randy asked. "Who's pointing fingers?" His tone had the edge of a man with nearly two decades of dealing with the dead, for science and for the occult.

"You don't want to know, Randy. Give me the god, and I'll let you go and make sure no one knows about this. Just tell me where it is."

"You might as well tell *me*, Stephen," the medical examiner said, his tone sharp with anger. "I don't know anything about any god."

Crowley stopped his pacing and gave a final, appraising glance at the medical examiner, who at that particular moment looked every bit the necromancer. Eyes sunken, lips pulled back in a snarl. What would he do with the information given to him? Would he lash out, seek revenge? This wasn't the best time to pour oil onto the fire. Then again, maybe knowing would break him down just enough to make him harmless.

"All right, but I warned you," said Crowley. "Erica came to me with some evidence . . . that she got from your niece."

For the second time since walking into the office, Randy McKenzie couldn't believe what he was hearing. Erica and Venus were two of his favorite people in the world. He knew Venus had suspicions about him, but he never thought they would go so deep that she would take action against him. And Erica, she had seen what was left of Gabrielle's body. How could she think him capable of such an atrocity? He could feel tears welling in his eyes. Through the watery haze, he could have sworn he saw a moment of regret on Crowley's face.

DANIEL

DAN WAS ALREADY running late when he stepped out of the house. Events from the previous week continued to leave him unfocused and thrown off of his normal schedule. As he walked to the car, he could see the front lawn needed cutting, weeds had begun to sprout between the cracks of the driveway, and nothing had been done yet about cleaning the flower beds. If his father weren't already preoccupied, there surely would have been loud reprimands.

These were petty concerns compared to the things that had been weighing on the teenager's mind, but right now he had to push all that aside to concentrate on making it to his summer job on time. He only had to sign some papers, but it wouldn't look good to be late. His manager, Luke, wouldn't care too much, but word would get back to Daniel's father. Stephen Crowley might forgive and forget some neglected yard work, but it was best not to add more reasons for a conflict. Especially since Luke was doing him a favor by employing Dan in the first place.

So when the teenager saw the car parked behind his white Civic, a flare of characteristic Crowley rage sparked inside of him.

"Get that thing out of my driveway!" he yelled a split second before realizing whose vehicle it was.

It was an old Dodge Caravan. Wine red. As clean as a new car but with the bumps and scratches of a vehicle that had seen years of heavy use. Daniel had been in that minivan many times since he was a child, riding to and from swim classes and soccer practice. More recently, he'd ridden inside it whenever his own car was too small for him and his friends.

If that minivan could talk, it would get him in trouble.

Dan knew upon seeing it that he was in for a different kind of trouble. The vehicle belonged to Sasha's mother. Reflexively, he touched the phone in his pocket. There were at least a dozen unanswered voice mail messages from Sasha stored on the device and twice as many text messages.

"We need to talk."

And there she was. Standing next to the van, peeling off a pair of sunglasses from her face, dark eyebrows twisted into a frown. On the very rare occasions when she was angry, Sasha looked strange. It wasn't a natural disposition for her. Her mouth would tighten and go slack, as if she wasn't sure what to do with her lips. Her sunny demeanor was one of the qualities that Daniel enjoyed most about her. Right now, however, there was no trace of that oasis of tranquility.

"Yeah, huh . . . about that," Dan said. His eyes darted between Sasha and her van, worried about whether he would make his appointment. "Can it . . . wait?"

Sasha came within a foot of him and stopped, unsure what to do next. It looked like one moment she might strike him, and another jump into his arms. She seemed relieved and infuriated by his presence, but mostly puzzled.

"What? No! Daniel, I thought you were fucking dead!"

"Oh, come on, I just missed a few phone calls . . . "

"A few phone calls? You never miss people's phone calls, least of all mine! Now you disappear for a week, and what? I'm supposed to shrug that off? Do you even realize where you live?"

He did. Saint-Ferdinand. Home of the Saint-Ferdinand Killer. A monster with a reign of terror stretching back almost two decades. A murderer with a body count that might end up rivaling that of Andrei Chikatilo, the infamous Butcher of Rostov. Here, more than anywhere, a teenager, especially one as straightlaced as Daniel, did not ignore phone calls from his parents or friends. Here, the boogeyman was real.

"Okay. You're right," he conceded, his hands held up in surrender. "I should have at least—"

"Dead, Daniel! I thought you had been killed! You think I don't know what's going on? That everything happening here is so damn well hidden? I read the news. I know what to look for. Your dad doesn't have that tight a lid on things!"

"Whoa there. What do you mean?"

"That woman who died in the forest? Now that boy who's gone missing yesterday? I thought your dad had caught the killer?"

Boy? Dan hadn't heard anything about a missing boy. Granted, his focus had been on other things, but his father always told him about any new cases he was handling. Crowley would be furious to know that the news had leaked out to the media. Then again, Saint-Ferdinand had brought the spotlight on itself when the local serial killer was finally apprehended. It was only a matter of days before it became national news. With all this attention building up, the presence of a copycat killer, or worse, proof that they'd caught the wrong man, would send the story into a media frenzy.

"I . . . I didn't know anyone else was missing. Do you know who it was?"

"No. Just a note about a missing boy suspected of being a runaway, and that his parents wanted to remain anonymous for some reason. Which is how I know your dad's involved; who wouldn't want to broadcast their kid's face all over the news if he were missing?"

They've found his body, then, thought Daniel. That was his father's style: keep the media one step behind. Wait until something else popped up before releasing anything new. By the time the grisly details were made available, it was old news and journalists had moved on to juicier things. Daniel had never questioned his father's methods. Until now.

"Look, Sasha, I need you to move the minivan."

"What?" Her eyes expressed shock, but her voice was full of anger. "No! Screw that. I drove all the way here; the least you're going to do is give me an explanation for why you've been ghosting me for a week!"

"I don't have time. I have to go meet with my boss. If I want to have a job, that is."

"First give me an explanation. And it better be a good one, or so help me, I will slash your tires."

"I'm not cheating on you if—"

"I never said you were, Daniel."

"God dammit! Fine!" Again, the Crowley temper welled up inside him, but he managed to rein it back in. Rubbing the back of his neck, a nervous habit he'd picked up from his dad, and looking down at the grass, he took a deep breath. "Look. It has nothing to do with you, but it's complicated and, frankly, it wouldn't hurt if I had someone to talk to about it. Just . . . let me go meet my boss and as soon as I'm done, I'll meet you at Daisy's Diner and tell you everything. Okay? Sasha? Does that work?"

When he looked up, she was staring at him dead in the eyes. Her pupils burned with frustration. There was no question that her patience had been stretched well beyond what should have been its breaking point. Every romantic gesture, every favor he'd done for her, any good faith he might have accumulated in the three years they'd been together, was spent. Not knowing what else to do, he stepped forward to take her into his arms.

"Don't touch me," she said, taking a step back. She pulled out her keys and walked toward the minivan, never breaking eye contact. Even as she pulled out of the driveway and onto the road, she kept staring at Daniel's defeated face, distinctly seeing him mouth the words *I love you*.

SASHA

OF COURSE, she had every intention of hearing his side of the story. No sane girl would throw away a guy like Daniel Crowley before getting some sort of explanation. Knowing him like she did, there was every chance that his behavior was somehow justified. As she calmed down, turning up the air conditioning to help her cool off, she thought about what could be so terrible that he believed he needed to hide it from her. Once she heard his story, would she still be angry, or would she be comforting him through some kind of crisis? As she played with the various scenarios in her mind, she came very close to her own crisis.

"Oh shit!" she screamed, yanking hard on the wheel while crushing the brake pedal with her foot. Once the minivan skidded to a stop, she rolled down her passenger window. At first, all she could see was a cloud of dirt and acrid blue smoke from the burned tires.

Then a man walked through the haze until he was almost leaning against her window. His well-pressed black suit seemed to repel the filth floating around it. He appeared unfazed by his near-death experience.

"Hey there," he said with a cold smile. "You okay?"

"I . . . I'm fine. I'm so sorry. I didn't see you."

"That's okay." The man tilted his head by a degree. "My name's Chris Hagen. Say, you wouldn't be driving to the village, would you?"

HAGEN

THE PHONE WAS cradled precariously between Hagen's cheek and shoulder, while his hands were busy. This had been so much easier when he was a kid. The phones were bigger, huge plastic monstrosities that barely required him to angle his head at all. In those days, he could spend hours on the phone without any issue. Electronic companies made a point to brag about how thin their phones were. It was almost impossible to have a conversation without some headset or using the phone's speakers. Chris didn't own the former and the latter allowed too much ambient noise. For a moment he smiled, realizing how much like an old man he sounded to himself. Normally, this kind of minor annoyance wasn't a big deal. After all, long conversations weren't in fashion anymore. Nowadays, people used e-mail and text messages if they had anything of substance to communicate. But the discussion he was having now was too important to be held over text.

"Of course I'm being careful."

He managed to squeeze in the words between two tirades from the other end of the line. Hagen wanted to put the phone down and give his sore neck a rest. Looking down at his bloody hands, he decided against it for the moment.

"No one seems to know where *it* is, no." By this time, Chris Hagen had spoken to almost everyone in the village, or at least anyone who might have a clue where he could find what he was looking for. There were certain people he had strategically avoided, of course. The Bergerons topped that list, as did Inspector Crowley. The former were easy to avoid, grieving as they were for their poor daughter. But Crowley worked in the public eye. So Hagen had pretended he was hunting the man down to "ask a few questions." Predictably, the inspector had decided that any journalist who wanted to see him was probably best avoided as well.

Hagen looked around for something to wipe his hands with. His immaculate suit was nearby, carefully hung on a wooden hanger. The pants were neatly folded, the white-collared blue shirt buttoned on top, his favorite red tie meticulously looped around the neck, his black jacket pressed. Beneath the ensemble sat a pair of polished black leather shoes.

The ground was packed dirt. The walls, stained concrete. Apart from the single naked bulb that hung from the low ceiling, the cellar was completely empty. Well, empty except for what Chris had brought with him.

Grimacing in disgust, he wiped his left hand on his naked leg before using his now mostly clean fingers to switch the side on which the phone was cradled.

"No. No. You don't have to explain to me how important this is," he said, straining to remain courteous and patient. "But you're going to have to trust me. Or do you want to drive down and take care of it yourself?"

Hagen smiled as he listened to the expected answer, nodding along with the follow-up explanations, the details of which he was already intimate with.

Knowing the conversation could go on without his participation for a while, Hagen looked appraisingly at his handiwork. He'd never fancied himself an artist, and he'd certainly never thought he'd be working in this particular medium, but there was no denying the quality of his work. The end result was very much in line with the sketch he'd brought with him. Every curve, every angle was meticulously reproduced to mimic the drawing. Instead of ink on paper, though, he was working with flesh on concrete.

And there was so much flesh to work with. Blood and viscera and bones and sinew. Hagen would take a large fillet knife and slice out thin strips of skin or extract full lengths of veins. The tricky part was applying all these materials to the wall.

The process demanded patience. Using the coagulated blood as a makeshift adhesive, Hagen would apply a thin coat of tissue as the base for his design. Whether muscle or skin, each material had its own viscosity. Bones and thicker organs were even more challenging. He needed to be careful laying down his foundation so that they would be properly supported. Everything had to hold together until the mural served its purpose.

As tricky and unpleasant as the work could be, Hagen had had plenty of practice. Even as a child in Saint-Ferdinand, he had done terrible things to small rodents and the occasional cat. His curious mind pushed him to look beyond their adorable, helpless exteriors and wonder what was inside. What made them tick. What made them alive. It wasn't long before he became creative with his dissections, disassembling animals in a manner similar to how his father would take apart his firearm and hunting rifles, laying each piece in an organized pattern neatly on a blanket.

What he was working on today went beyond a child's curiosity. This masterpiece was about ritual.

The yammering on the phone died down a little, a signal that he should start paying attention again. Pausing in his work, he frowned with some amount of concern.

"The circus? What circus?" He listened to the answer. "No. I don't care. I want to go see Harry Peterson."

Absentmindedly, Chris dipped a finger in the pool of blood he was using for glue. Finding it too thick, he cupped his fingers and retrieved more of the still-warm liquid from its original source. He stirred it into his mixture, all the while listening with interest to the person on the phone.

"Yeah. I see how that could be a problem. You're sure they'd recognize me?"

Satisfied with his mixture, he started laying down the first few lines in a new portion of the pattern, painting broad, expert strokes of blood onto the damp concrete, like a child prodigy finger-painting a gruesome masterpiece.

"What if I just . . . get rid of this Cicero?"

His neck was again making him uncomfortable. This conversation would have to end soon.

"I've already told you what I think about this whole 'prophecy' bullshit. Especially when it interferes with my responsibilities. Besides, what's going to happen if Cicero recognizes me? He must be over a hundred years old."

Hagen listened to more admonitions. All things he'd heard a dozen times in the past. Impatient to get back to his work, he sighed loudly into the microphone, unleashing a stream of outraged anger.

"Hey! Hey! Sorry. I didn't mean anything by it. But I'm very busy here. No, I'm not done yet. Well, how could I be done if I've been on the phone with you for an hour?"

More outrage followed, but this time Hagen took advantage of the time to apply ever-thicker layers of blood to the branches and spirals of his pattern. Getting to the center of a particularly steady and regular spiral, he took a step back. Bloody fingers dripped as he admired his craftsmanship. Nothing about his work was remotely pleasant, but there was no reason not to take some pride when the results came out better than expected. Pleased with the appearance of the portion he had just completed, he decided it would be a perfect place to apply one of the eyes.

It always came back to eyes, didn't it? The whole point of this activity was to see. The boy hadn't been enough. Perhaps this would also be insufficient. It didn't matter to Chris. As distasteful as he found the ritual, he would do it over and over again until it showed him where to find what he was looking for.

"Are you calm now? Listen, I'm sorry for being flippant. I know how important this is, but you're letting it get to you. You know better than I do what's at stake, so if you say 'no Peterson farm,' then so be it. I'll stay away. Anyway, my battery is running out. I've gotta go."

Chris wiped his right hand on one of the last clean spots on his naked thigh and shifted the phone back to his right ear.

"Yes, of course I'm lying, but seriously I gotta go. My medium is going to spoil." He waited for the answer. "Of course. You too. Love you, Mom."

Satisfied, he tossed the phone onto a pile of clothes puddled on the ground. Denim shorts and a white tank top.

Again, he contemplated the work left to do. If all went according to plan, this elaborate pageantry would permit him to see where souls went in Saint-Ferdinand. Like dropped dye into water to observe the flow of a current, the sacrificed victims allowed Hagen to see where their essence would be drawn. The procedure was easier said than done.

The "journalist" picked up his filet knife and leaned over the body from whom he'd taken the blood and flesh he needed for the mural. Bending close to her face, he placed the tip of the knife just under the teenage girl's left eye.

"Well, Sasha, looks like it's just you and me again."

VENUS

IT WAS THE TWITCHING that got to her most.

Venus had been staring, paralyzed, into the tall, unkempt lawn of her backyard. Seconds, perhaps hours had passed as she stood motionless, her fingers shaking, unconsciously mimicking the jerking motions of her cat's back leg.

Sherbet was dead. He had to be. The unfortunate creature was lying on the damp ground, drops of dew surrounding his body like glittering jewels. At first glance, she didn't recognize him. His smoky black coat of long soft fur had been removed. In fact, every bit of skin had been flayed from his body, leaving the cat a mass of glistening red sinew and muscle. His ears had been torn off. His eyelids and whiskers, removed. His tail, a glorious feather duster that he'd so proudly swayed as he'd walked through the house, had been reduced to a bony rope of pink and red strands.

The only thing left to identify her pet was the nylon collar around his neck. Whatever had murdered and mutilated the animal wanted to make sure he was recognized when found. It wanted Venus to know what she was seeing.

His back leg kept twitching. A tiny back-and-forth motion that was probably caused by some death reflex. Venus knew that. Any other number of postmortem bodily functions could occur: gasps, coughing, spasms in the extremities as rigor mortis set in.

Despite that academic knowledge, the twitching punched at her heart with every movement.

Eyes wide and unblinking, her vision blurred by tears, Venus crouched down to inspect her flayed cat. His big green eyes seemed to be staring at her, plaintive and confused.

She observed his tiny chest, glad to see that he wasn't breathing. She reached out, fingers shaking, to touch Sherbet's neck. She held her breath for God knows how long, and sighed in relief when she found no pulse.

Venus looked up. She had a vivid awareness of her surroundings. The low hum of a distant lawn mower, the smell of morning humidity, the wet dew on her knees: all of it cut through the haze of her distress to remind her exactly where she was. Her eyes settled on the backyard shed looming only a few feet away.

Scottish blood from three generations past boiled in her veins. Her beloved but dim-witted pet had been attracted to the shed, probably by the smell of the birds that had perished inside. There he had met his fate, at the hands of a monster made of shadows and blood.

Glad to feel something other than sadness and fear, Venus scooped up her dead cat. At first she was surprised at how dry his muscles felt. She'd expected them to be sticky with blood, but instead they had the texture of thin rubber. She paused, the feeling of his twitching leg muscles making her stomach lurch, but quickly, she surrendered to the rage once more.

"What have you done?" Venus demanded as she burst into the shed.

The girl had been careful to fling the door wide open, hoping the light of the sun would reveal more of the elusive monster that kept itself hidden in shadows. Maybe it would even suffer at the touch of light, like a vampire turning to ash under the sun.

No such luck. The creature kept to its dark corner, its expression hidden in the shadows. Was it laughing at her? It was impossible to know.

But one thing the morning sun did illuminate was the monster's handiwork.

The mural had grown. The baby birds had been joined by the larger anatomy of their mother. Delicate, hollow bones had been affixed to the wood paneling by dried blood, bile, and viscera that had been torn from the animal.

Other body parts had been added too. Their level of dismemberment and decomposition made identifying the creatures difficult, though. Venus managed to pick out the distinctive ringed fur of a raccoon tail, along with the unique shape of a frog's skull. All visitors to the shed that had met their unfortunate demise.

This wasn't just art, Venus realized, but something more. Something powerful. Something that demanded sacrifice. She couldn't say what it was meant for, but her scrutiny was abruptly interrupted when her eyes wandered to the end of a spiral and were met with a patch of blood-matted smoky-black fur.

Like an elastic pulled to its breaking point, Venus snapped back into her anger. Still clutching the skinless body of her beloved pet, she turned to face the shadows. The god was there, watching. Glowing eyes slowly split open, pierced the darkness, boring into hers. There was a human quality in them that didn't belong.

"Do I have your attention now?" Its voice crept out from the corner, worming its way into Venus's thoughts.

"You killed my cat."

"Yes. It was slow. And painful." Each word stung at her heart. *"And while the body may be dead, the soul is not at rest. Do you hear it? Of course not, but I do. It cries in agony from beyond the veil. All because I granted you a favor, Venus McKenzie."*

The shadows shifted subtly. A physical form rustling among them. Venus checked that she was beyond the imaginary line that kept the god prisoner. She could feel her conviction waver with every moment. Her fist tightened as she clutched her own hatred. She had indeed asked for something from the god. But while she hadn't been bullied since then, that didn't mean it was because of any supernatural involvement.

"I can end it, though." Its voice had the sweetness of a rotting apple, tempting for but a second before the rancid stench of putrefaction ruined the appeal. *"I can give the animal back to you. You know my price."*

"No."

She was impressed by the stability in her voice. Usually it was Penny who was the strong one. But even as she took pride in her answer, Venus began to wonder what she hoped to accomplish by being in here.

"Listen . . . ," the voice said. In between the folds of its words, the sounds of a cat could be heard, screeching as if it were being boiled alive. Venus recognized that sound. It was like the time Sherbet's tail had gotten caught in a closing door. A terrifying and heart-wrenching yowl, stretched out to a torturous length. *"I can end this . . . I want to end this. For you."*

"No," she repeated.

"It was a mistake. I didn't know he was yours." The screeching could still be heard under its voice. *"Let me bring it back . . . for you . . . if you free me."*

"Yes." The words fell out of her mouth uninvited. She hadn't planned to agree, but there it was. What she truly wanted.

The glowing eyes narrowed and Venus felt the creature smile. She could almost hear the sound of teeth sliding over one another in the darkness.

There was no flash of light, no grotesque display of reconstituted body parts. Instead she felt a thrum move through the mutilated corpse in her arms. Eyes wide, she looked to the wall and saw that the pelt of matted black fur still clung to the bloody mural. The texture of the thing she held was still dry and rubbery to the touch. Half-dreading what she'd see, Venus slowly looked down at the body of Sherbet and, in accordance with her darkest, unspoken fears, it moved.

The god had brought her cat back, all right, but his body had not been restored. Sherbet looked up at her with watery, lidless eyes and mewed. Furless, skinless, he didn't seem to know what he was. He squirmed in an effort to be put down. There was no doubt that this was her beloved pet and that he was alive, but he had been stripped of warmth and had no heartbeat.

"*There,*" the shadow whispered. The screech beneath the voice was replaced by laughter. "*Are we friends again?*"

Venus didn't answer. Struggling to hold on to both Sherbet and her sanity, she walked backward and out of the shed. Even in the warm sun of the Saint-Ferdinand summer, she could feel every fiber of her body shivering and every hair standing on end.

DANIEL

IT COULDN'T POSSIBLY be earlier in the morning, thought Daniel as he stepped out of his car. The sun was barely above the tree line, casting a warm and pleasant pink glow behind the silhouettes of evergreens and maple trees. To the west, the sky was still dark and some of the brightest stars were still visible. It was an odd balance, and Daniel was surprised to notice how beautiful the contrast was.

Closing the door to the Civic, he took stock of his surroundings. He was no stranger to the Peterson farm. He'd once worked here for the summer, helping to tend the wheat fields. More recently, he'd had an unpleasant discussion with his father deep in the forest at the northern end of this very property. This morning, however, the usually empty fields were alive with activity. A small fleet of old, decrepit trucks was parked on one of the fallow fields. At least two dozen people swarmed around the vehicles, emptying them of a variety of materials ranging from large tarps to folding chairs to sacks of food to crates of decorations. Judging from the garish colors, the rickety Ferris wheel, the strange people, and the sounds of exotic animals, the circus was in town.

Daniel walked among the roadies, watching as they put together a small city made of canvas, wood, and hard work. Men and women of all ages worked feverishly to assemble their places of business from things that could fit on a flatbed truck. The sheer variety of their tasks was dizzying to behold. Brand-new portable toilets were juxtaposed with a wooden trailer so old, the paneling was nearly worn through in places. Antique games of chance were erected next to modern vending machines. A young boy who looked a little like a rat, dirty and twitchy, was helping an impeccably dapper old man put up a poster that advertised "Katrina the New England Oracle." Everywhere Daniel looked, a sense of familiarity assailed him.

On every surface was the symbol of the Craftsmen: the eye with a spiral iris. The icon was painted on chipped signs, printed on posters, and stenciled on each of the attractions. The eye was omnipresent. Watching.

No one bothered Daniel as he strolled around the fairground, drinking in the oddities. A man almost two feet taller than he was walked past, carrying a post as long and as thick as a tree trunk. For a moment Daniel thought he would drown in the strange sea of activity, but suddenly he stopped.

Right in front of him, getting dusted off by an impossibly muscular six-and-a-half-foot man with an old-fashioned handlebar mustache, was a popcorn machine. The same one from his father's picture. He could almost see Stephen Crowley standing in front of it with the young woman and the strange little boy. There was no doubt in Daniel's mind that this was the same contraption. It even seemed to have been installed in the exact same place.

A wave of nausea washed over the boy. His steps became sluggish as he moved toward the machine, as if he were walking through a vat of honey. Cold sweat beaded on his forehead and his back. Halfway to the popcorn machine, a voice snapped him out of his reverie.

"You won't find what you're looking for here, son." The voice was old, tired, and in control.

Daniel turned to face the person who had addressed him. He was an aged gentleman, wearing a clean but tattered old gray suit accented with a crisp, new, bright red vest. "Huh?" said the teenager.

"No need to badger me with your razor-sharp wit, son; I'm telling you the truth." The stranger held up both of his hands in mock surrender. "There is nothing here for you."

"How would you know what I'm looking for, sir?" asked Daniel. "I think I've already found it."

"This?" The old man walked over to the popcorn machine, gently laying a hand on the grease-stained glass. "I doubt that's what you're after. No, you're looking for answers, but they aren't here, Mr. Crowley."

"How do you know my name?" asked Daniel. He looked down to make sure he wasn't wearing his grocery store name tag.

"I know your father, and he looks just like you. Or at least he did."

"If you know my dad, then maybe you can help me."

"We've been through this, Mr. Crowley. Your answers are elsewhere."

"Let me ask and then we can see if you're right."

The old man scratched at his chin. There was something impish about his grin as he considered the question.

"Fine, but I'm going to ask something in return."

"Depends what it is," Daniel answered, trying to be cautious.

"Oh, nothing much. I just want you to deliver a message for me. A summons, if you will." The old man cracked a small smile that was paradoxically creepy and comforting. "Shouldn't be too difficult."

By virtue of his father's work, Daniel knew everyone in town and could easily find the old man's friend. "Sure," he said. "I'm looking for a man called Cicero."

"The proprietor of this fine organization? I warn you, he's a busy man, especially on a day like this when so much needs to get done." He winked. "And he's likely to ask you something in return."

"So you're him?" deduced Daniel.

"Sharp lad. I am indeed Nathaniel Joseph Cicero, at your service." The old man bowed deeply, with a grace belied by his wrinkled frame.

"You say you know my father," Daniel said. Cicero confirmed this with a nod. "Then do you remember him visiting your circus?"

The old man stared into the distance, a look of regret in his eyes. "He was here when last the circus was in town. That was almost two decades ago."

"Do you remember who he was with?" pressed Daniel, eager to discover the identities of the woman and child in his father's photograph.

"Let me think, Mr. Crowley. Two decades is a long time." Cicero looked around. Perhaps he was absentmindedly supervising the assembly of his circus; perhaps he was looking for something to jostle his memory. "Ah yes. He had his family with him."

"His . . . family?" The dizziness rushed back to Daniel's head and he reached out to steady himself, his hand landing on the popcorn machine.

"Yes. His lovely wife, Marguerite, and their son." Cicero frowned, then smiled. "Well, their other son, I suppose."

"'Other son'?" Daniel had to take a moment to compose himself. It had been difficult enough to deal with the revelation that his father was in a cult, but discovering that he had an older brother was an almost traumatic blow. It seemed like every day since Sam Finnegan had been arrested, another part of Daniel's life unraveled.

"I . . . ," he murmured, scrambling to form the next question on his mind. But there wasn't just one; there were dozens. Most of which he should be asking his father, not a worn-out old stranger.

"Are you feeling all right, Mr. Crowley?" inquired the old man with obviously feigned concern. "Perhaps these were not the answers you were expecting? Dustin!"

A large man with a serious demeanor but kind eyes approached. He wore overalls, carried a clipboard, and appeared vaguely bothered by the interruption.

"Yes . . . ?"

"Dustin, would you be so kind as to get this boy some water?"

Dustin sighed loudly, but turned on his heel to obey the request.

"I . . . I'm fine." Daniel took a steadying breath. "Maybe I can change the subject for a minute?"

"For the span of one question, Mr. Crowley. I have things to attend to."

"Fine, fine." Daniel was more than happy to leave the circus now. There was a lot of thinking to be done. "I just want to know: Why were you a suspect in the Saint-Ferdinand killings?"

Nathaniel Cicero's face turned to stone. "A rather rude line of questioning, Mr. Crowley. You are your father's son after all." His frown deepened. "I was from out of town, and there were several disappearances during my stay. But no charges were ever brought against me. To your father's great disappointment, I'm sure."

"Disappointment?" It was a strange word to use to describe his father's professional attitude.

"Don't you know, Mr. Crowley? There is no love lost between me and your family. You and I, we're supposed to be enemies." Nathaniel's face melted once more into a pleasant visage. "You look like a good kid. You don't have to inherit this little war between your father and me, but that's a choice you're going to have to make yourself."

Daniel nodded, already drawing up a list of questions for his father.

Dustin finally returned, carrying a plastic water bottle. Before he could get within arm's length, however, the old man waved his employee away. Dustin sighed once more and, throwing his hands in the air, walked back the way he came, water bottle still in hand.

"As you can see, Mr. Crowley"—Cicero indicated the bustling activity going on around him—"I really am quite busy. Shall we discuss that little errand you owe me?"

VENUS

"THIS ISN'T WORKING."

Penny was sitting cross-legged on Venus's bed, bent over a bundle of fur and limbs. Strewn around her were wads of stuffing, scissors, and most of the contents of Grandma McKenzie's old sewing kit. She was wearing an oversized T-shirt that served as a nightgown, cartoon horses printed on its front.

Venus stood at the bedroom door, marveling at what she was seeing. After her beloved pet had been stripped of its skin and fur and then brought back to unnatural, gruesome life, Venus had finally sought her friend's counsel. She explained everything she had discovered in the last week, ending with poor Sherbet's terrible resurrection.

Penny had taken the news rather well. She was fascinated with the flayed cat, fawning over the animal as if it were an adorable kitten. She had also grilled her friend with questions about the thing that was locked in the shed, begging to be allowed to see it. It was creepy, but at least her friend seemed to have forgotten their previous altercation.

Venus was embarrassed that she'd been charmed and seduced by a devil clothed in shadows. Being able to confess had taken her all the way back to her rational self once more.

But Penny's calm acceptance of the situation had Venus worried. It was one thing to take an unusual circumstance in stride, and another to treat a reanimated jumble of muscles as if it were a cuddly pet.

"Penny?" Venus said, nearly dropping a plate piled high with sandwiches. "What are you doing? Is that Captain Mittens?"

Captain Mittens was one of Venus's favorite plush toys, a gift from her paternal grandmother before she had passed away. From what she could see, the stuffed cat had been eviscerated, its eyes plucked out, the stuffing removed.

"This isn't working at all," Penny said, appraising the squirming thing she held in her hands. Clad in the remains of Captain Mittens, Sherbet was doing his best to escape the failed disguise attempt.

Venus burst into laughter. Penny's handiwork hung loosely from her cat's flayed frame. The poor thing could barely see out of the eyeholes Penny had cut, and seemed extremely uncomfortable having its limbs trapped in the furry sleeves. Despite the grotesque yet hilarious result, Venus could see the potential of the idea quite clearly.

"Oh my God, Penny," she said, catching her breath. "That is the single most ridiculous act of genius I've ever seen. The execution, though . . . "

Penny frowned and put the struggling cat down. Clumsily, it hopped and hobbled to the foot of the bed, where Venus picked it up. She removed the makeshift fur coat, leaving Sherbet to wander the room in his unnatural state. The sight still made Venus uneasy. She sat cross-legged at the foot of the bed, putting the plate of food between herself and Penny.

"We can probably fix this so it actually works," Venus said, examining the small costume. "It just needs to be tightened in a few places."

"It's just a prototype," Penny answered, taking her creation back. "Sorry about your toy."

"It's all right. Besides, it's for a good cause." She picked up a sandwich and took a bite. "Did you call Abraham?"

"Yeah." Penny grabbed a sandwich of her own. "I didn't tell him anything. I figure he'll see it when he sees it."

"So, uh . . . how are you coping today?" It was a question she asked often, trying to gauge her friend's emotional state. Penny wasn't particularly difficult to read, but Dr. Hazelwood had told her that getting more than surface impressions was important.

"Not bad. I can go a few hours without thinking about it, but then out of nowhere I'll feel all empty inside and start bawling my eyes out. I am getting better, though. Tomorrow I'm probably going to start talking with Dr. Hazelwood more seriously about what to do next."

Venus hesitated. She had just come back from meeting with Dr. Hazelwood and Inspector Crowley to discuss her uncle's possible involvement in the murder of Gabrielle LaForest. Penny had reacted to the news of Randy's arrest with disquieting calm. She'd called bullshit on the supernatural part of the story. Of course, Venus had kept secret some of the more intimate details of her encounters with the god, but after showing her friend Sherbet's state, the outlandish story became a lot easier to believe. Venus had gone so far as to show her the captive thing through the monitor on her computer. Even though it was an unsatisfying scene, the monster still hiding in shadows and darkness, the older girl had been fascinated. Between that and fawning over Sherbet, Penelope was almost back to her old self.

"So when's he getting here?" Venus asked between bites.

"Abe? I told him eight, so he should be here any minute. You were gone awhile, Aphrodite."

Venus frowned in jest. Penny usually called her by the annoying nickname for fun, which was probably a good sign. If she was able to tease her friends, then she was probably on the mend.

They chatted for a while about a few mundane things, like the television shows Penelope had been watching to keep her mind busy. She'd gotten hooked on reality television makeover shows, and she detailed how the two of them should subject Abraham to something like that. It was refreshing to enjoy subjects that didn't revolve around murder and monsters, loss and fear.

But always at the back of her mind, Venus was keenly aware of what she had in her shed. What she was planning to show her friends later that night. It was both important and dangerous, like stumbling upon an atomic bomb in the woods. If that happened, though, it would be much easier to get the authorities involved.

Once they finished their dinner, Venus moved to take the dish, but Penelope snatched it from her hand unexpectedly.

"I'll take care of that!" she said, and smiled. "You made the sandwiches—seems only fair I let you spend some time with your zombie cat."

Penny's sudden cheerfulness surprised Venus. Was there such a thing as recovering too fast from tragedy? How would she react if her own parents were taken away in such a brutal fashion? How long would she mourn them? Would she be able to put on a brave face? Smile and joke to distract herself? She wasn't as close to Paul and Virginie as Penny had been with her mom, but she did love her parents and would be devastated if they were killed so suddenly. How was her friend able to stay so upbeat?

Her thoughts were interrupted by a noise at the window. The familiar sound of a pebble hitting glass and rolling down shingles. Abraham. The large farm boy seemed to think he lived in a Mark Twain story instead of a semi-modern village where doorbells were common.

"Use the front door, you idiot!" she yelled out at him as she opened the window and looked down.

He'd obviously not bothered to change after working the fields all day. His overalls were filthy, and his T-shirt was stained with sweat. There was no doubt that he would have a ripe odor about him, but he didn't seem to care one bit.

"On second thought, stay there."

"Hello to you too!" He waved, flashing his usual warm and naive smile. "So what's it that you wanted me to see? Something in your shed? Got some critter you need me to remove?"

He started toward the padlocked door at the back of the yard. Night was falling, and the shadows of the trees made the twilight darker and more forbidding than it should be. A blanket of panic enveloped Venus's mind.

"It's locked!" she shouted, and a good thing it was. Venus didn't want her parents, her friends, or any random stranger to innocently walk in on the creature she was keeping prisoner. Seeing what it had done to Sherbet and the other animals made it clear what the shadow god was capable of.

"I know the combination!" Abraham yelled back, getting ever closer to the shed, still smiling, not knowing what he was approaching.

"Stop!" Venus screamed.

Before Abraham could open the padlock or even reach the door, Venus threw herself out of her bedroom window. This wasn't a completely new way of exiting the house for her. She'd carefully crawled out of her bedroom once or twice to hang out with a friend late at night. Not that her parents would have cared about her leaving the house, but like any teen, there were meetings she didn't want her parents to know about. This wasn't one of those careful, controlled descents, however. Venus slipped on the shingles beneath her window and slid down, face first, toward the gutters. Failing to stop herself, she rolled off the roof, landing flat on her back onto the lawn.

"Veen!" Abraham ran to where his friend had fallen.

Venus lay on her back, letting out a soft moan of pain and embarrassment as she stared at the darkening indigo sky. The wind had been knocked out of her, but she didn't seem to have broken any limbs. Wiggling her toes, she silently counted herself lucky there were no rocks hidden beneath the overgrown grass.

"Venus? You okay?" Abraham knelt next to her and grabbed her arm. "Don't move. I'll get your parents."

"I'm fine, I'm fine." She smiled at him warmly, glad for his concern but more so for getting him away from the shed.

The big teen helped Venus get up, and she dusted herself off. Her entire back felt bruised, and her right arm was raw from scraping against the shingles, a thin layer of skin having been sanded off. It hurt, and she expected it would hurt even more the next morning. She began admonishing herself for such a stupid action but stopped, realizing she would have gladly broken an arm, or worse, to keep her friend from opening that door.

"Damn, Venus, what the hell is in there?" Abraham's usual nonchalant grin was gone. In fact, she'd rarely ever seen him this concerned.

"You won't believe me when I tell you."

"Must be pretty bad if you're throwing yourself off roofs about it." A shadow of his goofy smile returned.

"Oh yeah, it's bad. Very bad." Venus took a deep breath. "It's . . . I think it's a demon? Yeah, it's probably more of a demon."

The farm boy didn't blink or flinch. She couldn't tell if he believed her or not, but it didn't matter. She intended to show both him and Penelope tonight.

"A demon?" he finally said, a sprinkle of doubt in his voice.

"You should see what it did to her cat," said Penny from the side of the house, adjusting her shirt.

Despite their topic of conversation, Abraham's face lit up. He hadn't seen Penny since the day her mother's body had been found, and it was obvious he had been worried about her. The two friends embraced. Penny, who was usually the first to complain about Abraham's lack of grooming, seemed perfectly happy hugging her filthy friend for as long as possible.

"Ahem," Venus interrupted, uncomfortable with the situation. "So? You guys want to see it?"

The two teenagers let go of each other, an awkwardness falling between them.

"Absolutely," answered the older girl, pulling away from the big farm boy. "What do we need to know?"

"Not much. Keep your backs to the wall, just like I do. It can't get at you there, but don't do anything that'll mess with the camera and don't, under any circumstance, agree to anything with it."

"What's with the camera?" asked Abraham. They were both treating the situation very matter-of-factly, as if they dealt with death gods on a daily basis. In a way, simply by living in Saint-Ferdinand, they had.

"It's under some kind of curse or spell. It can't move outside of the camera's line of sight. And I don't think it can move when it's being observed."

Abraham nodded slowly. Hoping they both understood, Venus went to work on the padlock. It was a simple combination, the date of her late grandmother's passing. Yet her nervousness made her fumble the correct numbers so that it took her several attempts to open the lock. She turned back to look at her friends and realized, even if they did seem to believe her, they had no concept of what they were about to see.

"Remember, backs to the wall," she repeated, and pushed the door open.

Before she could nervously hit the light switch, Venus was assailed by the stench of rotten eggs and spoiled meat. Her first thought was that the god wasn't immune to starvation or thirst, and that, being held prisoner for so long, the lack of nourishment had finally led to its demise.

That hope was quickly dispelled as her eyes adjusted to the darkness. The god was still alive, and for some reason the veil of shadows around it had been lifted. The god was crouched on its haunches, ignoring the teenagers as they filed in. Penny and Abraham stifled gasps as they saw the thing. Venus took note of its strange, inhuman proportions. Thin limbs, too long to be human.

A genderless but sinewy frame with a body that defied anatomy. There was fresh blood at its feet.

Then she saw the source of the stench. Behind where it was crouching, the mural had grown ever larger. The beautiful and morbid design now extended to cover most of the walls and even the corners. How had it lured so many animals here? The bones and organs seemed too big to be from any local forest critter.

Finally deigning to acknowledge its visitors, the god rose to its feet in a single graceful movement, both standing and twisting to face them. Venus took a long, hard look at its face. High cheekbones, a lipless mouth, small ears. But most striking of all were its eyes—shining, red, and completely dead. No soul reflected out of those twin orbs. Nothing but the raw power of a god, ancient and alien.

"You've returned, Venus McKenzie." The whisper screamed into their minds. All three teens recoiled at the voice. *"And you bring me . . . gifts."*

Venus steeled herself, determined to keep her fears in check.

"No," she said firmly, taking a step forward but remaining behind the imaginary line that separated her from death. "We're here for answers."

"You lied to me. You don't get to make demands," the god said, dismissing her. *"Your friends, though . . . a deal with them, perhaps?"*

"We were warned about your deals." Abraham also stepped forward, keeping his body in line with Venus's. "But I'm curious: What are you?"

"Peterson . . . no. A new iteration. You don't know me? How interesting." The creature took two steps of its own, graceful and terrible. As it moved, it revealed more of the strange anatomy that clothed it. *"I am purity of purpose, ageless and vast."*

"Self-aggrandizing bullshit," said Venus, nodding in the direction of the dead birds. "You're just some beast that enjoys torture and death."

"You smell familiar." The thing addressed Penny, ignoring the younger girl a second time.

"Hey! Wait! I have more questions," Abraham interjected, nowhere near as scared as he should be. "Why is it you can't leave the shed?"

"A god keeps its promises."

The thing turned back to Penny, taking two more steps forward, until it was almost within arm's reach. The older girl stood firm, her face a mask of stoicism. Both of her arms were held behind her back, as if to keep them from straying within reach of the monster. Though it had no nose, the god cocked its head forward and mimed sniffing at air.

"Yes, I remember," the soft, screeching whisper echoed in their minds. *"I killed you just recently, didn't I?"*

Venus's mind raced. The impossible amounts of blood that surrounded the god. The atrocities perpetrated on her cat and the birds. This thing, which couldn't tell the difference between generations of human beings, had killed Gabrielle LaForest. She'd brought her best friend face-to-face with the monster who had made her friend an orphan.

"Oh God . . . ," Venus turned to warn her friend, but she was too late, the scene was already playing out without her.

"Step forward. Let me kill you again," the beast demanded of Penny, getting as close as the camera would allow it. *"I'll be quick this time."*

"How about I kill *you* instead!" was Penny's answer. In one swift, hate-fueled motion, she took out a large kitchen knife from the back of her jeans and rammed it into the god's midsection, giving the blade a nasty, wet twist. Tears finally broke free of Penny's eyes as she gritted her teeth into a smile of bittersweet revenge.

Surprised, the god froze. Black blood colder than ice ran down Penny's hands as she pushed the knife farther into the thing's chest. For an instant it looked as if she had actually slain the powerful being. But slowly, the thing conjured up a soulless grin.

"We kill each other and share our blood. What a beautiful dance," the god said with morbid sweetness. Penny closed her eyes. She seemed to realize that this small act, this brief moment of defiance, was as good as it was going to get, and she welcomed what was to follow.

But before the god could enact whatever terrible retaliation it had planned, Abraham shoved the thing away from his friend. Despite the large boy's considerable strength, the god barely took a step back. Yet it was enough to move them out of reach of the shadow creature. As it swiped at the teenagers, Venus pulled her friends back to the wall. Penny blinked, looking down in surprise at the black, blood-coated knife in her hand.

The god's frustration rented their minds as it tried to reach them. As it continued to wail, the three teens stumbled out of the shed. Penny seemed dazed by what she had done. Abraham busied himself by making sure the shed was locked again. Venus sank to the ground, hands shaking. All this time, she'd kept the god hidden, thinking of the creature as a pet, a friend, and more. A wonderful curiosity that was all hers, when in fact it was the monster responsible for ruining her best friend's life. The god she could outrun, but the guilt was already catching up to her.

RANDY

THE PEN CROWLEY had given him was running out of ink. It was already well past midnight, but his work was hardly complete. Randy was running low on both time and patience. While he doubted he would be in jail for long, things were coming to a head much faster than he'd anticipated. The accusations leveled against him wouldn't stick in the long run. He had a solid alibi. Should that somehow prove insufficient, character witnesses and his clean criminal record would be sure to protect him. The inspector would do his best to keep him locked up as long as possible, but eventually the creature would strike again, providing him with yet another layer of deniability with which to prove his innocence. The worry was who the next victim would be.

Crowley had been right, though. This rift between the two men was inevitable. He should have seen it coming and, like the inspector said, he should have prepared for it. While it was true that Crowley held all the judicial power in town, Randy was better equipped to understand and act upon the more arcane aspects of the situation.

Even so, Randy didn't regret turning down the inspector's invitation to join his club. He often wondered if Stephen Crowley realized how similar his Sandmen were to the old Saint-Ferdinand Craftsmen's Association. The rituals, the blood sacrifices, the attempts to find and control a living god . . . Crowley's efforts had been as unsuccessful as his old adversaries, but he would never admit it.

"What are you in for?" asked Old Man Finnegan.

"Murder," Randy answered flatly.

"Ah. Tried to keep it contained, did you?"

The two men were separated by a concrete wall, but the corridor that led to both cells bounced the sound of their voices nicely, making conversation easy. Randy hoped his new roommate didn't snore.

"No. It killed again. I'm just being blamed for it," the medical examiner explained. "*It*, assuming we're talking about the same thing, is still at large."

Finnegan clucked his tongue in disapproval. "Nah. It's locked up somewheres. Ain't no doubt about that."

"How are you so sure?" For the first time, Randy raised his head from the paper he'd been furiously scratching on for the past few hours.

"'Cause I ain't dead. It's like I'm a livin' barometer. That thing, when it's free long enough, it's gonna come straight for me, no hesitation. If I'm drawing breath, then it's locked up. I can guarantee that."

"Really now?"

"It hates me, Doc. Oh, oh, ohhh . . . it hates me so much." The old man's voice was laced with amused regret. "Y'see, I wasn't content just keeping it in that cave. I taunted it. Mocked it. Nothin' makes you feel as powerful as taunting a god like yer pouring salt on a slug. In hindsight, that might've been a mistake."

Randy thought about that. Taunting a god. Just how it had been held captive, the nature of the so-called Cicero's Curse, was a mystery to him. But how someone could mock an immortal being of such power for nearly twenty years, that was damn near inconceivable. Did Finnegan know the reckoning that awaited when the god finally caught up to him? The old man's body would give out long before the creature got bored with torturing his soul.

"That must have been . . . something," Randy mumbled, going back to his drawing.

"It was. Ain't sure it was worth it in the end, though." There was a short pause. Randy could hear the old man walking up to and leaning on the bars of his cell. "Whatcha doing in there, scratching away like that?"

"I'm drawing something. Or I would be if Crowley hadn't given me such a shitty pen."

"I didn't know you were an artist, Doc," came Finnegan's unsolicited comment. "My wife, she was an artist."

Randy looked up again. He didn't remember Sam having a wife during his almost two-decade stay in Saint-Ferdinand, nor mentioning he was married during any of their conversations. Finnegan was full of surprises, but this might go some way toward explaining why he was involved with this whole grisly affair in the first place.

"I didn't know you were married, Sam," the medical examiner said. "Did she paint or draw?"

"She painted birds. Beautiful birds. Bright and colorful and vibrant." Sadness and longing permeated the old man's voice. "Oh, how they sang, Randy. You should have heard them fill our little farmhouse with song."

Randy wondered if he'd somehow stumbled onto the source of Finnegan's madness. Most people knew that Old Man Sam once owned a farm, breeding ducks and dogs. He'd never spoken about his wife, though. And the mention of painted, singing birds teetered between the ramblings of an unhinged mind and the suggestion of another layer to the serial killer's story.

The medical examiner looked down at his papers. At first the drawings would have seemed meaningless to an outside viewer, but as time wore on, they began to resemble floor plans. Specifically, the floor plans of Sherbrooke University's medical center. His place of work and the office where he conducted his studies.

Randy was deep in concentration, trying to remember the number of rooms that separated his office from the main corridor. He didn't know yet how he'd get these plans out or who was best suited to execute his plan, but he wanted to get as many details right as he could. The medical examiner tried to focus as the voice continued from the next cell. Only now, it didn't sound like Finnegan.

"I miss riding my bicycle, but I guess I don't need it anymore. I don't even really walk now," an ethereal voice said, followed by a giggle.

"Well, how do you move around, then?" the old man said in a gentle voice.

"I don't know."

Audrey. Randy recognized the cadence of her voice despite the thick veil she seemed to be talking through. The medical examiner had worked with the dead for many years and had performed a lot of strange rituals. He could read whole histories in the eyes of the dead and see if their souls were still inside them. He had even reanimated a few corpses for a short time. However, he had never heard voices from beyond the grave so clearly.

"Y'know how when you want to go somewhere," the dead girl continued, "and you have to travel to get there? I just kind of think of where I want to be, and a little later I'm just there. Poof." She giggled some more.

Randy pressed himself against the prison bars, but he couldn't see into Finnegan's cell. His scientific curiosity was aflame with questions about Audrey's reappearance. It made sense that she could materialize here, in the police station. This is where her bear was. That had been the whole point of creating the totem for her.

"That sounds fun," the old man answered, adding his own laugh to the conversation. "But how is it where you are? Is it nice?"

"Nah. It's kind of . . . ugly? It's dark, and I think it's supposed to be cold, but I don't feel it. It just looks cold. Also, there's this shadow over everything, and once in a while the shadow gets really dark in one spot and then . . . something dies."

Randy heard Finnegan swallow hard. He didn't blame the madman. This "shadow" must be what could be seen of the god on the other side. At least the medical examiner's rituals seemed to have worked so far. Audrey's soul appeared to be safe from the malevolent deity. Just as it had been written in his father's notes, the postmortem acts that had been perpetrated on her tiny body anchored her to the living realm. Eventually Randy would have to set her free. Until then, perhaps this was something he could use to his advantage. Crumpling up his drawing into a tight ball, he cleared his throat.

"Audrey?" the medical examiner called out.

"Uncle Randy?" The bell chimes of her voice rang between the two cells.

Her appearance, though it could not be called "physical," was so similar to the ghosts he'd seen in movies that, at first, Randy wanted to think it was a trick. The reality of what he was seeing only sank in once he'd noticed the subtle details of the apparition. Though she was glowing and translucent, Audrey didn't behave like a cinematic specter. Her hair and gown did not flow as if untethered by gravity. Instead there seemed to be some wind, but it was only enough to put a light ripple to her clothes and locks. She didn't float above the ground, either; her feet looked like they were sunk half an inch into the floor. The girl was clearly subject to the rules and physical restrictions of another reality, while he and Sam were somehow able to see her image projected into their world.

"Audrey." It was his turn to swallow as he saw the iron nails piercing her eyes. His handiwork. "Tell me more about this shadow . . . "

CROWLEY

THE INSPECTOR OPENED the door to the studio. He felt like a man walking, uninvited, into a funeral. The loft of Harry Peterson's renovated barn was immense, littered with easels of various makes and sizes. The western wall was made up of tall windows that allowed for copious amounts of natural light to flood in during the daytime. Powerful neon tubes hung from the ceiling, bathing the room in a white, neutral glow in the evening.

Tiptoeing through the forest of paintings, each covered by an off-white linen sheet, Crowley wondered what each canvas in this private gallery had to show. The inspector was the kind of man who'd say he didn't know art, but he knew what he liked. The honest truth was that he didn't really like anything. Not that he couldn't appreciate beauty. In fact, that was one of the most painful memories from his past life. How Marguerite would sit with him simply enjoying a beautiful sunset. Before the kids, they'd take the small boat they owned, a much more modest vessel than his current craft, and they'd simply row to the middle of the lake to bask in nature's quiet beauty.

Art, however, was something he neither understood nor appreciated. A lot of it simply didn't make sense to him. All that postmodern, abstract, paint-splatter bullshit was better meant for wallpaper patterns than framed canvases. Impressionism just looked lazy. As far as his tastes were concerned, the closer to reality an illustration was, the better. Maybe that was why, despite some fundamental differences in opinions and personality, Crowley had always had a soft spot for Harry Peterson.

Both were single fathers trying to raise boys in a small village. Both had gone through the hardship of losing their wives (though to completely different circumstances), and both were heavily involved in the town's ancient, secret history. Before the cancer that was slowly killing Harry had done too much damage, the two would run into each other at high school sporting events, both there to encourage their sons.

But more than anything else, it was Peterson's paintings that brought Crowley back to him over and over again. Harry painted the kind of things the inspector could understand. Birds, trees, flowers: all in as realistic a style as was humanly possible. Sometimes, even a little more than that.

"Crowley?" came a raspy voice, echoing through the studio.

The inspector didn't bother answering. Instead he emerged from between the easels to stand in front of the windows. The sound of his boots reverberated through the room.

"Looks like old times, doesn't it?" the inspector said, crossing his hands behind him and looking out into the fields.

Outside, the circus was almost done setting up. Tents formed a makeshift village, crowding themselves around the big top. A bonfire was lit near the trucks, and Crowley could see a dozen or so people eating and relaxing around it. A few tents had light pouring out of them, and someone was testing out the Ferris wheel that had been assembled during the day.

The sight was a painful reminder for the inspector, of days that were better not only by virtue of their quality, but also because of how much simpler they had been.

"They're here legally," Peterson said, ignoring the inspector's nostalgia. "You can't kick them out."

That much was true. The circus had slid into town, filling in all their paperwork and getting all their permits behind his back. One more way in which the Sandmen had failed him. How could they see this happening and not notify him? By the time Crowley had been made aware that the cockroaches had crept back from the shadows, it was too late to stop them without breaking a few laws.

"Did you know they were coming?" It sounded more like an accusation than the inspector had meant.

"No. But even if I had, I wouldn't have told you."

Crowley turned to look at Peterson. He'd avoided all but the most superficial glances at the man thus far. Harry was actually two years younger than the inspector, but he looked like he could have been his father. Cancer had been burning him from within for a decade now. Disease, drugs, and radiation had made his skin gray and leathery, covering it with premature liver spots. In the past, the farmer could have snapped Crowley over his knee like a twig, but today he was little more than skin draped over a skeleton.

With a shaking hand, Peterson rinsed one of his brushes in a mason jar of turpentine. The fumes from the solvent rose and filled the studio. All the while, the farmer's brown eyes stared at the inspector over the rim of his glasses.

"What do you want, Stephen?" he finally said.

"I want you to ask them to leave."

A deep, wet cough rose from Peterson's lungs. It was meant to be a laugh, but the fit lasted for a full minute before the man got it under control. Crowley turned back to stare out the window. For a fleeting moment the temptation to go to the sink and get the man some water played in his mind. However, just as compassion was about to take hold, the coughing subsided.

"I . . . I can't do that."

"Why the hell not?"

"Because," Peterson said, still catching his breath, "if I do, they'll probably listen."

"They're leaving either way, Peterson. If you ask them, they'll leave peacefully. I can't promise the same if I have to get involved."

"Listen to me." With great effort, Harry Peterson got up from his stool and half-walked, half-dragged himself to a nearby canvas. "Look here."

With dramatic effect, the farmer pulled the linen sheet from the canvas. The frame rocked back and forth for a moment before settling again. It was a painting of a bird. A brightly feathered blue jay sitting on a branch among maple leaves. Everything about the portrait was photorealistic. Better than that, even. There was an element in the painting that couldn't be expressed through photography. For lack of a better word, the image had *soul*.

The life-size bird looked taken aback, as if it were trying to gain its balance again. It actually appeared to be reacting to the movement of the canvas, which was still wobbling slightly.

Then, to maintain its equilibrium, the bird flapped its wings.

Crowley's jaw went slack. He put a hand to the back of his neck, walking slowly toward the painting. The bird, noticing his approach, chirped in fearful response. When the inspector stretched out his finger to touch the miracle, the blue jay attempted to fly away. It strained and pulled against the canvas but couldn't quite break the seal between itself and the painting. No matter how much it chirped and flapped, the bird remained trapped in the oils and pigments.

"I'm almost there, Stephen. I still have a few kinks to work out, but I can do it. I can paint Audrey back to life, just as I promised, but I need the other Craftsmen. I can paint her body, but I need their help to find her soul."

Only once before had the inspector seen the miracles Peterson could perform with paint and brush. The results had been far less impressive back then, but still mind-bending. The skill was Peterson's life work, and he had improved greatly. If he could indeed paint the Bergerons' daughter back to life, then the Sandmen might lose one of its most influential members. William Bergeron may have been mired in grief recently, but he had been one of the strongest proponents of finding and capturing the god. If his daughter were brought back, even stuck in a painting, then he might abandon the quest. And Crowley couldn't afford for that to happen. Not after everything he'd been through. Not after all he'd sacrificed.

Crowley tapped the bird with the tip of his finger. Again, it chirped and flapped. Some imperfection in the painting kept it from fully manifesting in the real world. Neither could it flee beyond the borders of the canvas. What was described in paint strokes were the limits of its universe. Stephen stroked the blue jay, feeling the perfect texture of its feathers. He pushed against it, feeling it struggle under his hand.

"Stephen . . . "

But Peterson was too late. The inspector's finger punctured the canvas, silencing the bird after one final shriek.

"God dammit, Stephen!" Peterson coughed a little more. "You killed it."

"It's a painting, Harry. Now, are you going to tell Nathan and his cronies to get lost, or do I have to do it myself?"

Peterson stared him down. Ravaged by disease, his body prematurely aged from the cancer and treatments, the farmer decided to stand up to a man twice his size. A man he knew to be volatile.

"I'm sorry, Stephen. But Marguerite would never—"

Crowley's fist made contact with the painter's stomach, nearly lifting the man off the ground. Like the bird, he was silenced instantly. Peterson fell to the ground, clutching his abdomen and struggling for breath. Crowley looked down at him, pitiless. The rage was becoming more and more satisfying to obey.

"Don't you ever lecture me about her."

Peterson didn't answer. The effort of picking himself up off the ground was sufficient to occupy what little energy he had.

Inspector Crowley turned and walked away from the deathly ill painter. There was no way of avoiding it now. Crowley would have to meet with Nathan Cicero himself and once again throw the old man out of the village.

As the inspector walked out of the studio, he took a look at his right hand. Rubbing his thumb and index finger together, he noticed that they were stained with blood. Blood that smelled of oil and turpentine.

VENUS

"HE SAID HE had something important to talk about," Penny said, pacing the room quickly enough to dig trenches with her footsteps. "That big oaf better not be messing with me!"

"Penny, his father's in the hospital. In a coma," Venus answered from her stool.

It was the first time they'd returned to the ice cream shop since Dr. Hazelwood had delivered the news of Ms. LaForest's murder. Penny might have bounced back from that news rapidly, but Venus could see how much her friend had changed. The once calm, almost calculating girl was now brash and impatient.

The night she had shown her friends the god only drove that point home to Venus. Penny had attempted to kill a being of immense power, unconcerned by the consequences of her actions. If it hadn't been for Abraham's quick reaction, and courage, Penny might have suffered a fate worst than that of Venus's cat.

Earlier, the teenage girls had received a call from Abraham, telling them his father had been taken to Sherbrooke Hospital, but that he had very important news for them when he came back. However, he never made it to the shop, and his next call was to tell them that Harry Peterson had fallen into a coma. "So? He should have called by now." Penny stopped her pacing, eyes blazing with resentment and self-pity. "Abe said he had information on that thing in your shed. The monster that killed my mom!"

Venus took her friend by the shoulders, but the older girl retaliated by shoving her away. "What's wrong with you? His father is still alive," Venus said. "But who knows for how long? Abe wants to be with him if anything happens. I know you, Penny. You'd have killed for one more moment with your mom. Don't you dare take that away from him!"

Penny's frown evaporated. Underneath, Venus saw fear. More fear than her friend had shown when confronted with a living god.

"Oh God . . . ," Penny's eyes filled with tears. Her lips trembled and her knees faltered under the weight of realizing what she was becoming. "What's happening to me?"

"It's okay, Penny. You just got a little carried away. Under the circumstances, I think you're entitled to be a little selfish."

"No. No, I'm not," she sobbed, sitting on the stool next to her friend. "I almost got you both killed."

The girls sat in silence for a minute, with only Penny's shuddering breaths to fill the void. Venus couldn't find a sincere way to comfort her friend, and wondered if she even should. After all, Penny was right. No revenge could justify putting all their lives at risk.

"Well," Venus said, finally attempting to break the silence, "as much as I nearly pissed myself, I was kinda cheering you on when you stabbed that thing."

"It did feel really, really good," Penelope admitted with a half smile. "I know it shouldn't. I don't care what they say about revenge; that shit was pretty goddamned cathartic."

"I bet," Venus said, and smiled back. "And the look on its face!"

"I know! Venus, I stabbed a god!"

"You did! Right in the gut, too." Venus laughed. "When was the last time, in history, that anyone stabbed a god? They used to write songs about that kind of thing."

"And you're keeping it locked up!" Penny added, laughing right along with her friend. "Venus McKenzie: jailor of gods."

"Oh, wow. I hadn't thought about that. My résumé is going to be amazing."

The girls broke into a fit of laughter. It felt like they hadn't smiled in years. Like they had both forgotten how to laugh. So refreshing was the feeling, so overwhelming the relief, they failed to notice the door to the ice cream parlor swing open.

"Am I interrupting something?"

The customer was a young man, one year Penny's senior, with short, unkempt brown hair and an athletic figure. He wore plain jeans and a fitted gray T-shirt displaying the Saint-Ferdinand police department's crest in distressed white screen printing. Both girls recognized Daniel Crowley. Embarrassed, they stopped their fit of giggles, their faces a matching shade of crimson.

"Sorry, Daniel. It's been a slow day," said Penny, rushing to get behind the counter.

"Oh, don't worry about it," the boy replied. "I, uh . . . kinda heard about your mom. I'm really sorry."

"Yeah, it's okay. I mean, it's not, but thanks." Penny struggled to regain her composure. "Can I . . . Can I serve you something, Daniel?"

"Actually, I'm here to see McKenzie."

"Me?" asked Venus.

"Yeah. I have something to ask." He motioned toward the door, implying that the conversation was best held in private.

"Uh . . . sure. I guess." Venus looked back and forth between her friend and Daniel, then slowly got up from her stool to follow him.

The two of them stepped out of the ice cream shop. The weather was atypical for a Saint-Ferdinand summer day; instead of withering heat and humidity, the temperature was cold and rain had chased everyone indoors. It was one of the reasons Penny had decided to work; she needed to put some space between herself and the god, but this way she wouldn't have to talk with too many well-meaning but insufferable customers.

The teens did their best to stand under the awning that covered the front door. But even standing close together didn't keep them from getting splattered by rain.

"So, uh, what can I do for you?" Venus asked, uncomfortable being so close to an older boy she barely knew.

"A huge favor, actually," Daniel said. "I need you to give a message to your uncle."

"Randy? He's in jail."

"I know, and I understand you helped put him there."

"Wait. What?" Venus had been under the impression that reporting her uncle's suspicious behavior was supposed to stay between her, Dr. Hazelwood, and the police department. "Why do you even know that?"

"It's kinda hard not to overhear a few things here and there. With my dad being who he is and all," explained Daniel. "Anyway, you need to talk to him."

"Well, why don't you go talk to him yourself? Shouldn't that be easy, with your dad being who he is and all?" She wasn't sure she felt ready to confront the uncle she had put behind bars.

"Maybe I hear a few things I shouldn't once in a while, but that doesn't mean I can just waltz into the cellblock and speak with suspects."

"And I can?"

"You're his niece, McKenzie. The man has no wife, no children. You and your parents are the closest family he's got. C'mon, I'll owe you one."

Venus thought it over. It would be the perfect time to get some answers. She had sent Uncle Randy to jail, and it was only fair that she took some amount of responsibility for that. Especially now that she knew more. Perhaps she could, with his help, formulate a plan to somehow kill the monster in her shed. Still, she couldn't help but think that Penny would be a better candidate for something like this.

"All right, Daniel. What's this message you have for him?"

PENNY

AFTER VENUS LEFT the shop, there was little to no hope that anyone else would brave the downpour for a chocolate parfait or a strawberry sundae. Penelope LaForest decided she had more productive things to do with her time than wait for the weather to clear. Of course, the old Penny would have stayed at her post, ready to pour a milk shake no matter how unlikely it was that anybody would come in on such a dreary day. Or, at the very least, she would have called her boss to make sure he was okay with her taking off.

Today, however, things were different. She didn't know if her irresponsible attitude would persist, or if she was just taking advantage of the leeway granted by virtue of her personal tragedy. Regardless, she wanted some answers about her mother's death and the unusual circumstances surrounding it. A god. It was too much to believe and yet there it was, tucked away in the McKenzies' backyard shed, held prisoner by the most absurd means. It couldn't possibly last. Something would go wrong at some point. The camera would fail. There would be a power outage. And then it would come after her. It would kill Venus for keeping it trapped. It would kill her for having stabbed it. It would kill Abraham just because it could. It was only a matter of time. There was a certain peace of mind that came with the guarantee of imminent death. Not that Penny had given up. She was still hoping they'd somehow have time to figure out a solution, but if they couldn't, she was comfortable with the consequences. The best she could hope for was that it would be quick. The thought of such an end was the only way she could make herself walk all the way here. The only way she could keep the raw emotions from overwhelming her. "Here" was a small patch of forest, just off the road by the Richards orchard. The ground was sodden and muddy. Large droplets of water fell on her from the leaves above. She was already soaked so it didn't matter, though she felt a definite chill as she stepped over the yellow police tape that now lay among the foliage.

The hairs on the back of her neck rose in response to her surroundings. Apart from the rain and her own heavy breathing, the forest was completely silent. Thankfully, the smell of blood Penny had expected was either covered by the moist odor of the soil or had been washed away completely.

Slowly, Penelope made her way to the middle of the area delineated by the yellow tape. It was a comparatively clear part of the forest, probably as a result of a dozen policemen trampling the undergrowth during the investigation of her mother's death.

She was reminded of another walk in the woods she'd taken years ago. She and Abraham had been hunting for frogs near the lake when they were about nine years old. It had been a much nicer day, and although unsuccessful, they had enjoyed the excursion. On their way back through the forest, they had stumbled across sun-washed yellow tape, not unlike the one she'd just stepped over. The two had initially thought the discovery mysterious and exciting, but they soon came to the horrible realization that this was where Brandon Morris had been murdered the previous summer. They'd known Mr. Morris. He had worked at the hardware store and often helped his customers on whatever home repair or renovation project they were currently having trouble with. Abraham's father had employed him to renovate his barn loft. All that had remained of him were the copious bloodstains on the tree trunks and the unmistakable signs of a struggle. His body had vanished, only to resurface years later on Sam Finnegan's property.

Penny didn't know what she expected to find here. Perhaps just the reassurance that this was, after all, a normal patch of woods. And so it was, as normal as anything Saint-Ferdinand had to offer. Yet there was no further catharsis. Even standing at ground zero for the loss she'd suffered, there was no coming to terms with what had happened. Things would never go back to how they were.

Penny realized she was crying. The tears hadn't come in a couple of days, but now, under the rain, where even she had trouble noticing them, they streamed down her face. Her vision blurry and her breathing broken by choked sobs, the teenage girl leaned on an evergreen and allowed her emotions free reign over her. Before long she was balled up at the foot of a tree, sobbing.

Somehow sleep must have overtaken her. When she forced her eyes open, the rain had stopped and been replaced by the dull gray of twilight. Her muscles ached with pain as she forced them back into action. The cool, wet ground had sapped the warmth from her, and she shivered. It was oddly cold for late summer. So cold in fact, Penny could see her own breath.

Then she heard a sound.

It was a soft, echoing voice, like laughter through a tin-can phone. At first Penny assumed one of her friends had come looking for her. Then she saw it. An ephemeral glimpse of a white figure at the edge of her sight. This was where her mother had last drawn breath. Was it possible these visions were her ghost, trying to talk to her daughter? It was no crazier a notion than that of a god trapped in someone's backyard shed. But what if it was something else? What if the creature in Venus's shed had made its inevitable escape and hunted her down?

Between the cold and stillness of the forest and the approaching apparition, Penny finally lost her nerve. Taking little time to make sure she had picked the correct direction, she ordered her legs to run. Run and run and run. Get to the road, where she'd have at least the illusion of safety.

In her panic, she tripped on a root and fell flat on the ground, her elbows digging deep into the mud. Scrambling to get to her feet, she realized this was probably how her mother had died. Running scared and panicked, unable to understand what was happening to her and why. Penny did not want to die like that. If the god was going to take her life, she'd make it fight for the privilege.

She crawled toward her bag, grabbing ahold of one of the straps. As she did, the air around her became freezing cold and she could see her breath once again. Nearly hysterical, Penny reached into the bag and pulled out the large kitchen knife she'd used to stab the god. Getting a firm hold on its handle, she pulled off the T-shirt she'd used to cover the blade. The gruesome keepsake in hand, the object still covered in pitch-black blood, she spun to see what was behind her.

But there was nothing.

Nothing but empty woods, lush green foliage, and ever-growing puddles of water. No sounds except for the tapping of raindrops on the leaves above and her ragged, labored breathing. Obviously her fear had gotten the better of her, and her imagination was running wild. Or maybe she was going crazy. After everything she'd been through, losing her mind was to be expected, wasn't it? Crazy or simply on edge, the important thing was, she'd imagined the apparition.

"Penny?"

The teenage girl shrieked, twisted around, and slashed blindly behind her. She felt the blade bite into flesh, a sensation she hadn't been familiar with until she had tried to murder a god. This time only the tip of the knife found purchase. She worried that it might not be enough to stop her attacker, whoever it was. But before she had time to give another flourish, her mind finally registered who it was she'd attempted to cut to ribbons.

"Audrey?"

The little dead girl stood before her, a hand to her face. She wore a pretty white dress that glowed as if lit from within. Eerily, her clothes and her hair were dry, her skin pale and clean. The child's feet seemed to be planted deep in a puddle of dark water. Penny trembled in horror and disbelief, noticing large black iron nails had been driven into the child's eye sockets.

Yet Audrey seemed more upset by the cut to her cheek. She slowly lifted her hand to look at her bloodstained fingers. Audrey's wound wasn't long or deep, but it clearly hurt, as tears were welling up where her eyes should have been. The dead girl's lower lip quivered as she tried to swallow her sobs.

Penny's motherly instincts took over. Dropping the knife, she took a step forward and crouched so she could be level with Audrey. Slowly, she reached out to gently touch the child, but her hand passed through the little girl's shoulder. Penny's hand felt cold as it did so, as if it had been dipped in ice water.

To her credit, Penny kept her cool this time, focusing on the little dead girl.

"Audrey, baby?" Penny asked gently. "Are you okay?"

"No." The child took a step back. "You hurt me."

"I'm so sorry, honey. I really didn't mean to." Penny felt sick with remorse. "I would never hurt you on purpose, you know that."

Audrey looked Penny right in the eyes, the black nails in her skull almost hypnotic in their atrocity. Penny tried to stay calm. First gods, now ghosts. Was her mother's spirit also wandering around the forest? A lost spirit in the woods?

"It's okay," the little girl finally answered. "It's just a small cut. I thought you were mad at me."

"What . . . what are you doing here, Audrey?"

"I was looking for you." Her voice became cold and impersonal. "But it's okay. I found you now. I knew you'd come here."

"Why . . . why me?"

"Uncle Randy says he needs help. Can you help him?"

There was so much Penny wanted to ask. *Was* her mother also a ghost? Could she talk to her? She wanted to beg the little girl to let her see her mother again, but in the end she settled on the most pressing question.

"What kind of help?"

VENUS

"YOU'RE SURE YOU want me to leave?"

Venus had to crane her neck to look Matt Bélanger in the eyes. The officer was known for his calm nature and economy of words. Most residents of Saint-Ferdinand knew that he only ever spoke when he thought it was absolutely necessary.

She looked at the bars separating her from the two men. One was Old Sam Finnegan. It felt odd to see him. He sat placidly on his cot, looking at her with a gentle smile. Even now, after over two weeks in jail, it was hard to imagine he'd committed so many atrocities. Scruffy and thin, wrinkled and unkempt, he looked like a kindly grandfather, not a career serial killer.

The other man, of course, was her uncle Randy. Being behind bars suited him even less. His sunken eyes and ashen complexion made him look like he'd seen a ghost. She'd expected him to be angry or disappointed, but he looked confused and scared. Remorse filled her heart, seeing him like this, knowing his current situation was her fault.

"I'll be fine, Lieutenant Matt." She smiled confidently up at him.

The officer shrugged. "When you're done, or if you need anything, just hit the buzzer at the top of the stairs."

Venus waited until the door had closed completely before turning her attention back to the shell of the man that was her uncle. His lack of grooming and vacant expression painted him as more of a killer than Finnegan.

"I didn't know what else to do . . . ," she began, attempting to gauge his state of mind. "I've come to apologize. I . . . I'm trying to piece together a lot of stuff, but I need help."

Randy just kept staring at her. It made Venus nervous. She felt like running up the stairs and hitting that large red button, leaving this place, and never coming back. But she had a responsibility.

"Uncle Randy? I'm sorry. I connected the wrong dots, and I assumed you had something to do with Mrs. LaForest's death. I've come around, though. I guess that's why I'm here."

"What turned you around?" Randy McKenzie croaked. "The evidence you gave Crowley was pretty damning."

"It's hard to explain. I . . . I don't know that you'd believe me anyways."

"Try me, Venus."

She was relieved to hear emotion in his voice, even if it was impatience with a hint of irritation.

"I know what . . . who killed Gabrielle."

The dramatic reveal had the intended effect, just not on the target she expected. Sam Finnegan tilted his head and leaned forward a little. Randy, on the other hand, showed no reaction.

"It's not a person," Venus continued. Randy still didn't move, but somehow he seemed to intensify his stare. "It's a . . . it's a god."

She expected incredulity or even ridicule, but the reaction she received made all her worries seem pointless. Sam Finnegan sagged back onto his cot, his smile melting away, while Randy buried his face in his hands. Did they actually believe her?

"Actually, it claims to be a god. Maybe it's a demon or a mutant or some kind of monster . . . I don't know!" Venus added, struggling to get a further reaction out of her uncle.

"Oh, it's a god, all right," Finnegan said with a bitter smile. "Just not one of ours."

"Stay out of this, Sam," Randy said, finally lifting his head. His voice was raspy, like it hadn't been used in days. "Have you seen it, Venus? Have you seen the thing with your eyes?"

"It keeps out of the light," she said with some hesitation, "but it looks like it's made of shadows . . . and blood."

"When did you see it last? Where?" Randy was almost on the verge of panic.

"I have it trapped in the backyard shed. It's not happy about that."

"Trapped?" the doctor asked. "Are you completely sure about that?"

"Yes. One hundred percent."

Sam clapped excitedly and laughed. He seemed relieved while Randy seemed confused.

"Yes!" the madman cried. "She is very smart, isn't she, your niece?"

"No. I'm not," she said, throwing a look at the crazy old man. "It was luck. I had a camera set up in there. It can't go anywhere when someone, or I guess something, is looking at it, so it's stuck there. For now. But it killed Penny's mom and . . . other things, and it's trying to escape. It's making this weird mural, and I don't think it's just for fun. I don't know what to do next. I need a way to destroy it."

"That's a little ambitious, don't you think?" Randy said, standing and walking to the door of his cage. Venus was shocked at how haggard he looked. "You can't kill a god."

"Oh no, you can kill it," Sam disagreed. "You can kill it, but it doesn't have to die. Not if it chooses not to. It plays by a different set of rules. That's why the curse of Cicero works!"

"My friend Penny stabbed it with a knife about this big." She held her hands roughly a foot apart. "It didn't die."

"Or it did, but it doesn't mind or care that it's dead. Maybe it's been dead for years. Different rules," countered Sam.

"Okay. Whatever." Venus turned to her uncle again. "Why is he suddenly the expert on all this?"

"These are crazy days, Venus," the madman answered in his own defense. "And haven't you heard how crazy I am? I'm uniquely qualified—"

"Wait. Go back a little," Randy interrupted. "Penny did what? Venus, this is a god, a real god you've imprisoned. This isn't a game."

Venus clenched her fists. This was the kind of reaction she had been desperately hoping to avoid. She might be only fifteen, but there was no way she was going to allow herself to be condescended to. Not after everything she'd been through.

"My cat's been flayed and my best friend's mom is dead. Your god has threatened me, and for all I know, the entire world's at risk." She tried to keep her temper in check. "Apart from being mysterious and evasive, what the hell have you two been doing? I'm dealing with this better than either of you! I'm not the one playing games!"

"Okay. All right. I apologize," Randy said, trying to sound sincere. "I'm just . . . There's no precedent for this situation. I don't know how I can help."

"And I don't know if it can be destroyed," Finnegan added. "Other, better people have tried and died. I just know how to keep it locked up." Like her uncle before her, Venus was starting to wonder how much of the madman's persona was only a facade.

Venus calmed down and opened her hands. She hadn't realized just how tightly she'd been clenching her fists. Placing herself between the two cell doors, she tried to address both men at the same time. She knew her first priority was getting information.

"What can either of you tell me about this curse of Cicero?"

Finnegan looked away. Sadness and regret were reflected in his eyes as he stared at the wall. "It's a promise. A promise the god made to a man named Cicero over a century ago," he answered. His tone was neutral, but his voice was unsteady. "A promise to not move as long as someone looked at it. It started as a game, but now it's a curse.

"The Craftsmen, they used to take turns watching it. Then my wife painted the *eye*. When it all went to hell and she . . . When she passed and her painting was damaged, well, I had to come up with a different solution."

"'They are ever vigilant in death,'" quoted Randy. "That's why you took the eyes . . . "

Venus studied both men. Randy had stopped paying attention to her, suddenly swallowed by his own thoughts. Finnegan was no better, clutching his knees, his eyes distant. The young girl recognized that no matter what he'd told the police or his lawyers, this was Sam Finnegan's true confession. Obviously there was more to it than Venus understood at that moment, but Lieutenant Bélanger might be back any minute. She was running out of time.

"Uncle Randy?" she said, tapping on the cell bars to get his attention. "That man, Cicero? He's in town and he says he needs to talk to you."

"How?" the medical examiner answered. "There's no way Crowley is going to let Cicero in here for a chat."

"I don't know. I'm only the messenger, but if what I've been told is right, you only have until tomorrow. After that, he'll be gone."

It was starting to look like everyone had their own little piece of information about the god, but not everyone was on the same team. Which meant that not everyone could be trusted. She didn't want to be paranoid, but she could hardly open up to just anyone. So Venus had suggested that she and Daniel meet in front of the ice cream parlor, in the same place they'd spoken earlier. Venus had expected the shop to be closed, but Penny was back behind the counter. Her hair was a mess, her clothes were covered in mud, and her eyes were wild. Daniel had taken refuge inside, and the two of them had been talking.

"We need to talk," Venus said as she entered the converted trailer.

When discussing Daniel's request earlier that day, Venus had recognized that the inspector's son knew an awful lot about the goings-on in Saint-Ferdinand.

"That's an understatement," Daniel replied. "Penny's been telling me some really freaky stuff, McKenzie."

"'Stuff'?" Venus gave her friend a concerned look. "What 'stuff,' pray tell?"

"Stuff about gods, skinless cats . . . ghosts."

Venus shot Penny a withering look of accusation. Why the hell did she have to go and tell the inspector's son everything? They had agreed to keep things to themselves until they understood the stakes involved.

"Sorry, Veen. Daniel found me walking from the Richards place and gave me a lift. We got to talking again and, well, things just got a little more . . . complicated."

"How can things be more . . . Wait. Ghosts?" Venus asked, incredulous.

"It's Audrey, Veen. Little Audrey," Penelope explained. "Your uncle . . . did something to her."

"What?"

"He didn't kill her or anything. I think he . . . anchored her soul. With a spell or something."

"I just talked to him, God dammit! Why didn't he mention anything?"

"To be fair, you did put him in jail, McKenzie," Daniel said.

Daniel might be annoying, but he had a point. At least now she knew what her uncle had been doing in the cemetery.

"So Audrey's a ghost, and my uncle's a wizard?" Venus's tone was skeptical. "Sure. Why not?"

"It gets better," Daniel added.

Venus turned to her best friend. "Why is he suddenly in charge?"

"Just listen to what he has to say. You'll see."

When Venus turned back to Daniel, he gave her a look of patience and understanding that she did not expect.

"Right. So William Bergeron wants to bring his daughter back to life," Daniel explained. "Mr. Bergeron, my father, and a few other people in town have this club or cult or whatever you want to call it. My best guess is, they want to enslave this so-called god, then use it to grant Mr. Bergeron's wish. And maybe some other wishes too."

"That sounds crazy."

"Totally, but like I was telling Penny, I saw them. At church, doing some cult-y ritual."

"You said the god is always going on about granting wishes and making dreams come true," Penny added. "It's always angling to make a deal. They think they're getting a wish-granting machine. Like a genie in a bottle."

"Right," Daniel said. "And I think your uncle Randy and Harry Peterson are part of all this too."

"Abe's dad?" Venus said in disbelief.

Now she understood why her friend had been comfortable sharing their secrets with Daniel. It appeared that the older boy was aware of an entirely different side of the story, and had offered his own pieces so that they could be added to the puzzle.

"I gave Randy your message, but why didn't you tell me any of this before I saw him?"

"I didn't know if I could trust you."

"Fine." Venus couldn't argue that she had been just as secretive as Daniel. "He says he's okay with talking to Cicero but that there's no way they'll let that guy in the cellblock for a chat."

"That's another understatement," Daniel pointed out.

"I've got it," Penny said. "Audrey didn't just appear to me for no reason. She was giving me a message from your uncle. Now, don't get pissed, but he wanted me to get something from his office in Sherbrooke. But maybe she can help us get Cicero and Randy in contact."

"Hold up," said Venus. "What does my uncle want from his office?"

"A list," Penny responded. "People who were part of the Saint-Ferdinand Craftsmen's Association. He says all the information is in a wooden box on a shelf of the middle bookcase in his office."

"Perfect!" Venus said. "Let's go. We can catch up with Abraham."

"You'll have to say hi for me," Penny said. "I want to talk to this Cicero, and I think I know how to get him in touch with your uncle. You're going to have to go alone, Veen."

Venus had walked into the ice cream parlor confident that she was finally getting a handle on things, but now the situation was being flipped on her again. How was she supposed to make it to Sherbrooke? Penny was the one with the car and license. Venus would have to ask for a lift from her parents. It might take hours before they got around to driving her, assuming they wouldn't insist on waiting until morning. She was stuck in Saint-Ferdinand, unable to go comfort her friend and unable to do her part. Unless . . .

"Daniel?" she said. "You owe me a favor."

CROWLEY

THIS WAS THE second time in as many days that Stephen Crowley had made his way to the Peterson farm. Neither occasion was official business, though he wasn't opposed to stretching the limits of his authority.

The sight before him made his heart sink. As a child, he'd always loved the circus. Especially this one. Cicero's Circus didn't have any animals and only a few clowns. There was no freak show. It was the kind of traveling show that aspired not to disgust or terrify its audience, but to amaze. No one could visit Cicero's without believing in magic at least a little when they left.

It was also where Crowley had met his wife.

The inspector couldn't help but feel a little regret that Daniel had never been able to experience this circus when he was a kid. It was cruel irony that Crowley was the one responsible for that.

Back then, Cicero's came to town once a year, always at the end of summer, and had been doing so for years. Residents of Saint-Ferdinand waited for the old circus owner to roll down the street in his beat-up Volkswagen Beetle with the same anticipation most communities reserve for Christmas.

However, when clues started popping up that Nathaniel Cicero might be the Saint-Ferdinand Killer, it led to a series of events that chased the circus away and ultimately freed the terrible god from its cage.

Crowley had told Cicero to never come back. Yet here he was. With the capture of Sam Finnegan and the creature's release, the return of the circus was a bad omen and certainly no coincidence.

As the inspector walked through the game booths, tents, and attractions, Crowley expected all manner of angry stares. Yet it was as if they didn't recognize him or simply did not care. A fire-breather he remembered, Ezekiel, spit an impossibly perfect arc of flames above the inspector's head, welcoming him to the big top. He did so with the same smile he'd offer anyone. But Crowley wasn't just anyone. He was the officer who had chased Cicero's Circus into exile. Now he walked among them in full uniform— unmolested, unrecognized, virtually anonymous.

The inspector's heart ached as he entered the gigantic tent at the center of the circus. It was everything a big top was supposed to be: supported by two enormous posts and lined with rows of blue-and-white-striped seats. Two large rings lined the floor, in-tersecting where the ringmaster stood. The grandeur of it all was striking, and it made the inspector long for the time when he had enjoyed this strange monument to awe and wonder.

There was one individual in this place who could not ignore him. That person stood alone in the middle of the tent, illumi-nated on all sides, his back to the door. He wore a powder-blue tuxedo with a matching top hat. Old and frail, he leaned on a cane as he gazed up at his installation. He looked every bit like a human fossil, but Crowley knew better. Nathaniel Cicero was a man of unusual fortitude and foresight. He was here because he knew the inspector was coming.

As if he could hear this thought, Cicero turned around dra-matically when Crowley got close enough. Smiling with perfect teeth that did not belong in such a dilapidated body, he bowed deeply, removing his hat in the process.

"Mr. Crowley," he said. "It's been too long."

Without breaking stride, the inspector punched the old bastard square in the jaw, sending the frail ringmaster to the ground. Crowley stood over his victim, huffing as the adrenaline rush filled him with primal satisfaction.

"Still glad to see me, Nathaniel?"

Cicero got up and walked back, making sure he was a dozen feet away from Crowley as he did so. He smiled again, though this time more conservatively. He didn't want to appear smug. His guest was obviously not in the festive mood such a reunion should call for.

"I'm guessing this isn't a social call then, my boy?" he said, spitting blood into the sand.

"Didn't your fortune-teller warn you? I'm here to evict you."

"Katrina did tell me to expect you. Why else would I put on such theatrics?" He rubbed his bruised jaw. "She failed to warn me about this particular outburst, though. I must have slighted her somehow."

"It's only going to get worse if you and your people don't pack up and leave."

"Oh, I don't think so, Mr. Crowley," Cicero said, leaning on his cane. "We have business here. Legitimate business, and I have all the necessary permits."

The inspector shrugged. Taking a couple of quick steps forward, he took another swing at the old man and connected with force. Again, Cicero crumpled to the ground. This time he spat more than just a few drops of blood, and it took him much longer to climb back to his feet.

"Mr. Crowley, you misunderstand my intentions. I am here— we are here—to help. You're very much out of your depth. If you continue on this path, you won't survive."

True, the forces Crowley was setting out to control were vast to the point of being almost impossible to comprehend. But was there anyone alive who was equal to such a task? Certainly Cicero and his circus. Though they'd already tried and failed. Now it was his chance.

"You're not here to help me," he said petulantly. "You're here to shut me down."

"Oh, come now, Mr. Crowley. Surely you've grown wiser over the last two decades. You think you're the good guy here?" The smug, now bloodstained smile returned. "Jonestown. Aum Shinrikyo. David Koresh. Every cult is built on its own version of the truth. There's no such thing! The Craftsmen saw themselves as heroes and we were wrong. Your Sandmen thought the same thing when they took up our mantle, and they are making the very same mistakes. You honestly think you can succeed where your father-in-law failed so spectacularly?"

Crowley took a deep, exasperated breath, such as one would take with a child who refused to listen to reason. Then he took another swing at Cicero. This time, the old man moved out of the way so that his face was spared. Unfortunately for him, the inspector's left fist followed through with a solid jab to the stomach. To his credit, Cicero didn't fall to the ground this time, but he did spend the next minute doubled over, gasping for air.

"Eighteen years you kept the creature hidden from me. Under my nose!" Crowley yelled at the ringmaster. "Now you show up just as I'm about to succeed? You've taken too much from me already, Nathaniel. You ain't taking this, too."

To underline his statement, Crowley attempted one more attack on the old man. There was infinite satisfaction in releasing nearly two decades' worth of pent-up rage. Expecting the old man to try another dodge, Crowley threw a convincing feint with his left, then switched to a right jab that he hoped would drive the point home to Cicero: *you are not welcome here.* Then again, he thought, if more hitting was required, he'd be happy to oblige.

But this time the ringmaster of Cicero's Circus was prepared. Seeing the incoming jab, he lifted the end of his cane. Crowley's fist struck the pointed tip, perforating the skin between his index and middle fingers. The sturdy wood wedged itself between the bones of his hand and pushed them in opposite directions.

With a scream and a spray of blood, the inspector pulled back his fist, clutching the shattered extremity. Cicero, who had only been slightly imbalanced for his trouble, walked past the inspector, making his way toward the door in the big top.

"Feel free to kick me out of town, Mr. Crowley," the old ringmaster said without turning his head. "But please have the decency of doing it legally."

"I'm warning you, Nathaniel: don't interfere with my work," the inspector growled.

"Don't you know the prophecies, Mr. Crowley?" Cicero finally turned back to look at his attacker. "My meddling is almost at its end."

Then the old man walked out into the night, leaving Crowley with his agonizing pain.

VENUS

VENUS JOGGED TO the front door of her parents' house after Daniel dropped her off. The sky was an even, dull gray. The rain had slowed down a little, leaving puddles of mud in its wake.

As she stormed through the house, many thoughts raced through the girl's mind. She wasn't thrilled with her family's proximity to the malevolent creature imprisoned just a few dozen feet away, but Penny's manic behavior, Audrey's lingering ghost, and the burning need to find a way to end the god had her preoccupied.

"Would it be rude of me to ask if there's any chance you'll be cleaning up the yard at some point?"

The voice of her mother made her jump. Virginie never asked her daughter to do something if it sounded like an order. She and her husband had always been adamant about treating their daughter like an equal, never asking more of her than they would another adult. Of course, they never gave her more, either. Venus swung back and forth between being grateful for the freedom, and bitterly resentful of their neglect. In the past few days, however, the teenager had been glad of their hands-off approach.

"Not now, Mom," Venus replied, bolting past her mother. This wasn't the way the McKenzies usually talked to one another, but Virginie took it in stride. Venus didn't know how long she had before access to her uncle's office would be denied to her. It might already be far too late. She didn't have time to come up with a believable lie for her mother, and putting everything back into the shed was certainly out of the question.

On a good day, Venus's room was a monument to organized mayhem. She had long ago abandoned such mundane conventions as sock drawers, preferring to store endless yards of computer cables instead. Her clothes were usually sorted into neat piles inside her closet, the door of which she had had her father remove when she was a child. In the past few days, however, the barely contained chaos had devolved into a cesspool of wadded-up sheets, board game boxes, and empty snack containers.

Thus, it took a moment for Venus to locate her laptop. When it was found, she quickly looked at the webcam video feed, making sure that her "guest" was still safely confined to the shed. She was reassured at seeing the inky shadow of the creature writhing in the dim light. It seemed angry, the surface of its wispy presence undulating violently. Venus could swear it knew she was watching.

When she went to unplug the computer's power cord, she saw her mother leaning on the doorframe. Virginie looked concerned. Venus had always admired her mother's altruism and kindness. In a way, it made her even more resentful that such a kind woman had zero motherly instincts for her own daughter.

"Veen. What's in the shed?"

A cold shiver went down Venus's spine at the question. "It's . . . a project. I'm filming a bird's nest and I don't want it disturbed. I'll put everything back when I'm done." She had spent hours trying to figure out if she should say anything to her parents. At first, the independent spirit that Paul and Virginie had instilled in her had kept her from seeking their help. Then it was shame at having the creature gain such a foothold in her mind. After Penny had nearly been killed by the creature, however, her pride and shame became fear. She couldn't imagine what would happen if either of her parents fell into the hands of the monster. She knew from Daniel Crowley that her folks weren't part of his father's cult, but if she told them what was in the backyard, their first instinct would be to go to the police.

"You've been acting kind of spaced out lately, baby. I know it's been a tough few weeks, but Paul and I are getting worried." *Worried.* It had been years since Virginie had even used such a word. "This thing about you wanting to live out there. Coming and going at all hours. Randy being in jail. Now you're keeping secrets? It's not exactly your style."

Venus crouched down to put her laptop into its bag, her eyes hunting for a spare extension cord in case she needed it. Instead her eyes met with those of Sherbet. The horrifying, skinless cat narrowed its pupils as it poked its head out from under the bed. Ever since its encounter with the creature that had removed its pelt, the cat seemed rather self-conscious about its appearance. It also got cold more easily. This amounted to the animal spending more time hidden than usual, which suited Venus fine. Sherbet was a difficult secret to explain. Venus tried to shoo him back under the bed before he got noticed. Undeterred, the animal opted to clean itself, running its rough tongue over the raw, exposed muscle on its paw. The sight made Venus's hair stand on end.

"Mom," she said, hoping to draw attention away from the cat. "You wanted me to be independent? Well, here we are. Now I kinda need you to follow through on that."

Finally she spotted her power cord, which was resting at the edge of her desk under a half-empty box of cookies. Hoping to kill two birds with one stone, she snatched the cable and made the box of cookies fall off her desk, startling her hideous pet. Sherbet fled back to the shadows. Suppressing a satisfied smile, Venus stuffed her prize into her bag.

"Just tell me: Are you in any trouble?" Venus's stomach clenched at the concern in her mother's voice. "Whatever else we may be, Veen, we're your friends. If you need help with anything, we're here for you."

Venus let her demeanor soften and stepped forward to wrap her arms around her mother. She surprised herself with how genuine the act felt. It was a ploy, but right then the teenage girl wanted nothing more than to tell her mother the truth. Instead she broke off the embrace.

"I swear, Mom, I'm just trying real hard to keep Penny as distracted as possible. I'm fine." Venus forced a smile.

"Fine. Just be careful, honey," Virginie said, obviously unconvinced. But after a beat she managed to smile back. "And when you get home, you can explain to me why the Crowley boy is driving you around."

At those words, Venus's independent young woman mask melted away to reveal the awkward teenager beneath. She broke eye contact, clumsily adjusting her laptop bag. "It's not like that. He's got a girlfriend, and . . . I gotta go, okay? I'll, ah . . . I'll see you later, all right?"

In an even bigger hurry to get out of the house now, Venus bumped into almost every piece of furniture on her way out. Smiling, Virginie watched her only daughter slam the front door shut behind her.

VIRGINIE

VIRGINIE WATCHED THE Civic drive off, her only daughter riding along with the son of Inspector Crowley. Daniel was as good a kid as they came, and while he might have been a little old to be hanging out with a girl Venus's age, Virginie couldn't help but feel a strange pride in her daughter. Assuming Virginie's most gossipy presumptions turned out to be correct.

It was tempting to go check out the backyard shed. See what kind of setup Venus had in there. However, considering that the girl had shown the first sign of affection to her mother in a week, perhaps it wasn't the best time to go snooping around in her affairs.

Pressing her face against the window, looking out onto a now empty street, Virginie felt a short wave of optimism. For herself, for her daughter, and for their life in this little hellhole of a village.

"Meow?" came a pitiful, hungry cry from behind her.

"Oh, Sherbet, you poor baby. Has your mommy not been feeding you?" Venus's mother said, turning to look at her daughter's pet.

RANDY

RANDY COULDN'T BELIEVE his ears when he heard the sound of loose leather sandals slapping down the stairs. The doctor had become familiar with the unique signature of everyone's footsteps at the station. Jackie, who brought him and Finnegan their meals, had a light and nervous walk, while Lieutenant Bélanger's was slow and controlled. Crowley, who had been absent the last few days, had a heavy, purposeful step.

But only Paul McKenzie would visit a murder suspect while wearing sandals. The smell of freshly shaved wood and sweat confirmed the medical examiner's guess. "Paul," the medical examiner said.

"Hey, Randy," answered his younger brother, stepping into view. Paul McKenzie was a bit of a contrast to his sibling. Beyond their professional and educational divergence, Paul had a full head of hair, though his was graying prematurely, and he was thinner. Or had been. "You've lost weight, man."

It was true. The station didn't allow for food from off the premises, so Randy hadn't been able to indulge in his habits of pastries and snacks between meals. He still had his belly and jowls but they were diminished. His pants already hung on him loosely. As he wasn't allowed a belt, he was obliged to hold up his pants by hand.

"Yeah. When I get out of here, I'm going to have to get a whole new wardrobe."

"Or a hell of a lot of cheeseburgers."

The brothers chuckled, uncomfortable with the situation. When they were teens, the McKenzie brothers hadn't been known to raise hell. The worst brush either of them had had with the authorities was when Paul did a brief stint in jail for participating in a particularly agitated protest. He'd be hard-pressed to remember what it had been for. The legalization of marijuana or police brutality. It had been a long time ago.

"If Dad were alive, he'd skin you, you know that?" Paul said, attempting more humor to lighten the mood. His brother's expression darkened, however.

"If Dad were alive, I wouldn't be here in the first place," Randy said, bitterness tainting his words. "Hell, if you'd helped out at all, I wouldn't be in this situation."

"Aww, come on. Back off, man." Paul raised his hands defensively. "I've told you, like, a million times, I am not into that shit, dude. Look where it landed you. I bet this is just the tip of the iceberg too, isn't it?"

"Come on, Paul!" Randy said, stepping up to the bars. "You were the talented one. With Dad's notes—"

"Enough, Randy. I come in peace." The younger brother raised his hand to silence him. "Look, man, how bad is my daughter mixed up in all this?"

"Venus?" Randy should have anticipated this. While his brother and sister-in-law liked to practice progressive parenting, they still both worried about their daughter. "Why don't you ask her yourself?"

Paul sighed. Randy had never approved of the way his niece was being raised. She was a smart young woman and fiercely independent, but it seemed to the medical examiner that no matter how well the girl might be doing, without guidance, her potential was being wasted. When she'd been a child, she would hang out with Paul and Virginie. They'd talk about anything, and the girl's voracious curiosity made her quickly learn—and then get bored with—everything her parents had to teach. By the time she was a teenager, Venus had moved on to computers and electronics, subjects far beyond Paul's scope of knowledge. As his daughter's interests grew deeper, he was left to observe her from an increasing distance.

"Randy, she's a teenager. She's not gonna talk to me. Just tell me how bad it is."

"All right," his brother said. "I won't sugarcoat it; it's pretty bad. How much of Dad's notes did you even read?"

"Somewhere in the neighborhood of none. You know what I think of that crap." After the passing of Neil McKenzie, Paul and Randy's father, the brothers had inherited a foot locker filled with notes, old photos, and torn pages from books written in long-forgotten languages. There were also stacks of receipts from trips around the world, spanning decades of the man's life. The whole thing had gone a long way toward explaining why the McKenzie patriarch had gone, leaving his wife to raise two boys. When Neil was home, however, he was a controlling figure, prone to fits of anger at the slightest disobedience. His sons felt like an annoyance, something that distracted their father from more important work. When Paul found out that his father's "work trips" had to do with research into ancient religions and the occult, he simply couldn't come to terms with Neil McKenzie's failings as a parent.

"Yeah, well, the old bastard wasn't making it up," Randy explained. "He was part of a . . . gentlemen's club, and they were into some pretty heady stuff. Old gods, magic, prophecies . . . you name it: the stranger the better. You want to know why he went to Peru? Indonesia? Iraq? All over the oldest parts of the world? Why he spent all that time researching the most ancient and secret religions? Well, they were trying to take down an ancient, evil entity. But they failed, Paul.

"I thought I could figure things out on my own, but I can't. I need to find some of Dad's old associates, assuming any of them are still alive."

Paul shook his head. "I'll help you, then. Whatever you need me to do. Just don't get Venus involved."

"She's been involved her whole life, Paul. You know at least that," Randy said before his brother could voice any protest. "She's part of this, and I need her help."

"What? Why?" Paul wasn't a man who fell prey to anger easily. The back of his father's hand had taught him to hate violence. Even raising his voice would rack him with guilt. But if there was one thing he felt justified in getting angry about, it was his daughter's safety.

"Katrina told your fortune. You know the prophecies—"

"No, man. No. Fuck you and your prophecies."

"It's too late, Paul. I've already sent her to my office. Think about it. She'll be out of Saint-Ferdinand, where it's safe. For now."

Before his younger brother could protest, they were interrupted by Sam Finnegan clearing his throat from the back of his cell. So far, the Saint-Ferdinand Killer had stayed quiet. The brothers fell silent, listening for any further noise from the old man.

"Why don't you put things into perspective, Randy?" Finnegan rambled just as Paul was about to renew his protest. "Why don't you tell your brother what's in his backyard?"

CROWLEY

"I DON'T CARE, ma'am. No, I don't—" Crowley was starting to fume. He had stopped counting how many times the annoying woman on the other end of the line had cut him off. His right hand was beginning to cramp from holding the receiver.

The shrill creature on the phone was but the latest in a long line of irritants to the inspector. She was a reporter, one of many who were trying to get the story of how the Saint-Ferdinand Killer had finally been apprehended. She and others like her had been wasting enormous amounts of the inspector's precious time, and his patience was running short.

The media paled in comparison to a much larger problem, though. It was one thing to keep news outlets and television stations out of the town's business, but quite another to dodge the judicial system and his superiors, who were growing increasingly suspicious about the delays in processing Samuel Finnegan.

Crowley was no idiot. He'd prepared every document necessary for the Saint-Ferdinand Killer case. The forms were filled, reports filed. Should the pressure get too intense, the inspector could, in a matter of hours, have Finnegan, the evidence against him, and everything relating to the case taken out of his hands. Short of a decorative bow, everything was ready to be wrapped up.

But Crowley didn't want to let Finnegan go. Not yet. Sure, there would be consequences to his delay. Reprimands for mishandling the case. Maybe even a demotion. But whatever price he had to pay to maintain his access to Finnegan was worth it. Anything to get his hands on his prize.

But time was running out.

"Ma'am!" Crowley slammed his broken hand on the desk, paying another toll for his short temper. Channeling the pain, he continued. "We are concluding our investigation and will issue a full statement when we're done. But we're a very small department, and every minute I waste with a reporter too dumb to understand what *no* means is a minute I ain't getting things done here. Is there anything in what I just said that needs further explanation?"

The woman fell silent. Crowley considered that she might have hung up and was about to do the same when she finally replied.

"No, Inspector Crowley. Can we expect your office to get in touch with us when you are ready to issue your statement?"

"Yes, Ms. Shepherd." The inspector had to admit he was surprised. He had expected her to either be completely cowed or explode in self-righteous rage. Either way would have allowed him to finish the conversation. "I'll make sure someone gets in touch with you."

"Inspector?" she said, maintaining her measured tone. "Make it quick. The world is watching."

Then she hung up. Twice this week, Crowley had been put in his place by out-of-towners. He was not used to having his authority questioned or being on the losing end of a conversation. Still, it was all a small price to pay if his larger gamble paid off.

"Boss." Lieutenant Bélanger's voice cut through the inspector's thoughts. "What *are* we still looking for?"

Crowley had been having his staff investigate every little report that happened to make its way to the office. From Gaston's claims of strange lights waking up his dogs at night to reports of missing pets to drunken tales of ghosts prowling Main Street after dark, they were checking anything that might lead him to the Craftsmen's god. Anyone not following a lead had been assigned to keep an eye on Cicero's Circus.

"I'm just being prudent, Lieutenant. We caught our serial killer and got lazy. Then Gabrielle LaForest and the Ludwig boy get murdered. I'm not letting any more people get killed." Brad's body had been found yesterday, having been stuffed into several garbage bags and then dropped inside the drugstore Dumpster. The corpse was in such terrible condition that the time of death had yet to be determined.

"How many crazed killers do you think live in Saint-Ferdinand, anyway?" The question had an uncharacteristically sarcastic tone to it. Crowley was about to reprimand Bélanger but then saw that everyone on staff had stopped what they were doing to hear the inspector's answer.

"We got both our guys," the lieutenant continued. "I'm not one to tell you how to do your job, Stephen, but why aren't we gathering evidence on McKenzie?"

Because he didn't do it, the inspector thought. In fact, if they couldn't bring formal charges against Randy soon, they'd have to let him go. His alibi was rock solid; he'd been working at the hospital in Sherbrooke, over an hour's drive away, when Gabrielle had been killed. Plenty of people had seen and interacted with him there. The only reason McKenzie was still being kept in jail was the Ludwig boy. Crowley could only keep him incarcerated until the time of death was narrowed down. Sooner or later he'd have to let Randy walk.

"You're right, Matt," Crowley finally said, and sighed in agreement. "Let's get a warrant to search Randy's house and office. Hopefully we'll find something that'll help us hand that case to the courts faster."

Or enough proof that I'll have to release the bastard. Putting McKenzie in jail had backfired horribly. It took a while for

Crowley to realize it, but as long as there was no suspect in Gabrielle LaForest's murder, he could use his staff to look for clues of the god's whereabouts. But now that Randy's guilt was being called into question, anytime the inspector ordered Matt, Gary, or any of the other officers under him to investigate something else, he could see doubt in their eyes. Soon his staff would become useless to him.

"I'll start the paperwork, then," Bélanger said.

Crowley didn't bother acknowledging his lieutenant. It was moments like these that made him regret his course of action. Chasing after gods had been Marguerite's life. When she left, he'd grudgingly taken up the quest, using her old notes as a guide. He was out of his element. Crowley didn't know a thing about religion, magic, or miracles. If it hadn't been for people like Peterson, McKenzie, and Cicero, he'd probably still be ignorant of what really went on. Wouldn't that be grand? Unfortunately, he could no longer walk away from the things he'd seen or ignore the things he'd heard or forget the miracles he'd been promised.

It had all been too much to take on by himself, and so Crowley had surrounded himself with others. Ambitious, idiotic followers who did nothing to help him on his quest. All they brought to the table was an endless stream of demands. Everyone wanted to see the god, yet, after all these years, even he wasn't sure what he expected to gain from it. Power? *It grants wishes, like a genie,* he'd been told. Fifteen years ago that promise held much appeal, but after a decade as chief inspector, wielding as much authority as anyone could desire, he'd lost the thirst.

Perhaps that was why he'd never caught the killer that was right under his nose. Maybe, when all was said and done, he preferred things the way they were. Could it be that somehow he had known that by apprehending his killer, he'd sabotage everything?

It didn't matter. The hands were dealt now and it was time to play the game. Crowley's career, reputation, and what was left of his family hinged on this next play. If all went well, every problem he had would be solved. Should he fail and not find the god before it escaped, his whole life would topple like a house of cards.

Crowley's train of thought was interrupted when his office door slammed shut. The inspector was not a man used to intrusions, and he went from introspective to full-on furious by the time he'd spun his chair around.

His visitor stood before his desk. Her plump fists were propped stiffly on her waist in an almost cartoonish accusatory pose. A frown of disdain split her red face while perfectly coiffed, fading blond hair was held in a loose bun at the back of her head.

"Beatrice," the inspector said. He didn't bother to conceal his displeasure with Mrs. Bergeron's presence in his office. "What can I do for you?"

Crowley could have had the woman removed with the push of the intercom button. It was tempting. As his blood pressure rose, so did the pain in his hand. Dealing with William Bergeron was hassle enough, but when he sent his wife, the inspector knew the fat drunk meant business. Beatrice was less emotional, more calculating. She'd dealt with being married to an alcoholic, building no less than four successful businesses in town while her husband took the credit. To top it off, she had survived a troubled pregnancy only to have her beloved child snatched away at the tender age of eight. There was nothing the inspector could throw at her that would dissuade the woman. It was best to weather the storm.

"What the hell are you doing here, Stephen?"

"I work here," he answered, flexing his wounded fist. The pain helped him to stay calm.

"You should be in Sherbrooke, making sure Harry Peterson makes a full and quick recovery."

"He's in a hospital, Beatrice. I think he's in good hands."

"Then bring him his canvas and paints." The big woman slammed her hand on the inspector's desk for emphasis, her fingers like five malformed sausages covered in too much jewelry. "Or find someone else to do the painting."

There was no one else. The inspector knew it, and there was no reason for Beatrice to think otherwise. Even Peterson wasn't ideal. His birds were certainly impressive, but he wasn't good enough to paint a person back to life. Not like Amanda had been, but she was long dead.

The Bergerons had always been obsessed with finding a way to fix their daughter's poor health. Now that she was gone, they'd become fanatical. Beatrice didn't care if what she was demanding was impossible; all she knew was how to demand it.

"I think you should give up on Peterson . . . or anyone else to bring back Audrey," the inspector said coolly.

"Don't you dare go back on your promises, Stephen." By her countenance, Crowley might as well have killed Beatrice's daughter himself. "Without William and me, you would have nothing. Our contacts built your career. We gave you this job so you could do what needed to be done when the time was right.

"Well, that time is now, Inspector. You made promises to a lot of important people. You promised *me* my daughter! That is one obligation you don't want to back out of, Crowley." She spat his name out like it was sour milk.

Despite the frustration of the fat woman vomiting threats at him, Stephen felt calm. Relaxing his wounded fist for the first time in days, he took a moment to savor the taste of serenity. Then, keeping his eyes fixed on the overbearing sow who had dragged herself into his office, the inspector slowly leaned back in his chair. He could feel Beatrice growing more frustrated with every second of his silence. Her plump face was shifting to an ever-darker shade of red, and her breathing was accelerating to the point where she had to keep her mouth agape. Crowley was tempted to see if she'd fall over dead from a heart attack.

"I owe you nothing," the inspector said, then continued on before she could interrupt. "Before I brought the Sandmen's history to your attention, you and all the other beggars in this village had nothing. I blew the doors off your worldview. I figured out all that bullshit about the town's past, the Craftsmen, Peterson's paintings, and whatever weird stuff the McKenzies are into.

"So you listen real good, Beatrice, and make sure you tell your drunk of a husband what I'm telling you: back the hell off. You can either let me do my goddamn job and maybe, *maybe*, get your girl back, or you can go back to mourning your only child and living out your dull, ordinary lives. Forget the stupid painting and forget about Peterson. If you let me get on with what I gotta do, you won't need them."

Beatrice Bergeron closed her mouth, her lower lip still quivering with anger.

"Now," he said, savoring his next words, "why don't you drag your fat ass home to think that over? If I don't hear from you, I'll assume you've agreed to my point of view. Or not. Frankly, I don't care."

Inspector Stephen Crowley didn't bother knocking on the door. Partly because this was his station. He was lord and master of these offices and had no reason to ask permission before entering any of them, even the ones that were being loaned to outsiders. But the other part, the part he could barely admit to himself, was the very real chance that he might chicken out if he didn't barge in.

Regardless of his justifications, his rude behavior did not go unnoticed by Dr. Hazelwood. In fact, she almost jumped out of her skin when he entered. Her high-pitched scream was followed by a mumbled string of profanities as she clutched her chest.

"God dammit, Stephen!"

"Are we on a first-name basis now?" he said in lieu of an apology, stepping into the cramped office to take a seat.

"We are if you're not going to bother knocking, Inspector."

"I'm sorry. Didn't mean to startle you, but I need your help with something."

With care equal to the brazenness of his entrance, Crowley closed the door behind him, making sure to lock it. The click on the handle was met by a raised eyebrow on Erica's part. Being shut in with the intimidating inspector was not her idea of a comfortable situation. His attitude and behavior had become increasingly erratic and belligerent during the short time she'd known him. Every symptom pointed to an overwhelming amount of stress and an imminent psychological breakdown. She half-suspected he was here to ask her for some kind of prescription to help him cope, something that was not in her power to do.

"I'll do what I can, Inspector, but I'm not sure there's much I can do to assist you."

Crowley covered his face with both hands, sighing loudly. He struggled for a moment to find his balance and unearth the proper words. What he was about to do, he'd never done before. It wasn't in his character and it made him uncomfortable, but after days, perhaps even years, of avoiding the issue, he'd come to an impasse.

Removing his hands, he locked eyes with Erica. She had a look of concern on her face. Concern and a little disgust.

"What happened to your hand?"

He'd forgotten about the wound, the pain having somehow become part of him. The burning, tearing sensation of moving his broken fingers fueled his anger, painting anew the portrait of his goals.

"Oh, this is nothing."

Who was he kidding? The bandage was so soaked with dried blood that it had come to resemble a red, rigid cast. Flowers of red with brown-tipped petals spread all over the gauze that wrapped around his fingers. He'd have to get it looked at sooner rather than later; otherwise, the bones would heal wrong and surgery would be necessary to fix the damage. There was no time now, however.

"I might be 'just' a psychologist, but I took enough medicine to know that this isn't 'nothing.' Who bandaged this?"

She walked around the desk to take a closer look at the damaged extremity. Crowley made no attempt to stop her as Erica carefully inspected the dressing. The inspector had wrapped the injury himself, with only the first aid kit from his car and his own left hand. As shoddy jobs went, it was one for the books.

"I did." He sounded like Daniel when the boy did something stupid.

"Wait here," Dr. Hazelwood muttered before unlocking the door and letting herself out.

Long minutes passed while Erica was gone. It was late in the evening, and the station was mostly empty. That had been part of his plan, to get the doctor while she was alone. No witnesses that way. No one to hear or interrupt them. It had taken a while for him to work up the courage to do this, and just as he had the young woman trapped, he'd let her simply walk out.

Crowley looked around the office. In the few days since her arrival, Dr. Hazelwood had turned the small room into a cozy work space. Copies of every report he'd allowed her to have were stacked into a pile on the corner of her desk. Other folders, neatly arranged by color and brimming with notes, bore the names of various villagers. From memory alone, the inspector could tell that they were all related to Sam Finnegan's victims. The thickest file of all was labeled PENELOPE LAFOREST.

The office door opened again. "Hold up your hand," Erica ordered as she walked back in.

Stephen did as instructed but kept his eyes fixed on hers. She pulled a pair of scissors out of the well-stocked first aid kit she'd found downstairs. With both care and frustration, she removed the bandage from his hand. The pain of dried blood being pulled and ripped from the raw wound underneath made Crowley draw a noisy breath between his teeth.

"This isn't why I wanted to see you, Doctor," the inspector said, gathering his courage again. In all his years of chasing murderers and gods, he'd never faltered like this. "I . . . need someone to talk to."

Erica looked up from her handiwork to study her new patient. It wasn't the hand that needed mending most. That was a wound of the flesh. As she slowly finished removing the blood-caked gauze, watching Crowley flinch with every pull on the wound, the doctor realized what he meant. Crowley needed her services as a psychologist.

Erica finished removing the old bandage, curling her nose at the smell of pus and infection. She stood and pushed the door closed. This time, she was the one who turned the lock. The inspector appreciated the gesture of having his sense of privacy respected.

"All right," she said, and walked back to the desk, taking out some fresh gauze and sterile solution. "What would you like to talk about?"

"Everything I say here stays here?"

"Patient-doctor confidentiality. Everything you say here stays here."

A sigh escaped his lungs once more. The doctor began to clean his wound, giving him time to gather his thoughts.

"I have a . . . very strict set of priorities, Doctor. I've always thought that everything I was doing was for the ultimate benefit of the town and above that, my family. Seems like the harder I work, though, the worse things get. How is that possible?"

Even cleaned up, the wound on Inspector Crowley's hand was terrible to look at. His middle and ring fingers stood at odd angles to each other. Not only had the bones been pulled aside, but the swollen, damaged flesh gave his fingers the look of two sausages. The gash between the fingers was no better. It had filled up with fluid, and the palm of his hand was a deep purple with a sick yellowish tint at the edges. The bones would need to be set properly, the wound disinfected.

"Well, you haven't been getting much, if any, sleep. That'll lead to impaired judgment and manic episodes. Think of it as a DUI; except, instead of a vehicle you're driving, it's your whole life."

"It ain't just the sleep."

"Okay, what else is there then?"

The inspector winced as Erica put some antiseptic ointment on his wound. It wouldn't do much, but it would slow down the infection. "I think my son hates me."

"What makes you think that?"

"Did Finnegan tell you what . . . what he thought was in that cave?"

"It's in my report," said Erica, wrapping a new bandage around Crowley's fingers. The clean, dry gauze felt good over the freshly washed hand. It wasn't just wrapped like a child's art project, either. The psychologist knew what she was doing, and the bandage was both tight and tidy. By the time she was done, the dressing was as immaculate and white as snow. "He rambled about some kind of god. 'A god of hate and death.' I told Randy about it, but he made it pretty clear he couldn't discuss that aspect of the case."

She was fishing. Perhaps she thought a tired and wounded Inspector Crowley would be more amenable to divulging information than a paranoid Randall McKenzie. If so, she was out of luck.

"Right. Well, I don't know about a god, but there's something in that cave. *Was* something. Something dangerous to the community. Maybe even more dangerous than Finnegan."

"And you can't tell me what this hypothetical threat is?"

The inspector shook his head.

"You should know that, if you start to sound too crazy, I will look into getting you some forced leave," she said, half-joking.

"Fair enough. But humor me. This hypothetical threat, as you put it: I have a duty to stop it, right? To do whatever it takes to stop it? I should expect my boy to understand that, right?"

The inspector wasn't asking for her moral judgment; he was asking her permission to chase this boogeyman instead of attending to his family. It was hard for Dr. Hazelwood to accept that there was still something for the Saint-Ferdinand police department to chase down, something so important that Crowley would knowingly put his son aside. However, she didn't know all the details of the case. Long before the inspector had started really going off the rails, he'd made it clear that he suspected one or more accomplices, and she'd seen where Gabrielle LaForest's body was found. A god of hate and death sounded stupid, but a cult that believed in human sacrifice? That was much more likely.

"That's up to you, Stephen," she said, making a point to add what the inspector thought was a touch of familiarity by calling him by his first name. "My recommendation would be to get some sleep and then take a good hard look at what your moral obligations are. In most situations like this, I find that it's less about picking one priority, and more about figuring out a good balance between the two."

"I have people who depend on me. Not just Daniel. I don't know that balance—*ow!*"

The doctor had just flicked her finger directly at Crowley's wound. Anger flared up in the inspector's eyes. Withering rage boiled up as his face turned a deep shade of red. Erica may not have been as accustomed to these flights of temper as Randy was, but she quickly realized she might have gone too far. Still, she soldiered on.

"Stephen." Like a tightrope walker, she balanced her tone between soothing and commanding. "Listen to yourself. Get your hand looked at. Get some sleep. Figure it out in the morning."

A tense moment passed before Crowley finally flexed his wounded hand into a fist. No doubt this would exacerbate the damage and reopen his wound yet again, but it was the only tool in his current arsenal that would let him focus.

"You . . . You're probably right."

He stood, still flexing his broken hand, and walked out of the office.

VENUS

"MY MOM THINKS we're dating."

It was an odd thing to announce, especially after a quarter hour of silence. Venus regretted saying it as soon as the words left her mouth, but she couldn't bear the quiet any longer.

She had told Daniel that they couldn't visit her shed. He wanted to see the god, to have tangible proof of what had made his father become so obsessed. But Venus wouldn't allow it. Not with her mother being so curious about her activities. The risk of her parents stumbling upon the thing in the shed was already too high. So far, every visit to the god's prison had come at a cost. A life, a near-death experience, or, in Venus's case, something more personal and existential. Daniel appeared to understand, but he remained curious. His deluge of questions and her refusal to answer had quickly killed the conversation.

"Oh?" He sounded amused by the comment. The reaction of a boy who had gotten used to that kind of thing.

Venus felt foolish. Daniel Crowley was almost two years her senior, well respected, and an accomplished young athlete. He was handsome and popular in a nonthreatening way that appealed to the opposite sex. He was also currently dating a gorgeous girl from Sherbrooke who was on her way to a prosperous university career. Although he wasn't known to mock or bully other teens,

Venus knew how easy it would be to ridicule her comment. But Daniel didn't do that.

"I guess it makes sense from her point of view," he said, lowering the volume on his car radio. "We've never hung out, and I bet your other boyfriends don't have their licenses yet. Suddenly I'm picking you up to go who knows where without your usual friends in tow?"

He turned to her. His eyes were a piercing blue.

"Yeah. Makes sense." Venus felt awkward, but it was a good kind of awkward. Normal embarrassment over normal problems. She'd always thought movie characters were idiots for letting their petty issues cloud their judgment or distract them while they were dealing with alien invasions, giant monsters, or whatever other apocalyptic scenario was going on. Now she understood. While taking refuge from cataclysmic events physically, it was natural to seek comfort emotionally, like she was doing right now. Realizing that, she wished they were dating, if only to feel normal.

"Look on the bright side, though," Daniel said as if he'd somehow read her thoughts. "Means your mom's been spying on you."

"How is that a bright side?" she asked, frowning.

"Don't you keep complaining that your parents don't pay attention to you?"

He was right. Virginie had never before bothered to question the relationships she had with her friends. Venus had slept over at Abraham's house several times, and never a word was spoken about it. Something had changed. Venus had always been envious of those with "normal" parent-child relationships. Penny and Gabrielle had often been the main focus of her envy, but it was the relationship between Inspector Crowley and his son for which she wished. Everyone in town knew the Crowley boys were best friends. Yet the inspector was also intensely protective of his son. Venus had always imagined theirs to be the perfect household.

"What about you?" she asked. "How are you handling . . . all this?"

The question was more direct than she would have preferred. Penny would have come at it from an angle instead of jumping right to the point, but subtlety wasn't Venus's forte.

"I'm handling it."

If her goal had been to turn the tables, it was a success, but she was disappointed to see Daniel clam up so suddenly. He grew silent and taciturn, giving the road his full attention.

"You can talk to me, y'know," she said, though she was unsure where she wanted the discussion to go. "You clearly know more about me than I gave you credit for. I feel like I should return the favor."

Venus had never thought of herself as particularly empathic. She was smart, of that there was no doubt. Observant, when the subject held her interest. But gauging the mood of others was a skill at which she was mediocre. Yet she could tell from Daniel Crowley's silence, his furrowed brow, and his white knuckles on the steering wheel, that he was grieving. As far as he was concerned, he'd lost his father to this Sandmen cult a long time ago. She could only guess at his feelings of betrayal, confusion, and uncertainty.

"What do you see when you look at me, McKenzie?"

It felt like a trick question. Venus had never really hung out with Daniel. They'd spoken a few times at school and she knew a little about him because Saint-Ferdinand was such a small place, but they weren't friends.

"You're the star quarterback at school. I mean, whatever the hockey equivalent is, but you know what I mean. You're the cool guy. You have the cool car and the hot, smart girlfriend. I mean, I don't want to reduce you to a stereotype, but you're . . . you know, the guy! I don't know. I'm messing this up. Forget anything I just said."

"No, no! You're right. I am that guy. Or I was during the school year. Now? My dad's going insane, I'm pretty sure I'm not getting my summer job, and my girlfriend stood me up and won't return my calls after I ignored her for a week. I'm pretty sure we're broken up. It's not just all these murders and gods and ghosts. I'm messing everything up."

"Welcome to the club. The only requirement is being a complete mess." There it was, the patented Venus McKenzie lack of tact and empathy.

"Ha! You're right. This is a disaster." He laughed, nervously at first, but it built to a cathartic guffaw. "I don't know, McKenzie, at the end of the day, all I want to do is the right thing, y'know?"

Venus let the comment sink in. It was an awful cliché but exactly what she expected from Daniel Crowley. The star quarterback. That guy.

"After all," he continued, "that's kinda how he raised me to be."

A symphony of sounds wove together in harmonious purpose. The regular beeping of the heart monitor was supported by the constant hissing of a respirator. The careful ear could pick up the rhythmic drip of an IV while garbled PA messages served as occasional vocals. The music played was the beat by which Harry Peterson was slowly marching his way back to the land of the living.

Venus and Daniel had been allowed to go in, although visiting hours were coming to an end. The nurse at the front desk of the intensive care unit had asked them to wake up the huge farm boy who was sleeping there. He'd have to leave for the night and come back to see his father the next morning.

As far as Venus knew, Abraham didn't have anywhere to go in Sherbrooke. He'd spent the previous night sleeping in the waiting area of the emergency room and would probably do the same again tonight.

Her friend had been vague about the circumstances that had brought his father to the hospital. All she knew was that

Abraham's father had had some kind of respiratory failure and had been taken to Sherbrooke by ambulance. When she asked if it was the cancer, Abraham had been a little evasive before settling on a noncommittal "yeah."

She'd have preferred to be here sooner. Ideally with Penny in tow. They both knew about Mr. Peterson's condition and had expected a day would come when they would need to be there for Abraham. But the plan had always been to do it as a group. A trio of friends, supporting one another.

Light from the hallway illuminated Abraham's large body; the boy was sleeping on a chair too small for him. He was awkwardly slumped to the side, his head rolled back and arms hanging to the ground. Awake or not, the farm boy had never worried much about how graceful he looked. A tender smile made its way to Venus's lips as she moved to wake up her friend.

Suddenly her ears noticed a change in the symphony. The accompanying background noise of the respirator had ceased. Her senses on edge, Venus saw a shadow lurking next to Mr. Peterson's bed. And the shadow saw her.

Thankfully, *this* shadow was human. A short man of flesh and blood, wearing gray denim pants and a leather jacket. He had black hair and dark, leathery skin that smelled of ash. He bolted from the corner and made for the door, not realizing that Venus was accompanied and that her companion was an accomplished athlete.

Daniel did not hesitate. Without thinking, he tackled the intruder to the ground. His shoulder, its muscles hard from years of physical training, caught the small man in the upper chest, sending him bouncing to the floor. Lungs empty and his rib cage in agony, the stranger couldn't even cry out in pain. Worse, he'd landed near Abraham's feet, waking the huge boy immediately.

"Abe! Grab him."

Before even getting up from his chair, the farm boy reached down and gathered a handful of the stranger's jacket in his meaty paw. The man wasn't going anywhere.

Meanwhile, Venus tried to figure out what to do about Mr. Peterson's respirator. Quickly realizing that she had no idea how to restart the device, or even if that was the right course of action, she half-crawled, half-leaped over the bed to push the call button.

"Help!" she screamed.

The reaction was immediate. Whether the nurse's station had received her call, heard her scream, or was already aware that something was wrong with Harry's vitals, it didn't matter. Someone was rushing down the corridor with a cart.

During these scant few seconds, Abraham dragged the doubled-over body of the stranger out the door, passing by her and Daniel. A nurse quickly rushed in to take his place, questioning Venus.

"What happened?" she asked.

"I . . . I don't know," Venus croaked. "Someone turned off the respirator, I think."

Her words were lost in the crush of people rushing in. Another nurse, then a doctor, then more nurses. They all started exchanging medical jargon. The first nurse applied a breathing mask to Mr. Peterson's face. She squeezed and released the large bladder attached to the device at a steady rhythm, pumping air in and out of his lungs. A doctor was fussing with one of the many machines next to the bed, trying to bring the life-sustaining music back into harmony.

Shoved to the periphery, Venus watched, horrified. What had been meant to be a short visit on the way to her uncle's office, checking in with her friend to offer her support, had turned into a potential tragedy.

"What the hell do you think you're doing?" Abraham yelled from the hallway.

He had pinned the stranger to the wall, holding him a few inches off the ground by his fistful of jacket. Abe's left arm was pulled back, hand balled into an enormous fist shaking with rage. Venus had never seen her friend like this. All six feet and seven inches of him were tense with fury. His face had become unrecognizable. The usually soft features with a bit of a dull edge to them were contorted into an animalistic snarl. His eyes bulged from their sockets and the veins in his neck pushed out of his skin. If he were to follow through with his swing, his fist would crush the short man's skull into a pulpy mess.

Gasping for breath, the stranger lifted his head to form an answer.

"Abe . . . it's me . . . "

The farm boy blinked in recognition. "Ezekiel?"

Just like that, Abraham was completely disarmed. As he set the man down, he transformed back to his soft-spoken self.

"God . . . dammit . . . Abe . . . I make a living with . . . these lungs," he croaked.

"I'm so sorry, Ezekiel. Are you okay?" the large boy asked.

"I'll be fine. Ribs heal fast, right?"

Venus and Daniel approached carefully. The situation felt volatile. There was good reason to attract as little attention as possible, but at the same time, what they'd witnessed couldn't be ignored.

She put a hand on her friend's shoulder. "Abe? That man tried to kill your father."

"Him? Nah!" Abraham said with confidence, going so far as to throw his arm around the small man's shoulders. The stranger winced. "This is Ezekiel! He works with the circus. He's one of Dad's oldest friends. I've known him for years."

The enthusiasm and confidence drained from his voice the more he talked, to the point where he seemed to doubt himself completely by the time he reached his last word.

"Right?" he finished.

"Actually . . . ," Ezekiel said. "She's right."

Daniel stepped forward, ready to intervene should Abraham decide to murder Ezekiel for what he had almost done. Venus waved him back, fearing that his interference would make matters worse.

"Why would you do that?" the farm boy said.

"It's what he wants. Dying in Saint-Ferdinand . . . Harry deserves better than that."

"But he's not dead yet!" Venus said.

"Exactly," Ezekiel said. "He's going to get better. He'll go home to Saint-Ferdinand. He'll die there. I can't allow that."

Daniel put a hand gently on Venus's back, trying to nudge her down the corridor while giving a solid pat on Abraham's shoulder to encourage him to do the same, but the Peterson boy wouldn't have it.

"What is he doing here?" Abraham asked Venus.

"He's . . . my ride," she explained, signaling for him to follow. Again, the Peterson boy didn't budge.

"Your ride? Inspector Crowley's the asshole who beat up my dad! I'm not following orders from this son of a bitch."

"I'm just trying to help, man," Daniel said. "If you don't want your friend here to get cuffed and sent to jail, we have to get out of here."

There was a tense moment. Abraham wasn't an idiot, nor was he usually controlled by his emotions, but if there was any similarity between him and Daniel, it was how close they were with their fathers. Venus could tell it was a struggle for her friend to keep his belligerent urges under control. He'd already managed to suppress them once, and it was to his credit that he'd succeeded in doing it again.

"All right. I'm sorry." He shook his head. "You're right. It's just—"

Daniel gave the farm boy a light punch on the shoulder. "It's cool, man. I get it. I know it doesn't help or change anything, but my dad's been acting crazy these days. I don't know why he'd do that to your old man."

"I hate to break up this touching moment," Ezekiel said, and wheezed, still clutching his ribs, "but can we move along?"

Venus nodded. "We can go to my uncle's office. It's in another building, but we'll have some privacy there. And I need to pick something up."

"Shit," said Daniel. "I gotta go."

Venus turned to see that he had his phone out and was staring at the screen. His face was pale and his shoulders were slumped. There was a slight tremble in his lower lip as he kept his mouth agape.

"Dan?" she asked, worried that yet another crisis had emerged. "You okay, Dan?"

"No," he said. "I'll . . . I'll catch up with you in Saint-Ferdinand."

"Dan! You can't just leave."

"I'm sorry. I have to." He started to walk then jog away in the other direction. "Find me when you get back to town!"

"Daniel!" she yelled after him, tempted to try to catch up. "You're my ride home!"

RANDY

BOOKS.

In the short time he'd been jailed, Randall McKenzie had built a temple of them. Most of the tomes he'd read twice, some even three times. After all, there wasn't much else to do in prison. In fact, aside from his brother, Paul, Randy had received no further visitors besides Jackie, who brought him his meals.

They'd chat for a bit, mostly discussing some of the minor happenings around the village. On the second day, she showed him a rash on her upper arm, which he diagnosed as an allergic reaction. The doctor recommended a topical cream, and after a few days she didn't mention it again. Banal, boring stuff. But no matter how mundane, it was still better than attempting conversation with Sam Finnegan.

The madman had only been capable of holding a coherent dialogue on a few rare occasions. Usually when other people dropped by, such as Venus or Paul. Otherwise, the Saint-Ferdinand Killer kept to himself. Either quietly weeping or occasionally humming loudly. It was best not to disturb him, as it usually brought on his more musical moods.

There was no television and no Internet access. Randy had requested some notes and documents from his office, but Crowley had categorically denied him. So in the end, all he had left were the books.

These had been picked by Stephen Crowley. They tended to be a hodgepodge of bad cop mysteries, the occasional horror novel, and books on religion. Occasionally, an odd selection would make its way into the piles that were brought to him. One was an ancient book on gothic architecture. Another, a huge atlas of the United Kingdom, with details about every castle, abbey, and pile of stone on the island. These were not the inspector's books. These had belonged to his wife. Randy could tell because they were all annotated with scribbles in an elegant penmanship far beyond Crowley's ability.

Despite his boredom, it was not a welcome sound to hear the cellblock door open so late in the evening. Randy had run out of imagined scenarios in which someone came to announce that the threat in his brother's shed was neutralized. The only news he could think to receive was of more deaths. And the only way he could see Crowley releasing him was if the inspector had found a way to force the medical examiner to help him. In either case, it would be symptomatic that the village was tilting ever more toward its doom.

"Randall?"

The woman's voice preceded her. He heard her footsteps coming down the short flight of steps toward the cells, their hesitance all but confirming his worries.

"Erica," he croaked.

The psychologist finally turned the corner. She'd lost a significant amount of her radiance since coming to Saint-Ferdinand. The darkness of the town had taken its toll, stripping away her vitality and denying her sleep for days. She hadn't been born here and wasn't used to having secrets and mysteries as her bedfellows.

Right behind his old student was Venus's best friend, Penelope LaForest. The daughter of the woman Randy was accused of murdering in the most gruesome fashion imaginable. As one could imagine, the young lady had no joy in her face.

"How are you doing, Randy?" Erica asked.

"I'm as fine as can be expected. She shouldn't be here, Erica."

The medical examiner wondered if his niece's friend had received his message. If so, shouldn't she be in Sherbrooke, retrieving his notes? Or maybe Penny had brought them to him?

"Actually, I'm the one who asked to speak with you, Dr. McKenzie," Penny said.

"I know it's unorthodox," Erica added, "but Penelope wanted to confront you, as it were, to help her process—"

"I lied," the girl interrupted, stepping forward to stand a few inches from the bars. "Randy didn't kill my mother."

She was speaking to Erica but staring down the medical examiner. Sitting at the back of his cell, obscured by columns of books and magazines, Randall McKenzie frowned.

"I'm sorry, Dr. Hazelwood," Penny continued. "I didn't want to trick you, but you were my only way in here. And I have to talk to Dr. McKenzie. Preferably alone?"

Erica was stunned. Penny was a smart kid, but she'd never shown much in the way of guile. She simply didn't have the malicious bent for it, but clearly the talent was there. Dr. Hazelwood tightened her lips.

"No. I can't in good conscience leave you here."

"But he didn't kill my mother. I'll be fine."

"You've been anything but fine since the moment I told you about your mother, Penelope." Erica was adamant. "If you knew Randy was innocent, why didn't you say anything? He'd be free by now. We could tell Inspector Crowley, and he could be out of that cell before lunch!"

Randy could almost make himself believe that she cared for him as more than a friend, but he knew better. "Wouldn't have helped," he told her. "Stephen wants me where he can find me. He wants me contained."

"And he wants you away from Cicero's Circus," said Penny.

The medical examiner stood up from his cot. Careful not to knock over any books, he made his way to the cell door, both in order to lower his voice and to better see his visitors.

"What do you know of Cicero's Circus?"

"I know the owner needs to speak with you," Penny said. "And I know how to get you there."

The offer was intriguing. Randy could see that Erica, however, disapproved of the discussion.

"If you need to speak to someone, Randy, I can bring you a phone. Or better yet, get you released!"

"You don't understand," the medical examiner explained, shaking his head. "Crowley's been controlling everything that comes in or leaves here. I don't know what you're planning, Penelope, but I doubt there's a way to get me to see Cicero. I have a pen and paper. I could write down a few questions for him . . ."

He trailed off as Penny lifted her hands, showing him an object she'd held at her side this whole time. Audrey's bear. Still stained with soil from her grave and still wearing that red felt hat. The nails he had inserted into Audrey's feet were anchors, so that her soul couldn't be ripped away or dissipate. The nails in her eyes allowed her to see clearly into the world of the living. The bear, though, that was supposed to keep her from wandering. Forcing her spirit to remain near her grave so they could find it later and, ostensibly, bring it back.

Wherever the bear was, Audrey's spirit wasn't far.

"You buried this with her, didn't you?" Penny said.

Erica was shocked, but Randy paid her no mind.

"I had to."

"I know," the girl said in a voice of true understanding. "She told me."

"What are you two talking about?" Erica said, unable to follow the discussion.

"Erica . . . you should go," Randy said. "The longer you stay, the more in danger you are."

"Randall, you know I can't, from an ethical standpoint, leave this girl with you or him!"

The psychologist nodded toward the neighboring cell. There, Sam Finnegan had quietly approached the bars. He leaned his forehead against the metal rods, listening to their conversation.

Neither Randy nor Penny had seen him creep up, and while the medical examiner was surprised, Penny was even less comfortable. She might have been confident about Randy's innocence in her mother's death, but five years prior, when she'd lost her father, it was to the Saint-Ferdinand Killer.

Even so, the young woman managed to stay composed. Letting out a strained sigh to suppress both anger and tears, she continued.

"Dr. McKenzie," Penny said, "for all I know, I'm having a psychotic breakdown. I feel better with her around."

"You're perfectly sane, sweetheart," Finnegan said warmly. "I should know."

"You! Do not get to call me 'sweetheart'!"

"All right. I'm taking you out of here." Erica reached to take the girl by the arm. The teenager shrugged her off, focusing once more on Randy. He could see in her eyes, and from the way she shoved the stuffed bear between the bars and into his hands, that she wasn't beseeching him as a doctor. It was the necromancer she needed.

"She told me she had a way to help!" she said. "That there was a way to kill that . . . thing. She told me *I* could bring your soul to Cicero."

Randy took the bear out of Penelope's hands. With delicate care, he held it in front of him. It felt cold to the touch. He could see, in a way no one else had so far, that the toy wasn't completely "here." Part of it remained in Audrey's grave. In a fundamental way, Theodore Francis Bear, Audrey's favorite toy, was still very much with her.

In a voice so soft as to be inaudible, the amateur necromancer began to recite a chant. Something he'd taught himself along with the ritual that bound Audrey to the toy. The song had the rhythm of a nursery rhyme, but the words meant nothing to modern ears.

"Randy . . . ," Finnegan warned from his cell. "Do you know what you're doing?"

The medical examiner continued his chant. With every word, the cellblock grew a little colder. As if the bear was bait, he reeled in the spirit hooked to the stuffed toy. With every degree the temperature fell, his breath became easier to see and the ghost of Audrey Bergeron drew closer.

Erica stared in disbelief as she saw her old friend and tutor work his clumsy magic. From the corner of his eye, Randy saw her rising discomfort and fear. But it was too late to wish she had listened to him and left.

"No, Sam," he said after finishing his ritual. "None of us know what we're doing."

VENUS

VENUS WATCHED DANIEL walk then jog down the corridor. For a moment she regretted having confided so many of her problems to him. So much about the god that she had trapped. She didn't know the inspector's son that well. Who was it that could call him and make him leave with so little of an explanation? Was he going back to his father to report everything he knew? Had there been another death in Saint-Ferdinand? What if the god had gotten loose? But surely he would have said something if that were the case.

They walked down the corridor, making their way back to the first floor and toward her uncle's office. Ezekiel, still clutching his ribs, kept giving her knowing looks that made her uneasy.

"You must be Venus McKenzie."

Venus turned a curious eye toward Abraham, silently asking if he'd been talking about her. A slight shake of his head was all the answer she needed.

"Have we met?" she said to the circus worker.

"I've met your parents and I knew your grandparents. Particularly your grandfather Neil?"

Again, her grandfather's name had come up. The elusive and very much deceased Neil McKenzie. Spoken about with disdain by Venus's mother, with fear and respect by her father, and with hunger by the god in her shed. Neil had been a looming shadow over the family: seldom mentioned, except on the rare occasions when Paul would argue with her uncle Randy.

"You know, you're not the first stranger to mention my grandfather recently."

Ezekiel gave her a thin smile and then nodded toward the exit. The trio walked outside into the warm night. They passed a woman helping a limping child into the hospital. Across the parking lot, they could see the flashing lights of an ambulance on its way to deliver a new patient.

"There should be a statue of your grandfather on Main Street." Ezekiel took out a pack of cigarettes. A particularly foul-smelling American brand that Venus recognized from the occasional tourists who went through town. "He was a great man, after a fashion."

"I never knew him. I'm told that's not a great loss."

"Well, if I have to be truthful, he probably wouldn't have had much use for you. Never had much use for anyone. He was a very focused man."

"Focused on what?" Abraham asked, wrinkling his nose as Ezekiel lit up his cigarette and took a long pull from it.

"Hunting lions," he said, then exhaled.

"What 'lions'?" Venus asked.

"Maybe things like the god in your backyard," guessed Abraham.

Ezekiel paused mid-drag, his eyes bulging out in surprise. He followed it up with a weak attempt at keeping his cool and composure, but ultimately failed. "A god . . . in your backyard?"

"Maybe," said Venus. "Back up, though. What was my grandfather into, exactly?"

As Ezekiel took another drag, Venus's mind raced. Was Neil McKenzie the one who had introduced the powerful being to Saint-Ferdinand? If that was the case, it would explain why he was spoken about in such low whispers, but it would also mean that her parents knew about the god. That they knew about everything happening beneath the surface of the quaint little village, had moved her close to it, and had chosen not to warn her.

"Your grandfather, Cicero, me, your dad"—Ezekiel nodded at Abraham—"we were all part of the Craftsmen. Hell, half of Saint-Ferdinand was part of that particular enterprise at some point. I was trying to be coy, calling it a lion, but we were looking for ways to kill a god. And now you say it's in your backyard? Are you serious?"

"Yeah, but you can't kill it. We tried. My friend stabbed the thing in the gut. It did nothing! It barely slowed down."

Realizing that her voice had been getting louder as the conversation went on, Venus looked around. A few people in the parking lot had turned to look in their direction. Employees on their smoke breaks picked that time to return to work. Venus looked back at them defiantly, but Abraham lowered his voice.

"Venus has the god trapped in her backyard shed," Abraham cut in. "Go on. Tell him. I gotta go back inside in case they have news about my dad."

Venus reached for his arm. "You come and get me if you need anything, okay, Abe?"

The farm boy gave her a brief, crushing hug. Once he was gone, Venus sat on a concrete post. She and Ezekiel eyed each other for a moment. A soft, paranoid voice whispered in the back of her head. Ezekiel already knew about the god, but what if he wanted to take it from her? What if more people got hurt because of her?

Granted, there was no obvious reason to trust Ezekiel. Yet Abraham seemed to have faith in him. He'd been forthcoming with information and seemed to know about the history of Saint-Ferdinand. This weird, short cigarette-smoking stranger was exactly what she'd been hoping to find for the past week. Someone who could help them. An expert. So why did Venus feel like she shouldn't give him any more information unless he gave her some in return?

"Is it really . . . a god?"

"I don't know." Ezekiel tossed his cigarette aside. "Depends on what you're looking for in a deity. I mean, it's powerful enough to be a god, but what is it exactly? I have no idea. Cicero might know, but he doesn't speak to me. Neil probably knew, but he's gone. It doesn't matter."

"What about a way of killing it? You said my grandfather had been looking. Did he find anything?"

"We don't know," he said, and shrugged. "Neil kept his secrets. He had associates from all over the world, but he made a point of keeping his contacts to himself. The fewer people who knew, the safer we all were. That was his philosophy.

"The circus would come to Saint-Ferdinand once a year. The Craftsmen would get together and talk about what we'd found. Usually nothing. We'd all check in on the thing to make sure the bars of its prison weren't coming loose. But then people got greedy."

So it wasn't the first time the god had been held captive. Her own grandfather had been part of keeping the creature under lock and key somehow. Yet, in all that time, they hadn't been able to eliminate it. Now it was in her shed, under her tenuous control, and she had no way of stopping it should the monster get free.

"How was it imprisoned? I mean, before. What was the cage made of?"

"Oil and canvas. Has Abraham ever shown you his father's paintings?"

"Just the stuff at his house."

"No, I mean his real paintings." He smiled a little, like a kid with a secret. "The trick to keeping the god locked up, you see, is—"

"It can't move out of the line of sight when it's being watched. I know. I've got it locked up with a camera."

"A camera?" Ezekiel looked surprised. "Not a film camera, I guess. For an all-powerful being, it sure follows strange rules . . .

Well, we didn't have a camera back then. Not one that wouldn't run out of tape, anyway. I'm not even sure it would have worked. What we had were eyes."

He looked off into the darkness. "For the longest time, the Craftsmen, the original Craftsmen, mind you, kept a rotation of people going into the cave where the god was kept. They'd just look at it for hours and hours without stopping. There would be two of them so they could blink or take short breaks. Just the worst job in the world. That shit town should have gone bankrupt and closed down a dozen times over, but the Craftsmen kept the place running, just so they'd have a reason to keep the thing locked up. That's where it became kind of like a cult."

"What do Mr. Peterson's paintings have to do with any of this?"

Venus knew that Harry Peterson was a talented painter. His house was filled with beautiful tableaux of still lifes and farm landscapes. His paintings could be found in several homes around the village. Everyone knew about the huge studio he had built into his barn.

"There's a trick to painting something so real, so perfect, that the universe gets confused," said Ezekiel. "It doesn't know if the image is a fake or the actual thing, so it becomes real. Abraham's father is training to do something like that. He's almost got it. You should ask to see some of his stuff. It's absolutely mind-bending. His teacher, Amanda, though . . . she had the knack.

"She painted an eye. A great, big, human eye. It was so perfect that when she put on the finishing touches, the painting blinked. That's what we used for almost two decades to keep the god imprisoned. Worked like a charm! Until someone got greedy."

Venus could guess what happened. "Someone made a deal with the god for its freedom." It was the same deal she'd been offered. The exchange of power for freedom that she'd almost granted. *Release me,* it kept asking of everyone it encountered. For a moment she herself had been tempted to give it what it wanted.

"Exactly." Ezekiel pointed a finger, like a gun, at Venus. "A guy named Edouard Lambert. Greedy son of a bitch. One night he made his deal and everything went to hell."

"What about Mr. Peterson's teacher? This . . . Amanda? Why can't we ask her to make another painting?"

"'Cause she's dead. A lot of people died that night. But the greatest loss was Amanda Finnegan."

WILLIAM

WILLIAM BERGERON PUT down the glass he'd just upended over his mouth. It hit the granite counter in his kitchen with a loud impact. Not that it mattered. The noise coming from his living room could drown out the sound of a jet engine.

His guests, if he could call them that, were alternately arguing, eating his food, and drinking his liquor. William felt a pang of bitter satisfaction knowing that the really good stuff, the expensive stuff, was stashed away here, away from the collection of yahoos his wife had assembled in his house.

Taking a deep breath to steady himself, William finally summoned the courage to go face those who considered themselves his peers. Yes, they had all been his friends at some point. They'd come to comfort him and Beatrice when Audrey had been found dead. He'd had them over for barbecues, pool parties; he'd even gone hunting with some of them. But today—today they were nothing to him. Idiots at best, vultures at worst.

As he walked into his living room, they all slowly fell silent, each turning a pitying eye toward him. He knew what they saw: a bereaved father sinking back into the embrace of alcoholism to escape reality. Even Beatrice probably didn't know better. But he knew. He knew *they* were the ones who had lost perspective. They'd become greedy and stupid, forgetting the awe and fear they'd all felt almost a decade ago when Crowley, Peterson, and McKenzie had opened their eyes to a much wider world. A world stranger and more dangerous than any of them had ever imagined.

Oh, what promise the future held back then. They would put Saint-Ferdinand on the map, they told themselves. Power, money, health, success, even existential fulfillment: it was all at their fingertips. Nothing was outside of their grasp. There was magic in the world, and anything was possible.

"Don't we usually meet at the church? What about all that ritual nonsense?" he asked.

"We don't have time for pageantry, Will," his wife said. "We have important business to discuss."

"Fine. What business?"

William already knew what they wanted. His wife had already told him about her latest encounter with Inspector Crowley. She claimed that Stephen wasn't doing enough to fulfill his part of their arrangement, and she was probably right. The inspector did seem to be dragging his feet, but he was also the last of them who knew the fundamentals of their plans.

"We need to kick Crowley out," declared Sebastien Desjardins, his piercing blue eyes filled with annoyance and indignation. Beatrice nodded emphatically.

Bergeron gave the dozen people crowded in his large and elegant house an appraising look. Each had been instrumental in putting Crowley where he was, a position that was ideal for finding the proverbial genie in a bottle. It had been no easy task. Crowley's anger was legendary, and his methods as an officer of the law were dubious at times. A violent incident with the owner of a traveling circus almost two decades ago had also landed him on the wrong side of the former chief inspector. But they had done their part and gotten Crowley his promotion. Now they wanted answers, but William knew they were unlikely to get their way.

"I don't disagree with that," William said. Normally, he welcomed being thrust into the decision-making position. That was part of how he'd become the successful business owner he was today. He was easily the wealthiest man in the village. But those decisions had all been made when he was sober, a state that had ended the same day as his daughter's short life. "But getting rid of Crowley means giving up on everything we've been promised."

He expected them all to fall quiet at that. When they'd founded the Sandmen, Harry Peterson's paintings and Randy McKenzie's necromantic parlor tricks had served to convince the group, but it was Crowley who claimed to know where to find the real source of power. In the years that followed their agreement, both Harry and Randy had abandoned the cause, each for his own reasons. Thankfully, Crowley had been able to keep both men under his thumb. Without the inspector, none of them knew where to go from here. Yet the assembled crowd didn't seem to understand that.

"No, it doesn't." It was Alvarez, still smelling of blood and offal from his work. His crooked teeth did nothing to damage the sincerity of his smile. "We have a new expert."

At his words, the group parted to reveal a young, meticulously dressed man in his midtwenties. He smiled affably, both hands in his pockets. If William had been sober, he might have noticed there was something disturbingly familiar about him.

"So good to see you again, Mr. Bergeron. It's been too long." The young man extended a hand with delighted enthusiasm. William shook it absentmindedly. So he did know this boy, but from where? "I apologize for coming into your home uninvited, but when your lovely wife told me your situation . . . Well, I don't believe in destiny, but this seemed like more than a coincidence."

"You told him about the Sandmen?" Bergeron spat the question at his wife, attempting to drop the young man's icy hand, but it held firm.

"He already knew. He knows everything," Beatrice answered with a voice that was meant to be soothing. "In fact, he's been having trouble with Stephen too."

"I ran into Beatrice at the station," the young man said smoothly. "I've been trying to have a meeting with the inspector for some time now. He and I have, shall we say, a lot of catching up to do."

William was getting angry. All these parasites were looking at him with idiotic grins plastered to their faces, as if they were all in on some joke he didn't understand. Even his wife wore a simpering smile. William wasn't a man with many admirable qualities. He was, however, hardworking, and he knew his limitations. Above all else, he prided himself on being a keen judge of character. Yet he couldn't get a bead on this stranger in his house. He smiled too much to be sincere but talked too little for a con man. His features were uncomfortably familiar in a way that was distracting to William. *Crowley would have figured it out by now.*

Crowley.

"Don't worry, Mr. Bergeron," the young man continued without letting go of his hand. "I have all the answers you've been looking for."

Francis Crowley. The pieces suddenly fell in place. A young boy who drank too much soda and ran up and down the aisles of his drugstore, making noise while his mother shopped for cosmetics. Back then William and Beatrice had been desperate for children of their own. Crowley had been blessed with two sons, and Bergeron had been shamefully jealous of the younger man's good fortune. That is, until Marguerite Crowley disappeared, taking her firstborn with her.

"You're . . . Stephen's son?" Widening smiles confirmed that they all had known. Now that he saw it, the similarities were obvious. Not because of his slight resemblance to the inspector, but to his estranged wife. The round face and high cheekbones, the squinty eyes and broad mouth that smiled with ease. Over fifteen years had passed since William had seen either mother or child, but there was no doubt: this was Marguerite's son.

"Oh, Mr. Bergeron. I am so much more than that," said the young man, his cold fingers like a frozen vice on William's hand.

ANDRÉ

ANDRÉ WATCHED WITH trepidation as the rickety Volkswagen bus pulled out of the driveway. The vehicle's sun-bleached paint looked pink and orange, like salmon flesh, under the faint glow of the streetlamps.

Rural villages like Saint-Ferdinand attract a wide variety of people. From young families looking for affordable real estate to retired couples longing for a simple and quiet end to their days. Farmers and nature lovers were also common, as well as artists and oddballs who just didn't fit in and had abandoned larger metropolitan areas. As everyone in town knew, Paul and Virginie McKenzie fit into the latter category.

Ever since he could remember, André had heard his parents gossiping about Venus's mom and dad. *Hippies* was the term they most often used to describe them, though *lazy*, *dirty*, and the occasional *communists* were also tossed around. When he eventually met their daughter on his first day in school, she turned out to be nothing like he'd expected. She was smart, friendly, and just abrasive enough to be funny. Despite his parents' warnings, André became fast friends with her.

Then, at the end of middle school, Venus got pushed up a grade. Consequently, she began to spend more and more time with the older kids and less time with André. Bitter and hurt, he started picking on her. Almost overnight his best friend became the dirty, lazy hippie his parents had always warned him about. And he made sure she would never forget it.

While making fun of Venus had become a favorite way to show off in front of his friends, even André knew that stalking her from the bushes outside her house might be pushing things too far. His goal tonight wasn't to torment her, however.

Once the van was well out of sight, André slipped out from behind the hedge where he'd been hiding. He'd already seen Venus leave with Inspector Crowley's son, a detail that made him hate her all the more. He'd muttered something unkind under his breath as she was driven away by the older teen.

But now that mother and daughter were both gone, it left Paul McKenzie by himself in the garage. Most kids knew Venus's father as a rather friendly man, who was either too dumb to worry about the world around him or just couldn't be bothered with it. André's father thought he was simply too stoned to care. Either way, Paul made for an unimpressive authority figure. Two summers ago he'd caught André and his friends running off with eggs from Mr. Lee's farm. They'd told Paul that they had permission to take the eggs, a lie anyone would have seen right through. Not Paul McKenzie. He smiled and waved as they had run off to do their mischief.

Making his way toward the backyard, André took stock of the ancient lawn mower and vast collection of rakes and brooms that littered the overgrown lawn surrounding the wooden shed. Those and other gardening implements created a clear blast radius around the shed that dominated the otherwise simple yard. A quick glance at the back porch confirmed that the kitchen was empty, allowing him to creep carefully toward his goal.

He smiled upon seeing the heavy padlock on the door of the shed. It was all the confirmation he needed. The McKenzies owned an artisanal tea shop at the edge of the village. There they grew and dried their own leaves to supplement the large variety that was already available from various suppliers. Everyone knew the family was no stranger to hydroponic agriculture, and that made André very curious about what they could be hiding in a locked shed in their backyard.

Nervously, André searched the yard for something that could break the lock.

After a couple of minutes, he got his hands on a long crowbar that had been lying under a stack of broken carpentry tools. Pushed by a voice in the back of his mind, he slipped the crowbar slowly into the loop of the padlock, careful to make as little noise as possible. Then, when he was somewhat confident of his leverage, he closed his eyes and put his full weight on the crowbar. But despite his straining, the lock refused to give. Just as he was about to run out of breath, a thunderous crack burst from the door.

His eyes still closed, holding on to the crowbar but standing absolutely still, André listened for any indication that the noise had been heard. After what felt like half the night, he finally opened his eyes to inspect the damage. The results were not what he expected, but they would have to do. The padlock lived up to its promise of indestructibility and had remained intact, gleaming defiantly in the moonlight. But the panel to which it had been secured, however, had not fared quite as well. The old wood had given out, nearly disintegrating as the screws that had held the lock in place had broken free. The door to the shed hung open.

A soft neon-blue glow emanated from within. The boy nearly jumped out of his skin when a voice called out to him. *"Free me . . ."*

He knew immediately that this was not Paul McKenzie. In fact, before his eyes adjusted to the darkness within, primal fears were already urging him to run. But something else kept him rooted in place.

"You're new. Let me look at you."

The voice didn't come from the shed or the yard, but instead boomed directly into André's own brain. Whoever spoke to him wasn't using words but rather carving concepts and ideas directly into André's mind, painfully reshaping the boy's thoughts into a message.

Fighting his legs and bladder to keep either from running, André turned to look within the small shed. Perhaps the McKenzies were cooking up something even more potent than he had thought, and it was now affecting him. As his eyes scanned the cramped room, all they could see was a cacophony of bizarre horror. The walls were decorated with a complex lattice of bones and flesh and the stretched organs of small animals. The impressive, if revolting, artwork drew dizzying lines and spirals that instantly reminded him of the rosebushes his mother obsessively tended each summer.

Before the gruesome mural of stretched tendons and plucked eyes stood a figure. It was humanoid in form but featured an otherwise impossible anatomy. It seemed to be admiring the mural. Its dark, shadowy skin appeared to push away dust, air, and even light. At the thing's feet was a pool of dark blood.

"*Child,*" it said, its voice making André nauseous just to hear it. "*Free me.*"

André shook his head, eyes wide open, unblinking. His mind raced to comprehend what his senses were reporting. Though he was unable to come to a logical conclusion, every cell in his body agreed, as if the information had been encoded directly into his DNA: this thing meant to harm him.

No. It meant to harm and destroy everyone.

"*Free me, and you can have your heart's desire,*" it promised, turning around slowly. Once it faced him, the creature took three slow and deliberate steps toward the boy, stopping an arm's length away. André wanted to run, to void his bowels, to claw his own eyes out. But he couldn't. Was he frozen out of fear? Curiosity? For a second he knew, without the shadow of a doubt, that if he did not escape immediately, he would not live to see another morning. Yet he stood, transfixed by the thing's empty stare.

Bang!

André jumped, startled by the sound of the crowbar he'd unconsciously dropped to the floor. As he looked down to the source of the noise, a scalding cold hand closed around his left wrist and yanked him into the shadows.

The thing burned its message into André's brain like a hot branding iron: *"Free me!"* It screamed wordlessly into the teenager's naked mind: *"FREE ME."* But André, the boy whose weaknesses had led him to bully his former best friend, whose skull throbbed with the force of a god's command, whose eyes were blurry with tears of frantic terror, shook his head.

The thing was displeased. Calmly, methodically, without wasting time on further threats, it started to remove pieces of André's body. It began with his throat, taking great care to keep the boy alive during the process.

Unable to scream or beg, André could do nothing but watch as his muscles, bones, and organs were pulled from him, stretched into new shapes, and added to the beautiful, morbid mural in Venus McKenzie's shed.

DANIEL

THE DRIVE FROM Sherbrooke to Saint-Ferdinand wasn't unlike traveling through time. If Daniel's white Civic was the time machine, the roads that led him back home were like the pages of history, flipping backward the farther he drove.

Sherbrooke, despite its size, remained a fairly modern city. Being home to a respected university made it more vibrant than neighboring towns. It was the largest municipality in the Eastern Townships of Quebec, but it hadn't become too touristy. However, as one went south on the highway and passed Magog, the lights changed and then completely disappeared. The highway inevitably gave way to small country roads, and before long, civilization had been swallowed up by long stretches of dark forest and empty black fields.

While already taking great risks with his life by going well above the speed limit, Daniel was also committing the capital sin of occasionally looking at his phone. He wasn't in the habit of doing such things. This was the kind of behavior Stephen Crowley had warned him against and that Daniel had always obeyed. On this one drive, however, he simply couldn't help it. The words that appeared on his phone were too important.

Can I see you? Your place. 1 hr?

The text was from Sasha. The girlfriend whom he had neglected for weeks. When she had stood him up at Daisy's Diner, he assumed that their relationship was over.

He tried many things to keep his mind off his destination. Sure, he was driving home, but he was also driving back to her. He'd regretted how he'd ignored her. How he had kept her in the dark instead of seeking her support. Fortunately, regret still left room to learn. Seeing her name on his phone was an important reminder of that. If he was being given a second chance, he wasn't going to waste it.

Luck smiled on Dan during his drive. No stray animal jumped out in front of his car. No cops were waiting to catch people speeding. There was almost no traffic, nor did he get stuck behind a tractor hogging up the road. He made it home in record time.

A small part of him hoped he'd see both his girlfriend's minivan and his father's SUV parked out front. Then they could all talk together. Clear everything up with everyone at once, like a great big intervention. Unfortunately, the driveway was empty except for his father's boat trailer, covered in a tarp.

Standing under the porch light, he saw a single man, about his own height and build, wearing a crisp suit. Chris Hagen. He waved, revealing something in his hand. Sasha's phone.

For a second Daniel considered simply plowing into the reporter. This wasn't what he'd sped home to see. There was no logical scenario that explained why this reporter would have texted him from his girlfriend's phone. Instead he hit the brakes and jumped out of his car.

"Where's Sasha?" Daniel said.

A warm smile etched itself onto Hagen's face as he walked toward the car. "Daniel!" he said, extending a hand.

The teenager slapped it away, the Crowley anger burning hot within him. "Where is she? Why do you have her phone?"

"Hey, hey, calm down, buddy. That's what I'm here to talk about. Do you mind if we go inside?"

"Tell me where she is!" Daniel's fists were clenched, and he could feel his face turning red with barely restrained fury. He knew the posture well, having seen it in his own father.

"You are your father's son." Hagen sighed. "Calm down, Daniel. There's no reason to get excited."

The words only flared up the teenager's anger. He wanted to punch the smug grin off the man's face, choke whatever he knew out of him. Instead he took a breath. Recognizing his thoughts for what they were, Daniel Crowley managed to make the conscious decision to cool down. Like a man who's fallen overboard into the cold ocean, he fought back the initial panic. He pushed against the shock and confusion that might have caused him to swim in the wrong direction and drown. Instead he breached the surface of a sea of calm, took another deep breath, and brought himself back to center.

"Fine. Let's go inside."

Daniel unlocked and opened the door, turning on lights as he entered. His guest, however, stayed at the threshold. For once, his smile wavered and uncertainty flashed over his face.

"What are you, a vampire? Do you need an invitation?" asked Daniel sarcastically.

"No, I'm sorry. I was just . . . ," But he didn't finish the sentence.

Instead Chris Hagen stepped inside the Crowley home, setting his foot down like he was walking over a crystal floor. He looked around the entranceway and then the living room. The decor was sparse, as one would expect from the home of two bachelors. Only a few paintings and trinkets left over from the inspector's ex-wife added any flair to the house.

Yet the visitor's gaze passed over every detail as if he were in a museum. Every armchair, every table, its own exhibit for him to discover and learn from. He leaned in close to certain objects while ignoring others. The pattern was easy to notice. The items, decorations, and knickknacks that most attracted the reporter's attention were those most out of step with the rest of the home. Those things that had been left behind by Daniel's mother, Marguerite.

"Are you looking for something specific?" Daniel asked, unsure what to make of this behavior.

"Ah! Yes. I'm sorry. It feels strange to finally be in the home of the ever-elusive Inspector Crowley."

"You haven't been able to—You know what? I don't care. Why do you have Sasha's phone?"

Daniel had indeed had enough and decided to capitalize on his imposing stature, taking a few steps closer to Chris Hagen. Unfortunately, the reporter didn't seem intimidated in the least. In fact, the proximity had no apparent effect on him, apart from perhaps a softening of his features.

"Yes. Again, I apologize. I lack focus tonight."

Hagen fished the cell phone out of his pocket and handed it over. It was Sasha's, all right—a rather recent model tucked into a protective case of worn, dulled pink plastic jewels. A small charm in the shape of a cat hung from it. Daniel grabbed it from him.

"Where did you get this?"

"I found it off the road, not far from here. I'm shocked the screen isn't even scratched."

"So you don't know where she is, then?" Daniel felt the Crowley rage returning, but it was cut short by Hagen's next words.

The expression of detached amusement that seemed to permeate most of Hagen's moods evaporated, leaving in its place a frown of deep concern.

"I didn't say that. I think . . . the polite thing here would be to ask you to sit down for this."

The teenager took a step back. He could feel his heart pounding in his chest. For a moment, even though he was looking directly at Chris Hagen, he could no longer see the man.

Do you even realize where you live?

Those were some of the very last words he'd heard from Sasha. Clearly, Hagen had some bad news for him, and suddenly, more than he ever had in the past, Dan realized exactly where he lived. Saint-Ferdinand. The village where the boogeyman was real.

The town where people died.

"Just tell me," he said, his voice devoid of emotion.

"Actually, I'm surprised your father didn't tell you already. Probably trying to spare you from the trauma."

"Hagen!"

"Again, I'm sorry." Hagen extended his hand again, but this time to lay it gently on Daniel's shoulder. "Her body was found two days ago, in the cellar of one of Gédéon LaFrenière's warehouses."

The impact of the news hit Daniel like a truck, knocking him onto the couch. Try as he might, he couldn't put his thoughts in order. Should he be sad? Angry at his father for keeping such an important secret from him? It didn't take long for him to settle on self-loathing and remorse. Pain suffocated him. If only he'd paid more attention to Sasha, followed her advice, things might be different.

"Daniel? Dan?" Hagen's voice finally pierced through the haze. "Daniel. We can still save her."

The statement short-circuited the young Crowley's grief, snapping him out of his downward spiral. "Save her? You just told me she's dead."

"Daniel. Did you look into this?" Chris pulled something out of his jacket again, another business card. He tapped the winged hourglass logo printed above his name.

"I did, but . . . "

The god. He could bring back his girlfriend. In fact, maybe he could do more than that. Ghosts and gods, they were part of the fabric of Saint-Ferdinand. Myths made fact. If they were real, then why couldn't he defy the finality of death itself? Just like William and Beatrice Bergeron had planned for their daughter.

"Then you know that there's much more to this village than meets the eye." Hagen indicated the hourglass again. "Tell me what you've learned, Daniel. Together we can bring her back."

VENUS

VENUS HAD COME to Sherbrooke Hospital for a specific reason. Meeting up with Abraham would have been a short detour had they not interrupted Ezekiel's attempted "mercy killing." With that situation apparently handled, she could refocus on her true goal: to get into her uncle's office.

According to her uncle Randy, there was a wealth of information in there on the old Saint-Ferdinand Craftsmen's Association. Particularly about the more secretive side of the group. He'd made a crude drawing of where she could find the box that held his research. The illustration wasn't very good, and the pen he'd used had kept running out of ink. It looked like something a high school dungeon master might sketch for his players. But she and Ezekiel managed to reach her uncle's locked office after only a few wrong turns.

This was where the circus performer ended up being useful. When confronted with the locked door, the stranger produced a small set of picklocks. That he carried this kind of thing around as a matter of fact made him even more distasteful to Venus.

She assumed they would no longer need the crude drawing. How hard could it be to find an engraved wooden box in a small office? As the door swung open, though, she could see that her uncle Randy was a veritable hoarder, and his office was ground zero for several of his obsessions.

There were jarred specimens in formaldehyde randomly stashed on shelves. Innumerable books formed towers that had to be carefully navigated to get to the desk. Stacks of medical journals from around the world were piled in every available space. But what made the search most difficult was that her uncle collected wooden boxes. There were dozens of them, strewn in every corner of the space. Thankfully, the illustration made it easier to spot the proper one.

It was larger than expected. The size of a footlocker. The cover was inlaid with the symbol of the Craftsmen, the eye with a spiral iris. An image that had been ubiquitous in Saint-Ferdinand. Each corner of the box also had a distinctive carved decoration, depicting some sort of monster or demon.

Inside it, Venus had been told, was all the information she'd need to find the rest of the Craftsmen. She knew Nathan Cicero and her grandfather Neil had been members, but there were others. Randy knew precious little about the god and how to deal with it. Hopefully these others would be more helpful.

"What are we even doing here?" Abraham said, peering in at all the junk.

The large boy had caught up to them. He'd texted Venus that his father was stable again, but that they wouldn't know more until morning. She had quickly recognized that he needed a distraction, and invited him to join them.

"Help. I hope," she answered.

The box, however, was somewhat of a disappointment. The exterior might have looked like something from a wizard's hoard, but the contents were quite bland. Piles of paper. Receipts stapled together with airplane tickets. Maps and brochures from travel agencies that had probably gone out of business decades ago. These weren't the tools for fighting ancient eldritch horrors; these were the instruments needed to file one's taxes.

Venus had been told that she'd need to decipher the information, but she'd expected an ancient code or language, like the ones she'd seen in the movies. Undaunted, she quickly put together that the boarding passes corresponded to various destinations marked down on the maps in the chest. There were also several receipts for boat rentals that she managed to link to maritime locations also noted on the maps. She then pulled out her laptop and, using the university's Wi-Fi network, started researching the various locations on the maps. Then she shifted her focus to the boarding passes.

Ezekiel quickly got bored and excused himself to go smoke outside. Abraham, however, remained, watching over Venus's shoulder as she got to work.

She knew he didn't understand most of what she was doing. Browsing web pages and scouring social media sites, she took down copious notes. Within a couple of hours, Venus had zeroed in on two specific profiles. Both of them boarding agents for Air Canada. In front of her, hastily written on what could have been a hundred Post-it notes, were these women's names, addresses, work schedule, age, family trees. She had also written down personal details, from religious and political beliefs, to the names of their pets and their favorite colors.

When it looked like she could no longer distill another drop of useful information, Venus leaned back in the leather chair in her uncle's office and smiled nervously at Abraham. Her eyes were bloodshot and baggy, yet they gleamed with mischievous pride. At that moment she was a kid with a handful of firecrackers, about to strike a match. Putting a finger to her lips to keep him quiet, she picked up her uncle's desk phone, looked up a number from one of her notes, and punched it in. "Hi? Is this Sarah?" she said in a chipper tone once someone picked up on the other end. "Hi! This is Melanie Chagnon! We met at that Christmas party last year? Anyway, I need a huuuuuuge favor."

Abraham listened in awe as his friend, a fifteen year-old teenager, became a woman named Melanie working for a major airline. Her eyes darted between her notes, picking up details here and there to keep up with the idle chitchat coming from the other end of the line.

"I was supposed to pull out a passenger list for half a dozen flights for one of our travel agencies." She rearranged a few notes while listening. "Oh no, really old flights. Here, I'll give you the numbers."

Several more minutes passed while Sarah looked up the information. All the while, Venus gossiped about a coworker she'd never had and his horrible behavior at an event she'd never been to. Midway through the conversation, she had to scramble to look up information about some union rules toward which the conversation had gravitated. Finally the woman on the other line found what she needed.

"You've got them? Oh, you are awesome! Here, let me give you my e-mail address." Venus spouted off an address she had created moments before, and continued her small talk until she could verify that the information she had requested had indeed been received. She then politely concluded the conversation, claiming to hope that she and the poor woman on the other end of the line would run into each other soon. Once she hung up, she exhaled as if she hadn't been breathing for the full duration of the call.

"That lady's going to be having one awkward conversation sometime soon," Abraham said jokingly.

"Yeah, well, it couldn't be helped," Venus answered, rubbing her eyes.

"What do you expect to learn from this anyways?"

"Well . . . ," She started explaining while simultaneously copying the passenger lists onto a spreadsheet. "We know my grandfather was doing stuff for these Craftsmen. I'm betting that the reason all these receipts and boarding passes were kept was because these trips were 'business' expenses." With a series of rapid clicks on her mouse, Venus re-sorted the passenger lists and proceeded to highlight the names that came up in more than one of them.

"Assuming he didn't always travel alone . . . ," She turned the laptop so Abraham could get a better look. "We now have at least a partial list of members."

"Good God . . . ," Abraham pointed to the names highlighted in green. "Lucien Peña? Elijah Byrd? Sophie Courtier? These are all friends of my dad."

RANDY

SIMPLE TRICKS FOR complex problems.

Randy had been practicing necromancy for most of his life. Emphasis on *practicing*. There was no wizardry to it. No reason or logic. The only study of the art involved learning some tricks, incantations, and rituals by heart and repeating them verbatim. When he got it right, it worked. When he messed up, it failed. There were no accidental creations of monstrous, undead abomi-nations. The results were always exactly as described in his father's notes and nothing he did required any particular training or skill. If he knew the code, he could break the laws of life and death.

The only traits that made Dr. McKenzie stand out were his understanding of medicine and his own acquired comfort with the dead. When Randy put an iron nail to Audrey's eye and plunged it in with the strike of a hammer, his hands didn't shake. He felt some pangs of moral discomfort, but he had no trouble keep-ing his instruments straight. He'd seen enough cadavers moan or twitch on his autopsy table that he no longer was bothered by in-teracting with corpses. Gas escaping guts and lungs, postmortem reflexes. More scientifically sound than cheating reality, but with results that could be just as disturbing to the uninitiated.

Erica, however, wasn't quite as used to this sort of thing. She'd cut open her fair share of animals while taking biology classes and had been present for a few autopsies, but nothing could have prepared her for Audrey's apparition.

For a moment, the ghost materialized against its will, fighting the summons by twisting and distorting its form. Her limbs bent at impossible angles, and her face contorted like a demon's. It was unsettling to witness, a child so young undergoing such torture. Once she recognized the familiar bear that was being used to reel her spirit in, however, Audrey calmed down, accepting the summons smoothly.

But for Erica Hazelwood, the sight was a complete break with what she was willing to accept. Both hands covered her mouth as she stared, uncomprehending, at the sight before her.

Randy felt bad for her. Even though he'd insisted that she leave, she had chosen to stay without understanding the consequences. What must she think of him? he wondered. He'd exchanged being an overweight but admired mentor with being a creepy monster who dealt in the dark arts.

"It's okay, Dr. Hazelwood." Penny, who had kept her composure during the summoning, moved to comfort the poor psychologist. Erica would have none of it, stepping away from the young girl.

Audrey, ethereal and made of light, silently reached for her toy. Randy handed it to her, doing his best to smile at the girl. He expected her small hands to pass through the stuffed bear and that he'd have to comfort her because of it, but they didn't. For a brief moment, while both he and Audrey held the toy, the medical examiner felt a connection with the land of the dead. The toy became as cold as ice before his hands passed through its immaterial form.

"Thank you," the ghost squeaked while holding her bear tightly to her cheek.

"Audrey?" Penny said.

The diminutive apparition squealed in delight but quickly raised a hand to her cheek. The cut from Penny's knife was still visible. It made the girl wary of her former babysitter.

"Randy?" Erica finally found her voice. "What is going on?"

"This," he answered, attempting to stay clinical, "is William and Beatrice Bergeron's daughter, Audrey. She died, but I used some, uh . . . procedures, to anchor her spirit. I guess you'd call her a ghost."

"I'm not seeing this, Randy. Am I?"

"You are."

"This can't be. I'm having a breakdown. Lack of sleep can lead to visual and auditory halluci—"

"Erica. This is Saint-Ferdinand. You wanted to know more about its secrets, well, here you are. It only gets worse from here. You can still leave, and I very much hope you do."

His protégé's eyes darted between Randy and the ghost. They didn't reflect comprehension or understanding, only fear. Beneath that, though, the medical examiner could see a hint of amazement.

"No," she said, and swallowed. "No. I can't walk away from this. Even if I'm just going crazy."

Randy sighed and shook his head. He had no idea what the future would hold. He knew it would be dangerous, perhaps deadly, and that Erica was ill prepared to survive if things got ugly. But he had no time to explain everything, not at this very minute. With luck, he could convince her to leave town with him once he was done here.

"Audrey?" he called. "Penelope here tells me you have a way to help get my . . . my spirit to the circus?"

"Yes!" she said, her voice like small bells. "You want to know how?"

"Absolutely, honey. I'd love to give it a try. What do I have to do?"

"Well, you can't go alone, or the shadows will get you. The shadows eat all the ghosts."

The god, Randy thought. Even while imprisoned, it could still attract the souls of the dead to its location. He'd tried to use that as a way of locating it in the past, but he didn't know the correct rituals.

"Who would I go with? You?"

"I can't protect you. You need a body."

Back to square one was Randy's first thought. If he could simply walk out and meet Cicero in person, talk to him face-to-face with his own flesh and blood, there wouldn't be a problem. The amateur necromancer tried to think. Perhaps he could pretend to be dead. Have his body carted off and reanimated outside the jail. It was the kind of thing that worked in movies. Certainly there was something in all the tricks he'd learned that could simulate the effect.

"It doesn't have to be your body, Dr. McKenzie," Penny said, interrupting his thoughts. "Audrey can help you possess someone else."

"Don't do it, Randy," Finnegan warned from the next cell.

"How?" McKenzie directed his question at the apparition.

"You know how, when you're so scared, you jump out of your skin?"

"That's just an expression, honey."

The ghost shook her head slowly. "It's not. I see it all the time. I saw the lady over there do it when she saw me." Audrey pointed at Erica. "It's not for long, but if you do it to Penny, I can catch her."

Yes. This would leave the teenage girl's body empty, hungering for something to inhabit it. *The flesh abhors a vacuum.* Randy had read those words somewhere in his father's notes. It wouldn't take much for him to abandon his own. Just a simple near-death experience.

"Let me do it, Randy," Sam said. "I owe the village that much. Let me take the risk."

"I am not letting him possess me," Penelope answered. "You've been my doctor since I was a child, Dr. McKenzie. I trust you."

Hesitation was for the weak and time was slipping away, Randy tried to tell himself. And this was not a world that was kind to the weak.

"Close your eyes," he instructed the teenage girl. "Now hum a song. Something repetitive, preferably devoid of feeling. Maybe one of those pop songs kids your age like so much."

Penny gave him a disapproving look but was otherwise compliant. She began to hum something the medical examiner had heard a hundred times on the radio but still couldn't name. The tune was almost pleasant at first. The repetition quickly became grating as the experiment stretched into minutes. Dutifully, the girl kept on humming. As instructed, there was no emotion in her cadence. No passion. She simply repeated the melody along for what seemed like an hour. Randy had to quietly hush Erica as she began to protest. At long last, Penny's music faded into the background.

WHAP!

Without warning, Randy clapped his hands a mere inch from the teenager's left ear. As she popped her eyes open in shock, it happened. Penny's beautiful blue eyes went vacant. There was no name for what she lost in that moment. *Soul* didn't do it justice. The same spark Dr. McKenzie had been able to find in Audrey's dead body after her funeral was now absent from Penny's eyes.

"All right, Sam. You want to help? Now's your chance."

"God dammit, Randy, don't ask me to do that."

"You're the only choice," the medical examiner said, moving as close to the wall that separated the two cells as he could.

"God dammit. Good luck," Sam said before reaching through the bars and grabbing Randy's neck with both of his bony hands.

"Oh God!" Erica screamed, but Randy, already choking, waved her off.

It was excruciating to endure. At first the medical examiner was confident in what he was doing, but as the moments passed and his lungs burned, his faith wavered. He pulled at Finnegan's hands, the hands of an experienced killer, but they expertly cut off his air supply. Randy's vision became increasingly narrow and blurry, spots obscuring his sight. As consciousness slipped from him, he began to wonder if this had been a good idea after all.

PAUL

PAUL DIDN'T DRINK. A long time ago, when he and Randy had been teenagers, their father had caught them shoplifting beer at the convenience store, stuffing bottles into their winter coats. Neil McKenzie had never been a kind man, and no one had ever accused him of being tolerant, either. So it had come as little surprise to the McKenzie boys that their father had made them go through all the clichés as punishment.

First he had the boys bring the stolen goods back to Harland, the proprietor of the store. Not satisfied with the humiliation, Neil decided to teach his sons about the vices of alcohol, too. Purchasing a twenty-four-bottle case of the nastiest beer on the market, he had Paul and Randy drink every last one.

Randy, being older and larger, weathered the ordeal with little more than a nightmarish hangover the next day. Paul, who'd always been scrawny even for his age, did not fare so well. The only silver lining to his intoxication was being spared the hangover, but only because he had vomited up the entire contents of his stomach over the course of the night. Even when he had nothing left to barf up, he would dry heave until he spat up bile. Though the boy had clearly learned his lesson, Neil would be waiting next to the bathroom door with a bottle. This went on until Paul had drunk his half of the beer.

As a result, both boys had stayed away from alcohol until they were in their midtwenties. Once Randy built up the courage to drink again, he took to it like a fish to water, though with a marked preference toward wines and whiskeys. Paul, however, never touched a drink again, the very smell still dredging up feelings of nausea.

Despite the psychological scars of that lesson, Paul had recently purchased a large bottle of the cheapest malt whiskey at the local liquor store. He pulled it out of its hiding place under the kitchen sink and removed the brown paper bag.

He decided a few days back that he needed the liquid courage. Prophecy had told him the booze would come in handy, and it did not disappoint. The moment he saw the door to the shed was open, saw an eerie glow leaking through the opening, he knew his time had come.

This isn't so bad, he thought as he cracked open the metal screw top on the bottle. Paul had assumed that when this moment came, he'd be filled with dread. That courage would fail him and he wouldn't live up to his destiny. Instead he felt almost relieved. Then again, fate was a strange thing, wasn't it?

He took a quick, tentative whiff of the bottle. Surprisingly, he didn't feel like retching. The smell was more medicinal than intoxicating, like rubbing alcohol with a hint of sugar. Still, he wasn't looking forward to having it go down his throat. The more he contemplated it, the less he felt it necessary. Before he could make a decision, a wet, bloodcurdling scream came from outside.

Resolute, Paul put the bottle down on the counter. He made his way to the back door and kicked it open. He grabbed a rake that had been leaning against the porch and ran to the shed. Without looking, without thinking, he walked through the broken door, brandishing his makeshift weapon.

The sight that welcomed him was everything he had been told it would be and more. There was no doubt in his mind that before him stood a god, both beautiful and terrible to behold. In its grasp was André, the boy Paul had been told he would attempt to rescue but be doomed to fail. Even knowing all this, Venus's father raised his rake. He could see that the boy, who had been relieved of his extremities, finger by finger, arm by arm, was barely alive yet staring directly at him.

"*Neil McKenzie . . . ,*" called the creature.

Paul didn't bother to correct the mistake. Didn't take his eyes off the young man who was dying in the god's clutches. There was still hope in those eyes. Hope either for rescue or a quick release from his torment. Unfortunately, Paul knew both of them would get neither. Yet he charged forward with a glad heart, swinging his crude weapon wildly, knowing that he was meeting his destiny with nobility. He was defending that shred of hope in the eyes of his daughter's former friend, at the cost of his own life.

After all, what else was he supposed to do?

VENUS

"ARE YOU SURE you don't want to stay?"

It was the third time Venus had asked Abraham this question. Not that she was particularly looking forward to driving over an hour alone with Ezekiel. He reeked of cigarettes, and his truck looked like an absolute deathtrap. Rickety and old, the thing appeared to have been through a war that it lost. There was no doubt in her mind that many of the pieces for the vintage piece of junk were well out of warranty. To top it all off, the circus performer gave her the creeps. She couldn't forget the event that had brought them together, and it was a little difficult not to hate the man for attempting to kill Harry Peterson.

But above all, Venus wanted to make sure her friend wasn't accompanying them out of misplaced chivalry. His father's health had finally stabilized, but while he remained in the intensive care unit, there was no way to tell what his condition might be when he woke up. Abraham would want to be there when that happened, and Venus didn't want to take that from him. But the farm boy shook his head.

"Dad would want me to do what's right. If that means going back home and helping where I can, then that's what I'll be doing."

Venus took her friend by the arm, pulling him away from Ezekiel. The circus performer raised an eyebrow but continued rubbing his bruised ribs while playing with his keychain.

"Abe, your dad is going to need you when he wakes up, but we're also going to need him. If he knows of anything that can help, anything at all, we need to know." She squeezed his hand for emphasis. "Listen, I'm not exactly thrilled to be going alone with that guy, but like you said, we have to do what's right. For me, that's going back to talk to this Cicero person. For you, it's finding out if your dad knows where to find the people on that list."

"Fine. But I don't like it," he answered, his jaw clenched.

"Me neither."

They walked back to the truck just as Ezekiel was catching his keys one last time before jumping into the driver's seat. The vehicle swayed under the added weight, the suspension complaining of its old age. As Venus went around and got into the passenger side, the engine roared to life like a demon pulled from the depths of hell.

"You coming?" Ezekiel asked as Abraham got near his window.

"Staying with my dad."

"Let him know I, uh . . . dropped by when he wakes up."

"Want me to mention how you tried to do him in?" the farm boy asked without a trace of humor.

"Might want to leave that part out. Better I tell him myself." Ezekiel smiled and winked, then pressed on the accelerator and drove away from the hospital parking lot, leaving Abraham standing alone under the streetlight.

"You shouldn't joke about that." Venus didn't bother to hide her dislike of Ezekiel. He was part of the god's history and, by association, part of the problems plaguing her. Like everyone else, he kept his secrets and perpetuated the sense of paranoia that crippled her and her friends. Most of all, he seemed very unconcerned by his attempted murder of Harry Peterson, a man he claimed was a friend.

"Yeah, well, I'm not joking," he answered over the uneven roar of the truck's engine. It was going to be a long ride home.

"You tried to murder his father! Maybe show a little more compassion."

Ezekiel smiled at that. It was the kind of smirk one wore when he knew something others in the conversation didn't. Venus loathed how condescending it was.

"Harry's not dying in Sherbrooke."

"You don't know that."

"I do. I work in a circus. And what do all good circuses have?"

Venus was tempted to punch him right in his tender ribs. "I don't know. I've never been to one."

"You've never been to the circus?" Ezekiel was shocked. She might as well have told him she'd never enjoyed a hot meal or a warm summer day.

"No. I almost went to Cirque du Soleil once, but tickets were sold out."

"That's not a proper circus."

"I'm asking you about the death of my friend's dad, and you're being an elitist about what makes a real circus?"

"Trust me, it's relevant. You have to understand: these modern shows *flirt* with magic, often without even realizing it, but a real circus? A real circus loses itself in it!"

Ezekiel was obviously excited to talk about his livelihood. There was a sudden spark to his eyes and a sincerity to his grin that broke through the prior smugness and cynicism. He was no longer a would-be assassin but a child regaling his friends about some grand discovery.

"I've had my fill of magic, I think," Venus said.

"Well, brace yourself then. Cicero's Circus is all about magic. That's why we have that one thing that truly brings the mystique of the production together!"

"Get on with it. What do you have at your magic circus that has anything to do with Abraham's dad?"

"A fortune-teller!"

"A fortune-teller?" Venus repeated the words, punctuating the question with a heavy sigh.

"Don't tell me, after everything you've been through, that you don't believe in fortune-tellers?"

"I don't believe in destiny."

"Whether you believe in it or not doesn't make it any less of a reality."

"So I'm supposed to take it from you that I have no free will? That there's a big book somewhere and everything I'll do is written down and nothing can be changed?"

As much as she resented it at times, the one constant theme of Venus's existence had been freedom. Either how much she enjoyed or how little her friends had. The very concept of destiny made a mockery of that.

To his credit, Ezekiel took her seriously, stowing his enthusiasm for the subject in order to better explain. "Destiny doesn't undermine free will. That's one of the weird things you learn getting your fortune told enough times. Free will is the instrument of destiny."

"That makes zero sense. If I know that by crossing a street, I'll get hit by a truck, I won't cross the street. Free will beats predestination." She shook her head. "What does this have to do with you trying to kill Mr. Peterson?"

"We'll get to that. Ever wonder where the cliché of fortune-tellers giving either vague insights or predictions only about momentous events comes from? You can't predict something that *won't* happen once it's predicted. So destiny, the destiny we can see, only describes those events that won't change."

"You can always change events," Venus stated in defiance.

"You're not listening. I'm talking about your own personal decision. What if crossing the road and being hit by a truck was the only way to save your best friend? You would cross that street, get hit by that truck, and you would do so of your own free will.

That's destiny. The result of a great calculation that encompasses all possible variables including—no, *featuring*—our personalities and individual decisions. The big book where all future events are written is the entire universe, and our actions are the words that make up the story. And a fortune-teller can read that book."

"And Harry Peterson?"

"Harry Peterson will die in Saint-Ferdinand. I wanted to avert that, but I couldn't go against the wishes of Abraham. I don't have it in me to do so."

"Destiny," Venus said in grudging understanding.

"Destiny."

They drove a little longer in silence. Venus sensed that she had only scratched the surface of this weird man and, at the same time, had discovered another layer to Saint-Ferdinand's history. A tragic one. The contrast between how excited Ezekiel had been talking about magic and his sudden mourning of a friend who had yet to die made Venus thoughtful. Any talk of the supernatural, she supposed, contained these contradictions.

"How do you know about Mr. Peterson's fortune, then?" she asked, hoping to distract Ezekiel from his own dark thoughts.

"Eh," he said, and smiled. "A circus is a funny place. The moment you find out the owner's girlfriend can predict the future, you start asking questions. Doesn't take long for things to get dark. Everyone winds up knowing when and how they're going to die. The gallows humor sets in pretty quick after that."

"So, what? Impending death is like a joke to you?"

"Yeah. Maybe it makes us monsters, but we had fun with it. At least until it started to become real."

The circus performer shrugged, keeping his eyes on the road but his sight clearly elsewhere. While Venus might have been put off by the morbid amusement he described, Ezekiel seemed nostalgic. There was something else, though, and she couldn't put her finger on it.

"So, Mr. Peterson . . . "

"We knew he'd die in Saint-Ferdinand. In the nest of a thing that eats souls. The lion's den. I can live with one of my friends dying. I've buried enough of them. It's the eternal torment part I can't swallow."

The words struck a nerve. Penny's mother. Was that what had happened to her? What had happened to all of Sam Finnegan's victims? That would explain why the old man had gone mad. Sending dozens of souls to a literal hell would be enough to unhinge anyone. Venus had been close enough to the god that she knew such a thing was possible.

"Who else?" Venus wondered aloud. "Did you know how my friend's mother would die? Do you know how my parents die?"

"Nathan might know about the others. Katrina, she definitely knows. I only know about Harry and . . . I know about you."

Venus stopped breathing. Why would he know about her death? Was her demise so noteworthy that it had been important for a stranger to learn it? She must have made a noise or given some sort of outward sign of her distress because Ezekiel turned his head from the road and put a hand on her shoulder.

"You okay there?"

"What . . . what do you know about my death?"

"What do I know?" he answered, putting his hand back on the wheel, his knowing smile making a comeback to his lips. "I know you don't die."

RANDY

RANDY MCKENZIE COULD remember the first time his father had introduced him to the stranger things of the world. It was a day filled with wonder and curiosity. A moment in time where a young Randy had first discovered that there were cracks in reality, some only big enough to look through and some that could swallow him whole. If one knew where or, more important, how to find these cracks, they could interact with the other side. They could reach in and pull things out. And if they knew the proper tricks, they could wedge themselves into those cracks and break them wide open.

Unfortunately, that day wasn't one where father and son bonded over a coming-of-age experience. Randy's father hadn't walked up to him, tossed him the keys to the family car, and told him he was old enough to learn.

Instead Neil McKenzie, quiet and forbidding, had given his other son, Paul, a stack of notes and instructions and commanded him to learn. The younger brother had refused, and the discussion quickly devolved into an argument between the two. Meanwhile, Randy had leafed through the notes. A pile of mismatched papers. Most were scribbled in Neil's handwriting, but others, older and more yellowed, were written in a script he didn't recognize. Wherever these instructions, this mythology, had come from, they immediately took hold of young Randy's imagination.

Since then, he'd learned so much from that stack of aging paper. In fact, he'd transcribed most of it in order to preserve the information it contained. Over the years, the medical examiner had animated dead animals, spoken with the dead, and performed a few other parlor tricks. His dabbling in the dark arts led him to study medicine in the first place, and his particular set of skills was largely responsible for his grades and academic success.

Yet, despite the power he had, Randy had never been able to leverage it to help find the Saint-Ferdinand Killer. He couldn't interrogate the spirits of the victims, since all who died within reach of the god had had their souls consumed. It was frustrating.

Walking around Saint-Ferdinand in Penelope LaForest's skin, however, he was able to see a much more disturbing truth. He could have found the god had he dared to simply dip his head into the realm of the dead. A dangerous prospect to be sure, but one that would have yielded all the answers. For this was a god of hate and death, and the world beyond life was its domain.

A disturbing aspect of using someone else's body wasn't just how ill fitting the limbs and bones were. Randy also shared Penny's brain, borrowing neurons and synapses to think. The magic tricks he used didn't ignore biology; they hijacked it. Penny was still attached, still tethered, to her body. There were moments when Randall couldn't formulate thoughts because she was using what he needed.

The final and most disturbing problem, though, was with his eyes. They could not stop seeing. When Penny's eyelids were open, he saw through her flesh. The light of the living world hit her retinas and sent signals to her brain, where Randy's consciousness would pick them up. But whenever he closed her eyelids, even if it was just to blink, it was the other world he saw, and it was nothing like he'd expected.

Terrifying, seductive whispers beckoned him to leave his host body. He knew not to listen, that these were the temptations of the god calling to him. He also realized that the god wasn't in his niece's backyard shed at all. Or rather, what was locked up there amounted to the tip of a limb poking through a hole in reality. It was merely dipping a toe into the sea of the living. The real god was here, with the dead, and it was immense. Randall was like a mite crawling on the deity's skin. The world around him bristled at his presence, aware of him but unable to swat him away, though the intention could be felt all around.

This was Randy's experience all the way to the circus. Driving was especially difficult. Every blink reminded him how insignificant he was, how precarious his situation had become, and how little any of it mattered when faced with a power so vast and formless. Through luck, urgency, and the empty night roads, the medical examiner, clothed in the flesh of a teenage girl, made it to Cicero's Circus.

In the dark, with only moonlight to guide him, Randy made his way between the striped tents of the circus. He was greeted by an old popcorn machine that had traveled with the circus for decades. The mountainous big top, looming overhead like a castle keep, blocked out half the night sky. In the cold indigo night, a square of warm amber invited him into a small tent.

"Hi, Nathan," Randy said with Penny's voice.

"Desperate times, Doctor?" An old man, sitting behind a fold-out desk at the back of the tent, lifted his head to greet his visitor. He smiled, showing off a hole where a tooth had recently been knocked out.

"Desperate measures."

"Didn't know you could do that particular trick. Kinda thing that would have come in handy in the past."

"Just learned it today myself. From a ghost."

Cicero raised an eyebrow and broadened his smile. "Full of tricks, aren't they? The dead, I mean."

"You sent for me, Nathan. I don't have to tell you I went to great pains to be here." Randy gestured at the body he wore, self-conscious of his hands, careful not to touch Penny. "I would have rather done this over the phone. What do you want?"

"We've failed, Dr. McKenzie. Katrina's prophecies are all coming true, one at a time. The god is released and will be free soon enough. Harry Peterson is out of commission, and Marguerite's boy is lurking around the village, planning God knows what. It's all playing out as she said it would."

A wave of despair washed through Randy. At long last they had come to the end. His heart was in free fall as the meaning of Cicero's words calcified in his mind. A net of sympathy saved him from being overwhelmed by despair. The prophecies were true, but someone understood his pain. Penny, still clinging to the back of his mind, understood.

"So . . . Paul?"

"Is dead, Dr. McKenzie. Or close enough." Cicero gestured in a callous, almost dismissive manner. "He knew what fate had waiting for him, and knowing your brother, he probably charged in like some noble idiot. What a waste."

A pang of anger, shared by the original owner of the body, flared up but was immediately shut down by Randy. With disquieting efficiency, he compartmentalized his grief into a neat package that he would deal with at a later time. Cicero wasn't detached because he didn't care; he simply had bigger worries weighing on him. The medical examiner understood.

"What about you, then?" Randy asked.

"Me? I've made my peace with what the next day holds. I'm far more concerned about what's in store for the rest of the world if we can't stop this thing from escaping. We've had so much time and we've accomplished so little. Help me out, Doctor. Tell me there's something we can do in the next few hours. Tell me we can save some lives."

Randy scratched Penny's chin, finding smooth skin instead of his unshaven stubble. He'd had a lot of time to think about this problem. Days spent in jail, avoiding conversation with a madman and reading bad books and magazines. His mind had often wandered, straining to find ways to avoid the inevitable.

"I think maybe we can contain it."

"Again?" Cicero sounded doubtful.

"You know how ancient cultures dealt with their own gods?"

"Pyramids, mausoleums, grand tombs meant to keep their horror from escaping. That sort of thing."

"Yes, but that's not the common thread," Randy explained. "I've always thought that the answer was vessels. Getting the creature to adopt the same limitations we have."

"Go on . . . ," Cicero's eyes narrowed in partial understanding.

"This!" Randall waved at the young woman's body he wore. "We trap it in human flesh."

"Ambitious, but how do we keep it in there?"

Randy had no answer to that question. He knew Cicero had little interest in yet another imprisonment scheme for the god. The creature, which, through too many decades, had become his nemesis. While the god of hate and death craved revenge against Sam Finnegan, Nathan Cicero was the one who had invented the rules that had kept it bound. Randy had no doubt that it was thoughts of the circus owner's death that fueled the god's rage.

"That, I don't know," Randy admitted.

"Neil's notes talk of a way to destroy it. He'd been very close to a solution when we last spoke. I'd hoped you'd have figured it out by now."

"The only thing I have is what you already know: 'god-touched metal.' A weapon imbued by a god to kill a god. Dad spent his whole life looking for something like that, and it got him nowhere. He and Harry came close in Scotland, but that didn't pan out."

"A god-touched weapon. Might as well go into battle with unicorn horns and seven-league boots."

He was right. There was no such thing. And if there ever had been, it was lost to history. Randy had long theorized that what his father and the other Craftsmen had been looking for was another god, or a being of similar power. From that they could forge their weapon and slay their god once and for all.

"I have it," Penny's lips said without Randy working them. In fact, the medical examiner's very essence was being pushed aside by the teenage girl's sense of urgency.

"I have a knife soaked in that monster's blood," she continued. "It cut Audrey's ghost like she was real flesh. Will that do? Can we kill that thing with it?"

Randy felt her anger literally shoving him aside. His soul was being pulled back to his body, like elastic that had been stretched to the breaking point and was about to snap. The last thing he heard was Cicero answer with a rare hint of hope.

"Perhaps not, but it's as fine a start as any."

CROWLEY

"WHY DIDN'T YOU tell me about Sasha?"

When Daniel stormed into the station, it was obvious to Stephen Crowley that his son was distraught. Regardless, he was glad to see the boy.

The inspector had considered Dr. Hazelwood's advice. Get his hand looked at, get some sleep, and figure out his priorities. Of course, seeking medical attention for his wound was out of the question. He couldn't trust Randy or afford to drive an hour out of town to get stitches. Erica had done a good enough job bandaging him up. His maimed hand could wait another day.

Sleep had also been postponed until later. The pain in his hand made it hard to keep his eyes closed, and again, he couldn't afford the time. He'd already wasted days sitting in his office, looking at case files and trying to get into the mind of the creature he was hunting. Staring at a map of Saint-Ferdinand and the locations of all the murders. Those of Sam Finnegan, of course, but also the more recent bodies found. It all seemed like a dead end, but something in his gut told him that he was getting close. That all he needed was one final piece of the puzzle and he'd find his god.

Or perhaps get a lucky break like he had in the Finnegan case.

All that remained was to figure out his priorities, which he was about to do until his son asked about his girlfriend.

"I didn't think you needed to know yet," said the inspector.

"Didn't need to know? This is my girlfriend, Dad! Not just some girl. Three years! Three years we've been dating. That's most of high school! She gets murdered and you don't even think to tell me?"

Stephen kept his cool. The boy had the right of it: he should have told him. But how? Even after eighteen years of experience delivering bad news to the people of this village, Crowley still couldn't get used to the idea of telling someone their loved ones were dead. He simply wasn't wired for it. And how could he deliver that kind of news to his own son? The inspector felt compassion for Daniel, but there was just no way to properly communicate it. As far as Crowley was concerned, the best way to deal with grief was to sit quietly with a beer, watch the sunset, and wait for it to pass. Dr. Hazelwood would have a field day with that one, but it had worked when his father had died, and it had worked when Marguerite had left. He simply couldn't deal with the crying, the yelling, and all the hysterics.

"You're right," Crowley conceded. "I should have told you. I should have told you when I found out and I should have told you how it happened."

Daniel swallowed, shaking his head. When had he ever admitted to Daniel that he was wrong about something important? "How . . . how did she die?"

"Something similar to Gabrielle LaForest. Less brutal but just as calculated. I don't think you need too many details."

"Was it the god?"

It was the inspector's turn to be taken aback. How long had Daniel known about this? How much did he know? Had he been snooping around his affairs, spying on him?

"Who told you about that?"

"Was it the god, Dad?"

"*Who* told you?" Crowley snapped.

Daniel was unflappable. When had the boy learned to stand up to him like that?

"Dan! This is important! Who told you about a god?"

The inspector slammed his hand onto his desk, a typical gesture for him to underline his frustration. He'd often do it when chewing out an officer. The loud bang was meant to shock and intimidate. This time, however, he was met with a flare of pain up his arm, and a look of disgust and pity from his son.

"Jesus, Dad . . . your hand."

The force of the blow had reopened the wound. As Stephen raised the extremity to his eyes, he could see red blossoms of blood seeping through the gauze.

"Well, shit," he said, wincing at the throbbing in his fingers.

"What happened?"

Crowley considered telling the truth. Laying it all out, from the circumstances that had led to his wife leaving him all the way to how he'd gotten in a fight with an elderly circus owner and lost. Perhaps his son would even help him find the god.

But that would put the boy, the only family he had left, at tremendous risk. *Get your hand looked at. Get some sleep. Get your priorities straight.* He'd failed at the first two tasks, but he could still get the third right.

In lieu of an explanation, Crowley used his good hand to pull open a desk drawer. He took out a thick, letter-sized envelope. Judging by the size and shape of the bulge in the paper, it contained an impressive stack of cash. Crowley slid the envelope over to his son.

"Take it. Put it in your pocket and go."

Daniel looked at the contents. Crisp, bank-fresh bills in denominations of hundreds and fifties were stuffed into the overflowing envelope. Thousands of dollars in cash, easily. Crowley had initially taken out the money for bribes, but he'd decided it would be better in Daniel's hands. Getting his priorities straight.

"Go where?" the boy asked, confused.

"Anywhere. Go hang out with your friends in Sherbrooke or take a trip south of the border. Just get out of Saint-Ferdinand for the rest of the summer."

The inspector could see the struggle behind his son's eyes. He'd seen the same thing in his own face during the last weeks. The desire to leave it all behind warring with his responsibilities. Hopefully, Daniel was smart enough to listen to the former.

Reluctantly, the teenager took the envelope. He tried to put it in the back pocket of his jeans, but it turned out to be too thick. Instead he pulled out a business card and placed it on the desk, mirroring Crowley's gesture of sliding it over.

"This guy's the one who told me about Sasha." Daniel tapped his finger over the name. Chris Hagen.

"He the one who told you about a god, too?"

"Yeah."

The inspector could see his son wasn't telling the whole truth. That didn't matter anymore to Crowley. He'd find the god. His gut reassured him of that every time he felt so much as a hint of doubt. The important thing now was that Daniel leave Saint-Ferdinand tonight.

"You know I didn't tell you about Sasha for your own good, right? We're the Crowley boys, Dan. We don't let things get between us."

Daniel seemed to consider the question with care. He tapped on the card again, his finger landing on the Sandmen logo. "This Hagen guy says he's a reporter. He was still loitering around our place when I left. He says he's been wanting to talk to you for a while."

Hagen. The name hadn't crossed his desk or been brought to his attention at all. No one like that had requested an interview or a statement. He also wasn't part of the group that met with Crowley at the church once a week. Yet there it was on his card: the Sandmen logo.

"I'll take care of him," Stephen said, picking up his car keys from the desk. "Get out of Saint-Ferdinand. I'll call you in a few days when I'm done here. I . . . I have a lot that I need to tell you." His son nodded glumly, then turned and left the police station.

DANIEL

IT WASN'T OFTEN that people would call a Saint-Ferdinand summer "cold." "Cool," perhaps. "Refreshing," for the rare optimist in the area. But mostly the season was referred to as "insufferably humid" or "goddamn hot." This morning, however, after a full night of sleepless worry, driving, mourning, and arguing, Daniel Crowley stepped out of his car and found that it was, indisputably, cold.

The moisture in the air had condensed into a thick fog that hung low to the ground. The carpet of smoke added a layer of mystery to the circus, making it that much more forbidding.

When last he'd come here, Daniel hadn't exactly felt welcome. The owner, Cicero, had made it clear that the teenager would find no help between the tents and attractions. This was enemy territory for a Crowley, but this time, he would insist on walking away with answers.

The hope of bringing Sasha back to life had been short-lived. The truth that Daniel could sieve from the night was that Hagen had tried to trick him into revealing where the god was held, or perhaps pit him against his own father.

In spite of the early hour, there were already signs of life at the circus. Shadows moved in the fog, and lights were being turned on here and there. The strong man with the handlebar mustache was making his way back from a porta potty. He seemed alert but unsurprised to see Daniel.

The smell of bread and eggs cooking mixed itself with the thick cold air, traveling out of a big open tent. Daniel's stomach began to growl as he realized he hadn't eaten anything since the previous day. Guided by either logic or hunger, the teenager decided that the best place to get directions to Cicero would be the mess tent. Other performers were also gathering there, eating their fill before the long day of preparing the circus for its grand opening. One would expect a sense of excitement and anticipation, but everyone hung their heads as if they were attending a funeral.

"Have a seat."

The voice was from Dustin, the man Cicero had sent to get Daniel a water bottle. He was pointing to a folding table that could seat up to six people. There was a pile of utensils at the center, along with salt and pepper shakers and a bottle of ketchup.

"Actually, I'm looking for—"

"We know what you're looking for," Dustin interrupted. "Sit and I'll get him for you."

Resisting the urge to argue and hoping to get something to eat in the bargain, Daniel did as instructed. He took a seat at the end of the table, his back to the exterior of the tent so he could keep his eye on the rest of the people there.

An old woman emerged from the growing crowd. She walked on wobbly legs, carrying two plates of food while a cane she obviously needed hung from her right wrist. She wore the accoutrements of a classic circus fortune-teller: innumerable bracelets of beads and hemp covered her arms, and her head was crowned in an elaborate turban. She wore a dress made from half a dozen layers of colorful fabric, which were all covered by a thick wool coat to protect her frail form from the morning chill. Daniel stood to help her, but she waved him off.

The fortune-teller put down the plates of food and lowered herself into a chair with much effort. In a habit born of years of repetition, she reached for the salt and pepper, adding very little of the first and too much of the second. Then, without bothering to look at Daniel, she grabbed a fork from the middle of the table and started to eat.

"Bacon and eggs. No toast," she said, pointing at his plate with her fork, a piece of egg flopping at its end. "All protein, no carbs. Right?"

"I'm looking for Nathan Ciccro," Daniel said while getting his own utensils. The eggs were overcooked, but the bacon was crispy without being burned. The food was welcome, and it surprised him how much filling his stomach helped get his thoughts in order.

"I'm his secretary. Talk to me."

"I don't know if you'll understand. I need to talk to Cicero. We met earlier this week, and now I need his help."

"We all understand, Mr. Crowley."

Daniel was done being surprised that people knew his name. They knew his father and they knew him.

"I don't think you do. I need to talk to Cicero, or people are going to die."

The old lady raised her eyebrows in what might have passed for surprise but was more a vague acknowledgment of an already-known fact. She nodded while chewing her last bite.

"Oh, we know about the deaths. We've known for a long time."

"Are you here to stop them?"

"I'm afraid not, Mr. Crowley. We could no more stop these deaths than we could stop the sun from setting. We are here either to play our part or to bear witness. Do you know why *you* are here?"

"I'm here to understand what's going on so that I can put a stop to it."

The old lady let out a long sigh and pushed away her empty plate. She then proceeded to steeple her bony fingers and rest her emaciated chin on top of them. Her skin was gray and had the texture of paper, thin and fragile, but her eyes were piercing and focused.

"Look around you, Mr. Crowley. Hardworking men and women. Acrobats and freaks. Some performers, some toiling behind the scenes. All of them know more than you do. Most of them have been at this for longer than you've been alive. Some, like Cicero, have been dueling with this god since before your grandfather was born."

She nodded at Daniel's disbelief. "That's right. Nathan is older than any man alive. Older than any man should be. Older than he cares to be. We've all been touched by the god of Saint-Ferdinand somehow. We're going up against something far greater than we are. Lives will be lost."

Daniel did as instructed, and looked around at the others in the mess tent. He was surprised to find each one of them looking back at him. The old woman was right. There was something unique about these people. A hodgepodge of athletic trapeze artists, strong men, dwarves, extensively tattooed curiosities, and even a few clowns. A man wearing the attire of a carnival barker nodded at him, and a beautiful girl with sad eyes, dressed in a lavish Victorian-era costume, gave him a smile. Such a diverse crowd had not been assembled in Saint-Ferdinand for as long as Daniel could remember.

Yet there was also something unnatural to them. A haunted look in their eyes. The acrobats moved with a precision that didn't happen in nature. The ink on the illustrated man seemed to move ever so slightly. A stage magician in full regalia tipped his hat with a gloved hand, his eyes glowing slightly beneath the chapeau. There was more to these people than Daniel had first thought.

"Are these the kinds of gifts my father is hoping to get from that thing?" Daniel said.

"Do you know what's the worst thing about this creature here in Saint-Ferdinand?"

Daniel shook his head.

"It's not how it can kill with a gesture or torture the souls of those who are already dead. It's not the vast power it wields or the terrible gifts it can offer. You'd think it might be that it's alien to both our way of thinking and how we interact with reality. That it sees us and knows us but doesn't care. All of that is terrifying in its own right, but what really makes this thing terrible is how it changes us. Not just by its touch but by how we react to it. It makes us into monsters, just as we made it into a god of hate and death."

The teenager contemplated that statement. It had happened to the Craftsmen decades ago. It had happened to William Bergeron and the rest of the Sandmen years after that. And, over the course of the past few weeks, it had happened to his father. All of them, monsters.

"Eat," said the old woman, pushing herself to her feet with her cane. "When you're ready, I'll take you to see Cicero."

RANDY

WHIPLASH DIDN'T BEGIN to describe it. In fact, comparing what Randy had been through to any physical experience would have come up short. Like saying that suicidal depression was a close cousin of exhaustion.

The medical examiner's soul had been stretched, pulled like taffy across a distance both physical and spiritual, between his body and that of Penelope LaForest. When the link was severed and the girl ejected him from her flesh, the one end of his essence still attached to the physical realm yanked him back.

A soul had no nerve endings. Randy had studied the dark arts long enough to know that, but that didn't mean it didn't feel. It just did so in a much more raw and fundamental way.

Randy felt the full force of that spiritual pain. The experience would have broken a mind unprepared for the peculiarities of working with the dead. But even for the amateur necromancer, the episode was traumatic. One moment, he'd inhabited a body completely unlike his own; then, through tremendous torment, he'd been forced to fill the flesh that had been empty. His own body now felt alien. Too skinny and too frail, it wasn't the vessel he'd spent most of his adult life inhabiting.

His eyes and mouth were dry. Nobody had bothered to close them for him. Muscles cramped, finally released from the position in which they'd been frozen. His mind, though, was pleased with the return to the status quo. Penny's brain had been young and supple, but too different for him to use efficiently. It was a new car filled with modern gadgets: capable of so much, but nearly useless to a driver familiar with a beat-up old manual-transmission truck.

"Whu . . . huh . . . Erica?"

Randy blinked rapidly, trying to moisten his burning corneas. He opened and closed his lips to secrete sufficient saliva to help him speak. Through his blurry vision, he could see the psychologist's worried face.

"Randall! Oh my God, are you okay? I thought you were dead."

He was resting next to the bars at the corner of his cell closest to Sam Finnegan's. The very spot where the old man had choked him. The place where he had died. Or near enough to loosen the bonds of his flesh. Erica's eyes were wild with fear, her cheeks wet with tears. Yet she was still there, more worried about his safety than her own.

"He is dead. We're all dead," Sam Finnegan said from his side of the wall.

Randy sat up, head spinning, his throat in agony. His tongue felt swollen, and he couldn't hear well from his left ear. Even with his medical experience, he was having difficulty deciding which symptoms were from being choked half to death and which were from having abandoned his body for the better part of an hour.

"Has he been this chipper the whole time I was gone?"

Erica glanced at Finnegan. "He's been mostly quiet. Muttering to himself. I . . . I did most of the yelling. I'm surprised no one's come down to check on me."

"I had Penny tell Matt everything was fine on my way out."

"You never left your cell, Randy," Erica said. "Please don't ask me to believe all this . . . supernatural nonsense."

"Erica . . . ," Randy reached between the bars and gently took her hand in his. He rubbed his thumb on the tops of her fingers in a circular pattern, trying to soothe her. "You saw Audrey's ghost. How much more do you need?"

"No." She shook her head. "I imagined that. We're people of *science*, Randall. How can any of this be real?"

"Ask myself that question on the regular," Sam said. His voice was lower to the ground, suggesting he'd probably sat down on the floor. Randy tried to ignore him.

"It's real, and it happened twenty years ago, too," the medical examiner said. "But you should forget everything you've seen, and leave. You're a smart woman, Erica. Please save yourself."

"You're not answering my question," she said.

"I can think of two options," Finnegan interjected again. "My favorite is like you said, Doc—none of this is real. It's all just a figment of my deranged mind, y'know? Maybe when Amanda passed away, I just . . . pop! Blew a breaker. Now I'm just makin' up stories for myself in a nice padded room. No one got hurt. No one gonna get hurt. And I didn't have to hurt nobody."

It was a terrible thing, thought Randy—to long for a broken mind in exchange for erasing all the horrors he had committed to keep the god contained. It only served to highlight how horrible the last two decades must have been for him.

"I'm sorry, Sam," he said. "I'm sorry you were left to deal with it on your own."

"Ain't no changin' things now," the madman said with a chuckle. "Lotsa people gonna die, no matter what."

"Why do you say that, Sam?" said the psychologist.

"Don't matter why, Doc. McKenzie's right: you need to leave. Saint-Ferdinand ain't safe. It never was, but it's going to get much worse, real soon."

Randy squeezed Erica's hand in his. His fondness for his protégé had always been something he'd kept in check. She was his student, of course, and any kind of relationship with her had been forbidden. After she graduated, age became the excuse. Then social differences. In time, the medical examiner had accepted that having her as a friend was good enough. But now, with the gravity of the situation pressing down on him, he regretted never doing more than admiring her from a distance.

"Please," he said to her. "You need to go."

"No. I want to know what's happening. I want to know how to stop it."

"Ain't nothin' you can do," Sam explained. "But that don't matter, does it? You're one of them people. Yeh just can't leave well enough alone, especially if you think you can help. One of them 'heroes.'"

"I don't believe in doing nothing if I can help."

"Ain't that what I just said?"

Erica pulled her hand from Randy's. He hoped she would leave. Forget him. Forget Saint-Ferdinand. With any luck, they'd all overestimated the god's rage. Perhaps it would be satisfied to butcher only those who'd imprisoned it for so many years.

Then she turned her head to where Audrey's ghost had stood. Randy knew what his one-time student was thinking. It was the trait that made her such a skilled therapist. That goddamned compassion. Not just for Audrey or for Penny or even for him. It was her empathy for the entire town that motivated her decision to stay.

"What happened eighteen years ago?" she asked him.

"Greed," Randy answered after a deep sigh. "The whole point was to destroy this thing. This god of hate and death. The Saint-Ferdinand Craftsmen's Association was the first to try. People like Cicero and my father scoured the globe, looking for secrets, making up their own."

"We do love our secrets, don't we?" Sam mused.

"Right." Randy cleared his throat. "Well, then came Edouard Lambert."

Erica gave him a confused look. It was a name she hadn't encountered in all the files she'd read and the people with whom she'd met.

"Lambert split from the Craftsmen. Started his own thing," Randy continued. "The Sandmen, he called them. Whereas the Craftsmen, they were originally more of a social club. It's when they stumbled upon the god that their purpose changed. The Sandmen, though, are a beast of a different nature. They didn't want to kill the god. They wanted to keep it sleeping and have it do their bidding."

"Stupid idea," Finnegan said from his side of the wall. "Like any god'll listen to us."

Erica was riveted. Whether she believed him or not, Randy couldn't tell, but considering all she'd seen so far in Saint-Ferdinand, she'd be crazy not to lend him some credence.

"Then what happened?" she asked.

"Same thing that's happening now. Some idiot thinks he's smarter than history, and he's going to try to take the god for himself. It's going to backfire like it did for Lambert."

Finnegan nodded. "Got himself killed, that one. Not just a little killed, neither. Ripped to shreds by a god! Hell, his body's been dead for eighteen years, but I bet ya his soul's still being killed to this very day."

"Tell me more. How were these Craftsmen going to kill this thing?"

"Ha!" laughed the madman in the next cell. "Never figured that out. Think we'd be spinnin' our wheels if they had?"

"Fine, then how do they keep it locked up?" She turned to Sam. "Can't we just go back to how it was before Edouard?"

"Wish we could, Doc, but that ain't gonna work this time. Y'see, the only power we ever had over this god was Cicero's Curse. The eyes, the camera, whatever form it took—so long as something was watching it, it couldn't escape. But a curse can only last so long, and soon, Ms. Hazelwood, soon that curse'll be broken for good."

VENUS

THE DRIVE FELT longer than it actually was. Between the smell of cigarettes and the poor suspension on the old truck, not to mention the feeling that the ancient piece of junk would fall apart at any moment, Venus felt like time had almost stopped. In reality, it only took a little over an hour to reach the circus.

It was still early morning when they arrived at the fields behind the Peterson farm. The big top loomed ominously above the farmhouse, alternating stripes of colored canvas reduced to gray in the dawn light. As they pulled into the farm's driveway, the whole area felt abandoned. Venus would have believed it was, too, if not for Penny's car, which was already parked there.

"Friend of yours?" Ezekiel commented, tossing a cigarette butt out his window.

He turned the truck into an improvised parking lot, where a dozen or so other vehicles were hidden away. With little care for either the racket he was making or the comfort of his passenger, Ezekiel stopped the truck and jumped out. Venus couldn't help but feel some degree of satisfaction as he winced in pain, putting a hand to his cracked ribs.

"Ugh," he complained, before stretching. "You hungry? From the smell of it, they're making breakfast already."

"I'm fine," she lied, ignoring her empty stomach. "Just take me to Cicero."

"Suit yourself."

Ezekiel waved at her to follow and walked into the forest of tents and kiosks. For a moment he resembled a fawn or satyr, beckoning her into the woods to disappear. Everything surrounding Venus felt out of place too. Not only in Saint-Ferdinand but in this day and age. She should be running away from all this, she knew. But there was an odd comfort in this old-fashioned circus.

Perhaps it was the smell of eggs and bacon that made Venus feel safe. Or maybe it was something more subtle, like the familiarity of the eye with a spiral iris, which was festooned onto everything here. Whatever it was, Venus felt more protected the deeper she walked among the attractions. The shadow of the big top enveloped her like an embrace. She knew, deep in her empty gut, that if something were to happen here, the strangers that lurked in these tents would defend her.

The scent of warm tea and alcohol filled her nostrils the moment Ezekiel pulled back the canvas. Sitting at a rickety folding desk was an old man with even older eyes. In front of him were ledgers of paper, candles, and a half-empty bottle of some amber drink. On the floor, sitting on a pile of blankets and cradling a large mug of steaming tea, was Penny. The older girl went from deeply contemplative to joyful at the sight of her friend.

"Aphrodite!" Penny smiled and rose up to embrace Venus.

"Shut up!" She smiled back.

Penny's smile faded quickly as she tightened her grip.

"I'm so sorry . . . ," the older girl said as she pulled away from her friend.

"Why? What happened?" Venus had been living in fear ever since she'd found the trapped god. She knew it was but a matter of time before the thin wooden door and cheap padlock were no longer enough to hide the creature within. Her eyes fell on the old man, who held a small bundle of quivering flesh in his arms.

The flayed cat lifted its skinless head, calling out to its owner with a raspy mewling.

"Oh God, no . . . ," She turned back to her friend, pleading, "Why is he here? Why is Sherbet here?"

"Your mother brought him to me," came a voice from behind Venus.

She turned to see an old woman dressed in too many robes and too much jewelry. Her skin was like sagging leather, and her eyes were like that of a husky dog, a pale, icy blue. Daniel Crowley followed her into the tent. Venus could see that something was wrong. There was too much understanding in his eyes. An unwelcome sympathy that spoke of a tragedy that mirrored her own.

Supporting herself with a cane, the old woman made her way to Venus. Stunned and perhaps a little intimidated, Venus allowed her face to be grabbed by the woman's bony fingers. It wasn't a gentle touch. The old lady twisted her head this way and that, appraising what she saw before letting go.

"You turned out to be a beautiful child," she finally said, a broken smile settling onto her wrinkled features.

"What happened to my mother?" Venus asked.

The old lady crossed the room without answering. She nodded to the old man before slowly lowering herself into a chair in the corner. With much pain, she gathered the various layers of her dress and cloak onto herself, shielding her frail body from the morning's cool humidity. After she was done, she beckoned Sherbet over. Without hesitation, the cat leaped from Cicero's lap and transferred itself to the old woman.

"Your mother is fine. Have a seat," the old man instructed, doing his best to sound sympathetic.

Looking back and forth between Penny and the old man, Venus did as requested. "Will someone tell me what's wrong with my father, then?"

The old man looked drunk, or at least very much in his cups. The bottle of bourbon before him was almost empty. As Venus settled into the rickety folding chair, Cicero emptied his own glass, putting it down with a ridiculous amount of care until it stood balanced on one edge.

"Nathan . . . ," the old woman admonished softly.

Cicero shrugged, producing a second glass from apparently nowhere and filling it halfway with the golden brown liquid. After sustaining Venus's blistering glare for another moment, he pushed the glass in her direction.

"Your father is dead," he said. His voice was calm, but resigned. "Drink."

There was a moment of disbelief. Venus turned to Penny, who confirmed the bad news with a sad nod.

It hurt. For so many reasons, it hurt. Her body felt too big, too cold, like she'd suddenly become but a pinprick of a person, lost in the uncaring, infinite galaxy that was herself. This must be how Penny had felt when Dr. Hazelwood had given her the news about her mother. Or maybe it was different for everyone. Penny had given out an agonizing wail when she'd heard. Venus remained silent. Her senses and her voice felt distant, out of reach.

There was no way to know how long she sat there. Parsing the information. Cataloging her emotions. No one dared interrupt her, though from the corner of her eye, she could see Penny wanted to lend comfort. Then it happened.

In the span of a thought, the pain went away. Her mind, struggling to deal with the situation, pulled a trick she didn't know it was capable of. Without her agreement or her prompting it, all her emotions about Paul, about her father, were suddenly packed up, indexed, and archived. More pressing issues took the place of her grief.

With a trembling hand, she reached for the glass of bourbon in front of her and raised it to her lips. She grimaced as she drank some of the liquid, the smell of it reminding her of the turpentine Abraham's father used.

"I have questions," Venus said in a quiet but unsteady voice.

"Maybe I have answers," Cicero responded.

"Ezekiel said I needed to talk to you. Why? Who are you?"

"My name is Nathan Joseph Cicero." He gave a mock bow from his chair. "I am the lucky one who found the creature that I'm told now resides in your shed. I am here to set you on your destiny!"

"Did my dad know he was going to die?"

"He did," the old woman said. "Even knowing that he would eventually perish here, he chose to build a life in Saint-Ferdinand."

"Why?" Venus still struggled with all this talk of destiny and fate.

"Because I described to him who his daughter would be. He said meeting a person like that was well worth the sacrifice."

Venus choked back a sob, but as quickly as the emotion had been dragged up from her mental storage, she pushed it back down.

"How do we kill that thing?" she asked.

"With this." Penny reached down to where she had been sitting. She unwrapped a bundled towel and carefully pulled out the kitchen knife she had used to stab the god.

"That didn't do much good last time."

"It's different now," Cicero said. "Imbued."

"What does that mean?" demanded Venus.

"Before your friend plunged the blade through the god's body, this was just an ordinary kitchen knife. But, as with all things, contact with the divine changed it. Nothing and no one can be in the presence of a god and remain the same. That knife, your shed . . . you."

Venus felt a wave of self-consciousness wash over her. She'd never admitted to anyone how close she had been to the god in her shed. Even her best friend, who had soaked her hands in the creature's cold blood, wasn't aware of the depth of contact between Venus and the beast that had killed Gabrielle LaForest.

"Is that how Dr. McKenzie was able to do . . . what he did?" Penny asked, still haunted by her out-of-body experience.

"No." The old ringmaster scratched the side of his face thoughtfully, deciding how to handle the question. "During his travels, Randy's father had collected a rather long list of . . . *tricks* I guess is the best word for them. The list is not a spell book. There's no magic in what Randy's been doing. Just a series of ways to con the universe into doing certain preestablished things. Things that have been woven into the fabric of reality since the very beginning."

"Like a back door in a piece of software . . . ," said Venus. "So, what now? We just take this knife, go back to my place, and stab the thing? Again?"

Cicero took a sip of his drink. A thoughtful smile hung on his face as his ancient eyes looked into the distance, or maybe the past.

"Oh, I'm afraid not. Today isn't about heroics. Today is about tragedy. By the time we get to the creature's jail, it will have broken free. And there's no need to go after it, because it will be coming to us."

WILLIAM

WILLIAM HADN'T STOPPED drinking. Sitting behind the wheel of his Lexus, he'd hoped that with enough booze, somehow the world would change. That perhaps he could, through sheer intoxication, turn back the hands of time a few weeks.

A month ago he had been sober. His wife had been a world-class homemaker instead of a carrion-feeding harpy, and his sweet, innocent Audrey had been the bright sunlight of his days.

William had considered driving to the drugstore. He had the keys in his pockets and could get his hands on whatever he wanted there. Carl, the pharmacist who worked for him, often talked about which drugs did what, idly discussing which ones had the most interesting and unusual side effects. A Valium and Percocet cocktail would make for an easy enough exit, especially with the alcohol already in his system.

In the end, however, his car brought him to the Crowley house. It was a large, luxurious domicile. On the side of the house, Bergeron could see a trailer with a decent-sized boat on top, waiting for a sunny day to go fishing.

All of it, William knew, Crowley owed to him. The inspector was good at his job, but life wasn't a meritocracy. The man had gotten the job because William, a powerful and influential man, wanted him to have it.

Crowley, Peterson, and McKenzie had shown up one evening, not long after Audrey's eventful birth. They made wild claims about how they could help his daughter, heal her weak heart, each offering a more outlandish option than the last. William hadn't believed a word of it. Not until they'd shown him what they could do. Peterson had carefully pulled out a painting of a blue jay so convincing, the bird actually moved and chirped on the canvas.

It was Randy's trick that had really sold him, though. The doctor had with him a white lab rat inside a crude iron cage. Without taking the animal out, Randy reached in and snapped the poor creature's neck. When William was convinced of the rat's demise, the doctor had proceeded to insert a series of dull black metal needles into its body. Without ceremony or fanfare, the rodent had reanimated, despite its still-severed spine.

These were "cheap parlor tricks" the three of them had claimed, compared to what was actually possible. All they needed was to get their hands on a god. So, with William Bergeron's support, they had rebuilt the Sandmen.

Today Randy McKenzie was rotting in jail, accused of murder; Harry Peterson was dying up in Sherbrooke Hospital; and Crowley, after years of promises, was about to lose everything he'd worked toward over the last decade. And William and his wife had lost their precious daughter anyway.

Consumed by his thoughts, William didn't notice the large SUV that made its way up the road until it was about to turn into the driveway. He hadn't intended on confronting the inspector. In fact, he didn't really know why he was here in the first place, but seeing an exhausted Crowley get out of his car and stroll purposefully toward him fired up something in William's soul.

Stumbling out of his own vehicle, the drunken businessman tried to affect a confident demeanor as he weaved forward to meet the inspector. He didn't want this any more than he'd wanted the impromptu meeting at his house the previous night. Yet here he was, and it was time the inspector knew who was really in charge.

"Will. If you're here to apologize for your wife, you could have done that over the phone," Crowley said.

"I'm not here to apologize for anything, Stephen. In fact, I'm here . . . ," Why was he here? What reason could he possibly have for upsetting such a volatile man as Crowley? "I'm here to tell you that you've been kicked out of the Sandmen!"

"Really, now?" The inspector flashed a humorless grin. "You're drunk. Get in my car, William. I'll drive you home before you get hurt."

"I'm not going anywhere. You owe us, Stephen." William's anger and grief were overwhelming. When Audrey had been born prematurely, with a weak and fragile heart, they knew she would always live in the shadow of her condition. They did their best to give her a normal life. With her being such an energetic child, it was easy to forget that their precious daughter was living on borrowed time. Until Erica Hazelwood had informed him that his baby was dead. He begged and pleaded to have her brought back to him, whatever it took. The only person to answer that plea had been Crowley. "You owe me!"

"Owe you? I don't owe you a goddamned thing!" Crowley's face was turning crimson, a sure precursor to his legendary wrath.

"You owe me my daughter!" William spat. His own face was a deep shade of purple, half-drunk, half-furious. When William had gone to identify his daughter's body, Crowley and Dr. McKenzie had repeated their promise from eight years ago. A chance to bring Audrey back. The medical examiner claimed he knew how to anchor the child's spirit to the world of the living. The inspector said that he could get Peterson to paint a living portrait of the girl. One more convincing, more alive than his stupid birds. Together, with the god under their control, they would bring her back. William had clung to that promise with all his emotional might.

"Oh yeah? Well, if you want me to keep that promise, you better back the hell off!" Crowley winced as he reflexively curled his wounded hand into a fist. The pain did nothing to quell his anger. "In fact, why don't you get your fat wife and the rest of that stupid social club you recruited to back right off with you?"

"Oh, oh, oh . . . ," William was emboldened by the drunken realization that Crowley was injured. "I don't think so. In fact, I think you're off the case, 'Inspector.' In fact, we already found someone new to fill your position. The Sandmen don't need you anymore."

"Oh really? Who's going to help you get your daughter back, then?"

"Your son!" William grinned triumphantly, expecting his opponent to be stunned into silence.

"Daniel?" Crowley was more confused than defeated. "You piece of shit! You leave my boy out of this!"

"Not Daniel. Francis." This time, the businessman got the desired effect. Crowley stared at him, his mouth agape in shock as William continued. "Oh yes. Your prodigal son. He's been in town a few days, and he's chosen to help us. Consider yourself fired."

Crowley now clenched both of his fists, ready to beat the insolent drunk into a pulp. The pain that shot through his right hand, however, nearly caused him to black out. When his vision cleared, all he could see was Bergeron's drunk, triumphant smile on his round red face.

Without thinking, the inspector pulled out his firearm and, in a single, fluid motion, fired a warning shot a foot to the side of the fat businessman.

Or so he'd intended. His aim was off from firing with his wounded hand. The 9-mm bullet hit home, punching into William Bergeron's right eye, tearing through his brain before exiting the back of his head and taking a sizeable chunk of his skull with it.

The fat man didn't fly back dramatically. Instead he crumpled to the ground like a rag doll that had been dropped. Through his remaining eye, William looked up at the sky. The trees in

Crowley's yard reached to the heavens, framing a tableau of sky and stars. He couldn't blink, he couldn't think, he wasn't even sure it was his eye that allowed him to see. After less than a second of lying still, he saw his daughter kneel down beside him. Her eyes had been replaced by black iron nails, and a shallow cut marred her beautiful face, but it was her. His beautiful Audrey.

William tried to smile, but his muscles wouldn't let him. Finally he was reunited with his daughter, but this time it would be forever. He searched his little angel's face for a sign that everything would finally be okay, but all he saw was worry and grief.

That was when he heard something else approaching. Something terrible and cold, ancient and evil. He tried to move but couldn't budge. His daughter put a hand on his cheek and mouthed, *I love you, Daddy,* before the darkness consumed him.

VENUS

THE WAIT WAS killing her. Venus had retreated to the floor, to the same place Penny had been when she'd first entered Cicero's tent. Still holding on to the now empty glass, she stared into the distance, trying to unravel her feelings. It was a juggling act. One moment she was desperate to go check on her father, hoping that she'd get to the house and find him alive and healthy. Then she'd think of what it would mean if the god were free, and instead longed to escape Saint-Ferdinand. Abandon this circus, abandon her friends, and simply run away. The compromise, waiting there for the creature to come to them, seemed like the worst option.

Penny had left the kitchen knife on the lone table where Cicero sat, drinking. The old man wouldn't touch the thing but couldn't tear his eyes from it either. Such a mundane tool. It was difficult to imagine that this was what they'd use to make their final stand.

Who would wield the thing? None of them were warriors. Penny had asked if the circus had a knife-thrower, or even a juggler. Surely someone who used blades in their act would be capable at fighting with one, but Cicero seemed uninterested by the idea. In fact, he seemed unmotivated to put up a fight of any kind.

Penny had tried to offer comfort, but Venus had quietly turned her down. While the sympathy would have been welcome, it would only serve to pull her grief out of the shadows and distract her from the present.

Instead her friend had gone to see Daniel Crowley. The inspector's son hadn't spoken so much as a word since his arrival. Through overheard conversation, Venus could make out that he, too, had suffered a great loss.

Cicero was paying close attention to the boy, stealing frequent glances in his direction. So when Daniel suddenly got to his feet and walked toward the old man's desk, the ringmaster frowned, attempting to pull himself to his feet. Old, gnarled fingers knotted themselves into fists as he stumbled over his own chair.

"Mr. Crowley . . . ," he began.

But even he noticed that this wasn't the same Daniel he'd previously met. Not even the same boy who'd driven out of Sherbrooke mere hours ago. The Crowley boy looked devastated. A husk had replaced the "that guy." His arms hung from slumped shoulders, and his back curved under the weight of his grief. His eyes told most of the story. They were cold and withdrawn, only coming to life when they settled on the circus owner.

"Mr. Cicero?" he said. "We need to talk, sir."

"I've told you everything I could, Mr. Crowley. What else could you possibly need?"

Daniel stood across the table, towering over the old man. When he was all smiles and confidence, he was the most charismatic boy in the room. "That guy." But with anger and grief weighing on him, he became a threatening presence. Venus could see some of his father in Daniel now, and so did the old master of ceremonies.

"I don't need anything. I want to help."

For the second time, Cicero was surprised. He looked toward the old fortune-teller, who gave him a knowing nod.

"Didn't think I'd see the day when I'd welcome a Crowley into my humble home and be glad for it. However, I'm not the one who needs your help right now, Daniel."

The old man jerked his chin in Venus's direction. She didn't welcome the attention, preferring to stew in her own misery. When Daniel looked at her, she saw herself reflected in his eyes and blushed. She didn't want him to see her like this. Her face wearing the same grieving expression that Penny had been carrying with her for the past week, that hollow stare of loss. She broke eye contact, but he walked over and knelt down.

"McKenzie? You okay?"

"No. You?"

"No."

He went to embrace her, but as she had done with Penny, Venus recoiled at the gesture. She didn't want to be comforted. She wanted to taste the pain, make sense of it.

"What happened to you?" she asked as a way to distract herself from the awkward moment.

"Sasha is dead. She never made it to our date because she's been killed. My father hid it from me."

Venus remembered Sasha from school. They didn't share any of the same social circles, but Daniel's girlfriend had been popular and smart. She lived in the city, as opposed to the outlying villages. Whatever limited interaction the girls had, it had been polite and friendly. Sasha and Daniel had seemed like the perfect couple. Homecoming king and queen.

"I'm so sorry," she said, trying to inject as much sincerity as she could into her sympathy

"Thanks. I . . . I'm not sure how to feel anymore." He glanced sideways at Penny. "Do you believe them? What they say about your dad."

"Maybe. I don't want to." Venus looked accusingly at Cicero and the fortune-teller. There was no doubt. The costume gave it away, but it went beyond that. The older woman's ice-pale eyes looked around with a detachment brought only by knowledge. She watched the assembled group with profound sadness and infinite understanding, like she could already see them dead.

"I don't blame you for doubting what your ears tell you but that your eyes haven't confirmed," the old woman croaked. She dragged her chair from the desk to where the teens sat on the floor. "Should I have Ezekiel drive you home? See things for yourself? If I'm right, you die, but at least you'd have your certainty."

Venus had seen too much to take that chance. She knew in her gut that the old woman was right, but it was too soon to admit it to herself. "What about my mother?"

The question had been at the back of her mind for a while now. Virginie had brought her cat to the circus, and then for some reason she'd vanished. No one had mentioned her, and through her grief, Venus had almost forgotten about her mother.

"She's fine. She went back to your place to fulfill her own part of the play. She's stronger than I gave her credit for," the old woman said with something like pride in her voice.

"But she's alive? She's going to live?"

"We all die one day, but she will live tonight."

"How can you do this?" Daniel asked. "How can you all just let these things happen and do nothing?"

Venus shared his outrage. Of all the things she'd heard in the last weeks, the hardest to swallow was that things were immutable. In essence, Cicero had told her that the fortune-teller had predicted they would win. That in the end, the god would be vanquished. The old man wouldn't say how, only that the innocuous weapon on the table was supposed to accomplish the task.

"I see the price of victory and the path to get there," the old woman said. "Even if we could upset this balance, why would we? Knowing that things could easily get worse."

"So the ends justify the means?" Venus asked.

"That is one way to look at it. Or you could say that the means would not pardon the ends, should the god break free."

"How did you learn to do it, to tell the future?" Penny said. "Is it a trick, like what my uncle does?"

"Oh, it's no trick. This is a gift, one from the very creature you have locked up in your shed. Not the best gift, in hindsight."

"What do you mean?"

"I asked for the power to see the future, and in exchange, I would free the god from its bonds. One of a long line of fools who thought to match wits with a god. Well, it granted my wish, and the first thing I saw was the evil such a creature would sow upon the world. So I broke my end of the bargain, knowing full well what it would cost my friends and family."

Venus looked down at her empty glass. Her stomach lurched at the thought of what the old woman had gone through. Having to pick between those she knew and loved and the fate of the world, sacrificing others for the greater good—she wasn't sure she could do it herself. She thought she would vomit if her stomach hadn't been empty save for grief and bourbon.

"Why did my mother bring you my cat?" she asked, changing the subject.

"Your mother and I have known each other a long while, child. Long before you were born."

It seemed everyone knew everyone, and the villagers and circus people had intermingled at some point in the past. But exactly how was everyone connected?

"I still don't understand why we're just waiting here," Daniel said. "Shouldn't we be drawing plans? Preparing somehow?"

"We have spent our entire lives preparing, Mr. Crowley," Nathan Cicero said. "Now our time is nearly up. We should have passed this torch a long time ago, but the truth is, we don't know much more than you do. Never have."

"Pass the torch? What if we don't want that kind of responsibility?"

"No one does," Cicero agreed. "Circumstances don't wait for someone to demand the opportunity for glory. They show up when they will. I thought you were here to help. But perhaps you are more your father's son than I assumed."

"What's that supposed to mean?"

Venus saw Daniel's fists clench, halfway proving the old man's point.

"Normalcy doesn't lend itself to greatness, Mr. Crowley. The more tumultuous a life, the more chances one gets to leave one's mark. Life is only as rewarding as it is exciting. Someone your age should recognize that. See the gift for what it is. Through great tragedy, you have the chance to become a hero."

"I don't want to be a hero." Venus pulled her knees to her chest.

"I'm sorry, my child," Katrina said, and sighed. "In some cases there's the opportunity to decide, but the rest of us are forced into our roles."

"I've found a list of my grandfather's associates. I can continue his research. Why can't we just use this so-called curse of Cicero and trap the god while we find a permanent solution?"

"The curse isn't something that's cast, like a spell," the old woman explained. "It's a bargain, a deal struck between god and man. They are both bound by it."

"So if Cicero were to die . . . ," Venus looked toward the old man's strange blue eyes again.

"The bargain ends and the god is free, yes."

For the first time, Venus realized that among them, Nathan Cicero was the only one smiling. He raised his glass in a toast.

"Today, it seems, is as good a day as any to die."

Then the old master of ceremonies upended the last of the bourbon into his mouth.

CROWLEY

THE TWO MEN stared at each other intently. Inspector Stephen Crowley, driven by rage and purpose, and Chris Hagen, smug and in control. A few yards and fifteen years lay between them.

Unlike the other Sandmen, Chris wasn't surprised to see Crowley standing on the Bergerons' front lawn, pistol in hand, his face beet red and his uniform stained with sweat.

Immediately, Beatrice Bergeron put a protective hand on the young man's shoulder. Chris politely patted her hand away before stepping forward to meet his father.

"I was hoping you'd come," Hagen called out enthusiastically. "I assume William came to you?"

"I don't need to talk to you, boy," said Crowley, the spittle flying out of his mouth gleaming in the dull morning light. "I know a mouthpiece when I see one."

Chris reached for his heart mockingly, quickly straightening back up before calmly putting his hands into his pants pockets. The very image of nonchalance. "Ow! You wound me, Stephen. Can I call you Stephen?"

"I don't give a shit." The inspector flexed his wounded fist, feeling blood seep once again through the bandage. "Just tell me where your mother is."

"And why would I do that, exactly?" Hagen started circling his father, studying him from every angle like a lab specimen. "Did you bite off more than you could chew, Stephen? Do you need your wife to come home and fix everything?"

"Where?" Crowley insisted.

"Far. But you're right. I'm here on her behalf. I'm here to check up on you." Chris Hagen glanced back at the cult members behind him. Ordinary villagers, seduced by the promise of something greater than themselves. Sheep, most of them. "So far I'm not impressed with what you've achieved."

The young man turned back to the inspector, grinning with perfect teeth, beaming with arrogance. "But I think I can take it from here."

Crowley looked into Chris Hagen's eyes, but all he could see was his son Francis. The last time he'd seen the boy was on the day Marguerite left. She'd been depressed ever since her father's disappearance three years prior, but that evening she'd been particularly distraught. Raving about monsters and gods. Stephen, only a lieutenant back in those days, had to work that night. He'd left his wife, promising to be back as soon as his shift was over. But when he returned, she had gone, taking his elder son with her. All she'd left was a wooden chest, half-emptied on their bed, and little Daniel, crying in his crib.

The next day, Crowley had followed her trail back to the circus. Back to the owner—an old man called Nathan Joseph Cicero. A friend of Edouard Lambert, Marguerite's father. Tired, emotionally distressed, and desperate, Crowley hadn't had the patience to handle Cicero's ambiguous and evasive answers. The situation quickly escalated to blows.

A decade and a half later, just as the inspector felt like he was on the precipice of success, his firstborn had returned. And the son of a bitch was attempting to steal the fruits of his labor.

"You think those idiots are going to lead you to the god?" Stephen chuckled. "These morons couldn't find the ground if they fell off a chair."

"Tsk. You should show more respect to your constituents, Stephen. You're a public servant," Hagen said. "But no, I don't expect them to lead me anywhere. While you were on your wild-goose chase, Mother and I did our homework. I've studied. I've done the rituals, dropping souls into the river and following the current. A few more deaths, and I'll be able to track down the god, wherever it is. Maybe you can be useful for once, Stephen. How about it?"

Crowley swung his bloody right hand toward Chris Hagen. The young man danced to his father's left, light and agile, but didn't see the feint. Crowley's left hand closed viselike on Hagen's neck, nearly crushing his windpipe.

Leveraging his height and weight, the inspector threw Hagen to the ground without letting go of his throat. Placing his right knee onto his estranged son's chest, Crowley drew his face to within an inch of the young man's. The villagers who called themselves the Sandmen gasped in collective surprise.

"You want to push me into a corner, boy?" Spittle showered Chris Hagen's face. "Want to see what I'm capable of when I have nothing to lose?"

Everything he'd done, all his compromises over the years, were in the hope of finding Marguerite and Francis. Of figuring out why she had left. What had happened to her father, Edouard. The wooden box and its contents had opened up a world of possibilities and a thousand potential threads that might or might not have led to his wife and son. It had been an all-consuming obsession for the inspector, shaping everything in his life. The only place he'd ever found solace from his obsessive quest was when he spent time with . . .

"Daniel."

It was Beatrice Bergeron who'd spoken. The plump woman had come within a yard of the grappling father and son. Her voice cut through the blinding rage that was consuming Crowley as he crushed the life from his elder son. His son who had come back just to take everything away from him.

"That's something you have to lose, Stephen Crowley," she continued. "If you don't let go of Mr. Hagen right this instant, so help me God, we're gonna make sure to take Daniel away from you, too."

The inspector's first thought was to rip out the fat old woman's throat. In fact, at that very moment he would have gladly painted the Bergerons' front yard red with the blood of his former friends and allies. But she was right. He did have something else to live for. His wife's departure may have torn a gaping hole in his soul, but the boy she'd left behind had filled it.

Reluctantly, Crowley let go of Chris Hagen's throat, leaving stark white imprints where his fingers had been.

"That's right, Stephen," William's unsuspecting widow said as Hagen crept out from underneath the inspector's shadow. "Nice and slow."

Maybe I should tell you what I did to your husband, you cow, Crowley thought. He wanted to hurt her with some parting words, but he knew better than to incriminate himself. Soon this would all be over, and when the dust settled, it would do well to have been prudent.

The inspector backed away, slowly followed by the dozen people gathered on the lawn. He could see in each one of their eyes that they would gladly make good on Beatrice's threat.

As he started his SUV, Crowley consoled himself with the thought that they all believed they were safe from him. That they had neutralized him. The fools didn't realize what they'd really done. They hadn't reminded him of a reason to live. They'd given him a reason to kill.

VIRGINIE

THE CORDLESS PHONE hung limply in her left hand as Venus's mother beheld the spectacle before her. She could hear the voice at the end of the line, a weak crackling, as Jackie, the dispatcher at the station, tried to get Virginie to answer her questions.

The decision had come suddenly to her. Katrina had predicted she would meet her end trying to prevent whatever future had been foreseen for Venus. The old woman had also said that she would fail, but her prophecies were vague and made no promise about how or when Virginie would take part in this fatal game.

So while mourning her husband's death in a lonely tent at the traveling circus, Virginie had weighed her options. She could wait there for the inevitable, like livestock mindlessly awaiting slaughter, or she could choose to meet her destiny head on. She decided to see for herself what had become of Paul. To see how much truth there was in Katrina's predictions. Maybe even throw them out of balance.

"Mrs. McKenzie?" the voice scratched from the phone in her hand. "I have Inspector Crowley on the line. Should I patch you through?"

Virginie's hand shook to the point where she almost dropped the phone. She knew about the long quarrel between Stephen

Crowley and Nathan Cicero. While she didn't quite see the inspector as an enemy, she had always been wary of him. Seeing Venus with his son had been a surprise indeed. Yet she herself had never witnessed any kind of nefarious behavior from the Crowley boys.

"Yes."

"Mrs. McKenzie?" The inspector's voice cut through the static of the portable phone. He sounded worn-out and tense. "I understand you have an unusual problem?"

It was an understatement, to be sure. Virginie cleared her throat. "Yes. I think you should come here and have a look." She hesitated a moment before adding, "Bring . . . bring everyone."

The inspector acknowledged her, but she couldn't hear him. Her hand dropped to her side again, and the phone fell into the grass.

That was her first gambit. Crowley was the enemy, according to Nathan. A misguided fool who stood to let everything fall apart. But what if keeping him from the god in her shed was what allowed him to survive the coming events? What if, like so many before him, meeting the god would be his end? What if that was all it took to derail Katrina's prophecy about Venus?

Gathering her wits and courage, she took a step forward to address the creature before her. It was time to attempt her second gambit.

This wasn't the monster she had expected. At first glance, it seemed to be a mass of writhing tendrils of exposed flesh and bones. A living lattice of animal and human remains, but at the center, she could see the god for what it was. Its proportions were that of a child no older than her own daughter. If it were made of mortal flesh, she might have felt sympathy for the creature. But all she could see were blood and shadows, along with two glowing eyes. Every move it made, from the steps it took to the most subtle head turn, felt awkward and wrong.

Careful inspection of the beautiful cape of bones and organs it wore revealed the disassembled bodies of a teenager and her husband, Paul. Where one finished and the other began was impossible to tell. As the god stepped forward, more sections of the grisly robe peeled away from the wall of the shed. The horrifying garment subtly writhed and twitched, suggesting that not all its elements had been allowed to die.

Still, the monster worked on its creation. Moving this tendon or nudging that bone shard, ever perfecting its art. Virginie tried to make sense of it. Was it art? Clothing? Or did the garment serve some darker purpose?

"H-hey . . . ," Virginie called out. "I want to make a deal with you. That's what you do, isn't it? Make pacts?"

The thing kept working, its nimble, blood-soaked fingers moving swiftly and with calculated grace to readjust living flesh on its creation. Had it heard her? Minutes passed, the heat and stench in the shed becoming increasingly unbearable as the rising sun warmed up the charnel house.

"Not with you," it finally answered, its voice devoid of all emotion but hate and contempt.

"Why not?" Virginie felt almost insulted. What made her unworthy of being granted what so many others had received? Or was the god aware of her plans?

"You have broken your word to me. We are unbound."

"You've never met me! You . . . you don't even know who I am!"

The god halted its work and slowly turned to face Virginie. Her heart thundered under her breast, fueled by the adrenaline that surged in her veins. Surely the creature would reach out for her, take her flesh to complete its work. The idea, as terrifying as it might be, had a twisted appeal. To have her body merged with what was left of her husband. To have the pain, grief, and fear be obliterated along with her brain, mind, and soul. But the god just stood there. Studying her.

"I know you," the god said in its skull-splitting, unspoken voice. *"Katrina. You have broken your word before, and you will break it again."*

"What? No. Katrina is my mother . . . "

How did the thing even perceive the world around it? Images? Smells? Souls? No matter what she looked like to it, Virginie had to convince the thing that she was her own, unique individual. That she was trustworthy. That she could bargain with a god.

"*I* can free you! I can set you loose. *Please*," she begged, but the god turned back to its work, patient and uncaring.

She was still pleading with it when Stephen Crowley's SUV rolled into the McKenzies' driveway.

CROWLEY

STEPHEN CROWLEY STOOD in silent awe. For eighteen years he had been hunting down the thing that now stood before him. *A god of hate and death.* He'd read the line so many times, but now he knew the truth. As terrible as the powers before him might have been, they were contained. A madman had kept the creature jailed in a cave for eighteen years. A miraculous painting of an eye had come before him, and a cabal of fools before that. Now this so-called god was being held by an old garden shed and a fifty-dollar digital camera. Even with the door lock busted open, the thing couldn't move outside a limited perimeter.

All thanks to the curse of Cicero. Like a genie in a bottle, the god could grant one's deepest desires. Or so Crowley hoped. Marguerite had known more, of course, but after her father's death at the hands of the god, she had vanished. The inspector had always thought that fear had chased her away. Francis's return seemed to suggest otherwise.

The wound on his right hand tingled this close to the creature. It felt like his blood wanted to crack open the scab and ooze toward the god.

Not that the creature needed any more material. It had already turned the McKenzies' shed into a museum of horrors. Bones and guts and veins decorated the walls, seeming to pulse in time with Crowley's increasing heartbeat.

The inspector leaned down, turning off a portable phone that lay beeping on the ground. Virginie McKenzie, who had placed the call to the station, was nowhere to be found. It was difficult to know if she'd become part of the god's terrible artwork.

The god.

It turned to observe Crowley with its glowing red eyes.

"I'm, uh, here to free you." The inspector's voice came out weaker than he had intended. The creature did not answer but stood motionless. Expecting more than words. "In exchange for a few favors."

"You are . . . new," the creature spoke. Its voice was legion, each syllable a scream from hell itself, somehow harmonized into words and branded upon Crowley's brain. *"You presume to bind me in fresh chains."*

"No." Was there a point in lying? "I just want to help, but I know you have little love for humans. I don't want to suffer your wrath."

"My freedom for your safety? Done."

"And my son's!" Crowley was quick to add. It was said that to be touched by a god changed a man. Gave him power. His search had cost him so much already. He didn't just want more; he deserved more. "And . . . and your blessing."

The god cocked its head to the side in a gesture that was deceptively human. It stepped closer, the stench of fresh blood emanating from its crimson-slick body. Crowley could finally see through the gory lattice to the details of its face. It had no lips, no pores, and no nose. Only two burning red eyes. It was little more than a child's drawing of the human form.

"You wish to share . . . my power. To have my blessing . . . ," The god of hate and death pondered, amused. Each word like a knife through Crowley's thoughts. *"Step forward."*

VENUS

VENUS LOOKED AT her reflection in Penny's blade. Her emerald eyes were bloodshot and tired. Everywhere she and her friends had turned, hoping to find help dealing with the thing in her shed, they had been met with disappointment, failure, and horrid revelations. Each of them had suffered a terrible loss. And unless Katrina and Cicero were wrong, the god was now free, and it was coming for them.

It all came back to the old woman's predictions. Vague in places, precise in others, they were all unfolding, coming together. By tomorrow nearly every one of her prophecies would be fulfilled. Katrina could see little beyond the coming day, and even she could not say why.

"How much do you believe them?"

Venus looked up. Daniel Crowley stood over her, hands in his pockets, doing his best to look composed.

"I have no reason not to believe," she answered. "Everything else they've said is true."

"Except for the fact that it's all crazy nonsense, of course." He sat down next to her on the ground, giving her a sympathetic nudge with his elbow.

"Of course," Venus said. "There is that."

The morning had passed without further incident. The circus was meant to open that day, but no customers had shown up. Yet the performers and other employees went about their business, unperturbed. Popcorn was popped and cotton candy spun. The Ferris wheel was lit and turning.

"What are you doing with that?" Daniel pointed to the knife. "Isn't it dangerous if it can kill a god?"

"Katrina gave it to me." Venus brushed the tip of her thumb on the edge of the knife, appreciating how sharp it was. "She said I'm the one who is supposed to fight the god. She doesn't say if I come out victorious, though. I don't think I'm our savior."

"They do dance around their words, don't they? Like they're not sure what they're talking about."

"I don't think they do. I think that they gave up a long time ago. You'd think they'd have more to say about your situation, Daniel." Venus switched her focus from the blade to the inspector's son. She wasn't sure if her comment was meant as an accusation or a casual observation, but it was odd how Cicero had been shocked by Dan's appearance.

"Maybe it's because I'm the only one whose parents aren't dead so far," he said.

Without a word, Venus stood and walked away, leaving the knife on the ground.

"Aww, shit." The Crowley boy picked up the kitchen utensil and stumbled to follow her, cursing his insensitivity. "Venus, I'm sorry! I didn't—"

She stopped, and Daniel felt relief course through his mind. The last thing he needed was for some ridiculous faux pas to ruin his remaining relationships. His father was lost to him, his estranged brother was a psychopath, and Sasha was dead. He'd never felt so alone.

As he caught up to Venus, though, his relief melted into dread.

Flashing red and blue lights reflected off the tents near the circus entrance. Performers walked out from their stalls and canopies to stare, forming a large circle around a lone police SUV.

"Dad?" Daniel said.

Despite the silence, the air was electric. Performers and circus workers of every shape, size, and color gathered around the vehicle. Some were visibly hostile to the new arrival. Others were obviously afraid, huddled together like terrified animals. But all of them seemed to recognize that this was Stephen Crowley and that he was an enemy.

Venus stepped toward the entrance of Cicero's tent. Her eyes still blurry and her stomach still aching, she waited for what would happen next. Part of her wanted to run home, in the hopes of finding her father working in the garage and her mother drying tea leaves. Part of her wanted the inspector to reveal the whole thing had been a terrible prank, concocted by the cruel circus performers. But her legs kept her rooted in place. Morbid curiosity had taken over where common sense should have prevailed.

The driver's-side door swung open. Calm and purposeful, Stephen Crowley got out of his SUV. With tired, emotionless eyes, he surveyed the small crowd. Venus saw that his right hand was wrapped in a blood-soaked bandage. His uniform was dirty and grass-stained. It had been a rough night.

"Nathan Joseph Cicero!" Crowley called out. He placed his good hand on his sidearm.

Venus recognized something in his voice. Nails on a blackboard. Needles in her mind. The god was free, and part of it was now inside Stephen Crowley.

The inspector was here to kill the circus owner. Venus knew it, and so did everyone else in attendance. That was why the circus had come. This was the only performance they planned to give. To bear witness to the death of a man who had cursed a god.

Venus looked at the crowd. Each of these people had traveled with Cicero, some of them for decades. Each had a relationship with the old man, and each knew that this was his destiny. Yet they had followed him.

She was pulled out of her reverie as the old man walked past her. He had put on his powder-blue tuxedo and matching top hat. The ostentatious accoutrement, like its wearer, was ancient and faded. The circus owner supported himself with a wooden cane so old, it might as well have been fossilized. He continued on, without so much as a glance in Venus's direction. This was his time. His moment.

The circus workers parted as Cicero made his way through them. Some patted him on the back or shook his hand; some begged and pleaded with him. As the master of ceremonies approached the SUV, Crowley pulled out his firearm, holding it awkwardly in his left hand. That was when it dawned on Venus that this wasn't a confrontation; it was an execution.

"What the hell is he doing?" she asked no one in particular. "Why isn't anyone doing anything?"

"He's meeting his destiny," Katrina the fortune-teller answered from behind her.

"Screw destiny! There's one of him and two dozen of us! We can't just let him do this!"

"Why not?" It was Ezekiel who broke in this time. "Crowley could kill several of us before we got that gun out of his hands. We're all willing to die for Cicero, but none of us want to see one another be killed for him."

"Besides," added the old woman, "it's what he wants."

In the distance, Venus could see Cicero finish his walk toward the gallows. Perhaps it was the bourbon in his veins, but the old man was smiling. Not with joy or happiness, but relief.

"Why?" the teenage girl asked, grasping to understand.

"He's old, Venus. So old. He could be my grandfather," the fortune-teller said. "And he's been carrying the god's burden since he was a child. It's time he passed it on."

To us, Venus thought.

"I should have done this eighteen years ago, Nathan," growled Crowley as he raised his weapon. "Prepare to meet your god."

Venus wanted to turn away but knew she had to watch. Not out of morbid curiosity, but a sense of duty. To witness the passing of a man she'd met only yesterday, but who had had a profound impact on every aspect of her life.

There was a disturbance in the crowd. *Daniel.* The inspector's son was being held back by a handful of performers. Despite his athletic build, there was little he could do to escape the grasp of those restraining him. Venus felt sympathy for the boy, knowing that he was witnessing the final damnation of the man he admired most.

"Back off, Dan!" Crowley barked at his son. "I'm doing this for you."

Turning back to Cicero, who was leaning patiently on his cane, the inspector's demeanor changed. Venus couldn't hear them, but the old man said something to Crowley that softened his features. For a moment she thought the crisis had been averted. That the old master of ceremonies had been holding an ace up his sleeve all this time and that, through magic or convincing words, he had avoided his own death at the last possible minute.

Crowley gave a polite nod and then, without hesitation, he shot a bullet through Cicero's head.

RANDY

"LAST CHANCE, ERICA."

Randy had recovered from his ordeal. At least, as much as could be expected in the little time he'd had. He heard a commotion upstairs. Footsteps. Phones ringing. The few people in the station were scrambling for some reason. Considering the discussion he'd had with Cicero, there was every reason to believe that the shit had finally hit the proverbial fan.

As much as the medical examiner wanted to contain or kill the god, he was more concerned with Erica's survival. Actually, *survival* wasn't the appropriate word. Dying was one thing, but dying in Saint-Ferdinand was quite another. He'd have slit her throat himself if it meant she could escape the torment of what awaited her beyond the veil. But if the god was free, there was no telling how long its grasp had grown.

"I'm staying," she said. "I want to help."

There was courage in ignorance, Randy thought. She stood her ground because she was a good person, but also because she couldn't fathom what they were up against. Yes, she'd seen a ghost, but it meant nothing in the grand scheme of things. The die had been cast. The cards had been dealt. There was nothing to be done about it now. The medical examiner had never heard Erica's name spoken by the fortune-teller at the circus. Perhaps she was destined to live.

"You need to get us out of here, then."

"Both of you?" Erica was surprised. Seeing Finnegan strangle the life out of Randy had shaken up her belief that, despite his history of mass murder, the old man was relatively harmless.

"Both of us."

"Okay. How?"

Randy thought about that for a moment. Escape was another problem he'd pitted his intellect against during his incarceration. Unfortunately, he simply didn't know enough about the workings of the jail to solve it. He'd assumed that Crowley would have freed him by now.

"Maybe if you set off the fire alarms," he said. "I don't think the cell doors will open automatically, but someone will have to come check . . . "

His words trailed off. The commotion upstairs had stopped. All he could hear now was a single pair of feet walking across the station. Hurried and nervous and wearing boots. Like Pavlov's dog, his stomach gurgled at the sound.

Jackie. Bringing his dinner.

"Tell her I'm not well," Randy whispered.

A moment later the door to the cellblock opened, and Jackie's voice called down.

"Dr. Hazelwood? I'm going to ask you to come upstairs. I don't have enough staff to allow for visitors right now."

Randy nodded at Erica, prompting her to do as he'd instructed. Jackie would trust her. Jackie wouldn't let him suffer in his cell.

"I . . . I don't think Dr. McKenzie is feeling too well," Erica said.

"What? Let me have a look."

She didn't suspect anything. She was simply worried for his well-being. But the moment she was within arm's reach, Randy grabbed her from between the bars and pulled Jackie toward him, slamming her forehead on the cold metal.

"Her gun!" he called out to Erica.

The psychologist didn't hesitate. She made a grab for the firearm, but Jackie didn't go down without a fight. Surprised to be facing two opponents, she was quickly disarmed.

"Randy!" the officer objected. "Are you insane?"

"Open the door!" Erica yelled at the poor policewoman, pointing the gun.

Erica was clearly not used to holding a weapon. Randy didn't wait to see how the standoff would end. Holding on to Jackie's hair in one tight fist, he took the keys from her belt and tossed them to Erica.

After some fumbling with the wrong keys, the psychologist managed to get the door open. From there, it was a simple matter of tossing Jackie into his cell. Columns of books and magazines were knocked to the floor.

"I'm sorry. Really sorry, but Stephen did something stupid and I have to stop him."

"You don't want to do this, Randy!"

Furious, Jackie pulled her nightstick out and rushed the cell door, but she tripped on the tomes that littered the floor, smacking her head against the ground with a loud thud.

"Oh shit," Erica said. "Is she okay?"

Randy looked over at Jackie's unconscious body. Her chest seemed to be moving and there was no obvious wound to her head.

"Hopefully," Randy said before locking the door to the cell with the policewoman inside.

He then went to open the door to Sam Finnegan's cell, but hesitated. Instead of sending Erica away alone, he could escape with her. They could abandon Jackie and Finnegan, leave Saint-Ferdinand and its dark, bloody secrets behind. All they had to do was walk up the stairs and drive away.

What then, though? They weren't lovers who could go on the lam together. The whole point of having Erica leave was so that her life wouldn't be destroyed. They were well past that point now.

He placed the key inside the cell door lock. "Let's go," he said to the madman. "I have a plan."

"Do you now?" said the Saint-Ferdinand Killer, a toothy, curious smile splitting his face. "Let's hear it."

DANIEL

DANIEL RUSHED, KNIFE in hand, toward his father. They'd had their differences recently, but never had the boy expected that things would go this far. As far as he knew, Stephen Crowley had never shot or killed another man.

Before he could get to his father, however, Daniel was stopped again by the small crowd gathered around the SUV. Were they doing this for his protection or to keep him from interfering in what they saw as the inevitable? Their hands grabbed at him, holding him back as he attempted to push through. Only once the deed had been done would they release him.

"Dad! What . . . what have you done?"

He couldn't believe it. Standing before the amassed circus employees, his father looked up from the lifeless body of Cicero. Daniel could finally see the extent to which his father had gone. This was Stephen Crowley with his fury unleashed. He had become the embodiment of his rage. His skin was red with anger and his eyes burned with an intensity that no human should ever possess.

"Get in the car, Daniel."

Since the day he could understand English, Dan had learned the difference between Stephen Crowley's fatherly voice and the tone he used when he required immediate, unquestioning obedience. Now there was an edge to his voice that Daniel had never heard before. His fury had been given control, purpose. Something had changed inside him.

"I can't," Daniel answered, standing as he looked down on the serene corpse of Nathan Cicero, squeezing the knife still in his hand.

"You can and you will, buddy." Crowley's left hand tightened on his gun. "The Crowley boys aren't welcome here."

Daniel raised his eyes to his father. His fishing buddy, his best friend, the man who had raised him single-handedly. That man was gone. Only a shadow remained. The bloodied and bruised husk of Stephen Crowley, now brimming over with hate. Hate that had been given purpose by a god.

"Put the gun down, Dad," Daniel said, surprised at how level his voice remained. "I'll get Lieutenant Matt. You need help. You're . . . not yourself."

"Not myself?" The inspector took a menacing step toward his son. "I'm more myself today than I've been since your mother left! You don't know what I know, haven't seen what I've seen. This!" He waved his ruined hand in front of his face. "This is more *me* than I've been in years! *Now get in! The car!*"

The police inspector pointed his gun at Daniel to emphasize his insistence. For a moment, looking down at the still-smoking barrel of the shaking weapon, Daniel thought his father was actually going to shoot him.

Clearly, he wasn't the only one. The sound of a gunshot blasted through the air, coming from close range. The blast tore off the right side of Stephen Crowley's face, leaving behind a shredded mess. Blood, brains, and skull fragments spattered onto the SUV's windshield. Yet despite the mortal damage wrought upon his body, Inspector Crowley stood firm. He turned his ruined, dripping head to gaze at his attacker, who was standing behind Daniel.

He was a middle-aged man. One of those who'd held the boy back moments prior. By the looks of him, he'd been with the circus for most of his life. Perhaps he'd worked as a performer years ago, but now he wore the plain overalls of a stagehand. This was no hero, Dan saw. The man was terrified, probably of his own action more than anything else. He'd likely never shot the rifle at anything but empty tin cans sitting on a fence, but there he stood, trying to defend a stranger.

It took Daniel a moment to notice that his would-be savior's abject terror was spreading through the crowd. When he looked back at his father, he understood why.

Stephen Crowley hadn't been felled by the shot. Though half his head was missing, he seemed none the worse for it. Instead he stood tall, his shredded face twisted in a familiar mask of anger. Black wisps of pure shadow worked beneath his skin, pulsing through his raw flesh.

Without pausing to consider his wounds, he raised his own gun and fired. His left hand didn't afford him much precision, so his bullet missed the intended target, hitting instead a young trapeze artist at the base of her jaw.

Hysterical screams exploded behind Daniel. The crowd scattered as another shot blasted from his father's pistol, probably wounding another innocent, but the boy barely noticed. He could only watch, mesmerized, as Stephen Crowley's face began to knit itself back together in a gruesome display of crawling sinew and writhing musculature.

Another shotgun blast ripped through the inspector's right arm, nearly severing it above the wrist. However, before the broken hand could detach, tendrils of bloody tendons and shadows shot out of the wound, reattaching the damaged limb and mending the flesh before a single drop of blood hit the ground.

Stephen Crowley had freed the god and been rewarded. A blessing of shadow and blood that made him invulnerable. He was no longer human or even mortal. He had been touched by the divine.

Inspector Crowley pulled the trigger of his pistol until it clicked, then shoved a fresh magazine into his sidearm. Daniel hadn't taken note of exactly how many bullets his father had shot into the fleeing crowd. The absence of any return fire suggested that his old man had managed to kill his attacker. Yet the police inspector kept on shooting. The anger he'd spent his whole life keeping in check, especially around his son, had completely consumed him.

Feeling numb, Daniel Crowley watched his father fire. How many more would his father kill, cripple, or wound before he was satisfied? Would he stop once he ran out of bullets, or would he take the rifle from the car? Would he keep going until all of them were dead?

Suddenly the teenager remembered the kitchen knife in his hand. Tightening his fingers around the handle, he could feel the cold power of the weapon calling out with its own hunger. The god-touched blade.

Calmly, swiftly, Daniel walked toward his father. Suppressing all his emotions and memories, the son of Inspector Crowley plunged the kitchen knife into his father's throat.

The blade slid into the soft flesh of his neck, entering the left side and exiting the right. Daniel waited for his father to turn his gun on him, for the wound to close, for any sign that the knife, their secret weapon, was useless.

Instead ichorous black blood spurted out of the wound. The blade wasn't satisfied with simply cutting; it burned, corrupting and melting the flesh around it. The laceration quickly became a nightmare of decomposing meat. Before Daniel had time to see his father's reaction or even pull the knife free, Stephen Crowley's body began to fall apart, devoured by the very shadows that had inhabited it. The power of the god turning on him.

For a second, Daniel's father seemed to be at peace. He looked upon his son, trying to mouth something, but he couldn't push the air from his lungs. Daniel thought it might have been a question or perhaps gratitude for being freed of the god's grasp. Later he would decide that he'd tried to say, one last time: "We were the Crowley boys."

Then the inspector's face collapsed, devoured by the hunger of the knife blade.

AUDREY

THE LAUGHTER WAS terrible. Audrey wished that Uncle Randy had driven black iron nails into her ears to protect her from such a grotesque sound. It seemed to be all around her, and she recognized the voice. She'd heard it the night she'd died.

She never saw the god, though. After falling from her bicycle, she'd remained in her body, hiding and waiting. It wasn't the first time she had died. She couldn't remember before, but now she knew. Back when she was a baby, she had expired, just for a few minutes. But her soul had stayed put, hiding and waiting, and everything had been okay. So that was what she tried to do again.

She heard people talk at her funeral, and heard all the nice things everyone had to say about her. She thought she might cry, but instead it made her happy and satisfied.

Until the monster found her.

She could see it trying to reach into her body, to pull her spirit out of the decaying flesh. The thing was hard to describe. It looked like the smell of rotting flesh and sounded like shadows. It moved like lightning. Always a step behind her, yet everywhere, like the skin of the world.

That night, Uncle Randy had given her back her eyes. She couldn't see the creature anymore, but neither could it see her.

Uncle Randy had saved her from the monster, and now she had to be brave and return the favor.

Now that it had been released, Audrey could see its physical form moving through the police station. It had built itself a coat of flesh and blood, but instead of looking like a proper human being, it had spread itself into the garment of writhing sinew and bones, a mass of shadow and blood. It looked a little like a child, not much older than she was, hiding in a thornbush or a tumbleweed. It seemed to sense Audrey, looking in her direction but unable to see her. They had switched places—she was in its world and it was in hers, but only she could see it.

The only people left in the station were Jackie, Old Sam, Uncle Randy, and Ms. Erica. Audrey was sad to see that Erica hadn't listened to Dr. McKenzie's advice, but there was nothing to do about it now.

"Hey, sweetie."

It was an old, familiar voice that broke her reverie. She looked over and saw that Sam Finnegan stood next to his own body. Wispy tendrils of light and shadow still connected him to his mortal flesh.

"Sam!" she cried out, and threw her arms around the old man.

"Are you ready to help me fight the monster?" he asked.

"Yes," Audrey answered with as much confidence as she could muster. Deep down, she was terrified. "What do I do?"

"Well," Finnegan said, gently tapping the iron nail in her left eye, "first you gotta remove these."

Audrey understood a lot more dead than she ever had when she was alive. She knew that the nails in her eyes let her see the physical world, and the ones in her feet tied her to the world of the living. She knew her parents had planned this, to keep her between life and death until they could get her a new body. She also knew that removing the nails meant the god would see her. She knew what it did to the spirits it saw.

"Okay," she said.

Determined, Audrey grabbed the tip of the nail embedded in her right eye between her thumb and index fingers. She expected pain but was surprised to find the piece of metal slid out of her socket with ease. The sensation was beyond description. She could feel the nail rubbing against the inside of her skull, and once she had finished pulling it out, her vision became a little clearer. She could see impossible colors, superimposed over Randy's and Erica's bodies. The colors shifted as they turned toward the sound the nail made as it hit the floor, having found its way back into the physical world.

"Audrey?" called out Randy, panic staining his words. "Don't take those out, honey. You need those or the monster'll get you."

Saving Audrey's soul had been a great comfort to Randy when everything else in his life had fallen apart. He didn't want to see her consumed now. When the second nail fell, bouncing into existence on the police station floor, he closed his eyes in resignation.

"Randy?" Erica said nervously. "Where did those nails come from?"

"From Audrey. She's breaking the spell that's protecting her."

And now the monster can see me, Audrey thought. She tried to swallow, but her ethereal anatomy wouldn't allow it. Instead she settled for balling her fists nervously as she crouched down, reaching for the nail in her right foot.

"Don't," Finnegan's spirit interrupted. "Keep those in. They'll protect you."

The world around Audrey and Sam Finnegan rippled like the surface of a pond. Shadows grew darker, and light brightened for a moment.

"It knows you're here," the old man continued. "Remember, Audrey: it can see you, scare you, maybe even hurt you, but it can't take you."

The dead child nodded, determination etched onto her bright, delicate features.

"Good. Now hide in here." Sam pointed to his own empty body.

Ever obedient, Audrey moved closer to the old man's limp form. Unlike Randy and Erica, his body didn't glow with any color. It might as well have been another inanimate object, like the books piled up in Randy's cell or the handle on the doors.

She reached out her hand to touch Sam and realized she'd never tried to touch a living person since she had been dead. The feeling was strange and electric. She could feel a tingling sensation, like each cell in Old Man Finnegan's body was pulling her in. His motionless form was hungry for her soul, wanting to absorb it, assimilate it. Audrey found that she could resist, but that if she let it go, it would pull her in, force her to fill the vacuum.

As she let herself submerge completely into the pile of aging flesh and bones, she saw the door to the jail room explode.

Erica cried in surprise but choked on her scream when she saw the creature that walked through the doorway and down the handful of painted concrete steps. The lattice of human and animal remains slithered around the god, an aura of living decay that quickly spread tendrils around the room, crawling into corners and through bars. Audrey could see that, despite the vastness of its physical form, the creature was magnitudes larger on the wrong side of life, filling the jail and extending outward to cover most of the town.

The blood-covered monster grabbed Erica by the arm, twisting backward until her shoulder popped out of its socket. With a cry, Randy jumped toward his former student, in a futile attempt to pull her away from the creature. But before he could grab on to her, the psychologist was pulled within the garment of quivering animal parts. Erica Hazelwood cried out in agony and confusion as her extremities were pulled into impossible, bone-snapping configurations.

"Neil . . . ," the monster said with a thousand voices as it laid its burning red eyes on Randy.

For an instant, Audrey feared that Dr. McKenzie would suffer the same fate as Erica, whose screams had quickly turned to pleas of mercy and then into unintelligible gurgles as her body was crushed and lacerated.

Then Sam Finnegan intervened.

"Hey!" he said, his voice ethereal and ageless outside of its body.

The god turned. It saw the man whom, for decades, had held it captive. Who had tormented and mocked and lied to it over and over and over again. It cast aside Erica's body, and the world around it became dark with hatred—tangible, burning hatred.

It lunged at the Saint-Ferdinand Killer. The bloody creature in the living world reached to tear the old man's physical form apart, while it seemed as if the entire world of the dead fell upon Finnegan's spirit.

But it was to no avail. The god, despite all its power, all its anger, couldn't harm Finnegan's spirit as long as it remained tethered to his body, and it couldn't hurt his body while it was inhabited by Audrey's grounded spirit.

The creature quickly adjusted its attack, however. It poured its essence into Sam Finnegan's aging body. From Randy's point of view, the madman looked to be having a full-blown, grand mal epileptic seizure. An ocean of hatred and death flooded into the flesh in which Audrey had taken refuge, every drop of it now intent on consuming and destroying her.

This it tried, with all its immortal might. The god tore her soul apart only to have it coalesce again and again. There was no pain, not as the living would understand it, but instead an agony of loss, sadness, and existential despair. Without nerve endings to communicate the physical trauma, Audrey was rent and broken by her emotions. All the while, the nails in her feet kept her grounded, immune not to harm but to finality.

Just as Audrey began to give in to the never-ending assault, it was over. As quickly as it had arrived, the ocean of hate receded, and the little girl found herself standing beside the old man's spirit.

Once more, the god was trapped. Instead of a prison of promises and oaths, it was now held in one made of flesh. Confined by its own hatred and hunger.

Audrey looked up at Sam. His soul seemed serene, almost at peace. Glad to have sacrificed himself for a worthy cause.

"You did wonderfully," he said.

RANDY

THE GOD'S PHYSICAL form stood frozen, bent rigidly over the old man. The web of fleshy tendrils and bony tentacles quietly fell apart, no longer animated by the baleful will of the creature. The childlike figure that had stood inside fell over and burst like a water balloon, spraying the walls in black ichor.

Quiet fell over the jail room, with only the sound of a slimy blob of coagulating blood splattering onto the ground to break the silence.

Randy was frozen. As a medical examiner, he had studied the human body in almost every possible postmortem condition imaginable. Between his personal experience and the vast catalog of images found in medical reports and journals, he had seen just about every conceivable horror the mortal form might be subjected to. And as an amateur practitioner of necromancy, he was also no stranger to the supernatural. While he'd always shied away from truly delving into the actual art, Randy had toyed with the minor reanimation of small animals, out-of-body experiences, and whatever else his father's notes could teach him.

In spite all of his accumulated experiences, however, Dr. McKenzie had never seen anything as unimaginable as what had been done to Erica's body.

Perhaps it was that he'd known the young psychologist so well, or that he'd always seen bodies after they'd been mutilated, burned, or torn apart. Maybe there was just no way to find the detachment necessary to process what he'd just witnessed. Either way, sometime during the god's attack, he had fallen to his knees and clutched the iron nails he'd hammered into a dead girl's eyes. He found himself trembling like a dry leaf, hopelessly clinging to a branch in autumn.

Hearing nothing but his own heartbeat drumming in his ears, the medical examiner took stock of his surroundings, trying to piece together what had happened. As far as he could tell, Sam Finnegan, the Saint-Ferdinand Killer, had somehow tricked the god into his own body. Randy studied Finnegan's body, wondering what was going on beneath its skin. How much of his soul had the old man given up to forge this new prison for the malevolent god? How would the door to this new cage remain locked?

Suddenly Sam's eyes opened and Randy understood. It wasn't trapped. The creature was in there, of that there was no doubt. Empty blue eyes looked out of Sam Finnegan's skull, drinking in the situation, understanding it.

Without thought or hesitation, racing against the intellect of a far older creature, one with a complex and alien understanding of reality, Randy tightened his fists on the iron nails and then plunged them into those of Sam Finnegan's body.

The first one slid into the soft tissue of the old man's eye and brain with surprisingly little effort. Randy, ever the medical doctor, attributed it to the adrenaline still coursing through his veins.

The second nail was more of a challenge as the body, animated by pain, shock, and a supernatural presence struggling for freedom, thrashed about and sought to fight back.

All Randy could see in that blue void of an eye before he plunged the second nail in was hatred, hatred and death.

As soon as both of Finnegan's eyes had been replaced by the black iron spikes and pooling red blood, the body collapsed back onto the ground, leaving the medical examiner to stare at it.

"I gotcha," he said in a dry, exhausted rasp.

"No," came a smooth and relaxed voice from behind him. "*I* have him."

Randy McKenzie turned around slowly, trying to put a name to the vaguely familiar face. Flanked by Hector Alvarez and Gédéon LaFrenière, whom the doctor knew were part of Crowley's Sandmen, stood a young man. He wore a sharp but mud-stained suit, his features handsome despite the bruises and blood that darkened his face.

"Dr. McKenzie, I presume?" The man walked into the jail room, casually stepping over the leftover flesh and tissue that had been part of the god's extended form. "I've been looking forward to meeting you. Chris . . . I mean, Francis Lambert. It's a pleasure."

He crouched down to look Randy directly in the eyes, cordially extending a hand. The doctor took it automatically, dumbfounded by the turn of events.

Meanwhile, the other two men went to pick up Sam Finnegan's body. LaFrenière was a sickly shade of green and gave the impression that he might void his stomach at any moment.

"Wait. What are you doing?" Randy tried to interrupt, but Lambert's cold hand held him firm.

"Don't worry about it, Dr. McKenzie," the young man said with sincerity. "We'll take care of everything from now on."

Once the two Sandmen had left with the body, Lambert finally let go of Randy's hand. He stood, taking a calm look around the room and methodically drinking in every detail.

"Who are you?" Randy inquired, dark suspicion digging a pit in his guts.

"Your father knew my grandfather, Dr. McKenzie. I'm here to do what neither of them could."

"You're going to kill it?"

"Kill it? I'm going to use it." Lambert made his way back to the entrance of the jail room, both hands comfortably in his pockets. "Not in the clumsy barbaric way my father intended, however. My plans are far more ambitious."

His eyes finally settled on the body of Erica Hazelwood. She was buried under the putrefied remains of the god. Broken and limp. A bubble of blood formed at the corner of her mouth then burst. She was breathing.

"Tsk . . . what a shame. I don't think she's going to make it."

Erica was breathing! Ignoring Lambert's retreating footsteps, Randy crawled to his protégé's side. The strange young man was right: her chances didn't look good. Soon Lieutenant Bélanger would be back. He needed to escape, but he also couldn't leave Erica like this. Leaving her in the hopes that she might be found and saved in time wasn't an option. His mind flirted with putting the young woman out of her misery, but he simply couldn't bring himself to do it.

He wouldn't become like William and Beatrice, consumed by the need to bring back the dead. He wouldn't have to. Randy knew a little of the darker arts. He knew tricks. Parlor tricks if performed on rats. Miracles if he could pull it off on a person.

Shivering from an unnatural cold, the medical examiner began to pull at the tendrils of dead flesh, digging to free his student's body from the clutches of a dead god.

EPILOGUE

"I DON'T UNDERSTAND," Venus said, squeezing Katrina's bony hand.

For two weeks the young girl had stood vigil over the old fortune-teller. At first, the gunshot had appeared relatively harmless, boring a hole right through Katrina's shoulder. But when she saw the amount of blood pouring out, Venus realized an artery must have been damaged. She'd done her best to put pressure on the wound, soaking her arms to the elbows in hot, crimson liquid. It reminded her of the first time she'd seen the god she'd caught in her shed.

For a while it had seemed to work. By the time paramedics made it to the circus, Katrina still had a pulse, albeit a weak one. However, her old age and blood loss conspired to create a chain of complications that culminated in a series of organ failures and her current coma.

During that time, Abraham had come back from Sherbrooke. Harry Peterson was recovering remarkably well, as Ezekiel had foretold. Chances were that the old farmer would be back in Saint-Ferdinand within a few weeks. Abraham was hoping he could convince his father to move away.

Daniel, on the other hand, had completely disappeared. Before any of the authorities had arrived, he'd simply gotten in his car and driven off. Who could blame him? He'd been forced to kill his own father only minutes before. Much to Lieutenant Bélanger's frustration, the circus workers stonewalled him about Daniel's whereabouts and involvement.

There was also no trace of her uncle. Rumor had it that the jail room at the police station had been turned into a veritable slaughterhouse. Copious amounts of Erica Hazelwood's blood had been found at the scene, along with bones and organs from an unidentified number of other victims. Of the psychologist, Randy McKenzie, or Sam Finnegan, there was no trace.

"I thought I'd find you here."

Penny slipped her head through the doorframe, holding a bag from a local fast-food joint. The older girl had changed since the events at the circus. She'd snapped out of her grief and had focused her energies toward rebuilding her life and supporting her friends. Between meeting with lawyers and notaries to settle her mother's estate and serving as Abraham's chauffeur, she'd had very little time to devote to Venus directly. Indirectly, Penny had enlisted the help of a family friend and colleague of her mother to help ensure that the younger girl would keep financial control of everything her parents had left behind.

"How is she?"

"Dying," Venus replied.

"You think she knew this would happen?" Despite everything they'd seen over the summer, Penny had yet to be convinced of the old woman's prophetic abilities. She'd already voiced her opinion that, until they had further evidence, Venus should assume her parents were still alive.

"It's not over, you know," Venus said. "We've inherited this."

"You have. And Abraham and Daniel, maybe, but I don't think my parents were involved in any of this." She paused, putting down her bag of food. "Though if that crazy old man is to be believed, the scars from coming in contact with a god run deep, and there is no question that I've been cut by this one."

"Whatever it touches is changed forever. And we've all been touched by it. Some more thoroughly than others." Venus half-hoped that her meaning would be caught by her friend and half-hoped it wouldn't.

"Yeah," Penelope answered. "I guess I was covered elbow-deep in that thing's blood."

"Does that mean you'll help?"

"Aphrodite, please."

Venus frowned at the nickname but welcomed the reminder of simpler days. "Good," she said. "I need you to take care of stuff for me."

"Sure. What do you need?"

"Everything. At least for a while." She waited for a reaction, which came in the form of a raised eyebrow. "I'm going away for the winter."

"Venus McKenzie, skipping school? You *have* changed," the older girl said.

"I need to find the other Craftsmen, the ones who are still alive. I know a few of their names from that list I found in my uncle's office, and I have to meet them. That thing is out there somewhere, free and angry. I don't know why it hasn't done so yet, but someday it's going to come after us, and I refuse to be unprepared."

Penny considered her friend's words carefully and then nodded.

"Sure, I'll hold down the fort. Abe's father probably has some of the answers you're looking for too."

"Talk to him and Abe. Learn as much as you can."

"Wait. When are you leaving?"

"Probably later tonight. I'm going to take a bus to Montreal and maybe try to catch up with Ezekiel from there." She looked down at the dying old woman. "I'll have nothing keeping me here by then."

The girls fell quiet. Both turned to look at the old woman lying in the hospital bed. If not for the machines showing her faint signs of life, one could have mistaken Katrina for a corpse. Venus was both sad and angry to see her slip away, especially since she'd barely gotten to know her.

"I have one more favor to ask you," Venus said, breaking the silence.

"Don't get greedy," Penny warned her.

Venus nodded to Katrina. "Can you see that she gets a proper burial? Nothing fancy, but my family has a small plot in the Saint-Ferdinand cemetery, where my grandfather is buried. I think I'd like her to be buried there."

"I don't want to seem disrespectful, but shouldn't the people from the circus handle that? She's one of them, after all."

Venus bowed her head and turned toward the foot of the bed, unhooking the chart that hung there. On it was a long list of medical information, including the dying woman's diet and prescriptions and the hours for her nurse's visits. With a shaking finger, Venus pointed at the top of the chart, to the name under which Katrina had been admitted. *Elizabeth Lussier*. At first, Penny didn't understand, but looking into her best friend's watery eyes, she remembered—Lussier was Virginie McKenzie's maiden name. The fortune-teller was Venus's grandmother.

Penny reached out, wrapping her arms around her best friend. The younger girl dropped the chart to the ground, returning the embrace with a sob.

"I'm sorry, Veen," said the older girl. "I didn't realize you two were connected."

"Neither did I," said Venus.

ACKNOWLEDGEMENTS

THESE THINGS are always a chore to write. On one hand, I don't want to diminish the impact of those mentioned by making my acknowledgements boring, but I'm also not one to layer gimmicks on top of my words. This goes without mentioning the burden of a forgetful mind. I will miss a few names, and only once all is said and done will my negligence be brought to light. That's when the guilt will start.

Anyways, if you've enjoyed *A God in the Shed*, know that you owe everyone here a dash of gratitude, for they all participated.

Obviously, I'd be a monster if I didn't acknoweledge my family. My parents have shown the support and encouragement you'd expect, but they have, in their own way, gone above and beyond, providing me with the positive ground upon which to walk on this journey. Between my mom's peerless cooking and my father's eagerness to participate in any way he can, these two turned out to be pretty good at the job.

My brother is a specimen all his own. Thorough and pitiless, he's one of my best critics. His ruthless analysis and attention to detail is an indispensable tool when finalizing a manuscript. Never go soft on me, Phil.

On the opposite side of the scale is my best friend, David. The guy can't find flaw in anything I do. We've been through a lot together, and I'm proud to have him in my corner. Dave, why do you have to live so far away?

Speaking of living too far, Amy has been as hard-core a fan as one could hope to have without it being weird. I've come to depend on her unquestioning enthusiasm for whatever project I set my mind to. You've become quite the accomplice in many of my most hare-brained shenanigans, Amy.

Then there's the members of the Tadpool, the most supportive, distracting bunch of freaks on the Internet. I wouldn't have gotten this or any other book published if it weren't for them.

A similar accolade goes to the Diamond Club, a force of nature that leverages its will into improving the world in the strangest ways. I am thankful to be part of the collateral in this. To Justin and Brian, who spearhead the Diamond Club through their own creative efforts, I have a huge debt of gratitude.

Another luminary from that group is Renaissance man Andrew Mayne, who's shown unexpected and undeserved support of my work. Receiving the encouragements of such an accomplished individual fuels the fires of motivation.

I keep saying that none of this would have happened without this or that person, but I have to raise a glass to the people who helped me pull this story out of the cold, dark void and make it into a real thing: the folks at Inkshares. From the incredible opportunities that Adam has found for me, to the guidance Avalon gives all of us authors, the crew at Inkshares have shown passion and professionalism beyond what should be expected. You guys are awesome. I'm glad I hitched my fortune to yours.

It would be disingenuous to thank Inkshares without thanking the community. Brian Guthrie, my friend Paul Inman, Tal Klein, Amanda Orneck, and so many others that form our clique of Inkshares authors have become a core upon which we lean as we hew careers from the ether.

A special tip of the hat goes to Tom and Veronica of Sword & Laser. I got my start because of you guys and I'll never stop thanking you for it.

I need to drop a small thanks to Nicole, who caught mistakes that might have slipped by unnoticed. You are indeed an excellent and adorable human.

Finally, I can't forget Angela. From the very beginning, she's been there, gently nudging me forward on my path. I wouldn't have started—let alone achieved—anything as a writer if it weren't for her. She's always shown incredible patience whenever I get consumed by this or that project. I don't think I know how much you've sacrificed to be this supportive of me, Angela, but I will always appreciate it.

LIST OF PATRONS

Adam Gomolin
Amy Frost
André Brun
Angela Blasi
Angela Melamud
Avalon Marissa Radys
Brad Ludwig
Brian Guthrie
C. D. Oakes
Clayton J. Locke
Dave Barrett
Diogo M. Santos
Elena Stofle
Eric Bernier
Evelyn Robinson
Francine Garant
Inked Geek Studios
Jean.Tousignant
John Robin
Joseph Terzieva
Julie Kuehl
Kari Simms

Leanne Phillips
Lee Ajifu
Levi Krause
Matt Kaye
Max Wallace
Michel Dubeau
Mike Mc Peek
Montzalee Wittmann
Natasha Galea
Nathan Lawrence
Patrik Stedt
Paul Alejandro
P.H. James
Sebastiaan Van Dijk
Serge Tremblay Reader Writer
Simon C. Brooks
Stephanie D. Carlson
Steven Rod
Teras Cassidy
Terence Quinn
Ting Schweizer
Veronica Belmont

INKSHARES

INKSHARES is a community, publisher, and producer for debut writers. Our books are selected not just by a group of editors, but also by readers worldwide. Our aim is to find and develop the most captivating and intelligent new voices in fiction. We have no genre—our genre is debut.

Previously unknown Inkshares authors have received starred reviews in every trade publication. They have been featured in every major review, including on the front page of the *New York Times*. Their books are on the front tables of booksellers worldwide, topping bestseller lists. They have been translated in major markets by the world's biggest publishers. And they are being adapted at the biggest studios and networks.

Interested in making your own story a reality? Visit Inkshares.com to start your own project, connect with other writers, and find other great books.